# HAREM

*The spider spins her web in the palace of the Caesars.*

*a verse from Sa'adi*

## COLIN FALCONER

http://coolgus.com

Originally published by Hodder and Stoughton, a division of Hodder Headline PLC London and by Crown Publishers, an imprint of the Crown Publishing Group, a division of Random House, Inc.

ISBN: 9781621250708

# FORWARD

Many of the background events in this novel can be found in histories of the Ottomans in this period. What can never be known is what happened behind the iron-studded doors of the Sublime Porte to raise so much violence and passion. In this respect this is a work of fiction. Only the long dead could ever tell us how much is true.

The extract of poetry at the end of the book is from an actual work by Suleiman, the one they called The Magnificent.

Topkapi Saraya, Istanbul

Once there was silence.

A man would have had the flesh flayed from the soles of his feet for raising his voice above a whisper in this court of plane and chestnut trees, the sanctum of Allah's Deputy on Earth, the Lord of the Lords of this World, Possessor of Men's Necks, King of Believers and Unbelievers, Emperor of the East and West, Refuge of All the People in the Whole World, the Shadow of the Almighty Dispensing Quiet in the Earth.

Once, only the mumble of pages and viziers disturbed the grazing deer and parades of peacock, as the business of an empire that encompassed the Seven Wonders of the World was conducted in murmurs.

Once there was silence.

But today Mercedes buses rumble through the Sublime Porte, past the sleeping church of St. Irene, and the fountain where the bostanji-bashi washed the blood from his sword after an execution. Now grey-haired and superannuated executives from Frankfurt and Chicago and Osaka, armed with digital cameras and their wives giggling like schoolgirls, are ushered through the crush at Ortakapi by guides wearing Ray-bans who do not even

1

glance up at the niches in the wall high above them, to point out that they were once the resting places for the heads of the Sultan's viziers.

Beyond the Ortakapi, close to the Hall of the Divan, there is a sign on the stone wall that reads: "The Harem." Four matrons from Ohio pose underneath while one of their husbands focuses a camera.

"Don't lean on the wall, Doris," he drawls, "I don't know if it can take the weight."

The black doors swing open and the tour is herded inside, into the cool and cobbled darkness. A young Turk in an open-necked shirt and unpressed trousers, his English distorted by his lisp, stands to one side to address them.

""Harem" means "Forbidden"," he says. "Forbidden to men. Once the Sultan was the only man - the only complete man - who could pass through that gate. Any woman who entered there would never pass out again."

Once there was silence. It was broken not by the shouts of war and invasion, but by laughter, the laughter of a woman.

But first there was silence.

PART ONE

# THE SPIDER''S WEB

# CHAPTER 1

### Rhodes, 1522

Silence, but for the steady rhythm of the rain, splashing into blood-stained pools. Camels trudged through the mud; even the beasts of burden coughed at the stench of sick men and poor sanitation. The worst was the reek from the moat.

It encompassed the fortress, sixty feet deep and one hundred and forty feet wide, and was almost filled with the bloated bodies of the dead. The smell of putrefying corpses pervaded everything, it seeped into clothes and hair and skin, was pungent even in the silken sanctum of the Sultan's tent, despite the incense burners.

The assembled generals held perfumed handkerchiefs to their noses and stared at the ground. The young man on the mother of pearl throne looked as if he could murder every one of them. His lips were drawn back from his teeth in a snarl as he listened to the mumbled obeisance of his second vizier, Mustapha.

"How many of your Sultan's men did you lose today?" he said, referring to himself, as he always did in public, as if he were a separate person.

The second vizier's face and beard was crusted with black blood from a sword slash yet untended on his forehead. A dozen times that day he had led the charge against the breach in the wall below the towers of St. Michael and St. John, while the grizzled veterans of the Cross cut down his azabs with their broadswords and arrows. Even their women and children had torn up cobblestones from the street and hurled them down on their heads from the ramparts. He had even seen one pale priest take a turn at upending a vat of boiling pitch. Some of his men had run, it was true, their nerve broken. He had cut them down himself with his sword.

But now, for the first time that day, he was truly afraid.

"How many men?" the young sultan repeated.

Mustapha dared raise his head to look into the Sultan's eyes. "Twenty thousand, lord," he whispered.

"Twenty thousand!" The Sultan leaped to his feet and every man in the room - except one - took a step back.

In the long silence that followed several of the generals in the room thought they heard Mustapha trying to swallow.

When Sultan Suleiman spoke again, his voice sounded like the death rattle in a dying man's throat. "You advocated this expedition to me. For three centuries these infidels have taunted us from this fortress. Even the Fatih and my own father could not dislodge them. But you promised me this would be different."

Mustapha knew there was no excuse for failure.

The silk of Suleiman's robes rippled in the light of the oil lamps. A froth of spittle had formed at the corners of his mouth. "Another twenty thousand of your Sultan's army lie in the mud at the foot of this accursed rock, the rest are afflicted with pestilence, and still the walls stand! Winter is coming, the storms are boiling there out to sea, ready to shatter our fleet and leave us stranded here. Yet if Suleiman turns away now, he must drag the banner of Islam in the dirt. You brought your Sultan to Rhodes. What will you have him do now?"

Mustapha was silent.

"You advised this!" he screamed, and stabbed his finger at his second vizier as if it were an iron spike. He turned to the bostanji who waited in the shadows. He made a quick motion of his hands to give the order for execution. His butcher was a deaf mute, so he could not be swayed by screams of pain or supplications for mercy.

The Nubian strode forward and shoved Mustapha to his knees with one expert motion of his leg and arm. The bands of his muscle on his naked back tensed as he brought his killic above his head to strike.

Old Piri Pasha, the Grand Vizier, stepped forward, both hands held up in supplication, distracting the executioner. The killing blade glittered in the light of the oil lamps.

"Great Lord, please! A moment. Misguided this man may be, but he has fought like a lion for you in front of these walls."

"Quiet!" Suleiman shouted at him. "If you think him so worthy, then perhaps you should join him in Paradise."

A swift intake of breath from every man, like a wind guttering the lamps. Not Piri Pasha! He was an old man, the Vizier who survived Selim the Grim, had been Suleiman's own tutor as a child. He was one of the few dissenters against the attack on Rhodes. The assembled generals and counsellors fell on their knees in front of the young Sultan, put their foreheads to the carpets, and begged for his forbearance.

Only Ibrahim, his falconer, dared approach him. "Great Lord," he murmured and took Suleiman's hand. He knelt and kissed the ruby on his finger. "There is another way."

Suleiman tried to pull away but Ibrahim held his hand firmly in both of his.

"Tell it, then."

"The histories tell us the Greeks besieged Troy for fourteen years for the sake of a woman. Will not the Turk, then, oppressed by piracies and invasions from this rock for over three centuries, endure one winter's siege?"

The bostanji shifted his weight, waited for the final signal form the sultan.

"What is your counsel, Ibrahim?"

"They say that when one of the Roman Caesars invaded an island, he would burn his fleet on the beach. Great Lord, perhaps if you were to build a villa on this hill, in full view of the castle, the defenders will know there is to be no reprieve until the fortress is ours. It will crush their spirit. And if our soldiers know your conviction also, it will give them heart."

Suleiman sighed, and eased himself back onto his throne. He caressed a turquoise stone that was inlaid on the arm with his forefinger. "And what of them?" he said, nodding at the two men who knelt, heads bowed, below the killic. Only now did he realize that one of them was old Piri Pasha. He winced. How could he have contemplated such a thing?

"There has been too much Turkish blood spilled today already," Ibrahim said.

An almost imperceptible shake of the head and the bostanji moved silently again into the shadows.

"Very well," Suleiman said. "Perhaps you are right, Ibrahim. It is wise counsel. WE shall build the villa. Let winter come - the Sultan stays."

# CHAPTER 2

## The Eski Saraya (the old palace), Stamboul

The hawk rode the currents high above the city, its serrated wingtips tilting to each updraft and sheer. Two hundred feet below were the great sea walls of Stamboul and its squalid, cobbled streets, where legless beggars pleaded for alms and flies hovered in black clouds above the melon rinds. The domes of the mosques had turned rose-grey in the settling dusk.

Its golden eye focused on a young woman standing on the terrace of the Eski Saraya.

She was a striking figure, conspicuous even among the three hundred women of the Harem for the two braids, tied with satin, that hung halfway down her back. Her hair was the colour of fire, burnished yellows and golds and reds that shimmered in the sunlight, a stunning contrast to her green eyes and pale Tatar complexion.

Her face was turned to the north-east, towards the distant hills of Rumelia, to a place far beyond the violet horizon. Although it was out of sight, she saw it clearly; the dry grass reached so high in summer that it almost touched the rider's girdle, and you could ride three days and nights and not see another living soul. Salt marshes that gleamed silver in the moonlight.

She let out a small cry that startled the nightingale that lived under the eaves, trapped like her in an elaborate cage.

"I could spend my whole life locked up in here," she whispered, to the little bird. "They keep me for my pretty colors and my song, and one day my youth will be withered and gone, like a flower pressed inside a book. But I will find a way out."

There was really only one escape; but he was still at Rhodes, where they said he was building a new villa on Mount Philermus. She was his, he possessed her, even though she had never laid eyes on him and she had been in his dark and pretty prison for two seasons.

Well, there had to be some way. She would not spend her days idly dreaming of the miracle that might bring her to his bed. She would wake the Devil himself and light all the fires of Hell under this palace, but she would find a way to displace the Montenegrin and get out of here.

They would rue the day they allowed this hell-cat into their cage of pretty birds.


## Rhodes
## the Feast of Saint Nicholas

As he rode through the towns of St Nicholas and St. Angelo, three generations of Osmanli sultans rode with him. These old walls had been the cherished prize of his father, and his father before him, and his father, too - Fatih, the Conqueror. Already at twenty-eight years, he had achieved what they had only dreamed of. He had wrested the mighty fortress at Rhodes from the Knights of Saint John.

"They say the Colossus once stood here. Now here stands another."

Suleiman turned; it was Ibrahim, grinning, his Arab stallion prancing and fighting for its head.

"It was your wise counsel that prevailed."

"It is the Christian holy day! Do you think they will be celebrating our feat of arms in Rome?"

On the other side of the square a group of bearded knights were praying on their knees outside their chapel. They were scarred without exception, one with a pink cicatrix on his face, the skin smeared like mud around the place where his eye had been; another had a seeping bloody bandage on an arm without a hand. They mumbled their prayers together, oblivious to the yeniceris as they marched past with their banners fluttering green and white, ignored the cannon booming victory outside the gates. After all, they had not been the ones to surrender; it was the merchants who had sued for truce.

"Look at them. Did they not fight well?"

Ibrahim reined his horse closer, dropped his voice to a whisper. "My Lord, you perplex me. You have won the greatest victory for the House of Osmanli since the Fatih took Constantinople. Do you not rejoice?"

"It is our duty to Islam to conquer. We do not need to revel in it."

Ibrahim turned to the ranks of white plumed soldiers, distinctive with their long moustaches and harquebuses slung over their shoulders. "You will let the yeniceris have their day?"

"No, I gave my word. Not this time."

9

"They are like dogs feeding on scraps. You know what happens to a hungry dog if you take his scraps away."

"They must go hungry a while longer. There will be no looting here."

"You forget, we faced humiliation four short months ago, my Lord. You are extraordinarily compassionate."

Ibrahim was wrong. He had not forgotten what had happened here; how could he forget the reek of blood, the nauseating smell of corpses rotting in the mud, men dying in hedgerows? In the end God's will had prevailed. He had done his duty, but he hoped it would not be required of him again.

"What now, my Lord?" Ibrahim said.

Suleiman thought of the Eski Saraya, and Gülbehar . A woman's soothing voice and soft touch could help a man forget such nightmares. Perhaps she could help him forget the moment when he had discovered his own father in himself; if it were not for Ibrahim he would executed his first and second viziers together. Even Selim had never done that.

So the Beast was in him too, he owned that same mindless spite. Without Ibrahim he would have unleashed it, blindly, on the two men who served him most faithfully and least deserved his rage.

He shuddered. "Let us go home," he said.

# CHAPTER 3

## the Eski Saraya

When a new slave girl was brought to the Harem, she immediately received instruction in the language of the Osmanli court and the Qur'an; she was also assigned to one of the Harem functionaries for training in a specific duty.

Hürrem had been given to the Mistress - the Kiaya - of the Silk Room, an embittered Circassian with skin the color of leather. She was an old woman now but she still clung to the memory of one fruitless night spent with Sultan Bayezid, Suleiman's grandfather. She had spent every day since as the harem dressmaker, lost among the bolts of brocade and damask and satin, taffetas and velvet. Her temper was short.

Hürrem enjoyed her position; at least, she had decided to make the best of it, for now. She had nimble fingers and a good eye, and her handkerchiefs had evinced approving murmurs from the Sultan Valide, the Sultan's mother, the preeminent power in the Harem.

She hummed a tune as she worked, embroidering a square of green Diba satin - the best satin in the world, the Kiaya told her, from right here in Stamboul. She used gold and silver thread, sewing an intricate pattern of leaves and flowers into the cloth.

The tune she hummed was one she had learned from her father, a Tatar song about the steppes and the north wind.

She did not hear the Kiaya enter the room behind her, but she felt the stinging slap to her ear. She started with shock and dropped her silver needle to the floor.

She jumped to her feet and raised her hand to strike back. The Kiaya's eyes gleamed. "Go on, hit me, you little minx! I'll have the Kapi Aga put you to the bastinado!"

Hürrem flushed beet red to the roots of her hair and lowered her hand.

11

"You do not sing in here, I have told you before. This is the Harem, and there is always silence."

"I like to sing."

"What you like does not matter. It is what the Great Lord wants."

"He isn't even here. We could discharge a cannon in the courtyard and he would be none the wiser!"

Insolent little minx!" The Kiaya slapped her again, but this time Hürrem was braced for the blow. Her mouth twisted into a mocking smile, even though the Kiaya's open hand had left a pink imprint on her cheek.

"It is the law!" the Kiaya shouted.

Hürrem leaned close and whispered, "Keep your voice down. The Sultan might hear! You are supposed to be silent."

The Kiaya picked up the handkerchief she had been embroidering and looked for fault. Finding none, she dropped it back on the bench in disgust. "Get on with your work."

Hürrem shared the sewing room with a raven-haired Jewish girl who had been bought from slave traders in Alexandria. "Market meat," the Kiaya called her. Her name was Meylissa and she had long legs, thin wrists and the quick, nervous movements of a sparrow. Hürrem watched her out of the corner of her eye, bent over her needlework, trying to make herself invisible behind the chemises and veils piled on the table in front of her. But she was too tempting a target for the Kiaya in her present mood.

"Let me see that," the Kiaya said and snatched her work from Meylissa's fingers. "Look at this! The finest Bursa brocade and you have ruined it!" She slapped her around the head. "What were you thinking? Look at these stitches! A child could have done better!"

Meylissa bowed her head and said nothing. The Kiaya threw the piece of material on the floor. "Undo all these stitches and start again! And no supper until it's finished. Do you hear?"

She turned and swept from the room.

"Fat old hindbreath of a camel!" Hürrem hissed when she was gone. She sat down at her bench and started humming again, louder than before. Silence is the Law! What nonsense!

There was a tiny, muffled sobbing behind her. She turned around. Meylissa was crying, her head cradled on her arms.

"Meylissa .. don't let her upset you! She's an old hag!"

Meylissa only shook her head, and the sobs came harder.

"Meylissa?" Hürrem got to her feet, trying to curb her impatience. Really! Hadn't the girl ever been slapped before? She sat at the bench next to her and put an arm around her shoulder. "Now stop this!"

"It's not her."

"What then? Meylissa … ? Whatever is wrong?"

And then she saw it, plain in the girl's huge brown eyes. Terror; naked and raw. Whatever it was, it had nothing to do with that old bitch of a seamstress.

Merciful heaven, what had she done?

Meylissa searched her face, looking for reassurance. "I have to tell someone," she said.

"You can trust me," Hürrem said. "Whatever it is, I won't tell anyone."

"They'll kill me," Meylissa whispered. She clutched at the hem of her kaftan, bunching the material into a ball in her fist.

"Speak up! I can't help you if you don't tell me what the problem is!"

"I'm pregnant," Meylissa said.

Hürrem thought she had misheard. "That doesn't make any sense," she said.

"It's true. I missed my bleed."

Hürrem laughed. Pregnant? In this lady's prison? "Meylissa, it's all right, it happens. Sometimes they come late, sometimes they don't come at all. It doesn't mean you're pregnant."

Meylissa shook her head. "No, it's true."

"You need a man to make you pregnant!"

Meylissa looked over Hürrem "s shoulder to make sure no one could overhear. Until that moment Hürrem had thought herself the more worldly one, but in that unguarded moment her little Jewess was unmasked and she saw a knowing and a cunning in her she had missed until now. "The Kapi Aga," Meylissa whispered.

The Kapi Aga! The Captain of the Guards, the Chief White Eunuch! Hürrem "s jaw fell open in astonishment. Although he was in charge of the Harem Guard he was supposed never to be alone with any of the girls as he was not rasé - a complete eunuch - like the Negroes. She had heard that most of the white eunuchs had only been partly castrated, their testicles had been tied or crushed, like young lambs. Was it really possible …?

"But he's a eunuch," she said.

"Of course he's a eunuch! Do you think I would have fucked a whole man? In here?"

Hürrem was stunned. Not only at the word - prim little Meylissa! - but at her own ignorance. While she had been wrestling with the new language, thinking herself so superior to this market meat, as the Kiaya called her, this farmer's girl had already found a way to get herself bedded.

Well, at least I am not pregnant, she thought.

"But if he's a eunuch …"

"They say sometimes a man can … well, regenerate. Even the black ones, they check them every year to make sure it hasn't grown back."

"Nonsense! When you geld a horse, it stays gelded!"

"But the white eunuchs, you know, they are not rasé - their things are not shaved off, like with the Nubians."

Meylissa was calmer now; talking had helped her. Hürrem stared at her, appalled. Pregnant!

"But where did you ... do it?"

Meylissa continued in a whisper. "There's a courtyard at the northern end of the palace. It's surrounded by high walls and shaded with plane trees. There's a door in the wall but it's always locked and there's never a guard."

"What were you doing there?"

"I was learning my Qur'an, as we were instructed. He must have seen me, perhaps from the northern tower. I heard a key in the lock. I was going to run away but ..."

Hürrem cocked her head, waiting for this "but"; but Meylissa only shrugged. "He said I was the most beautiful woman in the whole harem. He said he would help me catch the Sultan's eye."

"How many times did this happen?"

"Just once. Perhaps twice." A breath. "Six times."

"Six times! Do you know what they would have done if they had caught you?"

"But they have caught me. Haven't they?"

Hürrem pondered this, wondered what she would have done if it had been her sitting in the shaded garden reading the Qur'an. Even mortal danger could be tempting besides the stifling boredom of this dingy palace. And the daily steam baths and massages they made her take had stirred something inside her. Indolence and pampering worked on the body and soul like an aphrodisiac. It was torment, for there was no man to take away the ache.

"What was it like?" Hürrem asked her.

"What was it like? What does it matter what it was like? They are going to kill me! They will tie me in a sack and throw me in the Bosphorus!"

"I'll help you," Hürrem said.

"How? What can you do?"

"I'll think of something. You'll see."

# CHAPTER 4

The room was as he had remembered it. For the first time since he had entered Stamboul in triumph three days before, Suleiman felt that he had come home. He threw himself on the wall couch. As he flung aside his silk turban he tossed aside that other self, the Sultan of the Osmanlis. He ran a hand across his smooth, shaved skull to the scalp lock at the crown.

Ever since he inherited the throne from his father three years before, he had the feeling of looking out at the world from a darkened room and watching himself, like an actor in a shadow play. He thought the feeling would pass as he grew accustomed to his new role, but instead it grew stronger. Even in his diaries he referred to himself in the third person.

He sighed. They called the Grand Vizier the "bearer of the burden." But the Grand Vizier was only a juggler, a balancing act of flattery, mathematics and duplicity. It was the Sultan who truly carried the load; the great weight of expectation, not only of the six million Turks that he ruled, but of Islam itself.

But here, in the silence of the Harem, there was respite; scented wood burned in the tall copper hearth; firelight rippled on the tiled walls; silver incense burners smoldered, chasing away the bloody ghosts of Rhodes. There were no viziers, generals, responsibilities.

And there was Gülbehar .

He heard the rustle of fabric as she entered through a rose damask curtain at the far end of the room. Her hair was tied in a single long braid down her back. She wore a chemise - a gomlek - of sheer sky-blue silk and two diamond buttons danced against her flesh. Her waistcoat was of blue Bursa brocade, her pantaloons a white waterfall of silk. She is like sunlight rippling on the water, he thought.

Gülbehar , Rose of Spring. What a perfect name they gave you.

She fell on her knees and touched her forehead to the carpet. "Sala'am, Lord of my Life. Sultan of Sultans, Lord of the World. King of Kings."

He motioned to her, impatiently. How many times had he told her there was no need? But she always greeted him this same way, keeping to the ancient formula. But he did not wish to be reminded of his role in the world. He was a man come home; that was all he wanted.

"Come here."

She ran the last few steps and buried her face in his neck. He felt the wetness of her tears on his cheek and the scent of dried jasmine from her hair.

"When there was snow on the minarets and still you had not returned I thought you were never coming back. I was so frightened without you. There are so many whispers." She pulled away from him and stared into his face. "You were not hurt?"

"No scars that will ever show. How is little Mustapha?"

"He has missed you. He talks of you often."

"Let me see him."

Gülbehar took his hand and led him through the apartments to the prince's bedchamber. A candle burned in a long golden candlestick at one corner of the bed, attended by a turbaned page. Another stood waiting in the shadows. Whenever the boy turned in his sleep the candle on that side would be extinguished and another lit on the other side.

Suleiman leaned over the mattress. Mustapha had fair hair like his mother, and the same serene features. He was nine years old now, growing tall, as skilled at throwing a javelin as he was at learning the Qur'an and reading mathematics. The next Osmanli sultan, Suleiman thought. Enjoy your youth while you can. It is good you are growing broad shoulders.

Such irony that his son looked so little like him, even less like one of the Turks he would one day rule. But every Sultan's wife was a slave and an infidel, since the Qur'an decreed that no Muslim could be sold into slavery. So every Sultan was the son of a slave yet divinely chosen as the Protector of the Great Faith. God's web was indeed a large one.

"He is well?"

"Sturdy and strong. He wishes to be like his father."

He stroked a lock of hair from his son's forehead. "Bless you little Mustapha," he said. He turned to Gülbehar . Her silhouette was outlined against the candle flame. Desire was like a physical blow. He wanted to have her now, pour his seed into her, like a flood, like a river. But that would not do.

Instead he said: "We should eat now."

Gülbehar brought the food herself; tiny squares of lamb cooked in aromatic herbs, pieces of chicken baked over a slow fire, eggplants stuffed with rice. Afterwards there were figs in sour cream and sherbet from a cold gold goblet. Silent pages refilled their cups and bowls.

"What is the talk around the Harem?" Suleiman asked her. It always amused him to hear the gossip.

"They talk of you as a great hero," Gülbehar said. "When the news came that you had conquered Rhodes, everyone said you would be remembered by history as another Fatih, a great conqueror. Some say you are destined to be the greatest of all the Sultans."

"The price of such glory was very high. We lost many men."

"Our army will soon be strong again."

The remark irritated him. What did she know of armies? "It was a terrible battle. If it were for a woman's ears, I could tell you things ..." He dipped his fingers into a silver bowl of scented rosewater. A page appeared instantly to dry them.

"You must not think about that anymore."

"By day it is easy not to remember. But at night, in the dark, it is harder not to hear the screams."

He waited, but Gülbehar did not encourage him further. How can I tell her? I have to tell someone. Or perhaps this is just another burden I must shoulder alone. He looked up at Gülbehar and smiled. How wonderful of God to make such a thing as blue eyes. He let his gaze fall to the shadow of her breasts beneath the silk chemise.

"When you were away," she said, "I would take out your poems and read them. It always made me feel close to you again."

\* \* \*

After so long with only hard things - the hilt of a sword, the saddle of a horse - it was a glory to again touch something soft. His hands clutched at Gülbehar "s body so that several times she squealed with pain and he remembered himself and drew his hand away. But the softness of her belly and her thighs! He spread her legs apart and she wrapped them around his hips. He lost himself in his pleasure, chased away the memory of freezing rain with an arm protruding like a claw form the mud, the tower of Saint Michael emerging from the clouds and smoke. Was it the smell of blood or the taste of near-defeat that haunted him like this? Gülbehar whispered soft words to him and he pushed inside her and with that one urgent movement he felt his body spasm, the bitterness pouring from him.

Like a flood, like a river.

As the roaring of the blood subsided, images tumbled in his brain, future and past; Gülbehar with another son if God wills; the smell of that reeking moat at Rhodes; the executioner's sword glinting in the lamplight as it hung over Piri Pasha's head. Mustapha's sleeping face became his own, and then his father's, a monster with its beard soaking in blood as he ate his own children. He groaned aloud and fell sideways, heard Gülbehar whispering soothing endearments to try and calm him. Her arms and legs snaked around him.

Then nothing.

When he woke there was only the silence of the Harem, the slaves standing mute at the foot of the bed. A single candle burned in the dark. Gülbehar was asleep beside him, still and silent in her sleep as she always was.

This is my Harem, forbidden to all men but me. I have my favorite asleep under my arm, these are my poems in the niches of the walls where Gülbehar keeps the manuscripts of my poetry, each a secret part of me enshrined in the rich language of the Persian. Even within the protocols of the Harem, I have kept these rooms like a sanctuary.

And yet I feel so empty.

She thinks she knows me but she does not. Even my poems are form and style, pretty words, but not truly me. There is no one I can talk to openly except Ibrahim but even with him I must play a role. He would make a better Sultan than ever I would and we both know it.

I have everything but it is not enough. When a man is alone in Paradise it is just the same as being alone in Hell.

# CHAPTER 5

Hürrem knew that she had been seduced when she began to anticipate the hammam, the morning baths, with pleasure instead of contempt. On the steppe bathing was frowned upon, even feared. Everyone knew it led to chills, sickness and death. And massage and oils! This was indolence, pure and simple.

But the Turk insisted the girls bathe twice a day and shave every hair from their bodies. At first this practice disgusted her; now she enjoyed it. She was getting soft. If only her father could see her now, damn his barbarian soul to hell!

There were three rooms: the camekan, or dressing chamber; the sogukluk, or warming room; and the largest, central room, the steam room or hararet. Hürrem stripped off her clothes and one of the negresses - the gedicli - handed her a perfumed towel. She slipped a pair of rosewood nalins on her feet and went into the sogukluk. The warmth banished her gooseflesh. There was a large marble fountain in the centre of the room with water that had been heated in the massive boiler below and a number of girls were sitting or standing around it, scooping up the water in large copper bowls and pouring it over their heads. Hürrem joined them.

She looked around, while pretending to be occupied with her own toilet. She never ceased to be amazed by the variety of flesh. Until she came here she had not known the world was such a vast place, and that human beings could be so different; hair, nipples, skin, eyes. Such a profusion of shape and color. There were the gedicli with tight black curls and mahogany skins; Greek girls with dark eyes and their hair teased in a thousand ringlets; golden-haired Circassians with blue eyes and pink buds of nipples; Egyptian girls with long, aristocratic profiles and nipples the color of a bruised plum; Persians with hair the color of night and eyes deep and dark as wells.

And so many shapes! She scooped another bowl of water over her head, silently comparing herself while pretending not to stare. Some girls had full, pale, blue-veined breasts like nursing mothers, except their bellies were tight and flat; others had breasts like teardrops, some mere buds. Many of the houris were young girls barely out of puberty, their bodies impossibly tight and smooth. Hürrem looked down at herself, slim and small like a boy, and wondered why they had chosen her for this place.

Well perhaps I am not as beautiful as some of these odalisques, she reminded herself, but I have golden hair like a fox and cunning to match. She picked up her towel and went into the hararet, her pattens clip-clopping on the marble.

Inside, the steam seared the lungs and clung to the skin in a scorching veil. Instantly, perspiration oozed from her skin in a thousand tiny droplets. Willowy shapes moved in and out of the mist like wraiths. The silence here was broken only by the clank of a copper bowl or the splash as a girl got in or out of the bath.

Light filtered from high windows in the domed ceiling, the vapor and walls of grey-veined marble bleeding into one another so that it seemed there were no walls at all.

Hürrem lowered herself into one of the warm pools and closed her eyes, the water lapping around her shoulders and breasts. She rested her head on the marble lip, scooped a handful of water over her face and pushed the damp hair from her eyes.

Look at all these women, skins flushed and tingling from the scalding of steam and hot water, flesh kneaded into suppleness by the gedicli, primped and primed in silks and purring like kittens. Yet there is no man to appreciate it. So much anticipation and so little satisfaction!

Hürrem felt movement in the water and opened her eyes. A tall fair-haired woman was sitting on the edge of the bath, while two odalisques scooped water over her body and massaged the muscles of her shoulders. She was leaning back on her arms, head thrown back, her hair almost touching the marble floor behind her. Such outrageous assurance! Gülbehar !

She felt an unexpected rush of hatred and envy. Why you? She thought. With all these women here at his command, why just you? Is it you who is so beguiling or is he just so easy to bewitch?

Gülbehar opened her eyes and caught her staring. What was the look on her face? Was it pity?

Hürrem turned her back and eased herself out of the water, leaving her bottom in full view a moment longer than was necessary. She immediately regretted such a childish gesture.

She has no need to pity me, she thought as she snatched up her towel. Fear me, perhaps, but do not pity me.

* * *

Marble columns and arches led off the steam room into the yeni kaplija, smaller side chambers with raised marble slabs where the gedicli tended to the girls, massaging their bodies and minutely inspecting their noses and ears, their legs and arms, their pubis, vagina and anus, ensuring no trace of body hair remained. Hürrem had long abandoned protest at such indignity. After all, they would do it anyway.

Her gedicli's name was Muomi, a pouting, sullen girl with tight jet curls. The other houris spoke about her in whispers, they said she was a witch and avoided her if they could. She had large hands that knuckled deep into joints and sinews and made the girls scream. Often a girl came out after a session with her, her face wet with tears.

Hürrem enjoyed such a challenge. She won't make me cry.

She flung herself face down on the marble. "Try to do it properly this time. Last time my shoulders were still knotted."

"Last time I go soft on you. I thought you were going to cry like a little baby."

"I'll give you two aspers if you can make me cry."

"You don't have two aspers." Muomi started to knead the muscles at her neck and shoulders. Hürrem thought her eyes were going to pop out of her head. She took a deep breath and endured. When Muomi shifted her position to start on her back muscles, she said: "They say you're a witch."

"Who says it?"

"The other girls."

"The other girls! When they bring girls here, they look for beauty not brains. They are all as stupid as camels."

"Are you a witch?"

Muomi's hands moved along her spine. It felt like she was driving her knuckles between the bones. Hürrem felt the wellspring of tears in her eyes and buried her face in her arms to hide them. She pretended to yawn.

"Well, are you?" she repeated.

"If I were a witch I would have cast some spells and got myself out of here a long time ago."

She pressed her knuckles deep into Hürrem "s buttocks. They found the joint of her hip and Hürrem bit hard into the muscle of her forearm to keep from crying out. "Your muscles are as hard as a boy's," Muomi conceded.

"A bit harder," Hürrem said. "I can hardly feel it."

Muomi chuckled. "Like that?" she said and Hürrem yelped aloud.

* * *

Meylissa found Hürrem lying on her back while Muomi performed her depilatory. She applied a paste of rusma, made with quicklime, and expertly scraped away small hairs with the sharp edge of a mussel shell. Hürrem "s breasts rose and fell tremulously with her breathing. Her cheeks were wet.

"Are you all right?" she said.

"I owe this witch two aspers."

"What for?"

"She wants the bostanji's job," Hürrem said. "From now on, she will be the Sultan's new head torturer. "Muomi ignored her, shoving her legs apart and examining the perineum minutely for hairs.

Meylissa folded her arms, all petulance. "What's the point of all this? Muomi is the only one who will ever see if we shave or not. The Sultan never will!"

"We must be ready. We cannot let one golden opportunity be lost for one golden hair."

Meylissa perched on the edge of the marble and lowered her voice to a whisper. She put a hand on her own slender brown stomach. "Soon I'll be starting to show." As soon as she said the words her eyes filled with tears.

Muomi's head jerked up. "What's wrong with her?"

"She remembers the last time you rubbed her back," Hürrem said. She clutched Melissa's arm, her nails sinking in so that the younger girl winced. "Don't talk about it here!"

"What am I going to do?"

"It's all right, I have a plan."

"What plan?"

"You'll see. Muomi here is going to help us. Aren't you?" Meylissa stared at them, afraid and astonished, but Hürrem said no more. She closed her eyes and gave herself up to the soft world of steam and Muomi's mussel shell.

# CHAPTER 6

For two months the Kapi Aga had known, by turns, abject terror, tremulous anticipation and delirious pleasure. He was a man with vivid imagination and he knew what they would do to him if his secret was discovered. But he could not stop now, even if one of God's angels had descended to earth to give him a written promise, signed in gold by God Himself, that he would be caught. The sexual pleasure - and she was a beautiful woman, made doubly so by being forbidden - was only part of it. It was the confirmation of a manhood he thought he had lost. He told himself he could endure any death, as long as he died a man.

Each Thursday afternoon, an hour before dusk, she would come to the garden to read her Qur'an. His whole week was precariously constructed around that dreadful, exquisite moment when he would turn the key in that rusted lock and enter the garden. Each time he pushed open the door he could never be sure if he would find Meylissa and her kittenish smile or his own soldiers, their razor-edged killic drawn. Even as Head of the Palace Guard and Keeper of the Girls, he could not pull off his own dogs if he were discovered.

The iron-framed door creaked open - Merciful God it sounded like a cannon shot in the silence of the Harem! - and he crept through, locking it behind him. He glanced up at the north tower. The only way they might be seen was from the room at the very top - it was from there he had first seen Meylissa himself - but he had just locked the door to those two rooms himself.

Then why did he feel as if every member of the Divan was watching him, while the sharpened the iron hooks that would tear him apart?

The garden was shaded by high walls, the paths flanked by columns of white Paros marble and overhung with cypress and willow. It was always twilight here, though above the trees he could see the late afternoon sun catch the tiles on the minaret of the Harem mosque, turning them rose pink.

He looked around for Meylissa, thought to find her hunched over her Qur'an as usual on a marble seat beneath the colonnades; but there was no sign. He felt a thrill of fear. He held his breath and listened; the only sound was a lone nightingale calling softly in the willow branches above his head.

Why wasn't she here?

"She cannot come today."

The voice came from behind him. He jerked around, instinctively drawing his killic from its leather scabbard.

The girl crossed her arms and laughed at him.

He did not recognize her, but then there were so many new ones. She was tall and slim with flaming red hair and green eyes. She wore a yellow cotton kaftan with a gold brocade jacket and a little green cap - a taplock - on her head. There was a single pearl tied at the cap's tassel.

She was so tiny a breath of wind might blow her away. Yet she had scared him badly and he could not stop shaking. "Where is Meylissa?" he said.

"In the Harem of course, safe from the attentions of men."

"What are you laughing at?"

"You are as white as your turban. It's all right, as you can see, I'm not one of the Sultan's yeniceris. What are you so frightened of? I'm just a sewing girl. Look, I'm unarmed. I don't even have my needle."

"Who do you think you're talking to, girl? I'll have you put to the bastinado ..." He grabbed her by the arm, put his sword point to her eyes to intimidate her. Hürrem smiled back and her fingers closed around his groin.

"Meylissa says they still work. I'm just an innocent little sewing girl, but I thought they weren't supposed to."

"What are you talking about?"

"Meylissa is going to have your baby."

She might as well have told him she had the pestilence. He took a step backward and his sword slipped from his fingers and clattered onto the marble. His eyes were as wide as a horse bolting from a fire. He tried to say something and couldn't. A thread of saliva spilled from his bottom lip.

"You are thinking it's not possible? That's what she thought, too. But I promise you, Kapi Aga, you have defied their efforts to unman you."

"Who are you? What do you want?"

"I'm Meylissa's friend." She looked at the killic lying on the marble. "Pick it up," she said, for no other reason than to test her advantage.

He bent to do as he was told. "What do you want?"

"I want to help you."

"I remember you now. You're the Russian girl. We bought you from the Tatars."

She watched him with amusement; each question, each calculation was written there on his face as plain as if it was an illuminated page from the Qur'an.

"Who else knows?" he said.

"It would be so easy to toss us both in the Bosphorus in the middle of the night and be done with the whole thing. That's what you're thinking, isn't it? That's why we have told one other. Someone whose name you will never know."

"I know you. The Kiaya calls you her little minx."

"I am my own minx. I belong to no one."

He sheathed his sword. He had the look of a trapped animal about him, cowed but still dangerous. "So you want to help me?"

"I want to help Meylissa, but it will help you too. Or perhaps you do not wish my help. You could marry her and raise a family together."

"Do not mock me!" He took a step towards her, bold again. "How do I know this is true?"

"You do not. You might never know for certain until it is too late. One night the Sultan will appear in your quarters with two sacks. One for my friend Meylissa when they throw her in the Bosphorus. The other sack will be to collect the pieces of his former Kapi Aga after the bostanji-basha has finished cutting him into small pieces."

"You're just a houri. What can you do?"

"I can eliminate your problem for you."

"Eliminate?"

"Completely."

"There is a witch in here who knows how to do this?"

"In return you will do something for me."

"How do I know you are telling me the truth?"

"How can you be sure I'm not?"

He wanted to throttle her, that was plain, but that would not do him any good. He puffed out his cheeks and then, to her astonishment, stamped his foot. "All right," he said, at last. "What is it you want? A better position? Clothes? Money?"

"You value your life so cheap?"

The sun was low in the sky now, and the minaret had turned blood-red. He should be reaching the sublime moment there in the shadows not bargaining with this impudent little slave girl. "What is it you are after?"

"I want you to get me into the Sultan's bed."

"What? But I cannot do that. It's impossible!"

"Then you must make it possible. Or else it is very possible indeed that the Sultan will discover your perfidy and have you hung on a hook and leave you to turn black in the sun. You know the punishment."

"The Sultan never sleeps with any woman but Gülbehar , you know that! What you are asking is not in my power!"

For the first time Hürrem  stopped smiling. "Enjoy your death. I believe the will give you plenty of time to savor it."

She walked away. The shadows crept across the garden and the Kapi Aga watched them come, frozen with terror.

# CHAPTER 7

The Harem dated back to the time when the Osmanli Turks were no more than nomadic traders living on the wild plains of Anatolia and Azerbaijan. The idea of the Harem was borrowed from the Persians, as a convenience for warriors who were away from the tribe for long months at a time. When the Osmanlis gave up their nomadic lifestyle, creating a capital first at Bursa, then Stamboul, the Harem had become an institution in itself and a rigid hierarchy had evolved, with its own protocols and government.

The Harem was not governed by the Sultan, but by the Sultan's mother - the Sultan Valide. The Sultan was bound as much by the laws of the Harem as any of the girls. It was she who governed this reclusive community of eunuchs and virgins, with the help of a Kapi Aga, the Chief White Eunuch, who was both Captain of the Guard and intermediary between the Valide and the Sultan himself.

A girl first arriving at the Harem would be given a position in one of the many departments, with the Mistress of the Robes perhaps or the Chief Kitchen Maker. She might rise through the ranks to a position of some importance in the Harem administration through her own merits, but the only way she might attain real power was by becoming gözde - "in the eye"; that is, if she caught the interest of the Sultan himself.

If he actually invited her to his bed she became iqbal, and was given apartments and an allowance of her own. She might have one night with the Lord of Life or a hundred. But it all counted for nothing anyway unless she bore him a son and became one of his wives or kadins. There were only ever four wives and no more; after that, the abortionist was called in. These four wives remained just a breath from real power, for only one of them would one day become the mother of the next Osmanli Sultan.

But Suleiman had broken with tradition. Even though he was now almost thirty years old he still had only one kadin, Gülbehar , and just one son. It was a tenuous thread for an exalted bloodline such as the Osmanlis, and Suleiman's mother fretted continually over this reticence on her son's part to ensure he had enough heirs.

Hafise Sultan, the Valide, was an imposing woman, feared more than loved. She received the Kapi Aga in her audience chamber, an immense vault of gleaming onyx and veined marble.

A yellow bolt of sunlight angled in from the glass cupola high above.

She regarded the Kapi Aga from a high backed ebony chair upholstered with rich purple brocade. She looked entirely regal, except for her face, which had the soft lines and gentle grey eyes of a grandmother. It was the sort of face one was tempted to confide in. This made her very dangerous.

"You wanted to see me, Kapi Aga?" she said.

The Chief White Eunuch licked his lips. He felt as transparent as gossamer. He had practiced his speech long into the night but now every word of it deserted him and he felt overcome with a black panic. "Crown of Veiled Hands ..." he mumbled, addressing her by her formal title.

"What's the matter? Are you unwell?"

"A slight chill."

"A visit to the apothecary perhaps?"

"I shall do as your Highness suggests." Great God, just get this over with!

"Something is troubling you?"

Troubling him! He had spent most of the morning spurting his terror at both ends. It was a wonder he had not turned himself inside out. "I have word of unrest among some of the girls."

The Valide frowned. "What kind of unrest?"

"Well, some of them, they are ..."

"The point, Kapi Aga."

"They are jealous."

"Harem girls are always jealous of something."

"This is not a passing envy. The discontent is growing. I think we should pay attention to it."

The Valide gazed at him steadily, and he had the uncomfortable sensation that she could see into him. "Go on."

"It is Gülbehar . She is well loved by everyone of course ..."

"Except me."

Well yes, except you, the Kapi Aga thought. But I was counting on that. "But some of the girls feel it is not right nor just that the Lord of Life ignores the rest of them in this manner. Some are becoming almost ... unmanageable."

"Well that is your job, and that of the Kislar Aghasi. To manage them."

"Of course, My Lady. But if only there was something I could tell them …
to encourage them."

The Valide tapped a jewelled index finger on her cheek. "What might
prove sufficient encouragement, do you think?"

"That perhaps the Lord of Life would have use for them one day very
soon?"

"Who is to say what he will or will not do?" The old lady's smile vanished.
He had touched a nerve. If anyone was unhappy about Suleiman's exclusive
attachment to Gülbehar , it was his mother.

"They all cherish the opportunity to serve their master as best they can."

"Of course they do!" She knew that, she had been a slave girl once, before
Selim had thrown his handkerchief across her shoulder. "Are any of them a
match for Gülbehar ?"

"They all think they are," the Kapi Aga said with a tight smile. Normally
he would have allowed himself many such small jokes in the course of an
audience, but it was hard to relax this morning.

The Valide looked through the window and across the gleaming cupolas
of the Harem. She tapped the fingers of her left hand against her thumb as if
she was silently calculating figures in her head. "I shall talk to the Lord of
Life," she said. "Thank you for bringing this subject to my attention."

The Kapi Aga wanted to scream: "Wait, I haven't said it all yet!" but he
knew when he had been dismissed. He bowed and backed towards the door.

"One other thing."

"Yes, Highness?"

"Do you have any particular girl in mind?"

He tried to hide his relief. He had thought she might not ask him. "There
is one girl I think might turn our Lord's head from the Rose of Spring. She
has the sort of quick mind and lively nature he may find more than pleasing."

"Her name?"

"Hürrem , Highness. Her name is Hürrem ."

# CHAPTER 8

The Qur'an decreed: "Virtue is at the feet of the mother." Whenever Suleiman came to the Eski Saraya, it was required by custom and by religion that he visit his mother first. He had always enjoyed his mother's company so this was one burden of office that did not sit heavy with him.

Hafise Sultan sat on the terrace in a flowered brocade kaftan, the spring sunshine sparkling on the dusting of baroque pearl and garnets in her hair. She seemed to enjoy these useless baubles more than real gems. It was an endearing vanity.

"Mother." Suleiman kissed her hand and raised it to her forehead. He sat on the divan beside her, holding her hand in both of his. One of her handmaids hurried to fetch sherbets and rosewater.

"You are well?"

"I feel the chill more than I once did. At my age you look forward to spring."

"You are not so old."

"I am a grandmother," she said. "At least - I have one grandson. I suppose that is the same thing."

Suleiman threw back his head and laughed. "So that's what's wrong. You are so transparent."

"I am saddened at how lightly you treat an old woman's fears." Hafise pulled her hand away and chose a fig from the bowl of fruit in front of her. "And what of the conqueror of Rhodes? Where does the Divan urge you to strike next?"

"You will hear no war drums this year. All my generals are still licking their wounds. It will be some time before they are ready to stretch their claws again."

"And what about you?"

30

He sighed. "The thought of another campaign sickens me to my soul."

"A Sultan who refuses to carry the banner of Muhammad into battle shall not remain a Sultan for long. The yeniceris will see to that."

"You do not need remind me of my duty, to them or to God. But for this season at least I have had enough of war."

Hafise chose another fig with care, sifting for the right words with equal delicacy. "A Sultan's duty lies not only on the battlefield."

So, here was the real business; her first words to him that morning should have warned him. They were to talk of Gülbehar again. "The Osmanlis have an heir," he said.

"And what if he sickens? A Sultan should have many sons."

"So they can murder each other when I am dead?" Suleiman thought about his father, Selim - Selim the Grim, they had called him. He had deposed his own father with the support of the yeniceris, then poisoned him on his way to exile. He then murdered his two brothers and eight nephews so his sultanate could not be challenged. He had murdered Suleiman's own brothers so that he would not be burdened with the same grisly business. Did he doubt that he would have had the stomach for it? Suleiman himself had not had a moment's ease until Selim's wasted and pain-racked body had finally succumbed to a stomach canker.

"You have a duty."

"I have many duties."

"And you should not neglect a single one."

She was right, of course. It was she, not Selim who had taught him that duty took precedence above all else. "Gülbehar makes me happy."

"We are not talking about happiness, we are talking about heirs to the line of Osman."

Suleiman turned away, staring at the panorama of minarets and cupolas that punctuated the jumble of wooden houses above the Golden Horn. He remembered his father's words to him before he sent him to Manissa as governor, his first official post: "If a Turk dismounts from the saddle to sit on a carpet, he becomes nothing - nothing."

But then his father was a barbarian.

"At this moment the house of Osman has only two heartbeats," Hafise said. "It is not enough."

"What would you have me do?"

"I do not ask you to give up your Gülbehar . It is only natural that you should have a favorite. But there are many girls in the Harem. Some of them must be pleasing to the eye."

"So I must play the bull for the house of Osman?"

"Indelicately put, especially in front of an old woman, but yes, that is exactly what you should do. Perhaps it would be different if Gülbehar had given you more sons. But she has been your kadin now for nine years …"

"She pleases me."

"And another woman cannot?"

Suleiman jumped to his feet. He saw Fatih, one of his mother's handmaids, glance at him shyly from under kohl-darkened eyelashes. He felt a surge of impatience, with her and with himself. What was wrong with him? Most men would not find it such an onerous duty. *Perhaps it is my way to rebel against the burden, how I demonstrate to everyone - especially myself - that I am different from the beasts who came before me. These hungry women make me feel shabby and degraded.*

Fatih saw she had made him angry and lowered her eyes.

"I will do as you ask," he said and kissed his mother's hand. *I'll bull them all, one at a time, if that is what you want,* he thought. *I'll fill the palace with cradles.*

*And then I'll go back to Gülbehar .*

***

The Kiaya snatched the cushion slip from Meylissa's hands, flung it on the floor and stamped on it. "What is this? Are you deliberately trying to provoke me?"

Meylissa shook her head miserably.

"Look at these stitches! I would not give this to a peasant in the field, never mind the Valide!"

"I'm sorry ..."

"What is the matter with you? These last few weeks you have been quite impossible!" She slapped Meylissa hard on the ear. The girl's howls encouraged her and she did it again.

Hürrem was contemptuous of Meylissa's surrender, but it was an opportunity to confront the old bitch. She got up from her workbench and snatched up the silk cushion at the Kiaya's feet. "It is not so bad. I can alter this easily."

"Ah, the little minx! You cannot sit still when you see fur flying, can you my sweet?"

"Leave her alone, she is not feeling well."

"Well, let's send her to the infirmary then. And if your stitching is so fine, you can do her work as well as your own!"

Hürrem flung the piece of material in her face. "Do it yourself, you old hag!"

The Kiaya slapped her hard on the cheek. Hürrem took a step back, then her own hand took the Kiaya on the side of the head, almost knocking her off her feet. The sound of the slap was followed by utter silence. The Kiaya stared at her, stunned.

Then her face split into a slow, triumphant smile. "For that you get the bastinado," she whispered. "The Kapi Aga will have them strip the flesh from the soles of your feet with whips. It is spring now. If you are lucky you might take your first steps again in the winter. I will teach you to strike me!"

Two guards appeared in the doorway. One stepped into the room and took Hürrem "s arm. "You are to come with me," he said in his high-pitched tremolo. "Bring your sewing with you."

Well, that was quick, Hürrem thought. Even the Kiaya cannot have her revenge served as promptly as this. She picked up her needles, her little bag of emery powder, and the green square of silk she had been embroidering, hoped the old hag could not see how her hands shook.

"Where are you taking her?" the Kiaya said.

"The Kapi Aga has given us our orders," he said and led Hürrem to the door.

"She must be put to the bastinado!" the Kiaya shrieked, but there was no conviction in her voice, only bewilderment.

Hürrem let the guards hurry her away down the corridor. If the Kapi Aga had sent for her, it could mean only one thing, and it was not the bastinado.

# CHAPTER 9

The courtyard was paved with almond-shaped cobblestones and dominated by an ornate marble fountain. Windows looked down from all sides. Hürrem felt as if the whole Harem was watching her.

This was the courtyard of the Sultan Valide! These were her apartments.

The guards hurried her to the centre of the court and there released her. "The Kapi Aga says you are to wait. And be sure to sing."

"Sing, why? What is happening?"

But the men had done as they had been ordered and they wheeled away without another word, the sickle-bladed yataghans at their waists rattling in their scabbards. Hürrem stared after them.

She waited there for an eternity but no one came. Water murmured in the marble fountain. Perhaps the Kapi Aga had arranged an interview with Hafise Sultan? she thought. But then why had they insisted she bring her needlework? What else was it they had said? "The Kapi Aga says you are to wait. And be sure to sing."

The Kapi Aga wanted her to break the sacred silence of the Harem?

She grew tired of waiting, found a cool spot in the shade of the fountain and sat down, crossing her legs beneath her, Osmanli style. She spread the handkerchief on her lap, took out her needle and went back to her embroidery. She chose to hum a love song her mother had taught her, about a boy whose horse had fallen in the snow, trapping him; as he died by inches on the winter steppe he told the wind how much he loved a certain girl and how he had never had the courage to tell her. He asked the wind to carry his words across the plain so that she would remember him. It was a stupid, sentimental song, Hürrem thought, but she had always liked the tune and after a while the words came back to her as well.

She soon forgot her initial anxiety and did not even notice the tall, slender figure in the white turban until his shadow fell across her lap.

"The first law of the Harem is silence."

She looked up, startled. The man was standing with the sun behind his back and she had to shield her eyes against the glare. He did not speak like a eunuch and he was not black like a Nubian. There was only one other man who might walk freely here.

"Perhaps we should cut out the tongues of all the nightingales then. And the bees. We should do something about them also. All this incessant buzzing. Don't they know the rules?" There. It was out of her mouth before she could stop herself.

For a moment he just stared at her. Hürrem remembered that her first action before speaking should have been to lower her forehead to the ground and make her obeisance. She put down her embroidery and went to her knees. She touched her forehead to the hot stones, a futile gesture, it was already too late. She should beg his forgiveness for breaking the silence. Well, there was no point now, he had spoken and she had answered him.

She was suddenly aware that the old Kislar Aghasi - the Chief Black Eunuch - was standing behind Suleiman, his face beaded with perspiration, fanning himself with a silk handkerchief. He looked as if he were about to faint.

"Do you know who I am?" Suleiman asked her.

"You are the Lord of Life."

"What were you singing?"

"It was a song I learned from my mother, my Lord. A love song. About a stupid boy who let his horse fall on top of him."

"He was singing to the horse?"

She giggled, then stifled it. "I think not. I dare to say the horse had lost much of its charm by then."

She heard him laugh. "What is your name?"

"They call me Hürrem , my lord."

"Hürrem ? Laughing one. Who gave you that name?"

"The men who brought me here. They could not pronounce my name. Though I suspect they were not intelligent enough to pronounce their own names either."

He laughed again. "Where are you from, Hürrem ?"

She squinted up at him. This was the moment for which she had gambled so much and all she could think about was the pain in her knees. How long would he make her squat here on these cobblestones? "I am a Tatar," she said. "A Krim."

"Do all you Tatars have hair of such amazing color?"

"No, my Lord. I was the only one in my clan so burdened."

"Burdened? I think not. It is quite beautiful." He stroked her hair and held a lock of it in his fingers, as if he were examining a piece of material in the bazaar for quality and strength. "It is like burnished gold. Is it not, Ali?"

The Kislar Aghasi murmured his agreement. Liar! Hürrem thought. You have only spoken to me once, and on that occasion you called me an undernourished carrot.

"Stand up, Hürrem ."

At last! She did as she was told. She knew she should lower her eyes, as she had been trained to do, but curiosity got the better of her. So this was the Lord of Life, the Possessor of Men's Necks, the Lord of the Seven Worlds! He was handsome, she supposed, but not especially so. There was the shadow of a beard on his face, which lent a certain majesty to his beaked nose. He had grey eyes.

He examined her head to toe, as the spahis had done the day her father had traded her. He did not seem especially displeased with what he saw yet when he had done he gave a long sigh. "What is that you are embroidering?" he asked her.

"A handkerchief, my lord."

"Let me see it." She handed it to him. "A fine piece of work. You have great skill. May I have it?"

"I have not finished ..."

"Have it ready for me tonight," he said and placed it carefully over her left shoulder. The Kislar Aphasias eyes widened in shock. Placing a handkerchief on a girl's shoulder signified that she was now gözde, and that the Sultan wished to sleep with her. No girl had been so favored since he had assumed the throne.

Suleiman walked away without another word. The Kislar Aghasi looked as if he would burst; then he remembered himself and hurried after him.

Hürrem stood there, frozen to the spot, long after they were gone. Her body trembled with triumph and excitement.

Gözde! I am in the eye! Now I just have to stay there.

\* \* \*

Suleiman hurried along the cloister, both angry and relieved. He had been forced to betray his own desires, but at least he had acted swiftly and decisively. After his mother's lecture to him that morning he accepted that he had neglected his duty, and had asked the Kapi Aga to arrange a suitable girl. This Hürrem that head picked out for him was appealing in an elfin way, she at least had an entertaining turn of mind. Most Harem girls were insufferably empty and vain.

And if she got pregnant his mother would be satisfied and he could return to Gülbehar and carry on his life in peace.

# CHAPTER 10

## Topkapi Saraya

A crescent moon trembled in the night sky. Suleiman and Ibrahim had dined well on sturgeon, lobster and swordfish, taken that same morning from the Bosphorus, all washed down with sherbets made with violets and honey. They had completed the meal with a bottle of Cyprus wine, even though it was forbidden by the Qur'an.

It was a small transgression, but one that gave him a measure of satisfaction, for in all other ways his life was proscribed by protocol.

At waking: the Parer of the Nails, and the Chief Barber to shave his head; then the Master of the Wardrobe, who laid out his day's clothes, each piece scented with aloe wood; then the Chief Turban Winder to curl yards of linen around his fez.

Five days a week he arose at dawn to attend the Divan; Fridays he rode to prayers along the Divan Yolu to the Aya Sofia, in procession with his Grand Vizier, his astronomers, his Chief Huntsman, his Chief Keeper of the Nightingales, the Master of the Keys, the Master of the Stirrup and four thousand of his yeniceris and Spahis of the Porte, his regular cavalry.

Afternoons: a short nap, required by custom, tired or not, reclining on two mattresses, one of silver brocade, the other of gold. He was attended at all times by five guards, deaf-mute eunuchs.

Within the confines of state, such small rebellions as a glass of wine were great victories.

Ibrahim was his greatest scandal, of course. During the siege they had slept in the same pavilion, had worn each other's clothes. He knew he outraged the whole court by showing such favor to a slave but then, for him, he was not a slave; he was confidant, confessor and counsellor. If anyone

37

helped him shoulder the burden it was not Gülbehar or Hafise, nor even the Grand Vizier. It was Ibrahim.

After they had the wine, Ibrahim sat cross-legged beneath the window. They were the same age, but somehow Suleiman felt so much older. Careworn might be a better word. But this betrays our heritage, he thought. I am the son of a man they called The Grim; Ibrahim is the son of a fisherman.

He had been born in a village on the western coast of Greece. He was stolen by traders and taken to the slave markets in Stamboul, where he was bought by a widow from Manias. She raised him a Muslim, and when she discovered his flair for music and languages, she had arranged for him to have a good education. He learned to play the viol and he could speak Persian, Turkish, Greek and Italian.

Later she sold him for a handsome profit into Suleiman's service when he went to Manisa as the new governor of Kaffa province.

When he became Sultan in 1520 he brought Ibrahim with him to the Porte and made him his hasoda-bashi, head of household. He sought him out for counsel now more often that he did Piri Pasha, his old Grand Vizier. After Rhodes he even made him one of his counsellors, just below Piri Pasha himself in rank.

This is why we Osmanlis are glorious, Suleiman thought. Even a Christian slave can rise by his own merits to become almost pre-eminent in the greatest Islamic empire the world has ever seen. What was it the Fatih had said?

"Our Empire is the home of Islam, from father to son the lamp is kept burning with oil from the hearts of the infidels.

"So solemn, my lord?" Ibrahim said, setting the viol aside.

Suleiman sighed. "Do you ever have regrets, Ibrahim?"

"Of course not. Look us here tonight. Good food. Good wine. What is there to regret?"

"But do you not sometimes wish you were someone else? Do you ever wonder what might have happened if the pirates had not come to the village that day and snatched you away?"

"I know what would have happened. I would be eating fish for breakfast and supper and mending nets on the beach all day. Instead I sleep in a palace, drink the best Cyprian wine and am held in favor by the greatest Emperor on the earth."

"Your life would have been simpler."

"My life would have been worthless."

"You enjoy all this, don't you? You enjoy going to war and you relish the endless politicking in the Divan."

"We are at the hub of the world, my Lord. We are writing history!"

"We are serving Islam."

"Well yes, that too." He picked up the viol again. "We are Islam's greatest servants."

Liar, Suleiman thought. You do all this for its own sake. That is why I love you and envy you so much. I wish I was more like you.

"I think sometimes you should have been Sultan and I the son of a Greek fisherman. We might have been happier that way." He got to his feet, rubbed his face with his hands.

"Shall we sleep now, my Lord?"

"You may sleep, Ibrahim. Your life is simpler than mine. I have yet one more duty to perform."

\* \* \*

Hürrem had been escorted to the Keeper of the Baths to be bathed and massaged. Her nails were dyed, her hair perfumed with jasmine, her skin pomaded with henna to prevent sweating, her eyes blackened with kohl.

She was then escorted to the Kiaya of the Robes, who dressed her in a rose-colored chemise and purple velvet kaftan, with a robe of silver and apricot brocade over the top. The Kiaya of the Jewels brought a diamond necklace as heavy as an iron collar and a string of fat Arabian pearls to plait into her hair, as well as a pair of heavy ruby earrings that reached to her shoulders.

They must all be returned in the morning, she was told.

A gedicli held up a mirror so that Hürrem could inspect her reflection. She regarded the apparition that stared back at her with something close to disbelief. "I look completely hideous."

The Kiaya of the Robes put her hands on her hips. "It is the way."

"It is the way to make a man fall on the floor laughing."

"You ungrateful little minx. Do you not realize the great honor that has fallen on you? Remember, it happened to me once, so don't think you are so high and mighty. You could end up Mistress of the Robes on day, and no more than that!"

"If you dressed this way on your big night, it's a wonder he didn't make you Mistress of the Royal Lavatory."

The Kiaya hissed with outrage and sent the two gedicli out of the room. "Now listen here! I don't deny that you and I ever got along too well, but I'm still willing to help you. This is a once in a lifetime opportunity. I know what it's like, I was gözde once, when Bayezid was Sultan. Let me tell you what you should do to please him …"

"I do not need advice from a failure. I know what I have to do. I have to get pregnant!" And she swept from the room.

# CHAPTER 11

There were two guards, the same pair who led her to the courtyard earlier in the day. They escorted her along a maze of gloomy, cold cloisters and down a narrow staircase. The hem of her gown and the trailing sleeves of her kaftan kept catching and tearing on the wood. She felt a chill draft of air on her cheek and she was propelled into the night through a heavy iron door. A boxlike carriage was waiting for her. She caught a whiff of horse and ancient leather and then a soft, fleshy hand pulled her inside.

The carriage jerked forward and the horse's hoofs clattered on the cobbles. As her eyes adjusted to the dark she made out the bulky silhouette of the Kislar Aghasi opposite her.

"Where are we going?" she said.

"To the Sultan. He is waiting for you in the Topkapi Saraya."

The curtains were drawn. Hürrem tried to shift them aside to peek outside but he snatched her hand away. "Is it far?" she said.

"No, not far." She could feel his eyes watching her, huge and yellow, like a cat. "The Kapi Aga arranged this for you," he said.

"Why would he do that?"

"A question I have been asking myself all day."

"And what answer did you come up with?"

"I have none. He looks very pale these days, like a man awaiting execution. Have you not noticed?" When she did not answer, he added: "Or perhaps he is unwell."

"Perhaps."

"Do not misunderstand me. Should the Kapi Aga fall into disfavor I shall not weep for him."

The coach clattered to a halt and the door was thrown open. Hürrem looked quickly around as she stepped down. So this was the Topkapi! The great tower of the Divan loomed above her and torches dotted around the gardens flickered among the bushes. A thousand trees rustled in the night wind.

Two halberdiers, the heavy tressed plumes on their helmets covering half their faces, ushered her through a massive iron-studded door and into the heart of the seraglio. The Kislar Aghasi wheezed and puffed as he struggled along behind. Hürrem was struck by how orderly and spacious it all seemed after the drabness of the Eski Saraya. The walls here were stone, not wood, and the corridors wider and better lit.

They reached two wooden doors, inlaid with mother of pearl and tortoiseshell, that led to the Sultan's private chambers. Two of his private bodyguards, the solaks, stood on guard on either side, their yataghans drawn.

Hürrem took a deep breath. This was the moment she had gambled everything for. Be calm, she told herself, you do not have to beguile him; just accept his seed and let it flower into freedom.

The Kislar Aghasi threw open the doors and led her inside.

\* \* \*

Hürrem looked around in awe.

The walls were decorated with Iznik tiles; peacock blue, orange and viridian in dazzling patterns of flowers and fruit. The ceiling rose to a high dome and below it censers on long golden chains glittering with turquoises and rubies. There was a fireplace shaped like a copper pyramid, and oil lamps glimmered in niches on the walls.

The bed was on a raised platform in the corner, hung with a canopy of green and gold Bursa brocade, supported on columns of fluted silver. There were quilts and cushions of crimson velvet, every one of them laced with pearls. Tapers burned in platinum candlesticks at the four corners.

Suleiman reclined on a divan of shimmering gold velvet. He wore an apple-green robe and a turban of pure white silk with a clasp of heron feathers and an emerald, the size of a baby's fist, glinting from the folds. One arm stretched languorous along the back of the divan. He looked faintly bored.

The door shut gently behind her as the Kislar Aghasi crept from the room. They were alone.

He stared at her for a long time in silence. She could almost hear him thinking: What have they done to you?

She should have trusted her own judgment. She had allowed the Kiaya to humiliate her yet again.

She untied the robe and let it slip to the floor, then unfastened the diamond buttons of the kaftan and pulled it over her head. She ripped off the diamond necklace and tossed it on top of the robe with the earrings. Finally she loosened the pearls from her hair and shook it free.

When she was done, she had on only her chemise and harem trousers. She pointed to the rich pile of garments at her feet. "The Kiaya of the Robes chose my wardrobe personally. Of course, these days she is half blind."

He shrugged. Why doesn't he do something, say something? she thought. And then it hit her; he was as much at a loss as she.

She must shake him from this torpor and she knew only one way to do that. She fell to her knees, covered her face in her hands and started to weep.

"What is wrong?"

"Lord of my Life, why did you choose me? There are so many beautiful girls in the Harem. I am not good enough for you. I know nothing about love or men.

He rose from the divan and put a hand on her shoulder. "Please, get up."

"I am too ashamed. You think I am ugly."

"I think you are … delightful. It is just that when you came in … you are right, the Kiaya must be half blind."

She let him lift her to her feet. She looked up into his face, searching for a clue to what he was thinking. "I never wanted this," she whispered. "I am frightened."

"Any girl in the Harem would change places with you right now."

"Then let them. They are far more beautiful than I."

"Hush now. Come and sit down." He led her to the divan and sat her down beside him, without letting go of her hand. "I think you are quite exceptional," he said and stroked her cheek.

She moved her head slightly to trap his hand between her cheek and her shoulder. "What should I do?"

"Just be yourself." He took her face in his hands, almost shyly. He brought her face towards him and kissed her. He tasted of wine. I have learned your first secret! she thought.

He pulled her towards him. His fingers gripped her shoulders so hard it hurt her. Yes, you like that, don't you? she thought. The Shadow of God Upon the Earth was a man like any other; he wanted to hear his woman moan a little.

He pushed her back on the Divan, tore at the pearl buttons of her chemise. She surrendered to him, murmuring softly, almost as if a man loving her could somehow bring her pleasure.

# CHAPTER 12

Now she was iqbal, Hürrem was given an allowance of two hundred aspers and her own apartment, and enough organza, silk, taffeta, brocade and satin for the Mistress of the Robes to outfit a complete wardrobe. She even had use of her own bath, carved from rose-veined marble, with its own cascading fountain of scented rosewater. Nightingales twittered in cedar cages on her private terrace.

She was also allowed her own gedicli. Hürrem asked for Muomi.

The girl seemed neither pleased nor surprised at Hürrem "s summons. On being presented to her in her new quarters, she looked at the carpets, shuffling her big splayed feet, her face a sullen mask of indifference.

Hürrem sat with her legs drawn under her on the divan. "Are you happy with your work in the hammam?" she asked her.

Muomi shrugged her shoulders by way of answer.

"As iqbal, I am allowed to choose my own handmaid. The work will be much easier than you are accustomed to."

Muomi offered no comment.

Hürrem got to her feet and put her lips next to the other girl's ear. "I want you to help me. Tell me what you want in return."

"What do I want?" She lifted her eyes. "When I was seven years old, the magic man in our tribe came to our family's hut with a stinging nettle. He parted my legs and rubbed the nettle into my cleft. That was to make it swell. The next day he came back and washed between my legs with butter and honey, then cut away everything that gives a woman pleasure and cauterized the wound with a red-hot ember. My mother pretended to cry with joy to cover my screams. When I married my husband opened me up with a knife to take me. Then he had me sewn up again, until the next time. It was the same when the baby came. When the traders stole me they took my baby away,

43

because he was a boy child. I do not know if he is dead or alive. If he is alive they will castrate him, the same as they castrated me. As for me, I will spend the rest of my life in this place, a slave, if not to you, then someone else. So tell me - what could you possibly offer me?"

Hürrem smiled and stroked her cheek, fondly as a lover. "Revenge," she said.

\* \* \*

The Okjmeydan, the Place of Arrows, looked down through groves of rosebushes the size of apricot trees to the dark waters of the Golden Horn. It was nearly summer, the time of year when the war drum beat in the court of the yeniceris, when the Grande Turke would set out again from Stamboul to raid the Lands of War.

But this year there would be no war; instead Suleiman was to remove the court to Adrianople for the hunting. He and Ibrahim went every day to the meydan with their arrows and spears for target practice. Ibrahim had set up the statues they had plundered from Belgrade along the slopes. The notion of using Greek Gods as targets amused him.

He ran to collect the arrows that had missed their mark himself, bounding through the grass like a small boy, crowing with delight when he discovered his aim was good and his arrow had split itself apart on Dionysius or Zeus.

Afterwards he and Suleiman rested in the broad shade of a fig tree and pages brought them olives and cheese and sherbets.

"If only our statues had been Charles or Frederick, I should have pierced their hearts a thousand times! I cannot wait for the hunt."

"Your aim is excellent, Ibrahim. If I were a boar, I should start running towards Russia now."

"Your eye is good also."

"No, you flatter me. My mind is on other things today."

Ibrahim drained his silver goblet, then carefully selected an olive, chewing it slowly as he placed the chalice an arm's length away in the grass. Then, with great theatrics, he spat the stone into the empty cup. He repeated this several times, without missing once.

"You are like a child sometimes."

"But it amuses you?"

"You always amuse me, Ibrahim."

"So what is troubling you today, my Lord?"

"Let me ask you something first. When we came from Manisa, you were able to establish your own harem?"

"Of course, though it is not as extensive as yours, my Lord."

"But you have a favorite?"

"Whenever I am with a woman, she becomes my favorite."

It was not the answer he had hoped for. How could he explain his problem to a man like Ibrahim? The night after he bedded Hürrem  he had chosen another of the Harem girls, fulfilling his duty to the Osmanli line, as the Valide had insisted. The girl was a simpering Georgian, with the most startling black eyes; eyes that must have taken up her whole head for when she opened her mouth she had nothing whatever to say. When he took her to bed she lay there pliantly, and the only time she had cried out was when he entered her.

She did not wake him three times during the night, as Hürrem  had done, begging for more.

The Georgian was classically, faultlessly beautiful but it was not enough. Not for him, anyway.

And what about Gülbehar ? She had been his favorite for nearly ten years, a slight, shy girl of fifteen when he first lay with her. Until Hürrem  she had satisfied all his needs. Now a door had opened on other possibilities.

The Possessor Men's Necks no longer had possession of himself. He had promised himself that he would not lie with any but Gülbehar  more than once, he was now tempted to summon Hürrem  once more; to hear her laugh, to hear her sigh and to discover if making love to her a second time might be as bewitching as the first.

But he hesitated. Surely, it was not good for a woman to find as much pleasure in the flesh as a man? This Hürrem "s soul was tainted by the sins of Rachel. If he encouraged her in her vice, was he then not tainted also? And what of Gülbehar ? He would be breaking the promise he had made to her, and to himself. He experienced the first sour gnawing of an emotion he had never expected to feel with any woman other than his mother.

Guilt.

"Does a woman have a soul, Ibrahim?"

"Does it matter?" Ibrahim sensed the shift in his mood and leaned in. "Is it Gülbehar  who troubles you?"

"No, it is another."

"May I enquire her name?"

"Her name is Hürrem ," Suleiman said.

Ibrahim raised an eyebrow. Another woman in Suleiman's bed? That was rare, though he himself had encouraged the Lord of Life to choose from his Harem more often. Then why this feeling of unease? It could be nothing. Suleiman often fell into these strange moods for no reason.

He aimed another olive stone at the goblet but this time it landed softly in the grass, a man's footstep wide of the mark.

# CHAPTER 13

Meylissa lay up to her shoulders in the bath. The milky mist of the hammam made it appear that her face was disembodied, like a ghoul. Her eyes followed Hürrem all the way to the water's edge. Hürrem stopped beside the pool to allow Muomi to remove her gauze shift, then lowered herself naked into the water.

"You look ill," Hürrem said to her.

"I am sick every morning. The Kiaya wants to send me to the infirmary."

"Don't let her."

"Do you think I'm stupid?" Meylissa moved closer. "Every day my waist gets thicker. I cannot pretend forever that it is the sweetbreads. You said you would help me!"

"Why do you think I am here?"

"I don't know. You have your own hammam now. Does the Sultan visit you every night?"

"I am going to help you, just as I promised."

"How? Will you plead for me with the Lord of Life while he shares your pillow?"

Hürrem nodded her head in the direction of her maidservant. "Muomi."

"Your gedicli? What can she do?"

"She is a witch. She is going to make you a potion, an abortive."

Meylissa" bottom lip quivered. The girl was living on her nerves, Hürrem thought, it would not take much for her to break down completely. "Be brave," she whispered to her. "It will be all right."

"It is too late."

Hürrem grabbed her arm. "Don't be such a milksop! Of course it's not too late. Do you think this is any easier for me? What if the Kislar Aghasi finds out about this? They'll kill me too!"

Meylissa bit her lip to keep from crying. "When?"

"I will send Muomi to you tomorrow. But you must tell no one about this."

"Of course I won't."

"Everything will be all right," she repeated, "you'll see."

Meylissa nodded and climbed out of the pool. Hürrem studied her silhouette through the steam. Great Heaven she was getting big. She had hardly any waist at all.

\* \* \*

Suleiman lay among the pillows and silks, Gülbehar naked beside him. He smiled; it was not just her beauty he appreciated but the familiarity of it. *Perhaps I am a creature of protocol and tradition, after all. I love order and repetition more than I know.*

He put a hand to her breast, and with his finger he tracked the blue vein from her nipple to the hollow of her shoulder. He watched the nipple tighten and constrict. *Another small miracle of the flesh!*

Gülbehar smiled at him, more in kindness than pleasure.

He felt a stirring of doubt. *This pleases her because it pleases me,* he thought, *and that is the proper way of it. But with Hürrem , she smiles because it pleases her also. The teachers say that is sinful.*

Gülbehar had painted her pubis with henna, as was the fashion. She moved her legs apart again, in readiness for him. He eased himself on top of her, watched her face intently for evidence of what she was feeling. *She is so eager to please me,* he thought. *She has never wanted anything more but to sate my hunger. Why should I ever want any more than that?*

When he was inside her he closed his eyes and Gülbehar "s face vanished, suddenly, shockingly. Instead he saw Hürrem , her head thrown back, her mouth open in a silent scream, the mane of gold-red hair splayed across the pillow, her body arched beneath him as if she were in the grip of some great torment. His sublime moment came swiftly.

He groaned and his strength left him. Gülbehar "s arms pulled him down on top of her in warm embrace. She was still smiling.

"It was good, my Lord?" she whispered.

"Yes. Yes, it was good."

But his hunger had not gone. *What more could he want? He wanted her. He wanted Hürrem .*

\* \* \*

Hürrem sat on the terrace, watching the dawn break over the city. A silver sliver of moon faded into the deepening blue of the morning as the calls of the muezzin broke the crystal silence. Another night passed without him, another night he had spent instead with Gülbehar , another night driven further into exile.

It had been almost a week since he had asked for her. One could not remain iqbal forever. If she did not become pregnant and the Sultan continued to ignore her, she would have to return to the sewing room and the taunts and lashes of the Kiaya of the Robes, and she would spend the rest of her life there, without prospect of more.

She could not allow that to happen.

# CHAPTER 14

The Kapi Aga had died a thousand deaths in the week since his encounter with Hürrem . He lived in unholy terror and every time he heard footfall in the corridor he thought it was the Sultan's bodyguard come to fetch him. He slept fitfully and dreamed about escape. But where could he hide where the Sultan could not find him when his empire spanned three continents?

So one warm-scented evening he went down to the garden once more. Nightingales sang in the plane trees. Such a pleasant hell, he thought. Every stone of this accursed place was dangerous, no matter how many birds sang in it.

He turned the ancient key in the lock and inched it open. He crept into the garden.

Hürrem knelt on the grass beside the fountain, a Qur'an, illuminated in green and gold, lying open on the wooden stool in front of her. She wore a green satin taplock, a chemise of emerald damask and white silk pantaloons so sheer she might as well have been naked from the waist down. He started to sweat.

She might have been desirable if she were not so terrifying.

"I did as you asked," he said.

* * *

Hürrem looked up, the intimation of a smile on her lips. She studied him with her piercing green eyes, then returned her attention to her Qur'an. He was not such a bad-looking fellow, she thought. Eyes as dull and savage as an animal's, but you would expect that in a Serb. They dressed him well: a pelisse of green velvet, yellow slippers, a white sugarloaf turban. The effect was not too unpleasant.

"I said, I did as you asked."

"Good."

"And now?"

"Now?"

"You must fulfil your part of the bargain."

She turned a page of her Qur'an. The Kapi Aga tried to control his temper. How thoroughly satisfying it would be, he thought, to slice off her head. Be done with this upstart right now. Watch her life's blood spurt over the word of Mohammed and up the grey stone wall. If only that would solve the problem.

"When does the Sultan return to the Eski Saraya?"

"Our bargain-"

"When?"

"He goes north to Adrianople tomorrow for the hunting. He will not be back until the leaves fall." He smiled at how the blood had drained from her face. How much longer do you think you will remain iqbal, you little witch?

"We had a bargain," he said.

"There is one more condition."

"I have done as you asked. You may make no more demands of me!"

"While I keep your secret for you, I may do as I please."

She is right. I am impotent in this. Yes, once more, someone has me by the balls. But I will see you squirm for this one day, Tatar witch. "You said you would help me."

Hürrem  closed the book, the heavy pages slamming shut like an iron door. She got to her feet and stepped right up to him. To his amazement she ran a fingernail down the length of his arm and took his hand.

"I will help you. After tonight, you will no longer have a problem. You will live in fear no more."

His mouth went dry. Hürrem  moved closer. He could feel the heat of her body and the softness of her thigh against his groin. "What do you want?" he said but his voice did not sound like his own.

Her breath was hot and sweet on his cheek. "I want some of your juice," she whispered.

\* \* \*

Meylissa was embroidering a kaftan the color of burnished gold for the young shahzade, Mustapha. She took her handiwork to the window to examine it in the fading light of the afternoon. She heard someone enter the room behind her.

"Did I frighten you?" Muomi said.

"No," Meylissa said and shook her head, but it was a lie. Muomi always made her uncomfortable.

"I have what you needed." Muomi put a small blue and white jar on her workbench.

Meylissa removed the rounded cork stopper and sniffed. "It's foul."

"Of course it is. It's a kind of poison. Swallow it all, it will make you sick and kill the baby."

Meylissa replaced the stopper. Her hands shook. "Thank you."

Muomi gave her a pitying look. "It has nothing to do with me," she said and shuffled out.

# CHAPTER 15

The Kislar Aghasi woke to the sound of a woman screaming. At first he thought it might be just one of the girls crying in her sleep - some of the new ones did that, and he would have to organize a beating for them the next day to encourage them to stop. But as he came awake he realized this was no milksop's nightmare. He had heard screams like that before, coming from the bonstanji-bashi"'s torture chamber. He swung his legs off the cot and reached for his wooden pattens. His hands were trembling.

The candle had not burned down far, so he guessed he could not have been asleep more than an hour. He took the candle and hurried out into the corridor, his belly shivering like jelly inside his nightshirt.

The screams came from the dormitory on the floor above. He summoned two of his guards and hurried up the wooden stairs.

Meylissa rolled naked on the floor, tearing at the bare wooden boards with her fingernails. Another spasm shook her and she curled her knees into her chest and retched. There was blood everywhere, soaked into her bedding and smeared across her face. There was a pink froth around her lips.

The other girls had gathered round her, pale and terrified. When Meylissa writhed again they screamed and jumped back as if she might infect them all. She tried to say something but her mouth just gaped open like a fish and the sounds she made sounded anything but human. She clutched her belly and screamed again.

The guards tried to pick her up and she kicked out at them. She stared up at the Kislar Aghasi and her lips drew back from her teeth in a snarl, like a rabid dog. He felt someone come to stand at his shoulder. He turned around; it was Hürrem .

Meylissa pointed a crooked finger at her and again tried to say something but then her mouth filled with blood and she choked on the words.

## Maritza River, near Adrianople

The hunting dogs flushed the partridge from its lair in the sagebrush. It exploded out of its hiding place, its short wings beating frantically at the air. Ibrahim laughed and raised the heavy leather gauntlet on his left wrist. The female peregrine falcon quivered with excitement.

Ibrahim removed the hood. The golden eyes blinked once, then the bird launched itself upwards, soaring on massive wings to its pitch in just moments.

Ibrahim and Suleiman spurred their horses and set after it.

The falcon dipped its wings. One moment it was riding the currents, as weightless as the air itself; the next it fell from the sky like a rock. The partridge flapped in panic but it had no chance of escaping; the peregrine hit it from above in an explosion of feathers and its talons took purchase on the spine with a blow so violent that its victim died mid-flight.

Both birds fell together towards the ground, the falcon releasing its death grip at the last moment. It wheeled away and the partridge fell dead into the swamp.

Ibrahim whooped and galloped to the edge of the black water; the dogs splashed in almost directly under his horse's hoofs, vying with each other to be first to retrieve the prize.

Ibrahim looked up and stretched out a gloved arm for his falcon, wheeling above him.

The boar watched the intruder from its sanctuary in a grove of wild rose, its yellow eyes bright with terror and rage. It backed further into the gorse and thorns. From one side came the yapping of the hunting dogs, from the other the thunder of horses and the shouts of the archers.

It was trapped. It had no choice.

Snorting with fear and rage, it charged from the brambles.

Suleiman saw it come and shouted a warning. The beast struck Ibrahim's Arab mare high on its flank, one yellow tusk piercing its belly and tearing a bloodied hole. She bellowed with agony and reared back. The boar charged again and Ibrahim was thrown to the ground.

Suleiman was fifty paces away. He pulled his bow from the leather scabbard on his saddle, and took aim. His first arrow buried itself in the boar's shoulder, throwing it on its side. It staggered to its feet, squealing, turning to face this new tormentor.

Suleiman reined in, pulling another arrow from the jewelled quiver. This time he hit the beast behind the shoulder, the steel tip angling in towards the heart, burying itself almost to the flight.

The boar's hind legs gave way.

In moments arrow after arrow thudded into its grey body and it died. The yeniceri archers cheered and ran forward and immediately Suleiman's horse was surrounded by solak cavalry. He ignored the captain's shouted apologies - for a moment the Sultan had been exposed to the boar - and jumped from the saddle.

"Ibrahim?"

The Arab mare was still on her feet, wheeling and bellowing, as the hunting dogs wheeled around her legs, jumping at the purple viscera trailing from her flank. Several yeniceris milled amongst them, one tried to catch her reins, another swore and slashed at the dogs with his killic.

The wounded horse, eyes bulging, galloped towards him. Suleiman staggered back, but then the dogs were at her again and she wheeled away once more and took off through the quince trees.

Suleiman looked around, dazed. Where was Ibrahim?

Suddenly he saw him, knee deep in the swamp, his white kaftan covered with mud. His turban was askew, lending an air of madness to his wicked grin. In his right hand he held the partridge by its bloodied neck.

"We have our prize!" he shouted to Suleiman.

"I thought you were dead!"

"While I have my Sultan to protect me, how could I die?"

There was such boyish innocence about him, Suleiman thought, as if it had all been a game. He looked so pleased with himself, and with his trophy, that Suleiman forgot his fear and his anger. He threw back his head and laughed, too.

\* \* \*

They were in Suleiman's pavilion; the music of Ibrahim's viol had to compete with the croaking of frogs from the swamp. The light from the candles rippled on the billowing folds of the tent.

Suleiman was elated from the hunt and could not sleep. He sat cross-legged on the divan listening to Ibrahim play, but his mind was not on the music. He had finally resolved, in his mind, a matter that had troubled him for some weeks. He had weighed his choice against the demands of court protocol, and had now justified his decision to his own conscience.

"I am replacing Achmed Pasha as Grand Vizier," he said suddenly.

Ibrahim stopped playing abruptly. "You are replacing him? He has been derelict in his duty?"

"No, he has not been remiss. It is just that ... I do not believe that he has the ability any longer ..."

"The ability? But he has served in the Divan these many years ..."

"Yes, yes. Once he may have been adequate for the position. But he has lost those powers he once possessed. I intend for him to be my governor in Egypt. I shall not humiliate him."

"Who will be his replacement?"

Suleiman felt like a father passing on a treasured heirloom to his son. "With you, Ibrahim."

"Me?"

"Yes, you will be my new Grand Vizier!"

Suleiman waited for the anticipated gush of gratitude, but it did not come. Ibrahim cradled his viol in his arms and stared gloomily at his hands.

"What's the matter?"

"Some of the Divan will wonder why you have elevated me to such a high rank at the expense of such an experienced man."

"It is not for them to question my judgment on anything."

"But what they will say privately concerns me."

"What they say privately cannot harm you!"

"It will seem that I have been appointed in his place only because of our great friendship."

Suleiman stared at him in astonishment. This was not what he had expected at all. He suspected Suleiman was not in the least concerned with the opinion of his peers in the Divan, or with Osmanli protocol. There was something else troubling him.

A night breeze ruffled the sides of the tent, like a long and drawn out sigh. The exasperation of God?

"I am afraid," Ibrahim murmured.

"Afraid?" He thought about him emerging from the swamp with the partridge clutched in his fist. "You are unafraid of being gored by a wild boar or trampled by your own horse but you are afraid if the Divan?"

"No, my Lord. I am afraid of you."

"Me?

"The Grand Vizier's neck is always under the sword, my Lord."

Suleiman was shocked that he should think this of him. Suleiman's own father had disposed of eight of his viziers in as many years. A common curse among the people at the time had been: "May you become vizier to Selim the Grim!" But he was nothing like his father.

Or at least that was what he had told himself. Yet hadn't he, blinded by his own rage, almost executed poor old Piri Pasha?

"You have nothing to fear from me, Ibrahim."

"You do me great honor. I always thought that I wanted this, until now. But you should not raise me so high that when I fall, I will die."

Suleiman placed his hands on his shoulders. "I give you my word. While I live, I shall see that you never come to harm. May God be my judge!"

Ibrahim took Suleiman's hand and kissed the ruby ring. "Very well," he whispered. "In truth you have brought me fame beyond my wildest dreams. I pledge myself to serve you until the day I die."

# CHAPTER 16

## The Eski Saraya

Where was she?

The Kapi Aga looked around the shadowed court and felt his guts turn to ice. She is not here, she has betrayed you!

The body is traitor, also, he thought. Drawn by pleasure like moth to a flame but what does it bring us to? The searing destruction of the fire. I could not help myself, even though I knew where it would lead me. This same flesh that brought me to ecstasy will offer me up to all the torments that Satan - or the chief, which is the same thing - can devise.

What was he doing here? She was the Devil's spawn, that girl. But killing her now was not the inconsequential it might have been before she was iqbal. Besides, then he would never again feel her warm breasts pressed against him, or the hunger of her mouth, all the forbidden delights he thought he would never taste again when Meylissa died.

Even food, money or power could not replace what he had found in this shadowed court, among the whispering fountains and marble walks and long-fingered plane trees. Here he was no longer a eunuch, and the razor's edge of danger that accompanied their trysts made his enjoyment only sweeter.

What if Hürrem became pregnant also? There seemed no end to this dark tunnel of lust and its consequence. How many times had he promised himself he would never return and how long did his resolve withstand the lure of just one last time?

She had enslaved him with her bite, her scents, her writhing, her yielding. It blotted out all else. These few snatched moments had become the purpose of his entire life now.

How easy to pretend they would never be caught, that this might never end. He heard someone behind him and span around.

"Did I frighten you?" Hürrem whispered.

He felt as if his heart would lurch out of his chest. It was beating so hard it almost hurt. "Where did you come from?"

"I was watching you from behind the pillar." She wore pantaloons of white silk and a gomlek of sheer emerald silk, open to the waist. The valley between her breasts deepened with each breath. She looked so composed. Was she never frightened? She wore a gauze veil attached to the green taplock she wore on her head and she pushed it aside with a practiced motion of her right hand. Her breath was hot on his cheek. "Let's do it, quickly."

He glanced up at the north tower. The doors were locked, he reminded himself, but he pulled her further into the shadows anyway.

Hürrem lifted up his robe. "How does it feel to be a man again?"

"You killed her," he said.

"It was not my fault. The abortive was too strong."

"You meant to do it."

"What if I did? Would you despise me for it? You would have killed us both if you thought it would save your neck. I saved you the trouble."

The pantaloons lay on the marble. She unfastened the three diamond clasps of the gomlek. "She was your friend," he said.

"While you two were practically strangers. You made her pregnant as she passed you in the cloister." She leaned back against the wall. His mouth was dry. Her nipples were hard; but then it was cold in the shadows.

He took her roughly by the wrists and pressed her back against the wall. "Perhaps one day I will introduce you to the Bosphorus." He put his right hand at her throat. It was a small neck and his hand could have enclosed it easily. He traced the contours of her shoulder to her breast, squeezing as hard as he could, tried to make her cry out. But she made no sound, staring back at him with cold, green eyes.

"They say it's rough this time of year," she said. "You should take care you do not fall in yourself. The Sultan might miss his Kapi Aga less than his new iqbal." She wrapped her thighs around his hips, guiding him into her. She took a fold of his robe and stuffed it into his mouth to keep him from crying out when he reached his sublime moment. The fountains alone could not disguise such a sound.

The Kapi Aga bit down on the silk, hating her for the power she had over him, hating himself for his weakness. Hürrem wrapped her arms around his neck and moved her hips slowly in time with his. "Give me your juice," she whispered. "I want it all."

A moment of shuddering bliss. For a few scarlet moments he was free of her and free of his servitude to women, and he gave himself up to it. He slipped through a break in the clouds and never wanted to return. Like a little death.

But then he opened his eyes. The cold evening drew on; only the terror remained.

Life was a trap. There was no way out.

\* \* \*

The Kapi Aga did not hear of his success from Hürrem herself. One day he woke and found the palace alive with rumor; the iqbal was with child!

So what should he do now? Surely he could not go to the garden again. She was kadin now, and to be discovered alone with a kadin was an offense to heinous to contemplate. But if he did not, what would the witch do then?

And then another thought struck him: what if the child was his? No, impossible. He could scarce credit that he had got Meylissa with child. Not Hürrem too?

He was a pawn in a game he no longer understood. From the first moment he opened that gate to seduce one of the Lord of Life's odalisques, he had lost all power over his own fate.

There was nothing to do now but wait.

# CHAPTER 17

Hafise sat on the terrace overlooking the shaded, eastern court of the Palace and regarded her son's new iqbal with a practiced eye. She could tell at once that this one was a different proposition to Gülbehar , you could see it in the way she walked, the way she held herself.

They said she was more clever than beautiful. But that was perhaps not such a bad thing. She had not survived so many years in the harem of Selim the Grim without a certain quickness of mind herself.

"Hürrem ," she said warmly, extending her hand. "I am delighted with your news. Come and sit here beside me."

It was a warm afternoon and finches twittered in the ornate cedar cages hanging from the eaves. Sherbets and melon and rahat lokum were laid out on the low table in front of them. Behind them the city shimmered in the afternoon haze, the cupolas of the mosques shining like diamonds through the dust.

"Suleiman is hunting at Adrianople, as I am sure you have heard. I have sent a courier today with a message for him. He will be overjoyed with this news."

Hürrem put a hand to her stomach. "We must wait many months to gauge the extent of his pleasure."

A good answer, Hafise thought. If it's a girl, we are all back where we started. "If God wills it." She reached out for the girl's hair, held a few strands towards the light. "You have beautiful hair. Not red, not gold. Where are you from?"

"My father was a khan of the Krim Tatars, Crown of Veiled Heads."

A khan of the Tatars. Listen to her! Perhaps she knows my own father was a Georgian peasant and thinks herself superior. "And how did you come to us?"

"My father saw an opportunity."

Hafise smiled. "For you, or for himself?"

"The Spahis tied him to the ground so they could force the money into his pockets. He struggled and screamed. I had to avert my eyes."

"You laugh when you say such things, but there is no laughter in your eyes."

"Why should I weep? He still lives in a tent, I am in a palace. In the end I won more from the trade."

"So you are happy here?"

"I will be happier when my lord returns."

"I was married to the Sultan Selim for many years. I can count the number of weeks we spent together on my fingers. It is a lonely life, Hürrem ."

"I shall heed your advice gladly. I will go back to my father, then. Can you arrange a horse for me?"

Hafise laughed, in spite of herself. The girl might be mocking her, but she had a point. Why be miserable over things you do not have the power to change? "Now you have the Sultan's child, this harem will be your home for the rest of your life."

"Then I shall have to arrange for larger rooms."

"Like mine, perhaps?"

"If God wills it."

"I should not be at all surprised if that is His design." Hafise selected a piece of lokum, flavored with pistachio nut, and bit into it. "If there is anything that you need, you must tell me. In Islam, the mother is sacred, and never more so than now. Everything will be done to ensure your comfort."

"There is one thing, Highness."

"Yes?"

"I want a bodyguard."

Hafise looked startled. "A bodyguard. Why?"

"I am frightened."

"Of what?"

"I have heard rumors that I will not live to see my baby born."

"Who dares threaten you - threaten the Sultan's child?"

Hürrem averted her eyes. "I don't know. It might just be gossip."

She is lying, Hafise thought. She knows who it is but dares not say. There is only one person who would wish her dead. Gülbehar ! But surely Gülbehar was not capable of that?

"If you think such rumors might have any base, you should have your servant girl taste all your food, even try on your clothes before you wear them, in case the fabric has been impregnated with poison. As a precaution I will have the Kislar Aghasi assign you one of his eunuchs."

"Thanks you, Crown of Veiled Heads."

"Nothing - nothing - must endanger the Sultan's son. Do you understand?"

"Yes. Yes, I understand."

* * *

The Kapi Aga watched from the North Tower as she appeared from the long shadows and sat down on the marble bench beside the fountain. She opened her Qur'an on her lap. She had come to the garden three days in a row. There was only one reason to go there and that was to speak to him alone. But why? What was she thinking? Soon she might be Suleiman's wife - so what more did she want? They could not continue with their trysts; but if he did not go down to meet her, what might she do then?

She could not betray him without betraying herself. But then, who knew what she might do? It had never occurred to him that she might harm Meylissa. It struck him for the first time that she might be mad.

He must know what she intended or he would never rest.

He scurried from the room, locking the door behind him, then went down the wooden steps to the courtyard.

He hesitated when he reached the iron gate. This must be the last time, he promised himself, the very last time. He put the key in the lock. The key and the lock! he thought. Just like men and women; you place it here, you find the fit, the tumblers fall and you open the way to dreams and nightmares. There was nothing as compelling as a locked door.

He slipped inside. Hürrem looked up at him and her eyes widened in surprise. She dropped the Qur'an, stood up and screamed.

The Kapi Aga froze. He heard moaning and realized it was him. He turned to run, fumbled with the keys and dropped them on the marble flags.

She screamed twice more as he fumbled on the ground for the keys. He fumbled with the lock and when he finally threw open the door he found himself staring into the startled face of one of his own guards.

He ran back into the garden. "You little whore," he shouted, and drew the jewelled dagger from his pelisse and slashed at her. Hürrem shouted and fell back, the stroke scything the air inches from her face.

The guard rushed at him. The Kapi Aga heard the blade scythe the air and then the dagger was gone, and with it his right hand. There was no pain, just the horror of it; the stump and the spurting of bright blood.

He fell to his knees and tried to prise the dagger from the fingers of his own severed hand. If he could kill her now, it would be all right. They could do what they wanted with him as long as he knew she was dead. But then the guard dragged him towards the gate and he screamed again, this time at the sudden white hot pain in his arm. Puddles of his own blood soaked the cobblestones around the little witch in the green taplock. He tried to scream a curse at her but then another guard appeared and struck him with the hilt of his yataghan and he groaned and his head fell back.

\* \* \*

The hawk soared on the updraught from the baked cobblestones of the city, then wheeled towards the Bosphorus, hovering again over the walls of the Topkapi Saraya. Its golden eye picked out the twin towers of the Gate of Felicity, where the head of the Kapi Aga was turning black as an olive high in its niche in the wall. His decapitated body still hung from the steel hook where it had been tormented for three days, its point penetrating the ribs and the thigh, a rope lashed from the scaffold to hold it upright. It would be there till the carrion crows had finished their work and the meat and sinew rotted from the bones.

The hawk wheeled again, now towards the Golden Horn and the wooden palace high on the hill beside the great mosque of Bayezit. On a balcony among the brass domes stood a woman with hair the color of fire. She was smiling.

The months would pass quickly, she thought. She stroked her belly. Let it be a son.

\* \* \*

The day of the birthing there was snow on the roofs of the Harem.

A birthing chair and swaddling bandages were brought to Hürrem "s apartment. Incense was burned and rose petals strewn over the marble floors; amulets and blue beads were hung around the room to ward off the evil eye.

Hürrem had never experienced such pain. When the baby would not come the Harem midwife, a terrible Nubian who weighed perhaps as much as three odalisques, sat on her stomach to force the child from her womb.

Hürrem screamed. The midwife jammed a stick of ivory between her teeth to silence her. "Bite down!" she hissed. "Bite down and be silent!"

Crouched over the chair, supported on each side by the midwives, she delivered up the child, the Nubian receiving the infant in a cloth of linen while she recited the declaration of the Faith.

The Kislar Aghasi watched, as Osmanli law demanded, to ensure that no substitution was made. He took the child himself to the white marble fountain and washed the baby three times, according to custom. Sugared oil was placed in its mouth to ensure a sweet and amiable tongue; kohl was smeared around its eyes to warrant a profound gaze and a diamond-encrusted Qur'an was touched to its forehead.

Hürrem clutched the midwife's shoulders. "What is it? Just tell me what it is!"

It was the Kislar Aghasi who answered her. "You are delivered of a son, my Lady."

"A son!" Hürrem repeated. She smiled at him, then fainted dead away.

# PART TWO

DARK ANGEL

# CHAPTER 18

## Venice, 1528

She was a vision in black velvet, a dark angel with hair as black and lustrous as coal. She had skin like ivory and her lips were so full and plum-colored, it appeared as if they were bruised. The bodice of her vesture was fashionably low-cut and the small gold cross at her throat - he could imagine the soft pulse just below it - seemed to taunt him.

White and Christian; twice forbidden.

The street was crowded, and rang to the cries of the hawkers and the cursing of the sailors - Armenians and Dalmatians along with Venetians - gambling in the arcades. An Albanian pushed past in baggy trousers, chewing a nub of garlic like a sweet; several people saluted the passage of a togato in the purple robes of a senator and he replied with a casual wave of the hand.

Abbas pushed through the mob, following her to the portal of a church. She ascended with elaborate grace, her eyes to the ground. She looked up just once, and their eyes met. Her lips parted, just slightly, and he told himself that his presence had affected her in some manner. God alone knew how.

The old hag who escorted her gave him a contemptuous look as they walked through the doors of the Santa Maria dei Miracoli.

"Did you see her?" he whispered to his friend, Ludovici.

"Of course I saw her. That's Julia Gonzaga."

"You know her?"

"My step-sister knows her. She's her cousin."

"Her cousin?" Abbas grabbed Ludovici''s saion - the fashionable waist-length scarlet smock he wore over his shirt - and pulled him towards the steps.

"What are you doing?"

"I want to get closer."

"Tu sei pazzo - you're mad!"

"Come on!"

Ludovici pulled him back. "Do you know who her father is? Antonio Gonzaga - he's a consigliatore!"

"I don't care."

Ludovici was alarmed, but not altogether surprised. Abbas was the most headstrong man he'd ever known. Reckless, his father called him. If it was his fault it was also his charm. Perhaps it was in his blood; a Moor is a Moor. But this time Ludovici would not let him make a fool of himself, and besides, there was real danger in this.

He pushed his friend against a wall and held him there. "Abbas, no!"

"I just want to look at her."

"You are not meant to look! She's a Gonzaga!"

"You cannot stop me," Abbas said, jerked free of his grip and sprinted up the steps.

To hell with him! Ludovici thought. It was his funeral. He started to walk away, then changed his mind and went in the church after him.

* * *

The saints watched, disapproving, from the gilt ceiling. A bust of the Vergine della Santa Clara frowned from her balustrade on a wall of pink coral marble. Putti and sea monsters cavorted on the pilasters.

It was cool after the warmth of the piazza. A shaft of light from the vault pointed to the altar like the golden finger of God. He had picked out the two figures kneeling at the prie-dieu before the altar. Saint Francis and the Archangel Gabriel stood guard on either side.

Abbas heard Ludovici"s footsteps echo on the marble as he came to stand beside him. "She is the loveliest thing I have ever seen," Abbas whispered.

"She is not for you, my friend."

The old hag heard them and raised her head from her prayers. Abbas and Ludovici ducked behind one of the pillars. Ludovici put a finger to his lips.

When they peered out again, the two women were gone. The old woman was hurrying her charge out through a side door. Julia Gonzaga looked back once before her duenna pulled her away.

"There, you've had your look," Ludovici said. "Now forget about it!"

* * *

The Captain General of the Republic put both broad, dark hands on the balustrade and watched the sun set behind the snow-capped peaks of the Cadore, setting aflame the backdrop of mushrooming clouds. The gondolas and galleys faded into dark relief against the pearl of the lagoon. Such a harbor, such a city; sometimes it was easy to feel a part of it. But he was only paid to love it for as long as they paid his hire. They did not belong; his son sometimes forget that.

"It is quite impossible," he growled. "You still do not seem to understand the first thing about them!"

"We can protect their lives but not marry their daughters? Is that it?"

"Marry? Is that what is on your mind?" He rounded on his son, who fell back a step. Mahmoud was a bear of a man and his thick frizzled beard added to his size and his ferocity. "There are reasons for our presence here and they are purely commercial. No Venetian wants a black Muslim son any more than I want a white infidel daughter."

They would not be in Venice at all, of course, if the Doge could trust his army to the command of one of his own noblemen. The Captain-General of Venice was rarely even Italian and sometimes, as now, not even a Christian.

"They treat us like dirt," Abbas said.

"The magnifici treat everyone like dirt. They mean nothing by it."

"But we have royal blood!"

"What do you think the royal blood of a Muslim means to them?" Mahmud crashed both fists onto the walnut table between them. "We are mercenaries. That is all we are. We have no rights and no place here. You may live in a fine palazzo and dress like the son of a togati but you are still a foreigner. Even if you may sometimes forget that, I assure you that they never do."

"Then what am I to do?"

"Do as the other young bloods do and find what you need on the Ponte delle Tette - the Bridge of the Tits!" Abbas knew the place, it earned its nickname from the women who stood stripped to the waist in its doorways, calling out to the young men who passed. "You are too young to think about a wife."

"No. I want to meet Julia Gonzaga."

Mahmud sighed. He was not angry any more. What was the point? Abbas was like a spoiled child petulantly demanding his own castle to play in. No Gonzaga would entertain the thought of his daughter even breathing the same air as a blackamoor and besides, there was a statute in the Republic forbidding a Venetian nobleman or woman to marry outside their peers. A magnifico of the Council of Ten, like Gonzaga, could not even speak to a foreigner in private, even the Captain General of the Army.

"It is just youth, Abbas. Believe me, it will pass. Tomorrow you will have forgotten all about her."

"You judge me poorly," Abbas said.

"I hope not, for you sake, for this can never be. Put it aside. Now."

* * *

Julia Gonzaga watched the theatre of the Venetian evening from behind the latticed screen of her loggia. The lanterns hanging from the sterns of the gondolas left rippling tracks on the surface of the canal and she heard voices and laughter echo along the fondamenta as a young couple vanished arm in arm through a dark sottoportico.

Julia felt a stab of envy.

She thought again about what had happened that afternoon in the church of Santa Maria dei Miracoli. Why had that boy stared at her like that? A blackamoor, too, like a gondolieri, though he did not dress like one. He had a jewelled bareta on his head, and his linen camicia had been open at the front, in the manner of a fashionable young nobleman.

So who was he?

Another mystery to add to mystery on top of mystery. Her life was like living in a great house where all but one room was locked to her; there was the mystery of her father, a sombre man who was rarely seen even in his own palazzo; there was the mystery of her mother, dead in childbirth and never spoken of; but most of all there was the mystery of men.

Her father had intimated to her that one day she might marry one of these exotic creatures. The notion provoked in her both dread and excitement; according to her duenna - her governess, Signora Cavalcanti - young men were the Devil's work, and they would put her very soul in jeopardy. Yet sometimes she wondered with a blush if even damnation might be better than this. She was already buried alive. What could be worse?

Signora Cavalcanti's tirades against the fecklessness of men had stirred a terrible fascination in her. She wanted to know what it was they were hiding from her. Despite her trepidation, she was eager to discover more about the world outside her loggia.

But how?

# CHAPTER 19

The girl stank of wine and sweat. She collapsed, laughing, onto Ludovici"'s lap. He put his hand inside her dress and popped out her breast, weighing it in his hand as if it were a fine vase he was displaying to a guest. The nipple, Abbas noticed, had been rouged.

"Now look, Abbas!" Ludovici shouted. "What are you getting so upset about? They're all the same underneath!"

The girl cuffed Ludovici playfully around the head. She pulled up her bodice in a feigned attempt at modesty.

"She's like a whale drawn up on the beach," Abbas said. "All that's missing are the gaffer's hooks."

The prostitute's laughter died in her throat. "Bastardo!" she hissed. "Black devil. I suppose you'd rather fuck a camel!"

She got up and flounced away. Ludovici shook his head. He picked up his goblet and drained the thick rosso, some of it spilling on his white camicia, where it spread like a bloodstain across his chest. "You don't have to be mean to a girl just because you don't love her," he said.

Abbas nodded, abashed. What had made him say that? No good taking out his frustrations on some poor whore. He looked around. The tavern was crowded with the sons of togati and their tarts. The girls were a riot of color beside their young suitors; under the strict laws of La Serenissima only the working class and prostitutes could wear what they liked, the wives and daughters of patricians always wore black with perhaps a white linen camicia. The young noblemen rebelled in their own ways; they wore their shirts wide open in front and their black baretas glittered with gemstones.

"You take life too seriously," Ludovici said.

Abbas wondered what they were doing there. The dive reeked of sour wine and cheap perfumes; from the back of the inn came the even less alluring aroma of stale urine.

"What is wrong, Abbas? You were never so fussy before."

It was true, there were enough times he had paid these doxies for their feigned endearments and easy-parted thighs but tonight the very thought disgusted him. Some of the girls made him pay more because he was a Moor; others charged less because they were curious. They were all either very drunk, very coarse or very old, God forgive him.

"I'm tired of all this," Abbas said. He stared at his friend; the red wine had stained his teeth and he looked ridiculously young. He pulled him to his feet. "Let's go," he said. Ludovici"s goblet clattered onto the wooden floor.

Ludovici protested but he was too drunk to resist. Abbas stood him against the wall of the tavern, holding him up by his shirt. It was sodden with wine. "Listen" he said, "you have to help me."

"Help you? Help you do what?"

"Julia. Can you get a letter to her?"

Ludovici started to laugh.

"I'm serious! Will you do it?"

"But Abbas ..."

"Will you do it for me?"

"I told you before, Gonzaga will kill you!"

"I don't care about Gonzaga. I want to meet her, just once."

"No!"

"You said she is Lucia's cousin."

"It makes no difference ..."

"Then she can take the letter for me."

Ludovici sagged in his arms. "It will come to no good."

"Please, this once. Do this for me. I beg you."

Ludovici groaned. "All right, I'll ask her. Now let me go." He felt suddenly sober again. "It's dangerous, Abbas."

"Danger gives meaning to life."

"More often it ends it. Don't do this. If you do meet with her - and that is impossible for she goes nowhere unescorted - even your father will not be able to help you. You cannot toy with the honor of a man like Gonzago."

"What of my honor, Ludovici? My father may be content to be the Doge's lapdog, but I am my own man!"

By the balls of all the saints! Ludovici thought. Love and rebellion; when did any good come from such a heinous mix?

"I will write the letter tonight!" Abbas said and put a hand around his shoulder and led him down the ruga toward the Piazza San Marco. Ludovici cursed himself for a fool for ever mentioning that he knew Julia Gonzaga. He would regret it. They both would, he was sure of that.

* * *

Julia draped her lacework across her knees, feeling the warmth of the yellow sun on her skin as she worked. Lucia sat beside her, whispering the petty gossips she had heard from her brother. She visited her often during the summer - escorted by her duenna of course - to chatter and to sew. It was a welcome relief for both of them from the monastic solitude of their lives.

Lucia was a dark, thickset girl with the beginnings of a faint moustache on her upper lip; yet her older brother, Ludovici, was fair and did not yet even have a man's beard. Life was not fair, Julia thought.

"I hear you are to be married," Lucia said.

"Yes. In the autumn."

"Is he handsome?"

"I have only heard my father speak of him." Julia pretended to examine her stitches. "He is a member of the Consiglio di Dieci also. His wife died three summers ago."

From the corner of her eye she could see the horror on Lucia's face. She leaned closer and whispered: "But how old is he?"

"He is in his sixtieth year. But he may yet be handsome." She fought to keep the tremor from her voice. What a match her father had made for her!

"What is his name?"

"Serena. Don't ask me his first name, I don't remember."

Signora Cavalcanti looked up sharply and frowned at her. Julia lowered her eyes.

"I have seen him," Lucia said. "He is very ... important."

They lapsed into silence. Signora Cavalcanti put down her embroidery and rubbed her eyes. "I think I shall rest," she said and went inside. Julia heard her pull the drapes at her bedroom window on the terrazzo above.

Sunlight bounced from the canal and threw dappled shadows on the walls of the palazzi. A line tagged with clothes danced in the breeze. On the other side of the canal an ancient duenna leaned out of her window to haul up a basket of provisions from a gondola moored below.

Lucia's duenna excused herself for a moment and the two girls were left alone. Lucia reached into the folds of her vesture and produced a letter, sealed with red wax. She almost threw it into Julia's lap, as if it were aflame.

Julia gaped at her, astonished. "What is this?"

Lucia glanced over her shoulder. "Quickly, open it!"

"Who is it from?"

"You have an admirer!"

She held up the envelope. There was one word written on the face, in black ink: Julia. She tried to swallow.

"Well, open it!"

Julia broke the seal. She read:

You are the most beautiful woman I have ever seen in my life. I must meet you. I will face any danger. Just tell me what I must do.

Her hands started to shake.

"What does it say?"

"Lucia, who is this from?"

"I don't know. A friend of my brother."

"What is his name?"

"He would not say. He just asked me to give it to you. Show it to me!"

Lucia tried to snatch it from her but Julia turned away, folded it and slipped it down the front of her vestura. She tore the envelope into small pieces and dropped them over the balcony into the canal.

"Why does this friend of your brother's send me letters? Does he wish to disgrace me?"

"Ludovici said it was the only way."

"The only way for what?"

"I don't know. The only way you might ever meet, I suppose." She gripped Julia's arm. "What did it say?"

Julia tried to compose herself. Her cheeks felt hot. If Signora Cavalcanti saw her now, she would know something was wrong. She fanned herself with her embroidery. She was startled by her own reaction to this outrage; a part of her had already started to form a plan. But this was madness, she told herself, you are bound to be discovered, you will disgrace the family name and your soul will be condemned to eternal torment.

And then she thought about Serena. Perhaps it would be worth it.

Yet it was impossible, to meet a complete stranger without introduction, without escort. No, she must burn the letter, she decided, as soon as she was alone. If the author of the missive were a suitable companion - husband even - for her then he would have arranged a meeting through her father; that he had persuaded a friend to smuggle his message this way only proved that he could not be a member of any noble family of note, or even a gentleman.

"What are you going to do?" Lucia whispered.

You are the most beautiful woman I have ever seen in my life. I must meet you. I will face any danger. Just tell me what I must do.

On one side disgrace and damnation and an ancient friend of her father's; on the other a young man who thought she was beautiful and would risk for her. Lucia looked over her shoulder, expecting her duenna to come back at any moment. She must decide.

"Signor Cavalcanti sleeps every afternoon between None and Vespers, while I study the Bible in my bedroom. Tell your brother ... tell your brother that his friend should have a gondola waiting by the canal at that time. If he is any earlier, or later, I will not come down, and he is not to bother me again."

"You are going to meet him ... without your duenna?"

"Yes, and I don't care if I am damned for eternity. It's better than being damned to marry a sixty year old consigliatore!"

# CHAPTER 20

Julia wrapped the long mantello cape around her shoulders and pulled the hood low over her face. It was not too late to turn back, she thought.

She could hear Signora Cavalcanti's snores coming from her bedroom window. She smiled to herself. There was a certain pleasure in outwitting her.

She opened the heavy wooden door and peered down the stone steps that led to the water stairs. The bright light hurt her eyes. Mary, Mother of God, forgive me, it is there!

The gondola was moored there, a line slung carelessly around the striped mooring pole. The gondolier was a tall Moor with a scarlet satin camicia with slashed sleeves, and his broad-rimmed hat was trimmed with scarlet ribbon. He leaned on his punta with arrogant ease.

She inched the door shut again and closed her eyes. She took a deep breath. It's not too late to go back. It's not too late to go back.

Go back to what? Go back to her dark loggia and open the great black Bible; go back to watching other gondolas like this glide by under her loggia, to peer at the curtained canopies and wonder …

To go back to waiting to marry a sixty year old senator.

She inched open the door, slipped through and ran down the steps. When she reached the gondola she pulled the curtains aside and jumped in.

She stifled a gasp.

He was a Moor, like the gondolier. She remembered him immediately; he was the boy who had stared at her in the church. This was why he could not approach her father!

He smiled, embarrassed; he must know, of course, what she was thinking. "They tell me I have all the makings of a fine gondolier," he said. "But my father would not permit it. He thinks the son of the Defender of the Republic should aspire to greater things."

"Your father is -?"

"-is the Captain General of the Army."

"If you find my appearance too shocking, my Lady, you may leave now and I promise you will never hear from me again. I guarantee it, because I will immediately throw myself in the canal."

He was young, almost as young as herself. His skin was the color of mahogany and his hair tightly curled; a ruby glinted in his left ear. He was at once forbidding and forbidden, and she felt the same thrill of excitement that she had experienced in the Santa Maria dei Miracoli.

"But that linen camicia you are wearing must have been fearsomely expensive. I should hate you to get it wet. Where are we going?"

"We can just pole around if you like. We can see nothing with the curtain drawn so it hardly seems to matter. I have everything I want to look at right here in front of me."

"I may only be away for a few minutes."

She sank back into the cushions. There were blue velvet curtains on all sides so they were safe from prying eyes. The only thing she could see outside the tiny cabin was the gaily colored hose of their gondolier as he stood at his position on the punta piede. The boat smelled of mildew and walnut.

He leaned through the curtain and said something to the gondolier. The boatman unhitched the rope and she heard the gentle splash of the pole as he steered them towards the centre of the canal.

"What is your name?" she said.

"Abbas."

"Abbas," she said, testing the exotic name and liking the sound and the feel of it on her tongue.

"It is not a Venetian name but as you can see, I am not quite a Venetian myself."

She reached inside her mantello. "Here is your letter."

"I do not want it back."

"It is too dangerous for me to keep. If you like I will burn it …"

"I do not want you to burn it." He took it from her. "I meant everything I said. Since I saw you I have not been able to think about anything else."

She felt her cheeks grow hot. "You know Ludovici Gambetto?"

"His father is a general and an adviser to my father. We are both renegades, I suppose. Outsiders."

"But the Gambetti are one of the noble families of Venice."

Abbas looked embarrassed. "You don't know?"

"Know what?"

"Ludovici came from outside the marriage. Signor Gambetto had a mistress. When she died Ludovici was still a baby. Signor Gambetto is a good man, he raised him as one of his own - but, you know, Ludovici can never really belong. That is why we understand each other so well. But perhaps I should not have told you. You are Lucia's friend and I assumed that you knew."

Why would she know? No one ever told her anything.

"I am sorry for ..." He spread his hands to take in the little velvet canopy. "... for this. I wanted my father to speak to your father for me, but he said it was impossible. But I am a man who believes nothing is impossible. And I had to speak to you." He reached up suddenly and pulled back her hood. She froze, thinking that he meant to touch her. But instead he just stared at her, studying her face with a frightening intensity.

"You are ... glorious," he said.

For a moment she thought she might laugh; it was the most wonderful thing anyone had ever said to her. She knew she was beautiful, of course. But what good had beauty had her beauty been to her, until now? Suddenly the risks of the afternoon were all worthwhile. She would have run the gauntlet of a thousand knives for this sort of adoration.

She had no idea what she was meant to do or say. She pulled her hood back over her face, overwhelmed. "I should be getting back."

"Not yet."

"If my duenna discovers I am gone ..."

"Just a few moments more." A shadow passed over the canopy as the gondola slipped under a bridge. She heard the shouts of urchins playing on the cobbles. "I have to see you again."

"I cannot."

"You must. Please. I feel as if I am on fire."

"What do you want from me? I am to be married in the autumn. My husband will return from Cyprus for the wedding at the end of summer."

"I cannot let this happen."

"Signor Abbas, it is what will happen and there is nothing you or I can do about it. Please take me back."

He took her hand. The shock of his touch made her gasp. No man had ever touched her before, not even her father. "Could you love a Moor like I love an infidel?"

"Just take me back," she repeated.

He sighed and leaned through the curtain and gave the orders to the gondolier. A few moments later she felt the boat scrape along the steps outside her palazzo. Julia stood up and the gondola swayed. She lost her balance and Abbas caught her arm to steady her.

"Let me see you just once more before you go."

"You can never see me again," she said and scrambled out of the gondola and ran inside. She did not stop running until she had reached her bedroom, where she threw herself on her knees before the wooden crucifix on the wall and prayed for forgiveness, and then prayed again for just one more chance to sin.

# CHAPTER 21

Antonio Gonzaga had noticed a subtle and worrying change in his daughter. He fretted over the flush in her cheeks and the nervousness in her manner. Such signs, small as they were, were not commensurate with a young lady whose time should have been fully occupied with religious instruction and lacework.

The maid set two plates of squazzetto, a broth made of rice and chicken, in front of them. Gonzaga watched his daughter take up her spoon. Her hands were shaking.

"Put your shoulders back."

Julia did as she was told.

He frowned, irritated. The sooner she was married and off his hands, the better he would like it. "Soon you will be the wife of a member of the Consiglio di Dieci. He will expect proper manners."

What could be wrong with her? He had seen such cow eyes on a woman before; his wife, on their wedding night and his mistress, whenever she was pregnant; something that happened with too frequent regularity.

He drank his wine, ignoring his food. Surely the thought of marrying Serena had not raised such a blush in her cheeks? The very idea that his daughter might entertain lewd thoughts about such a union was unlikely. So what, then?

The realization came to him and he gave a long sigh.

Julia looked up. "Father?"

"I feel unwell," he said to her. "I need to rest. You must excuse me." He left, leaving her to finish her supper alone.

\* \* \*

Ludovici and Abbas reeled out of the tavern, arm in arm and stinking of wine. Ludovici bent over, his hands on his knees, and retched on the cobbles. Abbas leaned against the balustrade of a stone bridge and stared at the moonlight at the canal. "I have never felt so alive," he said. "I love her, Ludovici."

Ludovici wiped his mouth. "You don't know anything about her. You are in love with the danger of it. If you are in love with anything, you are in love with your own daring."

"You live in such a bitter world."

"I am not bitter. I see the world as it is and no more. What is plain to me is that if you could marry this girl tomorrow with the blessing of her father and yours she would hold no more allure for you than a whore in a doorway."

"One day it will happen to you."

"Only if I lose my wits. Abbas, you are my greatest friend in the world. But I wish you would listen to me. A woman is just a woman and the world is full of them. She is something soft to lie on and a warm and giving place to spill your seed. I allow that a woman might be a boon companion and one day I shall have a wife to keep my home and children. But when I marry I will let my head do the choosing and not my heart. A man who does otherwise is a fool."

"Then I am a fool because I promise you I will love her forever."

"If you love her until next week I will give you two gold ducats."

"I feel sorry for you, Ludovici. You feel nothing inside. But one day you will, life will seek you out and make you feel again. As for me, I shall find the greatest part of me in loving truly."

"You're just in love with loving."

"You'll see, Ludovici. You'll see. You should give me the two ducats now."

Ludovici laughed and shook his head. He dropped the wine flask he was holding and it shattered on the cobblestones. Somewhere above them a man in a nightshirt ran up the shutters and called for the night watch. Ludovici and Abbas ran away down the calle, laughing.

\* \* \*

Gonzaga sat in his study, staring gloomily into the candle. A painting of the Death of the Virgin by Carpaccio dominated the room; two smaller offerings, a Virgin and Child by Bellini and a portrait of himself, for which he had commissioned Palma Vecchio five years before, hung on either side of it. Two bronzes by Il Riccio stood above the fireplace.

There was a timid knock at the door.

"Yes?"

"Signora Cavalcanti, Excellency."

"Enter."

The duenna crept into the room and bent to kiss the sleeve of his velvet gown. "You sent for me, Excellency?"

"I did. I am deeply troubled, Signora Cavalcanti."

"No failing on my part, I hope?"

Gonzaga examined the sumptuous alto e basso weave on his gown and picked at a piece of lint. He removed it with elaborate care. "I do not know, Signora."

She wrung her hands. "I assure Your Excellency I have been most diligent in my duties."

"Have you?"

The old lady looked terrified.

"I believe Mistress Julia is concealing something from you." The duenna was trembling, he noted with satisfaction. An old trick, of course, eliciting the fullest confession from mere suspicion, but it always worked.

"I do not think so, Excellency."

"Really? Has she spoken much to you about the joyous occasion of her wedding?"

"Very little, Excellency."

"The anticipation of it brings her no pleasure?"

"Well ... I am sure she is most overjoyed."

Gonzaga gave her time to think, or at least invent something. He busied himself with the stole that hung around his shoulders. "She is never left unattended?"

Ah, there it was! The slightest lowering of the eyes, the merest hint of a blush in her cheeks. He watched her prepare the lie. "No, Excellency."

He sighed and pretended to relent. "Keep an eye on her. A very close eye. Do you understand?"

"Yes, Your Excellency. I understand very well indeed." She turned with uncommon haste towards the door.

Well, that should do it, he thought. He had frightened her badly, as he had intended, and put her on notice. If there was something he should know, she would find out about it and bring her discovery back to him as an offering, like a dog with a rat. A murmured word of thanks and his great disappointment in his daughter would be her lavish reward.

He spared a glance for the Virgin in her extremis. He was sure she would approve of his intent, if not his methods. But then, she never had a beautiful daughter.

# CHAPTER 22

Julia and Lucia sat on the terraza, their lacework resting on their knees, as the late afternoon sun dipped below the roofs of the palazzi. The duenna had retired but Julia had not yet heard her draw the heavy drapes at her bedroom window, which was directly above them. She suspected it was a stratagem to try and eavesdrop.

Lucia leaned forward and whispered: "Did you meet him?"

Julia shrugged and mouthed: "Perhaps."

"Well?"

Julia smiled and said nothing.

A few moments later Signora Cavalcanti suddenly reappeared on the terraza. "What are you two girls whispering about?"

"Nothing, Signora," Julia said.

"I thought I distinctly heard voices."

"I was singing to myself," Julia said.

The duenna sat down and picked up her lacework, her face pinched into a scowl. The rest of the afternoon passed in silence. Julia felt two pairs of eyes fixed on her, watching her every movement, but she did not look up or say another word.

# CHAPTER 23

Julia drew back the hood of her cloak, slowly and deliberately, savoring the look on his face. It was just vanity, the vice of the Devil, but she so loved the way he stared at her.

She had not intended that there should ever be a second time. But one afternoon, a week or so after their first meeting, the gondola had appeared again by the water gate and the temptation had proved too great to resist. She just needed to feel alive again.

The second time had made it easier to do it a third time, and even easier the next. How many times had they met now? Half a dozen, more? She had never possessed a secret until now and it afforded her a feeling she had never experienced before; she had power. She was no longer utterly in the thrall of her father and Signora Cavalcanti.

"Just for a few moments," she said. She spoke the same words every time; it was like the bargaining chip that she tossed to Fate. Who could condemn for a few stolen moments? The rest of the day my Confessor will find me faultless.

He reached for her, his palms upwards. On the last two occasions she had allowed him to touch her and this was their signal. She put out her hand and he took it. He cradled it in his palm like a small, wounded bird.

"I love you," he murmured.

"You cannot love me. I told you, it is impossible. This will be the last time. We have to stop."

"I cannot stop. If they consign me to all the fires of Hell I could not be in worse torment than I am now. I will stop when they put me in the earth."

"Abbas, I am to be married soon ..." She wondered how she would live without this now. He had made her feel as if she were the most beautiful and important woman in the world. She felt more alive than she ever had. How could she ever go back to watching the world through her window now? In a way she wished this had never begun. Not knowing how life could be better was worse than knowing how it could.

"Come away with me."

"What?"

"I can arrange passage on a ship."

"Leave Venice?" She could not believe he could even contemplate such a thing. "No!"

"We can go to Spain. We will be safe from your father there. My father will give us money ..."

"Stop it. This has gone far enough. Take me back. Now!"

"You don't have to marry an old man! You don't have to spend your life shut up in a rich man's palace. You can be free!"

Julia was horrified. It had been easy, until now, to pretend to herself that this was just a game, to forget that the summer was passing quickly and that soon she would be married. But the game had gone far enough. Run away, leave Venice? To even contemplate such a thing was madness.

"What should I do in Spain?" she heard herself say.

"You will be my wife. I will find employment as a soldier there. My father knows many grandees who ..."

"You say now you would marry me but what if you changed your mind? What if you grew tired of me? What should become of me, then?"

"I should never grow tired of you."

"You say this now, of course. But Lucia has told me stories of men who have dishonored their women and abandoned them. This is madness!"

"You would rather spend the rest of your life trapped in an old man's palace?"

"At least I should be safe there. And what of sin, Abbas? Do you know of it, in your religion? If we should do this, God would punish us, if not in this life, then the next. I should never find absolution anywhere."

"Please Julia. Don't say these things! Ever since I saw you in the church, I knew I must marry you. I will do anything, anything! I would die rather than give you up."

He means it, she thought. He will stop at nothing now. Suddenly he terrified her. "Please take me back."

"Tell me you will come with me!"

"I cannot."

He took her by the shoulders and pulled her towards him. She felt his lips brush against hers, as gentle as his grip was fierce. She closed her eyes and kept perfectly still, hardly daring to breathe, aware only of the soft scent of his clothes and the sweet cloves on his breath. Finally he pulled away from her.

"Come with me," he repeated.

Oh, I will miss this, she thought. But I cannot throw away my whole life for the look in a man's eyes. "I must go back."

She jumped out of the gondola onto the water steps and climbed the stairs back to the palazzo in a daze. She looked back once, he had thrown aside the curtains and was watching her. He smiled and she smiled back.

She inched open the door at the top of the stairs. It creaked slowly open. The duenna stood waiting, her arms crossed across her chest. "So, you have deceived me," she said.

"Signora Cavalcanti!"

"What have you been doing?"

Julia turned around, slamming the heavy oak door behind her. She ran back down to the canal but the gondola was already gliding away from the steps. She would have shouted to him to come back, but then she heard her duenna's footsteps on the stone flags behind her and knew that to call out his name would be to betray him.

The old lady grabbed her by the arm and wrestled her back inside. She was surprisingly strong. Julia looked around a final time and thought she saw a movement of the curtains on the gondola as it rounded a bend in the canal, but she could not be sure.

* * *

Antonio Gonzaga wore the scarlet robes of a Consigliatore. He stood at the window, hands clenched into fists at his sides, staring over the roofs to the campanile of San Marco across the square from the Ducal Palace. What would they say about him there if word of this scandal ever leaked out? What would happen to his alliance with the Serena family?

His daughter! Behaving like a common prostitute! He wanted to cut her throat.

Julia stood in the middle of the room, one arm crossed across her chest. She would not meet his eyes.

"Who is this boy?" he growled.

She did not, would not, answer.

"I said, WHO IS THIS BOY?"

He saw Signora Cavalcanti waiting in the shadows, her eyes glittering with satisfaction. He would deal with her later. This situation would never have come about if she had done her job properly. Besides, if she had leave to wag her tongue, the story would be all over Venice tomorrow.

He crossed the room and slapped his daughter so hard across the cheek that the blow sent her crashing to the floor. He stood over her, daring her to stand up again and defy him. "I will beat you like a dog until you give me his name."

"Never," she said.

The unexpected steel in her infuriated him further. He grabbed her hair and shook her, then dragged her across the room to the window. Handfuls of hair came away in his hand. He kicked her in rage, then again because he felt like it. Julia put her hands over head to save herself from further abuse and curled into a ball on the floor, sobbing.

"Excellency," Signora Cavalcanti said, and even had the temerity to take a step towards him. She seemed shocked. Did she think a man of affairs did not know the way of the street? What did she think she might do - intervene? A look from him sent her scurrying back into the corner.

"You will tell me his name."

He hooked his fingers around the puffed sleeves of her vesture and pulled her to her feet. He cuffed her twice more around the head with his open hand while she twisted and writhed to try and escape the blows. Finally he released her and she crumpled to the floor a second time.

It seemed he would get no sense out of her tonight. Well, no matter, there was plenty of time to change her mind.

He had torn the sleeve and bodice of her dress, exposing her breast. "Cover yourself up, whore," he growled. Julia fumbled to reclaim her modesty but her hands were shaking so violently she could not do it.

"Take her to her room," Gonzago said to the duenna. "Lock it from the outside. Then come back here. I want to talk to you."

* * *

Signora Cavalcanti had never been so frightened in all her life. She had always revered His Excellency as a stern man; grave and menacing, a little like God, she supposed. But the scene she had just witnessed had shaken her. A righteous judge was within his bounds to pronounce sentence but to take a turn himself at the wheel of the rack was just plain savagery.

When she returned to the study Gonzago had composed himself. He sat at his desk, hands folded in his lap, and only his hair, still awry beneath his bareta, evidenced the violence that had taken place in the room just a short time before. "My daughter is shamefully stubborn," he said.

Signora Cavalcanti did not know what to say to that. She looked into the sorrowful face of Carpaccio's Virgin and felt ashamed.

"Is it possible she does not realize the extent of the injury she has done me?"

"I have instructed her faithfully in her filial duties, as well as her duty to the Republic and to God, Excellency."

"Perhaps." He pursed his lips and tapped a forefinger against his temple, as if deliberating a change to the tax on wool. "But if what you say is true, why does she defy me this way?"

The duenna realized that it was she who was now on trial. But what was there to say in her defence? Perhaps she should have kept her discovery to herself, handled it her own way. Well, it was too late now.

"Many questions arise from this," Gonzaga said. "For instance, how were these meetings arranged?"

Signora Cavalcanti swallowed the urge to say: "I don't know." It would be tantamount to expressing incompetence. "I will find out," she said.

"I hope so, Signora Cavalcanti," he said and smiled at her. "In fact, I rely on it."

She never liked it when His Excellency smiled. The effect was never pleasant.

# CHAPTER 24

Abbas followed the coach on foot from the palazzo. He lost it along the narrow calles but caught up again in the bustle of the mercato around the Campo Santa Maria Nuova. He barged his way through the fruit sellers and peddlers, vaulted a handcart loaded down with bolts of silk.

The church of Santa Maria dei Miracoli was one of the city's most beautiful churches, its façade built from yellow and antique white marble. The coach stopped below the steps, and Abbas watched two figures step out; one was short and stocky, the other tall, lean and graceful. She was dressed all in black, and her face was covered with a veil, but he knew it was her, just from the way that she moved.

"Please, Abbas. Don't do this," Ludovici said. He was out of breath after pursuing him through the streets.

"Have you really never been in love, Ludovici?"

"This is not love, this is an escapade!"

"I cannot live without her now."

"You breathe, you eat, you drink. That's all there is to living. It's simple. Anyone can manage it."

"That's not life, Ludovici! That's just taking up space." He started toward the church. "I just want to look. They will not see me."

Ludovici gave up. What was the point? He was headed for disaster and could not see it. At the very least Gonzaga would ruin Mahmoud, and he and Abbas would be expelled from the Republic - if they did not end up in prison.

He watched his friend bound up the steps, blind to everything but his own whims. Like a child, Ludovici thought. A headstrong, passionate child.

\* \* \*

The church was empty. Saint Francis pointed a long marble finger in his direction, as if singling him out for the Doge's soldiers. A frieze of naked putti danced above the main arch, mocking him. Where was she?

They were there, and then they were gone; shadows among shadows. They were already behind him, scuttling out of the doors. Why had they come and then left so quickly?

"Julia!"

She stumbled, dragged along by the old crone beside her. She threw back her veil and he saw the anguish on her face. He started to run after her, then stopped. What could he do?

When he came back outside they were already gone. He sat down on the top of the steps. Ludovici looked up at him, shook his head in frustration. Abbas supposed he had been right all along. A coach rattled away down the Via delle Botteghe, the horse's hoofs ringing on the cobbles. It had been a trap and it had fallen right into it.

\* \* \*

"Abbas Mahsouf? The Moor's son?"

Signora Cavalcanti nodded eagerly, revelling in her own mendacity. She had lured him out so easily. She was sure His Excellency would be delighted with her.

Gonzaga jumped to his feet, his oak chair crashing onto the tiles behind him. "A Moor?"

"He followed us inside, just like he did the first time. I saw him with my own eyes. He called her name as we left the church."

"The first time? What was the first time? You said nothing of this to me."

The duenna realized her mistake and her breath caught in her throat. "It seemed like a trifle."

"How did this ... trifle ... occur?"

"I thought nothing of it. Men stare all the time."

"That is why she has a veil."

"In summer she says it is too hot. Sometimes she pulls it back."

"And you let her?"

"She is headstrong."

"So do I pay you to be compliant?"

Signora Cavalcanti knew she must deflect his line of questioning, shift the focus elsewhere. "I saw someone else there."

"Who?"

"Ludovici Gambetto."

He stared at her, appalled. "You think she has had commerce with both of them?"

"No, of course not, Your Excellency! He was just looking on. I saw him watching as we left the  church. I believe the Moor is friendly with him."

Gonzaga went to the window, watched the gondolas and barges moving up and down the Great Canal. He need to think about this intriguing revelation. "So. My brother-in-law's bastard! You think this is how messages were passed?"

"His sister Lucia visits here often."

Gonzaga nodded. "Of course. I congratulate you on your discoveries. You shall have your reward Signora Cavalcanti. You may leave me now."

* * *

The door closed softly behind her.  Gonzaga stood there for a long time, thinking it through. What was he to do? If he brought the matter before the courts he would be the laughing stock of all Venice. His daughter and a blackamoor! They would force him from his seat on the Consiglio di Dieci.

He could perhaps bring the matter to the attention of Ludovici"'s father, but that was just as perilous. Old Gambetto's wife - his sister - had been a long time dead, and now he was maneuvering to be elected the next Doge, a rival to Gonzaga himself, and might welcome the opportunity to create a scandal.

The matter called for subtlety and patience. Ludovici could be punished in due course. The Moor must be dealt with now.

What was it that Signora Cavalcanti had said? "His sister Lucia visits here often." This was the key. Lucia was the conduit, then; but if water could flow one way, it could also flow the other.

But this time he would make it run to his own advantage.

* * *

When Lucia arrived that afternoon her duenna was dismissed and instead of being escorted to Julia's loggia or the drawing room overlooking the Great Canal, as usual, Signora Cavalcanti ushered her into Signore Gonzaga's private study where the Consigliore himself waited to greet her.

"Ah Lucia," he said. "How pleasant to see you again."

"Excellency," Lucia said, alarmed. She bent to one knee and kissed the hem of his sleeve.

"Come and sit here beside me," he said. He dismissed Signora Cavalcanti with a glance.

They sat together on the divan by the window and he watched her, his face frozen in the travesty of a smile. Lucia squirmed in the silence. She wondered if he knew about the letters. Why else would he wish to talk with her alone? And how much had Julia already told him? If he caught her in a lie it would go badly for her.

"I believe you have something to tell me," he said finally.

"I ... I did nothing wrong."

"I know you didn't. It's all right. Julia has told me everything."

"You are not angry?"

"With her, yes. With you? Yes, I am angry with you, too, my dear." He fixed his executioner's eyes on her, still smiling. "But you may yet find pardon in my eyes. You were, after all, only a messenger."

"You knew about the letter?"

"Of course," he lied.

"I did not know what was in it! My brother asked me to give it to her. That's all I know."

"You think this excuses your conduct in deceiving me and Signora Cavalcanti?"

She stared at her hands. "I don't know."

"Perhaps you are right. I think it does excuse you."

"You do, Your Excellency?"

"You were asked to convey a message from a friend. Where is the sin in that?"

"There is none."

"Of course. So you will not mind, then, extending me the same favors?"

Lucia stared at him, bewildered.

"Tell me, did you ever deliver letters to your brother from Julia herself?"

"Oh no, Excellency. Only that once through my brother to her. She never gave me anything to take back."

"Good. Because that is about to change." He unlocked the drawer of his desk and produced an envelope with a heavy wax seal. He passed it to her. "This is for Abbas."

"For Abbas? From whom, Excellency?"

"From Julia, of course."

She hesitated.

Gonzaga leaned across the desk and his smile vanished. "Understand me well. You will give this to your brother and tell him to hand it to Abbas, and you will say that you took this from Julia's own hand. You will tell no one - no one - of our conversation. If you fail me in this I shall inform your father of the role that you and your brother played in this infamous episode and bring down such calumny on both your heads that neither of you will ever be able to share polite society in La Serenissima ever again. The scandal may cost your father his place on the Council of Ten, and he will blame you and you alone should such a disaster befall him and your family. Am I making myself clear to you?"

Lucia nodded. The envelope trembled in her fingers.

"May I see Julia now?"

"I am afraid not. She is unwell and unable to receive visitors." He stood up and opened the door. "Signora Cavalcanti will show you the way out." He put a hand on her shoulder as she passed him. "Be sure that Abbas gets this message. I shall know if he does not. Count on it."

Lucia nodded, unable to find her voice. As the door closed behind her she clutched at a table for support. She felt dizzy with fear. She wished now that she had never let her brother talk her into this. All she wanted to do now was give Ludovici the Signor's missive and be done with this business forever.

# CHAPTER 25

*My dearest Abbas,*

*I am to be sent to the convent at Brescia until my marriage. Time is short. If you truly love me, as you say, I put my trust in you. I can get away but once more. The door that leads to the canal is now forever locked, but there may be another way. If you will wait for me at midnight tomorrow on the Ponte Antico I will come to you there. I will go wherever you choose to take me. My life is now in your hands.*

*May the hours pass swiftly until tomorrow night!*

*Julia*

Abbas read the letter twice more. Ludovici watched him, impatient. "What does she say?"

Abbas tore the vellum in half and held the pieces over the candle. Soon it was no more than a few wispy black leaves on the table. "Nothing," he said.

"Abbas?"

"You are a good friend," he said. "I can't put you in danger anymore." He stood up and walked out of the room.

***

Abbas was ushered into his father's council chamber at the Ministry of War, the Savio alla Scrittura. Mahmud glanced up from the charts on the table in front of him, maps of the Peninsula and the surrounding Ottoman possessions.

"What is so urgent that you disturb me here?"

"I am sorry, Father. But I need money."

"Is your commission as an officer in my army not enough?"

Abbas drew a deep breath. He imagined the Prophet must have been a little like his father, stern and courageous and proud, awesome in his mental and physical presence. He did not remember his mother - she had been a concubine in Mahmud's harem long ago - and so his father was all things to him now; mentor and master, teacher and confessor. This was the first time he had gone against his wishes.

"I have to go away."

Mahmud straightened up and stared, tucking his thumbs into the broad silver belt that was buckled at his waist. As he walked around the great oak table he reminded Abbas of a huge brown bear he had once seen in the forests near Belluno. On that occasion he had ten archers at his back. He wished they were there now.

"Go where?"

"Spain."

"Why do you wish to go to Spain?"

"I have been meeting a woman secretly. We plan to leave Venice together as soon as possible."

Mahmud put out a hand to steady himself against the edge of the chart table. He puffed the air out through his cheeks in a long sigh. "You little fool," he said.

"I love her."

"How you feel is meaningless to me. You have put both our necks on the block."

"I have already fought in two campaigns against the Ottoman and your name is known across the Mediterranean. I will find myself a commission and when it is done, Gonzaga will have to accept it. A year, perhaps two, and I will be back in Venice."

Mahmud shook his head. "Your resourcefulness far outweighs your intelligence. How you have managed to deceive Gonzaga for so long I do not know, but do not think he will ever forgive you when he finds out what you have done. Nor me. He is not a man who accepts anything that happens in this world unless it is of his own design. He was weaned on venom."

"Once we are married, what can he do?"

"There are many things he can do, you little fool. Does anyone else know of this?"

Abbas shook his head.

"Good."

The blow was so sudden and so unexpected that it lifted Abbas off his feet. He found himself suddenly on his back, staring at the vaulted ceiling. There was a buzzing in his ears and he tasted his own blood in his mouth.

Mahmud lifted him easily from the floor with one hand and pushed him against the wall. "Now listen to me! I love you and I will not let you ruin your life - and mine - by one rush of youthful lust. Buy yourself a mistress and leave Julia Gonzaga alone! Do you understand me?"

Abbas rested his head on his father's shoulder until his senses cleared. He felt his father's grip relax. When it did, he pushed himself away, swaying slightly on his feet. "Goodbye Father," he said and stumbled out of the door.

***

No Magnifico was allowed, by law, to speak with the Captain General of the Army alone. The Consiglio di Dieci was vigilant for any nobleman who might try to use the army for their own purposes, as Sforza had done at Milan. So Mahmud was accompanied everywhere he went by two senators, the Provveditori Generali delle Armi and they were with Mahmud early that morning when he burst into the private chambers of Antonio Gonzaga.

Gonzaga sat at the far end of the room, the lead-paned windows at his back. Behind him the domes of the San Marco loomed against a mauve sky.

"Most reverend Signore," Mahmud murmured and bent to kiss the sleeve of Gonzaga's robe.

"I am told you wish to see me on a matter of urgency," Gonzaga said, with a glance at the Provveditori. "A matter of private and not state importance, I presume?"

Mahmud fidgeted with embarrassment. Better to have discussed this with Gonzaga alone, but the law made that impossible.

"A matter of the utmost delicacy, Signore."

"Is it to do with …matters of the heart?"

Mahmud was in some ways relieved that Gonzaga already knew. It would make it easier to discuss this with the two senators present. He glanced at the Provveditori, who were almost licking their lips in anticipation of a scandal. They would have to be prudent before these two gentlemen. "You already have some knowledge of the matter?"

"All I know is that a certain lady has been impudent enough to pass letters between her friend and a young man who should have known better. I put it down to the tempestuousness of youth."

"I needed to be sure that you were apprised of the situation."

"Such indiscretions will never be allowed, of course. But I appreciate that you came here to warn me. I assure you all precautions have been taken to stop this foolishness from getting out of hand."

"I am most relieved to find you so informed."

"You have my thanks, General. But may I ask how you came by this information?"

Mahmud hesitated. Now that there was a way to contain this scandal it was not necessary to reveal to Gonzaga - or the Provveditori - that he had not seen his son since the last evening. "From the young gentleman in question. His duty is to Venice. As is mine."

"Do not upset yourself. All matters are in hand."

Mahmud bowed and made his leave. As he left the palazzo he persuaded himself that everything would end well. Now that Gonzaga had been warned there was no possibility that his son's life - and his own - would be ruined for the sake of something that could be easily purchased for a few dinari anywhere in the Republic.

# CHAPTER 26

Abbas kept to the shadows. All the previous night and this long day he had hidden, making his plans. With the little money he had, he had paid for passage to Pescati on a merchant galley that would sail with the morning tide. He did not know how they might reach Naples from there, but Abbas was sure he would think of something. All that mattered to him now was to get Julia out of Gonzaga's palazzo and escape Venice.

Abbas had hidden all that day in the apartment that Ludovici kept for his mistress at Guidecca. When Ludovici came to see him that evening he told him Mahmud's soldiers had been searching for him all day, turning out the inns and taverns.

"What will you do?" Ludovici asked him.

"Don't worry about me. I have already involved you too much in this."

"This game is deadly serious now. I warned you."

"It's not a game and I have always been deadly serious." He nodded at the somber, dark-haired girl watching them from a corner of the room. "I believe she thought you intended to share her with me. Reassure her that tonight I shall leave, your house and your mistress intact."

"Where will you go?"

"I cannot even tell you that." He embraced him. "Thank you. You are the greatest friend a man could ever have."

Ludovici pressed a purse into his palm. Abbas did not protest. Without it, he would have had scarce enough to buy a loaf of bread when they reached Pescati.

\*\*\*

He heard the clock in the Piazza San Marco chime the twelfth hour. He pulled his mantello more tightly around his shoulders. The gondola was moored by the steps below the bridge, waiting. Would she come?

You don't know anything about her. You are in love with the danger of it. If you are in love with anything, you are in love with your own daring.

Ludovici was right, he knew nothing about her. But that was not what love was; knowing everything about someone was marriage, it was contract and prudent alliance. Love was mystery and it was something even a beautiful friend like Ludovici would never understand. He was still at university and was already an old man.

You're just in love with loving.

He saw a shadow darting from the alley on the other side of the bridge. "Julia!" he said. He ran across the bridge, his arms outstretched. She saw him too and ran towards him. But just before he reached her, he heard footsteps on the cobblestones behind him. He looked over his shoulder. The milizia di note! The night police!

"Julia! Attenzione!"

Her hood fell back. In the light of the half moon he made out the crooked, bearded grin of a total stranger.

"Am I not the beauty you were expecting?" the man said. Abbas saw the flash of a blade, and felt the point of it jabbed hard between his ribs. "I may not be your Julia, but I know the way to a man's heart."

Abbas brought up his knee. The man squealed like a butchered pig and doubled over, collapsing at his feet. Abbas gasped. As he fell, the man had sliced into his side with the dagger.

He turned around, drawing his sword, knew the man's accomplices were behind him. He could not distinguish empty shadows from his enemy. How many were there? He guessed three, perhaps four.

He tried to run but the man in the hood grabbed his ankle. Abbas stabbed down with his sword, felt the blade crunch against bone. The man shrieked in pain and let go.

They had surrounded him. Abbas backed away, felt the cold stone of the bridge against his back. He heard his gondolier - God curse his yellow soul - poling away from the steps. Now the shadows came alive, two men rushed him from either side, neither as cocky or as amateur as the wretch still sobbing in his death agony at his feet. Abbas slashed with his sword, chest high, and they backed away.

Then he saw a third man come from the shadows. There was a shadow on the moon and something fell over his head and shoulders. He threw up a hand to protect himself. A net! He tried to throw it off, but tripped over the dying man and fell, enveloping them both in the mesh. His struggles only succeeded in working the net tighter around them both. Abbas remembered the dying man might still have his dagger.

He felt a searing pain in his face and screamed. But then they were on him, something clubbed him hard on the back of the head and he blacked out.

\*\*\*

When he opened his eyes, it was pitch black. He could smell bilge water, heard the slow slap of waves against the hull of a ship, the scampering of rats.

And there was something else he knew, something he remembered from the battlefield. The smell of corpses.

Whoever his assailants were, they were not cutthroats after his money. They had cudgeled him when he was tangled in the net, when they could as easily have killed him. He tried to move but they had bound his wrists and feet. His face burned like fire.

He tried to reason out his predicament.

These must be Gonzaga's men. If Julia had written the letter then she had deliberately led him into this trap; the other possibility was that it had come from her father's hand. He hoped so. Why hadn't they killed him and dumped his body in the canal? He supposed his father being Captain General of the Republic might have something to do with it.

There were footsteps on the companionway and men's" voices. A hatch was thrown open and torchlight flooded the hold.

He turned his face away and found himself face to face with the hooded stranger from the bridge. He was dead. Beside him lay another corpse, an old woman dressed in black. Her throat had been cut.

He heard a man laughing. Abbas turned to face his tormentors. They were bearded, shoeless sailors, the kind who could be bought at the Marghero wharf any day for a few dinari. One of them - Abbas smelled cheap wine and body stench - bent down and held the flaming torch a few inches from his face.

"Well, my boy, look at you. You don't look so pretty now. Bartolomeo here split your face in two with his knife before he died. Not that you'll care about that, soon enough."

The two men behind him laughed again.

He leaned closer. "See that other one next to Bartolomeo? She was Gonzaga's duenna. Put up a real fight she did. Not that it did her much good. Ever slaughtered a pig, have you? It was a bit like that." He grinned. He had rotten teeth and boils on his neck. "But she was luckier than you, that's a fact. You'll wish you were her before the night's out."

One of the men tugged down his breeches while the other sliced the ropes at his ankles. They gripped his knees and prised his legs apart. He shrieked in panic and tried to kick out, but they were too strong.

The first man drew his knife. Abbas twisted and bucked. Now he knew why they had not killed him on the Ponte Antico.

"You wanted Signore Gonzaga's daughters to play with these little toys, did you? Well, how about we give them to the Consigliore and he can give them to her himself."

"NOOOOOOOOOOOOO … !"

He let go his bladder in his terror and the men laughed.

"Say goodbye to them, Moor," the man sneered. The blade flashed in the light of the torch and the world sheered into a hot and infernal place.

\*\*\*

A milky dawn. A funeral procession of gondolas, draped with black velvet, emerged from beneath the Ponte Molino and slipped silently along the Sacca della Misericordia and across the lagoon toward the cemetery island of San Michele. Julia watched until they disappeared into the mist.

He was sending her to the convent at Brescia, to await the arrival of Serena and what her father referred to as "the joyous occasion of her wedding." The barge would be here soon to collect her.

She thought about that last afternoon in the gondola.

Come away with me. We can go to Spain. You don't have to marry an old man! You don't have to spend your life shut up in a rich man's palace. You can be free!

I should have said yes, she thought. It was my one chance and I threw it away. Now I am to be buried alive. Oh, Abbas. Where are you now?

# PART 3

## ROSE OF SPRING

# CHAPTER 27

## The Sweet Waters of Europe, near Eyüp

Fields of sunflowers dazzled the eye. On the other side of the Horn the city rippled in dusty amber behind its gray land walls. It was a view of the city some of the girls had never seen. Today the entire Harem had been transported in canopied caïques along the Bosphorus, a welcome respite from the oppressive monotony of the Eski Saraya.

The girls gossiped on the blue and crimson Persian carpets thrown in the shade of the cypress trees, while the gedicli fed them peaches and grapes from silver salvers. Musicians entertained them with flutes and viols; piles of silk cushions kept their pampered bottoms from the hard ground; dancing bears performed for them on the grass.

Gülbehar kept herself apart. One of her gedicli produced a mirror and held it up for her inspection. The handle was encrusted with sapphires, a gift from Suleiman after the birth of Mustapha. She studied her reflection and brushed an errant lock of hair back into place.

"Where is Hürrem ?" one of the girls whispered, watching her.

"The Kislar Aghasi says she is with Suleiman," another girl said. "Now he spends all his days with her, as well as his nights."

Sirhane, a raven-haired Persian, popped a grape into her mouth. "In the bazaars they say she is a witch, that she has cast a spell over the Lord of the Earth. How else could she have replaced Rose of Spring in his affections so quickly, and to the exclusion of all others?"

"Look at her," another whispered, watching Gülbehar "s gedicli combing out her hair. "She is so beautiful. If the Lord of Life will not look at her any more, what chance is there for the rest of us?"

"They say even the Grand Vizier fears Hürrem ," Sirhane said. "The Kislar Aghasi told me that the Sultan even goes to her to discuss politics and that she advises him on military campaigns."

"The Kislar Aghasi has a fertile imagination."

"He swears it is true!"

"The Grand Vizier would have her drowned in the Bosphorus!"

"Perhaps he cannot," Sirhane said and they all fell silent. Was that really the truth of it? Surely no one was more powerful than the Grand Vizier? "Anyway, I feel sorry for Gülbehar ," Sirhane added. "The Lord of Life has disgraced her."

"Gülbehar is still first kadin," another girl said. "And one day she will be the Sultan Valide. Her day will come."

"They say God is punishing the Lord of Life for making a witch his kadin. That is why his last son died in the cradle."

"But Hürrem has two sons still living. And she carries another child now."

"None of them will ever rival Mustapha!" another girl shouted and there the conversation ended. The girls" attention returned to the dancing bear and Sirhane kept to herself the other whisper she had heard from the Kislar Aghasi; that Hürrem was plotting to get rid of Mustapha also.

But that could never happen. The very thought was absurd.

## Topkapi Saraya

It was quiet here among the kiosks and the ornamental ponds. Only the sigh of the wind through the chestnut trees and the gentle murmur of water in the ornamental fountains disturbed the gazelles grazing on the lawns.

Suleiman had always liked to walk here to compose his thoughts and find respite from the endless demands and entreaties that came every day from the Divan and the Harem. Once he would come alone. Lately he brought a companion with him.

The last five years had been many times blessed, he thought. When he returned from hunting at Adrianople, shortly after their first union, he had found Hürrem already plump with new life. Early the following year she gave birth to a boy. At the insistence of the Valide, they called him Selim.

He had not quite shared his mother's excitement. While she celebrated the consolidation of the Osmanli line, he brooded over future conflicts. He knew what his father had done to secure his throne. He supposed now his sons would have to do the same.

Hürrem was now his second kadin, but she had replaced the first in his affections. Gülbehar had been his sanctuary for so long, but he had never been able to share the burdens of his sultanate with her. That had been Ibrahim's role.

But when Achmed Pasha rose in revolt in Egypt he had been forced to send Ibrahim to crush him, and while he was gone Suleiman had brought the problems of state to Hürrem instead. To his surprise he found her shrewd beyond her years and with an innate grasp of the intricacies of court politics. He continued to confide in her, even after Ibrahim's return. Her caution was now a counterfoil to Ibrahim's aggression.

She had opened a new world to him. While Gülbehar was pliant and predictable, Hürrem continually surprised him. On one visit she might be sullen but passionate; on another effusive and playful. She could soothe him with her singing and her viol or excite him with her dancing. She could dress like a slim boy in military doman or like a houri in gossamer. He never knew what to expect from her, though she seemed to have an uncanny ability to anticipate his own moods.

Her delight in lovemaking was still unholy and he knew he must one day send her to the mufti for education. But for now her infidel soul afforded him endless pleasures. One cry of ecstasy gave him more pleasure than all the groveling of foreign ambassadors in the Divan.

Hürrem was now his joy; everything else was duty.

The little Russian girl - he had taken to calling her, affectionately, "russelana" - had carefully cultivated her friendship with his mother, the Valide, and Nature had helped her cement the alliance by providing her with another son, Bayezid. She had failed in the labor chamber only once, when she had produced a girl twin. The boy, Abdullah, had died just last year; but his sister, Mihrmah, was now three years old.

She was not the devoted mother that Gülbehar had been, but that did not trouble him overmuch; he wanted her all for himself.

"I want to talk to you," he said to her as they walked in the garden.

"Yes my Lord?"

"It is the Hungarian question again. Frederick is sending an envoy to treat with us. He does not know that the voivoide, Zapolya, has sent his man also who has already met in secret with Ibrahim."

He did not need to explain the problem to her; somehow she already knew. Suleiman's army, marshaled by Ibrahim, had annihilated the Hungarians on the plain of Mohaçs just two years before. Their king had drowned in the swamp when his horse fell on him during the retreat. Since Hungary was too far away for permanent occupation, he had withdrawn his troops after the battle and it had since become a wasteland of warring bandits, coveted by noblemen such as Zapolya and the great Hapsburg family, under Frederick. But they could not have it without coming to terms with him first. Who should he treat with?

"What are your thoughts, my Lord?"

"We have slain the king and the horses of the Osmanli have set their hoofs in Buda, so it is now in the dominion of Islam. Why should I treat with either of them? I am the King of Hungary now."

"So every summer you must send your army to regain what it has conquered the year before. One day you will grow tired of it."

"The dogs are always at the door when there are scraps to be had."

"But you must guard every entrance to the house. If you become too preoccupied with one, the robbers may enter by another door."

"I shall not treat with Frederick. Then I would have exchanged a starving dog for a rabid wolf."

"What about Zapolya?"

"Zapolya is an upstart. He is no king."

"What is a king? It is not the crown that makes a king, it is the sword. Make Zapolya your gatekeeper and let him have a piece of iron for his head. In return demand his tribute and free passage for your army. While there is no border, you remain his master."

"He is not strong enough to hold back Frederick's armies."

"He can keep the borders until a real army is assembled against him, one that is worthy of your attention. You may even use Zapolya to lure Frederick into the contest and drown him in the swamp also."

Suleiman stared at the black waters of the Bosphorus, white foam streaked across the surface by the wind. On one side lay Asia, on the other Europe. She was right; one could not look too long at one side for fear of forgetting the other.

"Zapolya, then."

"If my Lord considers my counsel proper. In all things I defer to your greater wisdom."

Suleiman nodded, pleased with Hürrem "s diplomacy. Ah, she was a rare treasure indeed.

### The Eski Saraya

Suleiman and Gülbehar  ate kebabs of lamb on silver skewers with pine kernels and drank perfumed rosewater from goblets of Iznik glass. After the gedicli had removed the bowls they sat for a long time in silence.

"Have I offended you in some way, my Lord?" Gülbehar  said at last.

"No. Why?"

"You have not asked for me these many months. When you do come, it is only to see Mustapha."

"Do not deem to question me."

Gülbehar  hung her head. Suleiman felt sorry for her; she had been a good wife. All she had ever asked of him until now was some Venetian satin or Baghdad silk or a tortoiseshell comb. And she had given him Mustapha.

He had not wanted to hurt her this way. But each moment he spent with her, he compared her to Hürrem and his impatience grew. He could not be at ease with her; his frustration turned inevitably to anger.

He got to his feet. Gülbehar looked up at him, startled. "You are leaving, my Lord?"

"I have matters of state to attend to."

Gülbehar looked miserable. "Hürrem ."

It was an unpardonable breach of protocol but Suleiman decided to ignore it. "My Lady," he said and took his leave of her.

*** 

It was always dusk in the Eski Saraya. Even on a summer midday, the sun could not chase the shadows from the warren of dark paneled rooms and endless corridors. It was a world of dusty lanterns and baroque mirrors coated with ancient grime. Sloe-eyed women with dark rubies in their hair appeared on shadowed staircases like ghosts, ungratified and forgotten.

It infected Hürrem "s mood. I am a heartbeat from such a living death, she thought.

She had come so far. She had given him sons and somehow kept him from this neglected storehouse of pleasures. None of it had been easy. The strain of child-bearing had sapped her energies and after each confinement she had surrendered herself to Muomi's ministrations and to vials of the gedicli's foul potions in order to restore her figure. She had wet nurses for the children so her infants would not suckle her breasts dry.

Yet all she had won thus far could be snatched away from her in an instant. Only one woman in here had power over her own life and that was not the wife of the Sultan, but the mother. She could not wait for fate to be kind; to wait on destiny was to wait forever. She must force her own fortune.

"Muomi! Muomi!"

Her gedicli appeared instantly. She had been hovering at her post outside the door.

"Come here," Hürrem said.

Muomi sank to her knees beside her. "My Lady?"

"There is something I want you to do."

"Another potion?"

Hürrem nodded. "Yes. Another potion. I want you to make one that will kill Mustapha for me."

# CHAPTER 28

The stone kitchens below the Old Palace were cramped and hot, and smelled of spice, sweat and steam. Heat rose in waves from the open furnaces, and there was a constant clatter of pots and kettles. Cooks shouted at underlings and at each other, while veiled gedicli scurried through the fug of heat and noise with dishes and teas.

So in this hubbub the harried pages and servants and cooks paid no particular attention to the tall black girl carrying the tray of oranges; even if they had, even the most observant of them would not have realized that the platter of oranges she had with her as she left was different from the one she had brought in with her.

*** 

At fourteen years, Mustapha was everything Suleiman had hoped for in a son. Like every prince he was trained at the Palace School, with the elite of the boys recruited in the devshirme. He had proved an outstanding swordsman and horseman, and he was besides an outgoing and popular boy, already a favorite among the yeniceri who came to cheer him at the cerit - a horseback game using wooden javelins - in the Hippodrome.

He was also a talented scholar. He had already learned his Qur'an, Persian and mathematics. Suleiman was sure the Osmanlis could have no better shahzade than this.

Today he sported a plum-colored bruise above his right eye, which was almost swollen shut. Suleiman shook his head in feigned horror as his son knelt to kiss the ruby ring on his right hand.

"What happened to you?"

"It happens all the time," Gülbehar said. "He was hit by a javelin in the cerit. Tell him to take more care. Nothing I say to him seems to make any difference."

"Should I be more careful, father?" Mustapha asked him and grinned.

"You should take care not to get hit so often."

"He would spend all day on his horse if he could," Gülbehar said.

"There is nothing wrong with that. There was a time when the Osmanlis did not have fine palaces to sit in, or laws to make. It is good the next Sultan knows how it feels to have a horse under him."

Look how big the boy has grown, Suleiman thought. He was almost as tall as Suleiman himself, and he had the first sprouting of a beard on his chin. His eyes were bright with the optimism of youth; when I was his age I was consumed with terror, wondering when Selim's shadow would fall across my face. Thank God Mustapha will never know such a father.

Gülbehar sat on the divan and folded her hands on her lap. "Leave us now, Mustapha, I wish to talk to the Lord of Life alone."

Mustapha sala'amed to Suleiman, kissed his mother on the cheek and left the room.

"You are too severe with him," Suleiman said, after he had gone.

"I have to be. He is all I have."

"A young man should enjoy his youthful pleasures while he still can. He will have responsibilities soon enough."

"Every day he brings back from the Hippodrome some fresh injury. Last week he was thrown from his horse three times! What if he gets killed in that stupid game? I have no son and no master. My life is over."

"As God wills," he said.

"He is the shahzade. Do you not take a care to worry what may happen to him?"

"A Sultan must be a soldier as well as a statesman. A few scars from the Hippodrome will only make him stronger. What of you? Are you well?"

"What does it matter to you? You only ever come here to see Mustapha."

"That is my right."

"Do I no longer have rights?"

Suleiman knew she had him there; he had ignored the nobet gecesi, the "night turn" that was the prerogative of every kadin. He should by custom sleep with her at least once a week.

She had never questioned him before. He leaped to his feet and guilt made his fury even more potent. "You may be first kadin, but you are also still my slave. You will do as I say and you will not presume to question me!"

Gülbehar wilted in the face of his anger. "Once you would never have spoken to me so," she murmured and hung her head. "The little red-haired minx has bedeviled you. She wants dominion over the entire Harem - even over you!"

"Isn't that what you want also?"

She looked up miserably. "I just want to serve you."

"Then serve me by keeping your silence," he said.

He turned his back, his silk kaftan flapping about his heels. Like a great bird taking flight, she thought, leaving forever. The black mutes at the door watched impassively, staring fixedly ahead like statues. Kadins came and went. The Harem remained always the same.

\*\*\*

That night after the final prayer the killerji-bashi came to Mustapha's chamber and asked him if he would like to eat. Silent pages brought him his meal on a gold tray. There were tiny cubes of meat broiled in herbs, squash stuffed with rice, figs in sour cream and fresh oranges.

The meal was served in blue and white porcelain bowls each hand painted with hatayi scrollwork. The killerji-bashi tasted each dish for poison, as he did at every meal, then bowed and left the room. Mustapha sat cross-legged on the carpet and ate in silence. Occasionally he raised the index finger of his right hand and a page would step forward to refill his golden goblet with sherbet.

When he had finished Mustapha looked at the oranges. He chose one, peeled the skin from one side of it, and tasted it. It was dry and slightly sour. He dropped it on the tray and pushed it away.

Instantly another of the pages stepped forward with a bowl of perfumed water. Mustapha dipped his fingers in the bowl and allowed him to dry them. Then he got up and went to his bedchamber. It was customary for the pages to eat whatever he left and as he left the room he saw them fall on his leftover dishes like starving street dogs.

Other servants unrolled his sleeping mattress for him but he did not feel tired. He sat at the Qur'an stand and read two more suras by the light of the candle before the first spasm gripped his stomach.

\*\*\*

By the time Gülbehar arrived, the pages who had served the prince's meal were already dead. Mustapha was pale and shaken but still alive. The Palace physician had administered an emetic and Mustapha groaned as his empty stomach rebelled once more.

Gülbehar cradled her son in her arms. He must be really ill, she thought, for he lets me do it. "How could you let this happen?" she screamed at the terrified guards. "Who did this to my son?"

"We will find them," the Kapi Aga promised. By the prophet's Holy Beard, if Mustapha had died his own head would already be moldering on the Gate of Felicity.

Gülbehar rocked Mustapha in her arms like a baby, sobbing with rage and fear. "Who did this?"

Mustapha's chief food taster was delivered to the bonstanji-bashi who awaited him in his torture chamber below the Ba"ab-i-Sa"adet. He was examined closely, but he insisted on his innocence between his screams. However he was at least finally able to indicate which food had contained the poison, by the simple expedient of force-feeding him each morsel that remained from the shahzade's supper.

"It was the oranges," the bostanji reported. "Somehow they poisoned the oranges."

Suleiman ordered that everyone involved in the preparation of the prince's food be examined also; the two cooks and the pages who had brought the tray from the kitchen died screaming, pleading their innocence, begging for a mercy that never came.

# CHAPTER 29

Gold spigots dripped warm water into the marble bath. Naked bodies, alabaster, coffee and ebony, beaded with moisture, glided through the steam under a cavernous dome. Black gedicli in gauzy bath chemises scooped water into gold-plated bowls and poured it over the heads of the odalisques.

Hürrem perched on the edge of the navel-stone, a huge hexagonal slab heated from beneath by an underground furnace. Muomi soaped her back with rich lather. The other girls passed, their eyes averted, either from jealousy or from fear.

Muomi's knuckles worked the muscles in her back. Later she would have her work on her stomach and thighs. She would not allow herself to grow old and fat in here. A girl must have fangs in this snake pit.

She tried not to brood over her recent failure. The oranges had been her idea. She knew the killerji-bashi would not suspect a whole fruit. She had pierced the oranges with needles herself and Muomi had poured the hemlock in through the tiny pinpricks in the rind. Fate and a fussy nature had saved the shahzade.

Never mind, she would find some other way.

Gülbehar walked past. The bath chemise clung to her heavy breasts and Hürrem noted with satisfaction that her waistline was growing thicker. A slave girl hurried behind her carrying a silver platter of candied fruit. She supposed eating was all she had to look forward to these days.

"You will need a whole procession of slaves soon," Hürrem said.

Gülbehar had not seen her, but she recognized her voice immediately. She wheeled around. "You! What did you say to me?"

"I said you will need two more slave girls soon to keep your breasts from dragging on the ground. They can carry one each a silver platter. Like the fruit."

Gülbehar gaped at her, astonished by her effrontery. "How dare you speak to me like that!"

"I only say what everybody thinks."

"I know it was you! You tried to murder my son and now you insult me!"

"You are getting old. Your mind is playing tricks."

"It was you, little witch!"

"Why don't you run to Suleiman and tell him your suspicions then. If you dare!"

Gülbehar was on the edge of tears. But no, I will not give her the satisfaction! Hürrem was so certain of her hold over the Lord of Life! "If you hurt my son, I will kill you."

"I do not think so," Hürrem said and smiled. She patted her stomach. "How many more Sultans do you think I might grow in here?"

"Mustapha is …"

"Mustapha is all you have. I have two and another in my belly and I may yet have many more, since the Sultan no longer comes to your bed. Why is it you could not keep him, Rose of Spring? Because you are stupid or because you are dull?"

"Leave my son alone!"

Hürrem lowered her voice so that only Gülbehar heard her murmur: "Say goodbye to your little bud, Rose of Spring!"

Gülbehar lashed out. The slap stung Hürrem "s cheek. She struck back but at the last moment she pulled back so that she caught Gülbehar just a glancing blow on the side of the head. Gülbehar raked her face with her nails. Hürrem grabbed her and they fell onto the floor. The gedicli jumped back, screaming for the guards.

*** 

Muomi helped Hürrem back to her apartments. She was still dripping wet, just a thin bath chemise wrapped around her. Her hair hung in wet tangles and there were streaks of thin, watery blood on her cheek.

Hürrem slumped onto a divan.

"Shall I send for the physician?" Muomi said.

Hürrem shook her head but then a spasm of pain in her belly made her gasp and she doubled over. She had landed heavily when she had tussled Gülbehar to the floor. Well if she lost the baby that would still suit her plans. Two sons was enough. "What good is the physician?" she said. All he would be allowed to do anyway was examine her hand, and that from behind three rows of armed eunuchs.

"You are badly hurt."

"Fetch me a mirror."

Muomi brought her a jewelled looking glass. Hürrem held it up and examined her reflection. There were some small scratches on her cheek, two deeper ones on her forehead. Damn the bitch, she didn't even know how to fight properly!

"Scratch me," Hürrem said.

"My lady?"

"Scratch me!" Hürrem grabbed Muomi's wrist and drew her nails down her neck. "Like this. Harder!"

With elaborate care Muomi brought her fingernails to Hürrem "s neck and raked deep scratches almost to the collarbone. Then she made others, not quite as deep - she did not want to leave scars - on her cheek. She held up the mirror again. That was more like it.

"Are you satisfied?" Muomi said. She sounded breathless, as if she had just made love.

"It will do."

"Will your Sultan love you more, looking like that?"

"No, Muomi. But he will love Gülbehar a lot less."

# CHAPTER 30

The Eski Saraya trembled.

Suleiman strode through the cloisters, the Kislar Aghasi shuffling behind, face beaded with perspiration and babbling with fright.

The Lord of Life had come as soon as he had been told of the terrible incident in the hammam by his mother. He stopped in front of the doors to Hürrem "s apartment. The two eunuchs who guarded the entrance trembled when they saw him, but continued to stare resolutely ahead.

The Kislar Aghasi caught up, his breath sawing in his chest.

"Tell her I am here."

The old eunuch nodded and went inside but it was Muomi, not Hürrem , who was waiting to greet him. She sala'amed, and remained on her knees.

"The Lord of Life wishes to see your mistress."

"She cannot see him at present."

The Kislar Aghasi stared at her as if she had answered in a foreign language. "What did you say?"

"My mistress is distressed beyond words that she cannot accept the honor he does her by visiting her here. But she cannot receive him. She could not allow the Lord of Life to gaze upon her in her present condition."

The Kislar Aghasi felt the pain in his chest growing worse. He was getting too old for the tribulations this little Russian had brought to the harem. It had all been so easy when Gülbehar was the only kadin. How did the Chief Black Eunuch tell the Possessor Men's Necks that his second wife refused to see him? There was no precedent for this in the protocols.

"But she must see him," he said.

Muomi stared back and said nothing.

He hurried past her, into the private dining room. Hürrem was sitting on a divan of green brocade, a heavy veil covering her face.

"My Lady," he said.

She said nothing. This is just intolerable, he thought dabbing at the perspiration on his face with a silk handkerchief. They were toying with him, that evil-eyed black slave and this little red witch.

Hürrem  lifted the veil from her face and the old eunuch gasped. There were ugly red scabs over her nose and cheeks and her neck looked as if she had been clawed by a mountain lion. This was not the way he had heard it. He had been told that although the altercation had been unseemly, neither girl had been badly hurt.

He uttered a sob like the cry of a small animal and fled the room.

***

"Too disfigured to see me?" Suleiman said. He stared at his Chief Black Eunuch. The poor old man looked as if he was about to faint.

"It is as she says, my Lord."

"I do not believe it," he said. "I am here to see my kadin. I will see her." He swept past the guards into the apartments.

Hürrem  looked up from the divan. When she saw him she slowly raised her veil a second time. Suleiman took one look at the ruin of her face and said, "Gülbehar !" Then he turned on his heel and walked out again.

***

Gülbehar  could hardly contain her excitement. The Kislar Aphasias messenger had informed her that the Lord of Life was in the Eski Saraya. He had no doubt been told of the outrage the Russian minx had inflicted on her in the hammam. The snake had bared its fangs at last. Suleiman must see her now for what she was. She would tell him how she had tried to murder his beloved Mustapha; he would send her and her black sorceress to the and the truth would come out.

Then Suleiman would come back to her and everything would be as it was before.

She prepared the table herself, setting out sweetmeats and rahat lokum and sherbet, and then settled down to wait on the divan. Her hair was braided and brushed, and she was freshly bathed and perfumed.

She just could not wait to tell him how that bitch had provoked her, her whispered threat against the shahzade. Say goodbye to your little bud, Rose of Spring.

She was too impatient to sit still. She went to the window, stared through the grille at the glittering waters of the Horn and the red-roofed palaces climbing the hill of Galata. Sunny Stamboul that would soon belong, all of it, to her son. He had spent too long in the shadows.

The door crashed open.

There was no sweating old eunuch to usher the Lord of Life into her chamber, no time to settle herself. Suleiman stood in the doorway, his face ugly with rage. He slammed the door shut behind him, shattering the silence of the Harem, and advanced into the centre of the room.

Gülbehar dropped to her knees. "Sala'am, Lord of my Life, Sultan of Sult- "

He grabbed her arm and forced her to her feet. She gasped in pain as his fingers bit into the soft flesh of her upper arm. "Take off your veil."

Gülbehar felt weak. What was the matter with him? She pulled back her veil and his face twisted in contempt. "Not one scratch."

"I do not understand."

He slapped her hard across the face, then did it twice more. After the third blow she fell to the floor.

When Suleiman spoke again his voice was so soft she could scarce hear him. "If you ever again take from me the pleasure of looking on her face, I swear I shall kill you."

"Please, my Lord, I-"

"Your jealousy poisons the whole Harem!"

"What have I done?"

"Enough! You are the mother of the shahzade and one day you will be Valide. Be content!"

"What did that minx say to you? It was not I that-"

He struck her again, as she cowered on the floor. Then he held her by her arm and hit her again, kept hitting her long after she begged him to stop. It was only when he saw blood smeared on her white chemise that he realized what he had done. He let her fall to the floor, limp as a rag doll.

For a long time she lay at his feet, sobbing. He stood over her, panting with rage, appalled at himself. *Just like your father*, he thought. When she finally looked up her lip and eyes were swelling, and there was blood welling from her nose and her mouth.

"My Lord ..."

"Silence! You will never try to keep me from her again! Do you understand?" She nodded. Now that his anger was spent he felt sorry for her. He reached down to help her to her feet but she twisted away.

*I might have killed her*, he thought. *I came so close. If there had been a dagger in my hand, I would have used it. She has been my kadin for so many years, since I was barely more than a boy, and yet I might have murdered her in my rage.*

"You must leave her," he said, "it is best for you. I shall make the arrangements."

And he left the room, leaving her to her bitter tears.

# CHAPTER 31

## The Hippodrome

Güzül was a Jewess; once a month she was allowed inside the Harem to sell gems and trinkets to the odalisques. But that was not her true function; in the closed world of the Harem, Güzül was that most precious of creatures - a go-between. Over the course of the years she had become Gülbehar "s voice in the outside world.

She was no longer youthful. Her skin was the color of tobacco, and wrinkled; to compensate for her fading youth she dyed her hair with henna and tied it with bright ribbons, in the remembrance of vanity.

For her errand today she had chosen a cloak of scarlet silk with a small round satin cap, also scarlet, on her head. She had a gold damask waistcoat and white kid leather shoes. The silver bracelets on her ankles and wrists made her look like a brigand queen.

With the sunset the stone of Ibrahim's palace had turned a rose pink. The high walls and wooden shuttered windows echoed the splendor of the great Topkapi, which stood less than half a mile away. It was a reminder to everyone, from the horsemen playing cerit on the Hippodrome below, to the faithful filing into the Aya Sofia mosque, that this Greek was the greatest and wealthiest and most trusted Vizier the Osmanlis had ever known. They said the Sultan himself had built this palace for his Grand Vizier out of the public purse. He had even given him his sister, Hatise Sultan, in marriage.

The ivory and tortoiseshell throne, the silver candle holders and the copper-and-turquoise censers were all fit for a Sultan. With the thick band of gold around his sugar loaf turban and white satin robes, Ibrahim looked every inch as she had imagined the Lord of Life must look. The ruby on his finger was the size of a bird's egg.

This rising star had carried another with him, like a comet with its tail. He now sat cross-legged at the foot of the marble steps, facing away from her, so she could not see his face.

She had made discreet enquiries about him though, before coming here. They said Rüstem Defterdar was a Bulgar, brought to Stamboul many years ago by the devshirme. He had been educated in the Enderun, the palace school, and had excelled in mathematics. They said he rose quickly through the ranks of the Treasury Department thanks to Ibrahim's patronage. One might guess, she thought, how productive it might be for the Vizier to have his own money man inside the Treasury, helping him manipulate the purse strings. But none would raise their voice in complaint against a man like Ibrahim, unless they wished to make a closer inspection of the spikes on the walls of the Felicity Gate.

Ibrahim saw her glance curiously in Rüstem "s direction but he addressed her as if they were alone. "Well Güzül , tell me what brings you to my humble seraglio."

"My mistress, Rose of Spring, sends her felicitations. May your house always increase in wealth and prosperity."

"I thank her for her good wishes. May God always protect her and may her beauty never fade."

"Insha'Allah."

"I have heard whispers, Güzül ."

"What whispers, my Lord?"

"That your mistress quarrels with the Lady Hürrem in the Eski Saraya. One may only pray the conflict will be resolved to the satisfaction of all."

"She is to be exiled, my Lord."

Ibrahim did not seem surprised by this news.

"That is why I am here, my Lord. My mistress begs for your intercession."

"I do not have such power, Güzül ."

That's not what they say in the bazaars, she thought. There they say you are Sultan in all but name. "My mistress asks only that you speak for her with the Lord of Life."

"This is the business of the Harem, and no affair of mine. You know I would like to help your mistress if I could but this is beyond any small power I may have. She should perhaps take her case to the Kislar Aghasi."

"My mistress only suggests that you perhaps examine more closely the consequences of her departure."

Ibrahim leaned forward, one arm resting on the arm of his throne. "Go on."

"You have always been a friend to Mustapha. One day he will be the next Sultan. His mother hopes she will always remember you kindly."

"Is that a threat, Güzül ?"

"It is only human nature that we have a longer memory for our friends. And as she has always thought of you as a friend, she would like to extend a word of caution."

His eyes glittered. He glanced down at Rüstem .

"My mistress has never sought to challenge the power of the Grand Vizier."

He laughed at that. "Of course not."

"But Hürrem  might."

It was as if someone had dropped a horseshoe on the marble floor. Startled silence. Ibrahim stared at her for a long time, his fist clenched on the arm of the throne. Finally: "You think so, Güzül ?"

"In the bazaars they say she has bewitched him."

"The Empire is not ruled by carpet salesmen."

"He spends long days and nights with her, my Lord. Not all of their time together concerns the pleasures of the bedchamber. He talks to her of politics."

"More Harem talk?"

"My mistress believes you to be a wise and faithful counsellor. She wishes only for your continued well-being."

"Thank you, Güzül . You have made your point."

"My Lord." Güzül  crept forward and kissed the carpet at the foot of the throne and crept out again. Ibrahim watched her leave, his face creased into a frown of uncertainty. Hürrem , a threat? Impossible!

And yet …

He looked at the man kneeling patiently at the foot of the throne. "Well, what do you think?"

"It is always wise not to make more enemies than is absolutely necessary."

"He indulges this little Russian girl of his. But - challenge the office of Vizier?"

Ibrahim watched his defterdar. Can you see what I am thinking, Rüstem ? My real problem here is that the Harem is the only part of the Empire over which I exercise no control.

"As Güzül  said, Gülbehar  is the mother of the next Sultan. What should I do?"

"Perhaps a gentle word to the Sultan to gauge his thinking in this matter. How he responds to your advice should allow you to discover exactly the extent of this Hürrem "s influence."

Really? He had not even considered that. Suleiman would always be led by his counsel, he had never over-ruled him before. If he suggested to him that Gülbehar  should remain in Stamboul, then that is what he would do. As Rüstem  said, he could test him out on it.

Hürrem ? She was just a bauble, a whim.

Wasn't she?

# CHAPTER 32

## Topkapi Saraya

Suleiman stared gloomily into his hands while the servants removed the last dishes of rahat lokum - the sweet pistachio-flavored "rest for the throat" with which he finished all his meals. Ibrahim finished the ballad he was playing on the viol and laid the instrument on the carpet beside him. "Something is troubling you, my Lord?"

Suleiman nodded.

"Is it Haberdansky?"

Suleiman scowled. Haberdansky, the Hapsburg ambassador! Frederick had had the temerity to dispatch him to his court with no tribute and no terms, other than to claim Hungary was part of his empire by birth and demand its return. It had given him great pleasure to show him the rougher edge of Osman hospitality in the dungeons at Yedikule.

"No, it is not politics that wearies me, old friend."

"Yet the Hapsburg question must be resolved."

He sighed. Yes, a decision must be made. "What do you think of this Zapolya now you have met him?"

"He will make a poor king and a fine vassal."

That was what Hürrem had said, Suleiman thought.

"Very well. We can make him our gatekeeper. He may wear the crown, but as long as he gives us tribute, in gold and slaves for the devshirme, the kingdom remains ours."

"It is settled then?"

"Yes. Give his envoy our decision."

Ibrahim picked up the viol again and gently plucked at the strings. Suleiman felt a prickle of irritation. He could not rest, even here. All he could think about was the war of nerves taking place in his own Harem. He would not rest until Gülbehar was safely removed from it.

"There is something I must discuss with you. It is about Mustapha."

"A fine boy," Ibrahim said.

"Indeed, he shows great promise as a leader and as a warrior. He is fourteen years old now and I think it is time he is given a governorship, to test his mettle for the great burden he must one day accept."

Ibrahim put down the viol. So it was true, Suleiman wished to exile Gülbehar from the Harem and this was how he planned to do it.

"He is still young," he said.

"Only a year younger than I was when my father sent me to Manisa."

"A year is not a long time when one is forty, but a lifetime when one is fourteen."

"Still I think it is time. But I accept what you say about his youth. We should have his mother accompany him, to guide him. They are very close. Do you agree?"

"I would counsel against it, my Lord."

"No, I have made up my mind."

Ibrahim blinked in surprise. Months to make up his mind about Hungary, days to make up his mind about a woman? Suleiman had never before made a decision without his blessing on it. "There is danger in blooding him too soon. We should weigh this carefully over time."

"I cannot see anything further that we should trouble ourselves with."

"I would counsel forbearance. Can we not wait at least one year?"

"He is my son. I know him best."

"But to give him a governorship so soon -"

"Will you give me peace, Ibrahim! I have told you that I have made up my mind! You are a fine Vizier, but sometimes it seems you think yourself the Sultan!"

Güzül was right, Ibrahim thought; so was Rüstem . The little Russian has his ear as well as his balls. I should let this subject be, for now. It is too dangerous to provoke him further. "As you say, my Lord. I defer to your greater wisdom."

There was a tense silence.

Finally Suleiman got to his feet. "I shall go to bed now," he said. "I am tired."

***

His pages had laid out his sleeping mattress on the floor. Suleiman slipped under the coverlets. Two of his bodyguards took up their post by the candles at the foot of the bed; Ibrahim stayed where he was, strumming a melancholy tune on the viol.

As he played he closed his eyes, saw the music drift beyond the walls of the seraglio, over the seven hills of Stamboul, across the Black Sea and the Aegean and the Mediterranean; a phrase drifted on the hot desert winds of Africa; one sad note echoed along the valleys of Persia and Greece, and then over the wide slow rivers of the Danube and the Euphrates; a refrain was carried with the wind over the wide plains of Hungary and the steppes of the Ukraine, and even found its way along the winding streets of Jerusalem and Babylon and Mekka and Medina.

Princes and pashas, shahs and sheiks danced to the music for this was the empire the Osmanlis had built and it was here within the walls of the Topkapi that they plucked the strings. It has always been thus.

But tonight he heard another melody, discordant, competing with the harmony he and the Divan had created. It came from the old palace where the Sultan kept his Harem, and the hands that played it were soft and white, and the nails were painted scarlet.

For the first time in his life he was a little afraid.

\*\*\*

Suleiman sat astride a white horse in the cobbled courtyard, a dark topaz glittering in his turban, a heron's plume bending to the breeze. His face was drawn in a stern mask. It would have been impossible to decipher his expression, even if the pages and guards who stood nearby had dared look up at him, and on pain of death, none of them would.

Mustapha jumped into his saddle and nudged his stallion forward with the slightest pressure of his knees and reined in alongside his father. Suleiman put a hand on the boy's arm. "May God bless your journey and keep you safe."

"Thank you, Father."

"Do well."

"I shall do all I can to serve you."

"Remember it is not me you serve but Islam. Even Sultans and their princes are only servants of Allah. Go in peace."

Suleiman felt a great weight on his chest. How strange it will be to go to the Harem and not find Mustapha there! He turned around and saw three veiled figures hurry across the courtyard and climb inside a waiting coach, Gülbehar and her two handmaidens.

He waited until the tiny procession had left the court and the great doors of the Eski Saraya were shut behind them. He felt both sorrow and elation. Had he lost her or was he free of her? She was only a woman, as Ibrahim reminded him on so many occasions. Yet he wondered sometimes if a woman was not the other half of a man.

All the women in the world and he still did not yet feel complete.

# PART 4

## THE CUSTODIAN OF FELICITY

# CHAPTER 33

## The Ionian Sea

The galley resembled a giant water beetle, twenty seven sets of oars on each side like spindly legs pushing it across the surface of a pond. The Golden Lion of Venice hung limp from mast and stern, asleep in the sun. The elaborately carved poop was shaded with an awning of purple silk under which the officers and more gentle cargo reclined at their ease on rugs and low divans, perfumed handkerchiefs held to their noses to block out the appalling smells wafting from below.

The sails were braided along the two yards above the fore and main masts while in the bowels rows of naked slaves pushed her across the ocean. They were chained to wooden benches, their own feces swirling in the bilge around their ankles. They had been rowing now for eighteen hours without a break. An under-officer moved down the rows of benches with bread soaked in wine, cramming it into the gasping mouths of those wretches who seemed closest to exhaustion. Several men had already passed out in their chains. They were flogged back to consciousness with rope dipped in brine. Two who did not recover quickly enough were unshackled and tossed over the side.

Julia Gonzaga saw nothing of this from her chair under the purple tabernacle above. Brocade curtains spared the passengers such unpleasantness, though they had all caught glimpses of those unfortunates at the oars several times during the journey. Julia had never seen such despair, or such filth. It had haunted her all the ten days they had been at sea.

The captain explained to her and her duenna that she should not trouble herself as they were only heathen, captured Turkish sailors and Arab pirates and no better than animals. But she felt ashamed anyway. Whenever she caught a whiff from below she closed her eyes against the glare of the ocean and fingered her rosary.

She looked down at the beads, remembered how they had trembled between her fingers the night of her wedding, how she had sat there in the marriage bed staring at the walnut paneled door, hardly able to breathe, waiting for her new husband. Would it hurt? What was she supposed to do?

Finally she heard a timid knock on the door and when it opened her husband stood framed in the doorway, still in his wedding clothes. They stared at each other in embarrassed silence.

"I am accustomed to sleeping in my own bedchamber," he said. "I wish you a goodnight."

She had not entered his bedchamber until almost a year later when succumbed to a chill and could not leave his bed. He was running a fever and the physician was called and bled him. He sent for her afterwards and required that she sit beside him and read to him from Plato.

And so, day after day; Greek philosophers and holding a basin under his chin while he coughed up foul humors. If he had maintained his malady long enough she might have become a philosopher. To keep from despair she would think about Abbas and remember how he looked at her.

Serena was barely out of his sickbed when she was dispatched to another. Her father took to his bed autumn and did not come out again until the following spring, covered in a shroud. He died by inches, from the inside out, and at the end he was unrecognizable. She could still remember the smell. It was worth than the one coming from the slave deck. His breath would have stunned a dog.

At the very end a pale claw reached out from under the bed sheet and taken hold of her wrist in a death grip. "Heaven is waiting for me," he had croaked. "Let it be known that I have led a good and holy life and I have nothing to fear in the next world."

He looked like a cadaver. She could not bear to look at him.

"I have made you a good marriage. I die content."

She had leaned forward and whispered: "What happened to Abbas?"

"Abbas?" He looked puzzled.

"The Captain General's son. What did you do to him?"

He had smiled. "I don't know what you're talking about, my child," he said.

When he died her husband was away visiting his estates in Cyprus. He wrote to tell her his business might keep him there for some time and he had arranged passage for her to join him. Perhaps he needed someone to read him philosophy. More likely he did not trust to leave her alone in Venice, now that her father was no longer around to do it.

She had anticipated this adventure with great excitement. She reveled in the salt air and the wide expanses of ocean, the unexpected pleasure of seeing the bright spring flowers blooming on the islands off the coast of Greece. It was all a joyous relief from the cloistered palazzo, with its smell of must, the monotony of lacework and daily prayers. Only two things spoiled it for her; one was the stench coming from below; the other was the knowledge of what awaited her at the end of her journey.

She went to stand at the rail. Her duenna was below decks, seasick again; she was an unpleasant old woman, as most of them were. Like Signora Cavalcanti. Thinking of her drew her inevitably to wonder yet again, as she so often did, what had happened to Abbas. She had never seen Lucia again so she never had the chance to ask her about it. They sent her to the convent until her marriage, and afterwards she went to live in Serena's palazzo and there had been no way of finding out about affairs outside.

"You are ... glorious," he had said.

She remembered how he had pulled back her hood, and the look on his face as he had said it. She smiled at the memory. Sweet Abbas.

***

"Pleasant thoughts, my lady?"

She looked around, startled. It was the captain, Bellini, a plump young man with florid cheeks and furtive eyes.

"I beg your pardon?" Had he seen her smiling through the black lace of her mantilla?

"One has so much time for reflection on these long voyages."

"I was thinking of my husband."

"Ah." Bellini pointed to the sails. "Still no wind. But another few days and I am sure you will be reunited. The voyage has taken longer than usual, because of the calm. The oars are a poor substitute for sail." He held his handkerchief to his nose for a moment and breathed deeply. "How long since you have seen your husband?"

"It must be nearly six months."

"A long time. You must miss him."

"Not especially," she said and saw the blood rise to his cheeks. It was not the answer he had expected and she had embarrassed him.

"For a lady such as yourself-" She never found out what he was about to say. The sentence caught in his throat. "Corpo di Dio!" he shouted and ran across the deck to fetch his eyeglass. Another cry from the sailor in the yards confirmed his fears.

The triangular lateen sails of the galleot appeared suddenly from behind the cliffs of an island on their port side. The blades of its oars hovered and dipped, hovered and dipped again as she came on.

"Turks!" Bellini shouted, panicked. He ran down the companionway from the poop to the slave deck. "Row!" he screamed. "Make these scum row!"

The galley captains gave a blast on their whistles. Julia heard the slap of their whips as they ran up and down the rows of benches, kicking and lashing and swearing at the exhausted slaves. The ship lurched as the helmsman leaned on the long tiller, swinging them hard to starboard, away from the Turkish pirate.

Suddenly the deck swarmed with sailors, clambering from the yards to their positions in the prow and poop. Soldiers fumbled for their harquebuses and crossbows, cursing God and their luck in their terror.

The long beaked prow of the galleot came on: dip-pause-sweep.

Julia gripped Bellini's arm. "What is going to happen?"

He shook her off, looked right through her. "Corpo di Dio, where's our escort?" He searched the horizon for the warship escort he had allowed to slip away across the horizon.

"Can't we outrun them?"

"They're lighter and faster and their oarsmen are all freemen and rested." His eyes were wide, like a horse running form a fire. "They must have been waiting for us," he said, perhaps to himself, and then pushed her aside and ran to the bridge. The screams from below got louder as their galley masters worked the slaves with their whips.

She looked back to the stern and gasped. The galleot was almost on top of them.

***

A primitive wail came from the slave deck, over the cries of the pilot and soldiers and the thrum-thrum of the war drum. The galley slaves were defying the officers now, their voices raised in a strange guttural chant.

"La illah ilallah Muhammadu rasul allah ... la illah ilallah Muhammadu rasul allah ..."

God is great and Mohammed is his prophet.

The green flag of Islam fluttered at the mast of the galleot. So this was the heathen they had been fighting all her life, this was the Devil Islam.

Their rais stood at the poop, urging even greater effort from his oarsmen, while a huge Arab, bald and bare-chested, gave the stroke on the tambour. The blades rose and fell in perfect unison. A white puff of smoke drifted from the prow as the Turks opened fire with their harquebuses.

One of the soldiers on the bridge screamed, clutching at his face, and disappeared over the side. The galley slaves cheered.

"La illah ilallah Muhammadu rasul allah ... la illah ilallah Muhammadu rasul allah ..."

The galleot swept towards them from the starboard aft, safe from their own bow-chasers. There was a roar as the Turks fired their own cannon. The

130

water in front of them churned to foam and then part of the rigging in the main mast collapsed in a scream of cracking timber.

Julia was so frightened she could not think. Her legs shook and then gave way under her. She tried to cover her ears with her hands, but could not block out the sound of the chamade, the chant sent up by the Turkish rowers to frighten their enemy. "Allahu Akbar! Allaaaah!"

One of Bellini's officers pulled her to her feet and pushed her towards the hold. "For the love of God!" he screamed. "Get below, get below!"

She ran blindly where he pointed.

But when she reached the companionway she stopped. She could see the slaves chained at their benches, their backs ripped and bleeding from the whips of their galley masters, leaning on their oars watching the Turk's iron-tipped fighting prow, the rambade, scything through the waves towards them.

Within moments it crashed through the oars as if they were twigs, the looms snapping back into the chests and faces of the oarsmen. The bilges turned red, the screams deafened her. She saw one man trying to push his own viscera back into his stomach.

Then the rambade crashed through the starboard bulwark and the galleon lurched. She toppled forward into the hold.

***

When she came round she found herself lying on her back at the foot of the companionway. A filmy mist of white smoke drifted across the deck above her. She could hear men shouting orders, others crying in pain or begging quarter. The clash of steel and the boom of the harquebuses stopped abruptly. It was replaced by a terrible rattling and howling.

She realized it was the galley slaves, begging for their freedom.

She was too terrified to move. She crawled into a corner, hugged her knees to her chest and waited. She closed her fingers around her rosary and started to whisper a prayer to the Madonna.

"Holy Mary, full of grace ..."

She heard footsteps on the companionway. Three men were silhouetted against the hatchway. They all wore turbans and carried curved swords.

They stopped halfway down and stared at her. Then one of the men said something in a language she did not understand and the others laughed. They pulled her to her feet and dragged her back up to the deck.

# CHAPTER 34

## Algiers

The coast of Africa rose from the horizon, the village of Sidi Bou Said stark and white against the scorched red earth. As the galleot sailed past the headland the lateens filled with the sort of brisk wind that might once have saved the miserable huddle of humanity now chained together in its hold. They were dragged on deck one by one at sword point, blinking in the harsh sunlight.

The fortress of Algiers loomed from the sea. Below it, whitewashed buildings piled up the hillside like blinding white cubes, safe beneath the Osmanli cannon and the green crescent banner of Mohammed.

As they slipped into the harbor several of the prisoners gave an audible sigh, knowing their lives as free men were over.

Julia, being a woman, was kept separate from the others. She dared a glance at them now from behind her mantilla and gasped. They had been stripped naked, except for thin strips of material around their loins and their hands and feet were chained. None of them raised their eyes from the deck.

She barely recognized Bellini. He looked smaller and fatter without his uniform. Julia blushed and looked away.

The galleot moored at the quay in front of the harbor mosque. The men were led away first, the pirates shoving back the crowd that had rushed from the souk to gawk at them. They all wore burnooses and djellabas, and they spat at the Venetians as they passed, screaming curses at them in their strange, guttural tongue.

Then one of the Turks - Julia supposed him to be their captain - grabbed her by the arm and led her away, dragging her along behind him.

Julia had not given up hope. Her husband was a Magnifici after all, an esteemed member of the Consiglio di Dieci. Venice had brokered a peace with the Osmanlis, and her husband even traded with them, had once entertained members of Suleiman's court at his own table. The worst that might happen, she told herself, is that I will be shut up in a castle somewhere until they organize the ransom. I am accustomed to being shut up in a room. How bad can it be?

The crowd jostled her and one man hawked phlegm at her. She wanted to slap him. Heathen!

The rais ignored the jostling and curses and hurried her along.

The crowd followed them through the Kasbah, along narrow alleys piled with filth. The men were herded along in front of her. Julia kept her eyes down, ashamed to witness their humiliation. They were all proud Venetians, now they looked no better than ... galley slaves.

The Bey's Palace loomed ahead of them. They were all shoved through a gate, past the black slave corrals where caravans from the Sahara brought the Nubians and Sudanese for market. There were women and children among them, some of the women still had babies at their breasts and the men were quite naked ...

Corpo di Dio!

They led them into yet another courtyard, this one a vast esplanade of white sand enclosed on all four sides by arched colonnades. There were so many bodies packed together inside it created a great stink, worse than the ship. There was a din of voices all shouting in languages she did not understand, some shouting orders, others babbling in fear. She stopped, overwhelmed. The rais cursed her and slapped her across the shoulders with the handle of his whip.

Julia realized she had lost sight of the others and somehow felt abandoned. Desperate and helpless as they were, they were her last link to the world she knew.

The rais dragged her into yet another court. This one was smaller, but almost empty, though there were countless footprints in the bleached sand.

Julia looked around. A man sat in the shade on a pile of cushions, staring at her. He had dark skin, almost ,mahogany, and was hideously fat. His white kaftan was trimmed with gold thread and there was a large turquoise in his muslin turban. A young Nubian boy stood behind him, cooling him with a fan of ostrich feathers.

The rais and the fat man started shouting at each other. Julia heard one word repeated over and over: Gaiour.

The fat man lifted an arm, to signal that he was about to rise. The Nubian boy dropped the fan and helped the man to his feet. "Como se chiame?" the man said.

"You speak Italian?"

He smiled. "Of course. And many other languages beside. What do you think I am? A barbarian?" He came closer. "Do you speak Turkish?"

"Of course not."

He lifted her mantilla. Despite her situation Julia felt outraged. No Venetian gentleman would ever dare such a thing. Only a husband might lift a lady's veil. But she might hardly reprimand him.

She felt utterly humiliated and lowered her eyes.

The fat man glanced at the rais. "He is right. You are very beautiful. Again, what is your name?"

"Julia Gonzaga. My husband is a consigliatore in Venice. He will reward you richly for my safe return."

"The Sultan might pay me more." The Nubian boy shooed a fly from the fat man's face with his ostrich fan. "But allow me to introduce myself. My name is Mehmet Ali-Osman. I am Bey of Algiers, in the service of Sultan Suleiman, King of Kings, Lord of Lords, Emperor of the Seven Worlds." He effected a mock bow. "I am his lifelong servant. You may have the honor of doing the same."

"I am no one's servant."

"Ah, so proud! Pride and beauty often accompany each other. But that is no matter." He walked around her, inspecting her for flaws. She endured this new humiliation in silence, staring at the white sands with her cheeks burning. He faced her again and then with one pudgy hand he gently squeezed her breast, as if it was an avocado. Julia screamed and jumped back.

The rais growled at her but Ali-Osman thought this most amusing. He roared with laughter. "Your modesty will not be worth much to you where you are going, bellissima!"

He turned to the rais and the two men fell straight into a heated argument. Julia could understand none of it but from the expression on the pirate's face, and the angry tone of his voice, she dared to hope that he was about to draw his sword and pin this Ali-Osman to the wall.

But then suddenly they both laughed and slapped each other on the shoulders. The Bey reached into the folds of his robe and produced a leather pouch. He loosened the drawstrings and tipped a number of gold coins into his other man's palm.

The pirate walked away without another word, leaving her with Ali-Osman. "Julia Gonzaga, my bellissima, you are now a member of the Sultan Suleiman's kullar! Bless the day!"

"What's a kullar?"

"It is a family of slaves. Yes, you have a new family!"

"My husband ..."

"Your husband no longer exists. The Kislar Aghasi has a deeper purse than any Venetian, I assure you. I shall make a tenfold profit on our little transaction today!" He clapped his hands and two turbaned soldiers appeared from the shadows. "Take her inside and keep her under guard. Make sure she is given food and water. Treat her well, who knows, one day she may be the mother of the next Sultan!"

Mehmet Ali-Osman settled himself back on his cushions, and shouted at his Nubian to fan him faster, he was getting hot.

\*\*\*

First, an endless glittering ocean that hurt the eyes; then a sudden violent summer storm that left her weak with nausea with no escape from the vile stench of bile and vomit. For two weeks they sailed across the Osmanli empire, now and then glimpsing the inverted mirages of islands or a distant coast, stopping at this port or that dirty village to load a giraffe or a slave or a bale of silk.

Julia prayed to die. They had sold her as a whore, it was plain. The Turks watched her, their eyes bright and hungry and hard, but none dared offend her or tried to touch her. She was the Sultan's meat now.

They brought her food but it was not fit for a dog, though it was the same mess of rice and dried meat they ate themselves. They gave her a cabin below deck, guarded day and night by two of the crew. She could scream or she could cry; they just ignored her.

Once, when she was taking air on the deck, she contemplated throwing herself over the side. But a part of her would not give up hope completely. She was sure her husband would find a way to have her released for all of Ali-Osman's boasting. She convinced herself that when they arrived in Stamboul there would be a legation from the Venetian ambassador waiting for her on the dock to negotiate her ransom.

\*\*\*

Sunrise, sunset, on an endless blue ocean.

One morning she came up on deck and there in front of her were the mountains of Anatolia, shrouded in mist. Later that day they put in at Smyrna. The nightmare was almost over.

Two days later, at sunset, they sailed past Troy and through the narrow neck of the Dardanelles into the Marmara Deniz. They weighed anchor there and waited for dawn.

\*\*\*

The sea was as flat and as silver as the blade of a sword. Stamboul rose from the dawn like a hand rising from the mist, the minarets of the Aya Sofia like fingers pointing to the sky. The rising sun caught the golden domes of the mosques, burning off the fog that clung to the sea walls and the jutting arm of

Seraglio Point. The water teemed with fishing boats and fast caïques. She even spotted the golden lion of Venice hoist on one of the galleys and she felt a physical pain. So close.

Then they were round the point and inside the sweeping arms of the Golden Horn. There was no delegation from La Serenissima waiting for her at the quay. She closed her eyes, knowing that everything she had ever known was gone forever. Antonio Gonzaga's daughter was now a whore and a slave.

# CHAPTER 35

## Manisa

Gülbehar watched the riders from behind the latticed windows of the palace. The iron on the horses" hoofs rang on the smooth stones of the Roman road and echoed along the valley walls. It reminded her of the bells that rang every hour in the Eski Saraya. That was another world away now. She did not miss the dusty stairwells or the draughty rooms; she missed being close to him. Now, for all the freedom of her new life, her bed was always cold.

The evening sun dipped below the wheat fields. The breeze carried with it the smell of wood smoke.

The riders drew closer. There were a dozen of them, one riding ahead of the rest, she could hear his voice booming up the valley even from up here. He was dark, with a sparse beard and wore a loose fitting robe. A stag, its throat pierced by an arrow, lay across his saddle. Blood from the wound had stained the horse's flank.

Mustapha.

"So tonight we shall be dining on venison," she murmured. Her son looked pleased with himself.

He rides like a true shahzade, she thought. He shouted something to his spahis. It was lost to her on the wind, but his men shouted with laughter.

What a son! He hunts, he laughs, he excels in mathematics. He could speak Italian as well as he could speak Turkish. Four years as the governor here, and everyone loved him.

They said he would be the finest of all the Osmanli sultans, that he would even surpass his father. So many talents, so few flaws! Ah but they do not know you like I do, he thought. You have one terrible flaw and you are blind to it; it will kill you if I am not there to save you.

The riders dismounted in the courtyard below. Mustapha looked up at the window and waved. He could not see her, of course, but he knew she would be there, watching. He strode across the courtyard; he had a swagger about him, it reminded her of her own father, He reminded her of her father, a Montenegrin mountain bandit.

Such a lion; such a lamb.

\*\*\*

The years of exile had changed her. Not much physically; just the tiny lines that bitterness had etched into her eyes and the corner of her mouth, that was all. But it was the heart of the Rose of Spring that had grown thorns. It was not even the loss of Suleiman that had made her sour; it was the attempt on her son's life that had done that.

They ate in silence. Mustapha had described how he had killed the stag three times for her before he ran out of conversation. Elated with his success, he resented his mother's dark mood.

"The venison is good, isn't it?" he said, choosing another cube of the meat from the dish.

"Delicious."

Mustapha sighed. "What is it, Mother?"

"We must think about your future," she said.

"Not that again." He laughed. "I have the simplest future of any man living. For now I am governor of Kutahya. And one day I will be Sultan of the Osmanlis. What is there to think about?"

"Will you really be Sultan?"

The smile vanished. "Mother, please."

"It is four years now and your father asks to see you less and less. Meanwhile the witch insinuates herself further and further into his court ..."

"How he conducts his Harem is no business of mine."

"You are blind."

"You see conspiracy everywhere."

"She tried to have you poisoned!"

"There is no proof of that."

"Who else would want you dead?"

"The Osmanlis have many enemies."

Gülbehar slammed her hand on the table, startling him. "Of course it was her. You are all that stands between her and becoming the Valide!"

"My father would never betray me."

"I thought that once, too. "

Mustapha pushed his plate away. He had quite lost his appetite. "What would you have me do?"

"You have many friends at the Sublime Porte. Perhaps it is time you thought to use them."

"For what purpose?"

"Your grandfather knew the answer to that."

Mustapha turned pale. "I will not raise my hand against my father. It would be a sin before God."

"There are greater sins and they are being committed as we speak in the palace at Stamboul."

Mustapha raised a finger and a deaf-mute hurried forward with a scented finger bowl. He washed his fingers and held them out to be dried. "The throne will come to us as God wills. I will not turn against him." He reached across the low table and took Gülbehar 's hands in his own. "I love you, Mother. But you see phantoms everywhere. If Hürrem is my enemy then she will answer for it one day. But I will not harm him."

After he had left Gülbehar sat for a long time, brooding in silence. Then she clapped her hands for the servants to remove the dishes and had a maid send a summons to Güzül .

## The Eski Saraya

Julia had never seen anything quite so ugly in her whole life.

The Kislar Aghasi was young, perhaps not much older than herself. He wore a kaftan of flowered silk over which was an emerald green pelisse, lined with ermine, its long sleeves sweeping the ground. There were thick rubies on his plump little fingers. A white cat dozed in his lap.

But none of these refinements could hide the fact that he was grossly, obscenely, fat. There were scalloped rolls of it all over his body. Then there was his face; she wondered what might have happened to him to disfigure him so terribly.

Julia had taught herself a little Turkish on the way from Algiers. She heard him talking to one of the guards who had brought her. She heard familiar words: "Gaiour", "Bey of Algiers" and "woman".

He pointed at her. "Take off her veil."

Julia had learned during her voyage that she could avoid great humiliation by submitting to lesser ones. She would rather do it herself than have these heathen paw her with their filthy hands. So as soon as he spoke, she reached up and pulled back the black lace.

The Kislar Aghasi underwent a startling transformation. He jerked in his seat, as if he had been stabbed in the back. His mouth fell open.

Then he leaped up, spilling the sleeping cat onto the floor. It screeched and darted away. He pointed to her and bellowed: "GET HER OUT OF MY SIGHT!"

The guards hesitated, stunned.

"I SAID GET HER OUT OF MY SIGHT!"

But before they could drag her away he had already turned for the door. It crashed shut behind him.

How astonishing, Julia thought. And they had told her that the first rule in here was silence.

## Topkapi Saraya

The Kubbealti, the Hall of the Divan, was the hub of the Empire. For eighty years, in this small chamber under the watch tower of the Second Court, Osmanli Sultans had held court for four days in every week, receiving petitions, resolving legal matters, meeting foreign envoys, deciding foreign and state policy. Every decision, from the most humble legal dispute between merchants to the declaration of war, had been declared in this room.

On the morning of the Divan a long line would extend across the garden outside as petitions waited their turn to bring their case before the Sultan. Suleiman would sit on a cushioned dais opposite the door with the Grand Vizier on his right, and the Kaziaskers of Rumelia and Anatolia - the European and Asian provinces of the Empire - sitting directly behind him. Agas, pashas and mufti would sit in their proper order of rank to either side; secretaries and notaries would record the imperial decrees and judgments.

Only the Sultan had the right to speak. Others could offer their opinion only as requested, or when sought out on a particular point of secular or religious law that was their speciality. The Sultan's decree in all matters was final.

But Suleiman had grown tired of these tedious perquisites of power. Lately he had abrogated the duties of the Divan to Ibrahim and allowed him to preside in his place. He reported to the Lord of Life on his decisions twice a week, and the Sultan would ratify them. A small latticed window had been cut in the wall high above Ibrahim's divan so that Suleiman might watch the proceedings whenever he chose without being seen. It was a measure to safeguard Ibrahim's conduct, even though Suleiman rarely used it.

Ibrahim was increasingly troubled by the changes he had witnessed in the Sultan. Perhaps, he thought, he has come too far too quickly. He has conquered Rhodes and Belgrade, then crushed the Hungarians and their king at Mohacs. He had achieved what his father or even the legendary Mehmet Fatih had been unable to do, and so his greatness was already established.

He delegates too much to me, Ibrahim thought. It does not bode well for him, or perhaps even for me. It is the witch's fault. She has done this.

\*\*\*

On this particular morning the petitioners were made to wait as the Grand Vizier debated with his generals the matter of that summer's campaign in the Lands of War. Ibrahim allowed the mufti to speak first.

"Sooner or later the Lord of Life must deal with the Persian Shah, Tamasp, who dares shelter the Shi'a heretics and raids our border constantly. He offends not only the Osmanlis but Islam itself. It is the Sultan's duty to bring him to heel!"

Ibrahim bowed his head in deference to the Islamic judge although if he had his way he would have the charlatan's head on a spike at the front gate. He turned to address the other generals: "I agree with the mufti, the shah is indeed an offense against God. But should we use cannon to squash a mosquito? Though Shah Tamasp is a heretic, the greatest prize we might present before God is the capture of the Green Apple." The Green Apple was a reference to Rome; every Sultan, before he ascended the throne of the Osmanlis, was traditionally asked at the ceremony "Can you bite from the Green Apple?" Suleiman's achievements might already rank alongside those of his father and grandfather but in Ibrahim's opinion, he had the opportunity to stand in heaven next to Mohammed himself if he could take away the infidel's greatest prize.

Can you deliver us Rome?

Ibrahim paused to let his words take effect. "Surely our greatest threat must be the man who calls himself the Holy Roman Emperor? At this moment he is troubled on his southern flank by Francis; the Christian heretic Luther is inciting rebellion against the Pope and his own nobles are warring among themselves. The time to strike is when your enemy is weakest and there is no doubt he is deeply divided at this moment. Vienna's walls are ready to fall and when they do the whole of Christendom will tremble at our approach!"

He turned to the Aga of the yeniceris. "What say you, Achmed?"

"As long as our kettle is full, my Lord, we will eat. My men are restless for another chance to blood their swords."

Ibrahim turned to his other generals, Mahmut, Aga of the Spahis and Cehangir, Kazaskier of Rumelia. They, too, both spoke for Vienna.

"We can deal with the heretic Tampas at our leisure," Cehangir added. "But Frederick is ripe for the plucking right now. Let us lay Vienna at the feet of our padishah!"

Ibrahim smiled. It had been six years since their last great victory. No empire could stand still, the ghazis of old knew that as soon as a man stepped out of the saddle his muscles started to get soft. Perhaps on the long road to Vienna Suleiman would find himself again and forget this Harem girl who was making him weak.

"It is decided then," Ibrahim said. "This summer the Sultan goes to Vienna."

# CHAPTER 36

The first time she came her she had been aghast. She had never been naked anywhere except in her own private bath and even then she had felt sinful for not wearing clothes. But here, in this heathen palace, the women barely wore anything in the summer, even to eat.

When she arrived they took away her clothes, forced her to bathe and afterwards undergo the most humiliating operation any Christian woman might be subjected to. They shaved her completely - under her arms, her legs and then ... even now, she cringed when she thought about it. There were no words. They had outraged her utterly and she knew that even if she did somehow find her way back to La Serenissima she would never be able to look her husband - or any Christian soul - in the face again.

She had been defiled.

The ritual of the baths renewed her agony daily. She was made to undress in front of strangers, bathe with them and then subject herself yet again to the attentions of black women. She tried to avoid eye contact with anyone, ignored the whispered taunts made behind her back, though she soon understand them well enough. In just a few weeks she had picked up a great deal of the language. It was a challenge for her and she had nothing else to do.

She removed her bath chemise and slipped into the water. Two other girls - one an Egyptian with a hawk nose and skin the color of hazelnuts, the other alabaster-white with startling blue black hair - sat on the edge of the bath and examined each other for hair. The search became intimate and Julia knew she should turn away. But she continued to stare.

The Egyptian parted the other's legs, quite casually, and with her fingers traced the lips of her kouss and parted them gently. The white girl gasped and whispered what sounded like an endearment. She realized she was not grooming her after all; this was something quite different. Wait, her finger was inside her now.

Corpo di Dio! Another outrage! The girls heard her gasp and the Egyptian gave her a mocking smile. Her lover - for that was what she must be - had thrown back her head and her long, braided her brushed the water. She groaned and lifted her buttocks from the marble, her eyes closed, utterly without shame.

Julia got as far away from them as she could. She felt as if her cheeks were on fire. She splashed some water on them to cool them. She heard someone move towards her through the water and hoped it was not the Egyptian, come to taunt her more. Instead she found herself staring into the blackest eyes she had ever seen.

"You are the Gaiour," the woman said.

She nodded. Gaiour, she had learned, meant Christian.

"Don't be frightened. It must all be strange to you now but you'll get used to it."

It was the first kindness she had found since she had come here and she wanted to weep. "What are they doing?" she whispered.

"They are just bored and they are helping each other take away the hunger, that's all. There is no man to do it for them. Besides, some say that a woman can do it better anyway."

Julia looked up at the Nubian guards and wondered why they just watched and did not try to join in. And what was it that a woman could do better than a man? But she said nothing. She felt so stupid here, like a child.

"What is your name?" the girl asked her.

"Julia."

"I am Sirhane. I am from Syria. My father gave me to the devshirme."

"Devshirme?" So far she had understood most of what Sirhane had said, but this was a new word.

"It is like a tax, only instead of money you pay it with young men or women. The Sultan's men travel the empire taking the best boys and girls for royal service."

"So you are a prisoner, too?"

"Prisoner? A woman is always a prisoner, isn't she? I'm glad my father gave me up, I prefer my life here. Do you know what I would be doing if I was not lying here in this bath? Picking cotton in a field! Ask me where I would rather be."

"Do all of these women belong to the Sultan then? Are they all his wives?"

"Of course not! He has only two wives - we call them kadins - and one of them is far away in a place called Manisa. That just leaves Hürrem , but she is not young anymore, so that leaves hope for the rest of us."

"I do not understand. Speak slower, please."

Sirhane smiled and edged closer. To Julia's horror she put her arm around her. "You will need someone to take care of you in here. You don't know anything, do you Gaiour?"

Julia could not move; there was a naked Muslim woman with her arm around her in a warm bath. This was sin beyond measure, beyond imagination. So how could there be such comfort in it?

Perhaps because at last she had found a friend. She put her head on Sirhane's shoulder and the Syrian embraced her and held her as she wept. Julia thought about her Confessor in the Chiese Santa Maria dei Miracoli and wondered what he would say if he saw her now. She was slipping further from Venice and further from God. "I just want to go home," she said.

"You have a husband?"

"Yes."

"Was he good to you?"

She shook her head. "He's an old man. He was old when I married him."

"Then why weep for him, Julia? Perhaps, if kismet is kind, you will find yourself a much better husband. The best husband in the world - Sultan Suleiman, the Lord of Life!"

***

The Kislar Aghasi leaned against the lattice window that overlooked the hammam, closed his eyes and groaned aloud. What kind of cruel joke was this? What devil in all the hells could have devised a torture more exquisite than to take from a man all means of loving a woman but leave him the desire, as fierce as it was when he was complete? If he was not so weak he would have ended his life long ago.

Any man in the world would envy me for the view I have here; every day I see hundreds of the most beautiful women in the world, and all of them naked, or nearly so. They glide in and out of my vision through the misty hararet like it is all just a dream; or they sprawl on warmed marble sofas and braid each other's hair. The most lurid fantasy of the lowest debauch is my daily fare and yet these women remain utterly unattainable.

Light poured in brilliant tendrils from the small rounded windows high in the cupola and one picked out Julia's milky silhouette. His fingers curled around the iron lattice as if he would wrench it from the wall.

He would rather be dead than this.

***

Suleiman held the flickering candle above the crib. The infant looked so scrawny and so pale. He reached out a tentative finger and stroked the suckling's back, recoiled from the grotesque lump on his spine. He looked like a skinned quail and scarce bigger.

Hürrem watched him. She was surprised; he had never paid any attention to their other children when they were in the cradle. Yet every day he came to stare at the grotesque and deformed son she had delivered him.

"He eats?" he asked her.

"His wet nurse says he has little appetite. She does not think he will survive."

"You must pick him up every day and croon to him. It will help."

"Yes, my Lord." I shall do no such thing, she thought. She wanted nothing to do with the little monster. Birthing him had almost killed her.

Suleiman handed the wet nurse a gold coin. "Look after him well," he said and led Hürrem from the chamber.

When they were alone she helped him remove his turban and brought his head to her breast. He was unusually quiet.

"My Lord is troubled?"

"Matters of the Divan, russelana."

"You wish to talk?"

Suleiman sighed. "It is spring. Every spring my Agas press me for another campaign. This year they wish to go north again, against Vienna."

"And what does Ibrahim say?"

"Ibrahim clamors louder than any of them."

"He longs for glory. For Islam, of course. Yet I wonder if it wise."

"Tell me your thoughts."

"It is a long road to Vienna. Perhaps too far to take an army, even the army of the Osmanlis. If one goes through a door one must be sure one can get out again."

"The real prize is not Vienna, it is Frederick."

"He will not come out to fight you! Why should he risk everything in a battle against the greatest army in the world? He will quit Vienna when you approach and when you withdraw for the winter he will come and take the city back again and everything will be as it was before. You will have nothing to show for it but a long trek through the mud."

"I cannot hold the leash on the yeniceris for another year."

"The Persians have been raiding the eastern borders and murdering our mufti. Send them to Asia if they want a fight so badly. We could serve God by preserving his judges from the heretics."

"The Persians are just flies nipping at the rump of a lion. We only have to swat our tail to remove them."

"Perhaps God wishes us to be his swatter of flies even though there is little glory in it."

Suleiman laughed. "What I would not give to put you into a debate with Ibrahim!"

Hürrem stroked his forehead, felt the tiny pulse of blood at his temple. This is all I have, she thought. When this pulsing stops, life will stop for me as well, unless I can find a way to rid myself of the curse of this Mustapha.

"Do not go, my Lord. Let Ibrahim shoulder the burden and chase Frederick through the Austrian mud if that is what he wants."

"Impossible. If the army goes into battle I must be at their head. It is the way, the yeniceris expect it."

"Do you love war so much?"

"You know I do not."

"Then why?"

"It is my duty, Hürrem ."

"Duty has made the king of kings a slave then!"

Suleiman sat up, face flushed with anger. "Enough!"

Hürrem bit her lip, contrite. She cursed her own impetuosity. She should know better than to make him angry. A wasp was trapped with honey, not vinegar. "My Lord, I did not mean to offend you."

"The place of the Sultan of the Osmanlis is with his army. They cannot go to war without him. It is our way."

She cradled his face in both her hands. "Forgive me. It is just that I love you so much, my Lord. The summers are endless without you. And I am so afraid that one winter you will not return ..."

Suleiman stroked her face; then his fingers traced the line of her throat to her breast. "Enough of politics," he whispered. "We will talk of this another time."

She put her arms around his neck and smiled. "Three times in one day! You are truly a lion, my Lord!"

She drew her to him. Oh fortunate son of Selim! Tomorrow perhaps he would decide where he would take his army. Tonight he would take his might against a better yielding adversary.

## The Eski Saraya

The girls of the Harem were housed in a long dormitory next to a stone courtyard. The mattresses were kept in wall cupboards during the day and unrolled onto raised platforms at night. Only the iqbals had their own apartments.

Julia lay on her mattress in the darkness and tried to force the memories of the day from her mind. After everything that had happened to her in this place she felt little better than a beast. It was not that they had enslaved her to one man; her father had done that, also, in his way. But she had expected her slavery to be a private thing, that even if she were to become just one of many wives they would at least not parade her naked before other men.

She lay awake through the night, too bruised in her soul to sleep. Even God was no help to her in this infernal place.

# CHAPTER 37

## Pera

The quarter where the Venetian ambassador - the bailo - and the rest of the Venetian traders lived and built their palaces overlooked the Horn, looking directly south towards the city and the Topkapi Saraya. The suburb was known, with the humility typical of the Golden Lion, as the Comunità Magnifica.

Ludovici had built his own residence in the quarter. It had a marble terrace that faced onto the water and from there he could watch his own ships sail past Seraglio Point into the Marmara Deniz, loaded down with Turkish grain, Nubian slaves, Arab horses and Oriental spices.

He had done well by himself coming here. Being a bastardo the Venetian court was closed to him, so while his peers had donned the black robes of togati, he took himself to Pera, the foreign colony at Stamboul, and established himself as a merchant. Feeling no special allegiance to either his hosts or his former countrymen he had quickly learned to manipulate both to his advantage.

His father had assisted him, of course. Senator Gambetto appreciated Ludovici"s decision not to remain in Venice where his presence among the merchant community might have caused him embarrassment. It was Gambetto's zucchini that founded the business; but it was Ludovici"s acumen that expanded it.

At first it was difficult. The spice and pepper trades were dominated by the great merchant families of Venice and Genoa. He could not compete. He soon realized that greater profits were to made from smuggling wheat.

Suleiman had placed restrictions on the export of Turkish grain with a rigorous price-fixing policy. But a resourceful man could find a way around such regulations if he had daring and a little imagination. He chartered a fleet of Greek merchantmen to pick up wheat from Black Sea ports and ferry it to the Venetian colonies at Crete and Corfu. Avoiding the Turkish harbor patrols in the Bosphorus was simply a matter of knowing which palm to grease in the Topkapi palace.

The Comunità Magnifica regarded his success with a sort of benign contempt. He did not really care what they thought of him. He could do business here without their patronage. Lately he had become more Turkish than Italian and had even acquired a small harem.

And so tonight he sipped his Cyprian wine, well satisfied with the course his life had taken. He had money, he had a fine residence on the water and he had women. He was content.

The only thing he really missed was his friend. Not a day passed he did not think about Abbas and wondered what had become of him. His recklessness had been part of his charm; it had also been the end of him.

One of his eunuchs - the poor wretch had been razored in a slave camp on the Nile, but then it was next to impossible to find any young buck here who had not been put to the knife - appeared on the terrace. His name was Hyacinth - all these fellows adopted the names of flowers - and he was typical; obese and beardless with a tremolo voice.

"There is someone to see you, Excellency."

"Who is it?"

"He said to say he is an old friend of yours."

"What's wrong, Hyacinth. You look puzzled about something. Who is this fellow? Did he give a name?"

Hyacinth shook his head. Someone newly arrived from Venice, Ludovici supposed. More condescension to endure. Oh well. "Show him in," Ludovici sighed.

He was expecting some young togati fresh off the boat from La Serenissima, an old acquaintance from university; he was unprepared for the devilish apparition that presented itself on the terrace a few moments later. The man was wearing a black silk ferijde, and its hood covered his face. He was wearing soft leather boots; not a Venetian then. And he had no old friends among the Turks. What was this?

Ludovici got up, alarmed. "Who are you?"

The man pulled back his hood. It was difficult to tell if he was Moor or Nubian as his face had been so disfigured by the scar that slanted across his nose and right eye. He was also hideously fat, like Hyacinth. He wore a great sugarloaf turban, in the courtly style.

"Hello Ludovici," he said.

"Do we know each other?" he said, wondering at how this man might presume to address him by his Christian name when he was so obviously a slave.

"I am the Kislar Aghasi of the Sultan Suleiman."

The Kislar Aghasi! The Custodian of Felicity - Captain of the Sultan's Girls, and one of the most powerful creatures in the Harem. Ludovici was too surprised to speak.

"Don't you recognize me?"

"How should I recognize you? We have never met."

"Look more closely. I know I have changed greatly since we last saw each other but think back, if you will, about the warning you gave to a young friend of yours outside the Chiese Santa Maria dei Miracoli. Looking back on it now, it seems like good advice, I think."

Ludovici stared at him then slumped down onto the divan, speechless.

"Corpo di Dio," he murmured at last. "Abbas!"

## Çamlica

Suleiman reined in his Arab and watched the goshawk floating on the air currents at its pitch, waiting for its prey. Ibrahim walked his stallion through the long grass to flush out their quarry. The hawk twitched its wings, and hovered.

Then its golden eye found its target. Seeing it scamper from Ibrahim's approach far below, it tucked in its wings and swooped, its razor-sharp claws crushing the hare's back. The hare kicked and then was still. The bird beat its wings and then settled on its kill. There was a scarlet blossoming on the white fur clutched between its talons.

His pages ran forward to collect their game.

When it was done Ibrahim returned, grinning, the hawk held aloft on his gloved left arm. It was hooded now in its leather rufter. Behind him the pages carried their day's trophies; a dozen hares and rabbits, strung from poles, and a brace of pheasant. She was an efficient killer this bird. It had always struck Suleiman as curious that the female hawks were better at this deadly game than the males. All the falconers preferred them for hunting.

"A fine day's sport, my Lord."

"The sun is low, Ibrahim. We should return to the caïque."

"It has been a long time since we hunted together like this."

"There should be many days like today this summer."

Ibrahim's smile fell away. "I should like that also but the Divan has recommended another campaign against Frederick's brother, Charles."

"You did not agree to this? Because if memory serves two years ago, on your advice, we besieged Vienna. Frederick did not come then, and nor did his brother. What good will it do to go after them again? They will not fight us."

"We were stopped then by the unseasonal rains. If we had been able to bring our cannons to the walls-"

HAREM

"If we take Vienna, how do we keep it? If one goes through a door one must be sure one can get out again."

"But we must go back to the Lands of War. It is our duty to Islam."

"Ah yes. I forgot what a good Muslim you are Ibrahim."

Ibrahim bridled at this jibe. "We cannot leave the yeniceris inside the city for another summer. They grow impatient for battle."

"Perhaps we should look in another direction."

"Shah Tamasp?"

"He is trying to infect our eastern borders with his Shi'a heresy and he is still killing our mufti. He should be taught a lesson."

"He is nothing. We could crush him at our leisure."

"Glory is not always the same as duty. Sometimes we serve Islam better by crushing vermin that riding in futile quests against Emperors."

"Frederick's brother is the Holy Roman Emperor, the avowed enemy of our faith. What greater duty is there than to defeat him?"

"But if we take Vienna and he and his brother do not stay there to fight, what have we gained for God? A distant outpost that Frederick will retake as soon as we withdraw. The destruction of Tamasp should be our more immediate goal."

The goshawk on Ibrahim's wrist grew restless. She batted her wings and Ibrahim cooed softly to gentle her. "If we take Vienna, Rome is at our mercy. Should we threaten the Green Apple, we will flush out the Emperor then."

Suleiman fell silent. The scent of the pines lay heavy on the dusk. The pine needles formed a soft blanket beneath the horses" hoofs. Between the trees the Bosphorus was silver and pink behind the silhouette of the royal barge. "Well then you should decide this, Ibrahim, for it is you who shall lead them."

"As your seraskier, of course. But as Sultan -"

"No, Ibrahim. I shall not go with you this time. You will lead my armies. There is too much to do in Stamboul so I have decided to remain here."

Ibrahim was too stunned to speak.

"Speak up," Suleiman said finally.

"You cannot do this," Ibrahim said.

"Cannot?" Suleiman stopped and Ibrahim reined in beside him. "Who says to me "cannot"? Am I not the Sultan? Am I not King of Kings? The King of Kings, then, shall do as he pleases!"

"Your place is at the head of your armies."

"My place is wherever I choose to be."

"The soldiers take their inspiration from you. If you are not there-"

"They are my soldiers and they will do as I command."

"No Sultan has ever-"

"A Sultan makes tradition, he is not slave to it."

"You will lose their faith!"

151

Suleiman leaned across the saddle so that his face was inches from his Vizier's. "Ibrahim, you are my friend and my counselor. Please. I have had enough of war, take this burden from me. They just want blood so let them wallow in it. It does not matter whose blood it is, not to them. But I do not wish for another campaign."

"You must not contemplate this!"

"I have made up my mind." He put his hand on his friend's shoulder. "I trust you like I would trust no other. You are my brother. Do this for me."

He rode ahead through the trees. Ibrahim stared after him. Oh great God, he thought, he really means it.

## Pera

Even his voice has changed, Ludovici thought. The color of his skin, too. It was paler, and sickly looking. He was no longer handsome - far from it! - and the light had gone out of his eyes. It was Abbas and yet it was not.

Abbas stared at the sparkling waters of the Horn. "I should have listened to you, Ludovici. You tried to warn me."

"I never knew what happened to you. No one did. Though it was not hard to guess. I assumed you were dead. As you say, I did try and warn you."

"What about my father?"

"Gonzaga brought charges of drunkenness against him a short while later. The Consiglio dismissed him as Captain-General. I think he is soldiering in Naples now." Ludovici felt sick to his stomach. Better you had died, old friend. "I always hoped that perhaps you had just run away."

"As a wiser man would have done."

"I should have -"

"What? There is nothing you could have done."

"It was Gonzaga, wasn't it?"

He took a very long time to answer. Finally: "Do you remember giving me a letter? Lucia had handed it to you, she told you it was from Julia. But it wasn't, it was from Gonzaga. It was how he baited the trap. The letter said I should meet her on the Ponte Antico. Instead I made my rendezvous with four gentlemen he had hired on the waterfront. I fought them but there were too many of them.

They razored me Ludovici, right there in the bilge in the galleot. They thought I would die, I think. But somehow I survived and every day since I have wished I had not. I was sold in the slave market here in Stamboul and taken into the royal Harem to be trained as a page. The old Kislar Aghasi took a liking to me, he could see I had more learning than the rest of the poor wretches they sold on the blocks, I could speak Turkish and Arabic as well as Italian. He groomed me for better things, if you can call it that. So I learned my tasks well and when the old Kislar Agasi died the Sultan's mother appointed me in his place." He stopped and hung his head in his hands. Ludovici wanted to reach out and console him but found, to his eternal shame, that he could not do it. "I have wished for death often of course but if it is not your time you cannot make it happen unless you take a dagger to your own veins and make sure the job is done right. It is not easy to die, at least not for one like me. " Abbas composed himself. "They have made a ghost of me, Ludovici. A ghost who walks and talks and breathes, but a ghost just the same."

Ludovici did not know what to say to him. "Why did you not come here before?" he managed finally.

He laughed, with no humor. "We both know the answer to that."

"Then why did you come today?"

"Because I need your help."

"Name it. Anything."

"Do not be so quick to offer favors to a stranger, Ludovici."

 "You are no stranger to me."

"But I am."

Ludovici finally gathered the courage to touch this monster that once was his friend. "Abbas, I will never deny you."

"Ludovici you really don't understand. You can't." His fingers strayed to his cheek where the dagger had sliced him five years - was it just five years? - before. "It doesn't stop afterwards. You still want women. I thought the longing would go away."

"Just tell me what you want me to do."

"I thought I should never see her again, you see. But she is here, in Stamboul."

"Who?" Ludovici shook his head in astonishment. "Not her? Not Julia Gonzaga?" Impossible. If she had come to the Comunità Magnifica he would have heard of it.

"She is a slave in the Harem. She was captured by corsairs a few months ago. I have seen her, Ludovici, I have seen her with my own eyes. She is as lovely as ever."

"Does she know ..."

"No, she does not recognize me. I do not want her to know. I just want to get her out of there."

"But Abbas ... how? No woman ever escapes from there."

"There must be some way. I only know I cannot do it alone."

"It will involve terrible risk. Why would you do it?"

"Let us just say - I believe you owe me two gold ducats."

"You have risked too much for her already."

"Look at me, Ludovici. What do I have to lose?" When he did not answer, he went on: "You told me once that women were just women, that I was a fool to moon over just one. Perhaps you were right. But if I was a fool then I am a bigger fool now, do you not think so?"

"I don't know what to think any more."

"You know I also might ask you why you wish to help me. You owe me nothing Ludovici - or her. This could be dangerous for you as well. If we do this and we are found out, you won't be able to hide from the Sultan's wrath here in Pera."

"You are my friend, Abbas. I am yours to command."

" You are a good friend, Ludovici, for you have more to lose than I do. Why don't I give you time to think about this. You have a nice life here now. Why throw it away?"

"You were my friend, Abbas. I count you as one still. Just tell me what you want me to do."

Abbas seemed overcome. Finally, he said: "Very well. But I don't know how this might be done. I shall try and think of something. When I have a plan, I shall get a message to you."

"I would rather you come here yourself. I have missed you old friend."

"I cannot come again. If I am seen here, and something goes wrong, it will put you in danger. And also ..."

"Also?"

"It is painful for me even to come this once. I am sure you understand."

He left. Ludovici stayed where he was, staring at the black water. The great mystery of his resolved then, but now he wished he had never known, so he could remember the handsome and reckless friend of his youth without thinking also of what they had done to him since.

Why did he still wish to help this woman? Was it love then, or was it a personal redemption? He did not know; as he did not know why he had agreed to help Abbas to do it. Was it out of love?

Or was he looking for redemption, too? After all, he was the one who gave him the letter that sent him to the Ponte Antico. He put his head in his hands. Poor Abbas.

# CHAPTER 38

## The Hippodrome

Ibrahim stood on the balcony in the gathering darkness, staring at the rose-pink walls of the Aya Sofia and the cupolas of the Palace beyond, the distinctive tower rising above the Divan. Güzül thought he looked tired. His shoulders were hunched.

"I trust the Rose of Spring is well," he said.

"She is well in her body, my Lord. But she is sick at heart."

"I am her servant, as always."

Güzül hesitated. Gülbehar had impressed on her that her message should not be heard by any but the Vizier himself. This game grew more dangerous by the hour! "She has heard whispers, my Lord. About the lady Hürrem ."

"Go on."

"She believes that the witch conspires against the shahzade."

A cool wind accompanied the dusk, guttering the candles. "She has proof?"

"Not yet, my Lord."

"The there is nothing to be done, is there?"

"My mistress asked me to convey to you just one message. That if ever you were yourself threatened, Mustapha is ready to come to your aid at a moment's notice."

"If I am threatened? By whom?"

"She did not say."

"Suleiman loves me with his life! He is the only one who might threaten me. Unless you mean Hürrem ?"

He knows exactly what I mean, Güzül thought; knows that he is as much a threat to her as the shahzade Mustapha. But Ibrahim must tread carefully; should anyone know of their conversation he would find his head on a spike,

155

whether Suleiman loved him with his life or not. They were touching on treason here.

"Mustapha told you he would support me - or his mother did?"

"The message came from Rose of Spring but she told me that -"

"That is not the same thing," Ibrahim snapped. He shook his head. "You may give Rose of Spring my answer. Tell her I will do all in my power to help her, for I am as troubled by what is happening in the Eski Saraya as she is. But I will never, ever, do anything to harm the Lord of Life. Even if it cost me my life."

"I shall convey your words exactly."

"One other thing," Ibrahim said. "I am curious. Have you ever seen this - Hürrem ?"

"I have seen her many times."

"Describe her to me."

"She is pretty, or pretty enough. But no beauty. Yet she has a certain way with her. She is brighter and more spirited than most of the girls in there."

"What color is her hair?"

"Gold and red. Like wheat and rust."

"And her face?"

"Her lips are a little too narrow and her nose a little small. Her eyes are her best feature. Green and bright. Piercing, one might say, my Lord."

She could see Ibrahim trying to form a picture of his adversary in his mind. But it would be like trying to imagine the dome on the mosque by describing each tile separately. Hürrem was much more than the sum of her parts. You only had to be in the same room as her to know that.

He turned away and leaned on the balustrade, his forehead creased into deep furrows. "Thank you, Güzül , you may go."

Güzül touched her forehead to the carpets and hurried away.

\*\*\*

After she had gone Ibrahim stood very still and watched the night come. He had risen so far; his own barge, eight guards of honor, a salary twice that of the previous Vizier. And more power than any slave could dream of; he ruled the Divan, now he even commanded the army. And yet he had been more content when he had been in Suleiman's shadow; indeed there had been freedom in it. He had only really learned what shackles were when he became Vizier.

Was he really in danger from that little Russian? But Suleiman was his friend, surely, as well as his Sultan. He would never betray him for a woman. He might give up the Divan and give up the Army but he would never give up his best friend.

# CHAPTER 39

## The Eski Saraya

Julia had experienced many things since her capture by the corsairs; terror certainly, despair yes, and she had drunk humiliation to the dregs. There were long nights at the beginning when loneliness was like a physical ache in her belly. For a long time after that she had felt simply numb, overwhelmed by her situation.

But then one day she experienced something that was utterly unexpected. Joy.

She had never appreciated how miserable she was before; it was simply her life and she was accustomed to it. But now, even though she had, in many ways, replaced one cage with another, she realized she had found more freedom here than she had ever imagined for herself. She did not have to nurse an ancient and sickening husband that she despised and she also had other women to talk to; and although there was little of note to discuss inside the Harem walls, they were from all corners of the Empire, and many were Christians like herself. She was endlessly curious to hear about their former lives in Syria or Armenia or Greece.

Baths and massages were a daily event and she began slowly to awaken to her body's senses. Learning how pleasing it could be to be touched was a startling discovery. She even began to enjoy the sensation of being naked.

God would punish her one day, of course. The thought made her both fearful and angry. If he wished her to remain chaste why had He allowed the corsairs to capture their galley? And yet where was her sin exactly? She had committed no adulteries and she still prayed her rosary every day.

This morning she lay face down on the marble as Sirhane massaged her back with warm oil. It was stifling in the hararet and the sweat ran into her eyes and made them sting. Thinking about God and her Confessor made her

157

neck muscles tight but Sirhane's expert ministrations soothed the knots out of her shoulders.

*I never want to go back to La Serenissima.*

She looked at the black pages standing mute at the doors. "Why do they never try to talk to us?" she asked Sirhane. "Isn't it torment for a man to see a woman without her clothes and not be able to touch her?"

"Some of them do," Sirhane whispered.

"What if the Sultan were to find out?"

"Then they would find their heads on a spike outside the gate. Not that they can do anything. They are not really men anymore."

Julia hesitated. Sirhane would laugh at her, she was sure, but the question had been bothering her for weeks. "Why not?"

"You mean you don't know? They've been razored."

"Razored?"

"They've had their manhood cut off. They can't make love to a woman."

Julia closed her eyes as Sirhane squeezed the muscles of her neck, kneading them until tears welled in her eyes. "Sirhane, have you ever … with a man?"

"Of course."

"What was it like?"

Sirhane paused. "I thought you were married. Did your husband not possess you on your wedding night?"

"He did not seem interested. I think I was just a bargaining chip in a business or political arrangement with my father. He was an old man when he married me."

Sirhane began kneading her shoulders again, pressing her knuckles deep into the valleys along her spine. "I only did it twice. If my father had ever found out he would have killed him, and me."

"What happens?"

"A boy has a muscle between his legs. If you stroke it, it gets long and hard and then it will fit inside you."

"Where?"

"In your kouss, of course."

"Does it hurt?"

"A little. But Hanif was gentle. I liked the way he kissed me best. That is what I miss the most. He would kiss my breasts, too. I still remember the feeling."

Julia closed her eyes and tried to imagine Sirhane kissing her breasts. The thought made her feel sick. "Is that what the Sultan will do?"

"If you're lucky."

"Lucky?"

"Don't you want to be chosen by the Sultan? It's what every girl in here wants. But it's not very likely. It's a long time now since he chose a new girl.

He spends all his time with his second kadin." She put her knuckles into the muscles of Julia's bottom and she bit into the soft flesh of her arm to keep from crying out. "If the Sultan chooses you, you will have all the wealth and comfort you will ever want. Look at Hürrem . She is practically a queen."

Julia glanced back at the eunuchs at the door. Eunuch: so that's what it meant. She had thought it was just a name the Turks gave to the Nubians. Look at them. They stood there like statues. Once she had felt mortified to be naked in front of them, now she treated them as if they didn't exist.

"I knew a boy once, we met in secret a few times, he wanted me to run away with him. Do you think he wanted to make love to me?"

"Of course he did. It's what they all want. Roll over."

Julia did as she was told. She felt as if it had been pummeled with iron rods and yet all the tension was gone and she felt as if she was floating.

Sirhane stared at her. "You're so beautiful," she said and kissed her. Julia froze. Sirhane's wet hair fell across her face and then she felt her hand stroking her belly and sliding between her legs …

Julia pushed her away . She ran out of the hararet and into the pool, her mind and heart in  utter turmoil.

## Topkapi Saraya

Suleiman and Ibrahim dined off green and blue Chinese porcelain, a gift from some long-forgotten ambassador that had been found gathering dust in his treasure house.

There was honey from Wallachia; butter brought in ox hides across the Black Sea from Moldavia; sherbets iced with snow and carried in felt sacks from Mount Olympus; and to finish there were dates and plums from Egypt.

"My Lord, we have eaten our way around the Empire," Ibrahim said, when they had finished.

The dishes were collected by servants and Suleiman asked Ibrahim to play for him on the viol.

"My Lord, I hope you will pardon me, but tonight I am too troubled to play for you."

"But what troubles you, old friend? Is it the Army? Do you still wish for me to charge the walls of Vienna with you and help fill the moats with our soldiers?"

"It is a matter of greater import, my Lord."

Suleiman sighed. How Ibrahim had changed, always needing to talk about matters of great import. He seldom laughed any more. "Well, tell me, then. Is it to do with the Divan?"

Ibrahim shook his head. "It is a matter I should normally tremble to mention in your presence."

"You have mated with your horse?" Suleiman had spent the day with Hürrem and was in high spirits.

Ibrahim did not even smile. "There is talk among the Janissaries and in the bazaars."

"Rumors! You want to fill my head with rumors?"

"Rumors are like the pestilence. A few hundred cases a year are to be expected. When there is an epidemic one should take notice."

"An epidemic?"

"The talk fills the bazaars and even spreads along the cloisters of the Palace itself."

"What are these rumors?"

"They concern the lady Hürrem ."

Suleiman stiffened. "What happens in the Harem is of no concern to anyone but me."

"I only repeat what I hear."

"What is it that you hear?"

"They say ... they say she is a witch. They say she has enchanted you and clouded your reason and that is why you will not take the army to Vienna or attend the Divan."

Suleiman leaped to his feet, stamping the room in search of someone to strike down. "A witch, they say. A WITCH! Find me who says it! Find me these pigs and I will have every one of their heads hung on the gate!"

Ibrahim remained resolutely cross-legged at table while Suleiman paced the floor behind him. "The reports are brought to me by my spies. They do not bring me names."

Suleiman snatched up the nearest object within reach - Ibrahim's viol - and smashed it against the wall. "I WILL CUT OUT THEIR TONGUES AND MAKE THEM EAT IT!"

Ibrahim stared at the mess of splinters and strings lying about the carpet. He turned white.

"Leave me."

"My Lord?"

"GET OUT!"

Ibrahim scrambled to his feet. This had never happened before. "My Lord, let me sit with you a while and-"

Suleiman tore his own robe between his fists. He grabbed a eunuch who had been standing in the corner of the room and threw him onto the floor. The wretch cowered away, sobbing. He aimed a kick at his rump, sending him scurrying on all fours towards the door. Then Suleiman took the jewelled dagger out of his belt and sliced a hole in the fleeing man's robe leaving a bleeding gash on his buttock.

Then he turned around and stared at Ibrahim with the bloodied dagger clenched in his right fist. He was panting and his eyes were unfocused. "GET OUT!"

Ibrahim fled. By the morning the news was all over the Palace. The Sultan had gone mad and tried to kill the Vizier. It was like the bad old days of Selim the Grim all over again.

# CHAPTER 40

## The Eski Saraya

They had given her to the Mistress of the Robes; she had proven her skill with fine needlework - God alone knew she had had enough practice over the years - and the Kiaya had professed herself well pleased with her.

He found her hunched over a satin robe that was intended for young Bayezid, working a pattern into the cloth with gold thread. When she saw him she dropped to her knees to make the proper sala'am, but he stopped her.

"Just sit down," he said.

Julia did as she was told.

"Look at me," he said.

She raised her eyes and he saw her wince. The scar is not pretty especially in good light, close up. It would have been better if the dagger had taken his eye out completely than leave just the white of it staring at the world like this. He waited for some dawning of recognition but there was none.

"Do you know who I am?"

"You are the Kislar Aghasi."

"Yes, the Kislar Aghasi. Your well being is my responsibility from this moment on. Do you understand?"

Julia nodded.

"Do they look after you in here?"

"The Kiaya is very kind to me."

Abbas nodded; better than the last one by all accounts, and more fortunate, too. Apparently Hürrem had ordered that the foot that had kicked her be lopped off by the and then had her exiled to Diyarbakir.

"You have learned much of the language already. That is very good."

"I have an ear for it."

"You are clever then, as well as beautiful." But I always knew that, he thought. What would you do, I wonder, if I spoke to you in Italian, told you that you are still the most beautiful woman in the world, even though I spend all my days surrounded by beauty? "You are a Gaiour, a Christian?"

"I am."

"It will not help you here. No one will force you to give up your religion but you will rise faster if you learn your Qur'an. They have given you a holy book?"

"I cannot read it. It is in Arabic."

"Then you must learn to read Arabic." He lowered his voice and said more gently. "You must forget about Venice. That world is gone now. You can never go back there."

"I know."

He searched for something else to say. He understood how it must feel to be a ghost, to see the physical world and be unable to join it. She does not know me anymore and what difference would it make if she did? I don't want her pity, I could not stand that. And what else might she feel for me, after all this time and after what they have done to me? "If you need for anything, let me know."

She bowed her head. He hesitated. Once I waited a week just for the moment when you drew back the veil that covered your face, he thought. Now I see you naked every day, I watch you from my lattice window high above the hammam and I still burn for you. Dear God, how I burn!

I am ashamed for spying on you but there is no offense, for the only hurt I cause is to myself. I admire you now as a man might admire a great work of art. No sculptor could ever have carved anything as perfect as you.

Oh sweet Jesus, have pity. How can I live like this?

"My Lord?"

He realized he had groaned aloud.

"Is something wrong?"

"It is nothing." He turned and left the room. He made his way slowly through the darkened cloisters of the Harem to the tiny cell that was now his home. He sat down on his cot, hung his head and wept.

*** 

The Marmara Sea looked like rose-tinted glass, the gray humps of islands breaking the surface like spouting whales. Below the Valide's window, new fruit had bowed the branches of a cherry tree. She still loved the view from here, though she had seen it every day for most of her life.

Behind her three small boys in skull-caps and baggy trousers scuffed the marble floor with their soft slipper boots, impatient for the audience to be over.

"So have you boys been working hard at your studies?"

Bayezid and Mehmet looked at their older brother and waited for him to speak for them but he just sniffed and stared at the floor. So Bayezid took up the responsibility. "Yes, Grandmother," he said.

She studied them in turn; Bayezid and Mehmet were both fine looking boys, she thought, they had their father's long limbs and lean good looks. But I am not sure about Selim. When did he get to be so chubby? And why does he let his younger brother answer for them? He is eight years old, time he had a tongue in his head.

"Do you learn your Qur'an, Selim?"

"Our tutor beats us," he mumbled.

"Why does he beat you? Are you lazy?"

"I don't know."

The Valide picked up a silver salver from the table in front of her, arranged with her favorite sweet, rahat lokum. Her pastry cooks prepared it fresh for her every day using the pulp form white grapes mixed with semolina, flour, rosewater, apricot kernels and wild honey. She selected a piece and popped it into her mouth.

"Would you like a piece, children?"

The boys came forward eagerly. Bayezid and Mehmet, she noticed, took one piece each, Selim took three.

She wondered what the future held in store for them. None of them would ever grow to be as fine a prince as Mustapha, but if anything should happen to him …

"Tell me what you have learned at the Enderun."

"I can throw a javelin from the back of a horse!" Bayezid shouted.

"But you are only six years old!"

"And hit a target with an arrow!"

"What about your Qur'an?"

Bayezid lowered his eyes again. He nudged Mehmet, who, without looking up, recited ten verses from the first sura of the holy book. The Valide clapped her hands in appreciation and Mehmet flushed to the roots of his hair.

"And what about you, Selim? What have you learned?"

He shrugged and said nothing.

"Come now, Selim. You are three years older than Mehmet. Recite the first sura for me. You must be able to do that by now."

Selim mumbled his way through five verses and then stopped.

"Well, go on."

"I can't remember any more, grandmother."

She frowned, was about to coax him, then changed her mind. What a stupid little boy. "No wonder your tutor beats you," she said, "at your age Mustapha could recite the first chapter without taking breath!" She sighed. "I am tired, I need to rest for a while, come and kiss your grandmother, boys, then be off with you."

Bayezid and Mehmet dutifully kissed her. Selim was the last, his lips barely brushed her cheek, and as he left she saw him scoop up another piece of rahat lokum and hide it in his robe. She almost called him back to reprimand him but then changed her mind. What was the point? He was greedy and stupid and God had seen fit to make him that way.

She went back to the window and watched them playing in the courtyard below. Selim showed his two little brothers the sweetmeats he had stolen and when they threw out their hands for a share he laughed and stuffed all the pieces in his own mouth at once.

Praise God there was Mustapha.

\*\*\*

There is a currency in the Hall of Kings, Rüstem thought, and it is not jewels or gold. Money of itself has no value, he thought; the only thing that can be traded for power and for life is information.

Which was why the Kislar Aghasi was worth to him more than his own substantial weight in gold.

Abbas visited the Treasury once a week and was always ushered into his the defterdar's office without being made to wait, as most others were. While he drank Rüstem "s chai and ate his halwa, he gave him all the news from the Harem. Today it was the usual thing; Hürrem was making the lives of the servant girl and the other houris a misery.

"And the Valide?" Rüstem asked him.

"She sickens. The physician sends her potions but they do little good."

"May God protect her," Rüstem said.

"She is in all our prayers," the Kislar Aghasi said with little enthusiasm.

Rüstem tapped a finger on the arm of his chair. "I have a crumb for you to peck at."

"What is it you wish to know?"

"It is not something I wish to know this time. It is something I wish to tell. You have heard the war drum beating?"

"The blacksmiths in Galata keep their foundries burning day and night. Do we make war on Frederick again?"

"We shall. But this time the campaign will go a little differently."

"How so?"

"This time the Grand Vizier will lead the army."

"Of course. Who else would be seraskier?"

"Indeed, no one could replace me, thanks be to God. Especially when the Sultan himself will remain behind, here in the palace."

Abbas cocked his head. "This is true?"

"Another crumb for you. It was the Lady Hürrem who persuaded him to abandon his duties in the Lands of War. She means to sing and dance for him while his yeniceris bleed and die for Islam at the Gates of Vienna."

"He must be mad!"

"Something very like it." Rüstem yawned. "Soon the whole palace will know of it, Kislar Aghasi. But the Sultan Valide will remember you kindly if you tell her of it first." And then perhaps she will stand up to that poisonous little witch, Ibrahim thought. Pray God she does for who knows what will happen when she is gone, for she is the only one who holds sway with him now.

# CHAPTER 41

## The Eski Saraya

A gray mist of cloud obscured the neck of the Bosphorus. The branch of a honeysuckle scuffed against the window as an unseasonal chill ruffled the water of the Golden Horn. Just the day before the sun was shining. How quickly all life can change.

Almost ten years I have been in this prison, Hürrem thought. Somewhere beyond those clouds the wind is bending the long grass into banners of green and stirs the manes on the horses and hums through the nomad tents.

Ten years a prisoner.

She watched her nightingale sing in its lacquered cage. On impulse she snatched it down and carried it out to the terrace. She opened the tiny door.

The bird hesitated, cocking its head to the side, alert for danger. It hopped to the floor of the cage then back to its perch, startled and unsure.

"You've been in this cage too long, haven't you?" she said. "You wouldn't know how to survive outside now. That's what you're thinking. It's the only world you know, isn't it?"

She closed the door and put the cage back on its hook.

The steppes, the wind, the waving grass; they were far beyond her reach now. They might as well be on the moon.

Damn them, damn all men.

\*\*\*

Two odalisques were soaping each other's bodies, fondling each other without any self consciousness at all; here two other girls were perched on the edge of a marble sofa examined each other intimately for hairs; others sat alone, naked or wearing nothing but their gauzy bath chemises and cleaning their teeth with pumice, picking their noses or scratching without inhibition at their most private places.

Julia did not spare any of them a second glance. When had it all ceased to shock her? She no longer even remembered that it once had.

She found Sirhane lying on a bench of warmed marble, a gedicli massaging her with scented oil. Julia sent the slave scurrying from the room with just a glance.

She poured some of the warm oil onto her own hands and smoothed it gently across the Syrian's textured skin. Sirhane felt the difference in her touch immediately and opened her eyes, startled. "Julia?"

"I came to tell you I was sorry."

Sirhane rolled onto her side. "No, it is I who should be sorry. I was impetuous."

"I do not want to lose you as my friend."

"More than a friend," Sirhane said. "I love you, Julia."

Love: I suppose it is, Julia thought, though I had never imagined it with another woman. But until she shocked me with that kiss I looked forward to spending every moment I could with her. Is that love, then?

Sirhane ran her fingers through Julia's braids and pulled her face towards her. "Do it again," Julia breathed.

Sirhane kissed her. Her lips tasted of sherbet and fruit. Her skin was slippery and hot.

"What should I do?" Julia said.

Sirhane took her hand and put it between her legs, crushing her hand against the smooth mound. She closed her eyes. "Put your mouth there," she whispered.

Julia gasped. My mouth? No! The idea astonished her. Yet Sirhane had such pleading in her eyes; if I don't do this, Julia thought, she will shun me forever. She's the only friend I have here.

She took a deep breath and kissed Sirhane's belly and then the crease of her groin. The Syrian uttered a tiny sob and her body quivered.

I can't do this, Julia thought. Her Confessor appeared through the steam, in the long vestments of penance, a Bible clutched in his right hand. Her father stood behind him in the red gown of a Consiglio. Do this and you are damned for all time, he said.

Sirhane opened her legs wider, her heels slipping on the wet tiles.

"You will be cast into a fiery pit," her Confessor said, "and whipped with metal-tipped rods and boiling pitch will be poured into the wounds. Demons will roast you over a slow fire and there will be no escape from the torment …"

"You are worse than a beast," her father said. "Your name will be a byword for shame and depravity all through La Serenissima …"

"Please," Sirhane whispered. She was panting so hard Julia could see the outline of her ribs through her skin. "Please."

She arched her back, her fingers entwined in Julia's braids, pushing her down. Julia banished her Confessor, made herself deaf to her father's howls of outrage.

*I will do this for you, Sirhane.*

She touched her kouss with her lips, just a tentative brush of her lips. Sirhane wriggled and moaned. She found to her surprise that there was no taste to her, just a warm fragrant musk and silkiness. "Use your tongue," Sirhane begged her. "Please, please, please ..."

Julia stared at her. Could this really give so much pleasure? Was her touch really so unbearably sweet? Sirhane wriggled towards her until her legs hung over the edge of the marble. Julia lowered her head again, the pink tip of her tongue extended. She was timid at first, thinking someone must see them and stop them. But no one entered their cubicle and the steam of the hararet made a natural curtain.

Julia lowered her head again. Sirhane clawed at her back with her nails and moaned at the slightest touch. Suddenly her father and her Confessor were left far behind as Julia plunged into this strange new world of pleasure and moans, mesmerized by her own wickedness and new-found power. Unlike her old world this new prison had an endless vista that was yet to be charted and explored.

# CHAPTER 42

## Topkapi Saraya

There was a kiosk at the end of the long peninsula of Seraglio Point. Its silver-plated dome was decorated in arabesque with flower motifs in blue and white. The woodwork was inlaid with ivory and it had windows of stained glass in patterns of claret and pavonine. There were fretted gold sofas and even a conical bronze fireplace against one wall.

It was Suleiman's refuge from the furnace heat of the palace on these warm nights. The unseasonal storm had spent itself quickly and the days that followed it soon baked the city dry once more. But it was cooler out here, with the evening breezes from the Marmara Sea whispering among the plane trees.

Hürrem lay with him on the long divan, listening to Suleiman's musicians playing unseen somewhere in the garden.

She made a shadow play on the wall of the kiosk with her fingers. "Look," she whispered.

"A camel!" Suleiman laughed.

"Now this."

"A sheep?"

"It's a horse!"

"It looks like a sheep."

"Did you ever see a sheep with such a long nose?"

"I have never seen such a long nose anywhere. Perhaps Ibrahim," he laughed.

Hürrem frowned in concentration as she manipulated her fingers. Suleiman watched her, smiling indulgently.

"What about this?"

"A cat?"

"The Kislar Aphasias cat. See? It has nothing between its legs!"
This time he did not laugh. "You should not make such jokes."
"Why not?"
"You offend against Islam."
"Oh, you're such a hypocrite."

Suleiman was lost for reply. How dare she say such a thing to him? Did she have no sense of her place? But perhaps it was what he loved most about her. He would let no one else speak so freely in front of him.

In the garden tortoises with lighted candles on their backs ambled through the roses and carnations. A full moon threw long shadows through the trees. He closed his eyes to the music. Such peace here, I could stay here forever.

But then the breeze died away and in the stillness he heard the ringing of hammers on iron as the smithies at the Galata arsenal set to forging new cannon for the coming campaign in Austria. He was overcome with guilt. God forgive me. I should be going with them.

## The Eski Saraya

The Valide was growing old. Her once rich black hair was now dyed with henna to disguise the gray, and all her kohl and powders could not hide the pouches under her eyes and her chin. Her limbs trembled even when she was sitting down.

Abbas placed his forehead to the silk carpet in reverence before addressing her. "Crown of Veiled Heads."

"Abbas." The Valide sounded breathless even though she had been resting here for at least an hour. Her time must be close. "You wished to speak with me?"

"Indeed, on a matter which, I hope, will be of no import."

"Come now Abbas, I know you better than that. If you have come to me it must be a matter of some weight."

"It is merely a rumor that has come to me through my various sources."

The Valide sat forward, suddenly young and viperous again. "Concerning who?"

"Concerning the Lady Hürrem ."

"That one!"

"It is, as I say, only a rumor."

"I have more faith in your rumors than the official pronouncements from the Divan. Tell me what you have heard, Abbas."

"Soon the army will march against Frederick in Vienna."

"The whole world knows that!"

"What they do not know is that the Lord of Life will not lead his army to the Lands of War this year."

"What?"

"I am told the Lady Hürrem has persuaded the Sultan to remain behind - with her."

For a moment he thought she was going to choke.

"This cannot ...be true."

"I only repeat what I hear. I felt it was my duty to report it."

The Valide slapped the palm of her right hand against the divan. "She presumes too much! I warned him about her. First Gülbehar and now this little Russian. My son has not the faintest idea about women!"

"I hope I have not caused you offence," Abbas said.

"On the contrary, you have done me a great service." She picked up a cushion from beside her and threw it across the room with surprising force. The effort exhausted her. Her two maidservants rushed forward but she waved them away. "Get away from me! I am all right." She took some while to get her breath back. Then she said to Abbas in a quiet voice: "What happened to your face?"

"Madam?"

"Your face. What happened to it? Come now, Abbas, I have known you these few years now and I have never asked you before. I shall be gone soon and I should like to know before I die."

Abbas contained himself only with difficulty. Until now the old woman had treated him respectfully. Why would she shame him now, just to serve curiosity? The imminence of eternity was no excuse. "I received the injury in a street fight."

"A street fight. What were you fighting over?"

"My manhood."

She was silent for a long time, and he had the feeling that after five years she had seen him for the first time, as a man and not a slave. But it could have been just his imagination.

"I wish my son would fight as hard for his own manhood," she said. "Thank you for your service, Abbas. I will remember it. Leave us. I have business to attend to."

# CHAPTER 43

Suleiman was dismayed when he saw his mother. She seemed to grow a little older, a little frailer, each time he came. He had always thought her indestructible.

But age had not dulled her mind - or her tongue. "Have you seen your sons?" she snapped at him the moment he had settled beside her on the divan.

"I have seen them. Çehangir is still sickly, but the others prosper. Their tutor seems pleased."

The Valide scowled. "What do you think of Selim?"

Suleiman shrugged his shoulders.

"I do not like him," she said. "He is a sullen child. I do not trust him. He eats too many sweetbreads for a boy and he carps like a woman. He is cruel to Mehmet and Beyzid."

"You have nothing better to say about him?"

"In all other ways he is a model prince."

"Well his tutors have said nothing to me."

"Of course not, they do not dare. It is his mother's fault, she spends no time with him. It is only a wonder that Bayezid and Mehmet are as pleasant as they are."

"Ah! Do I detect some kind words?"

"You may laugh, Suleiman, but it is fortunate for you that you have a son like Mustapha. I should despair if Selim were our shahzade." She tapped her finger on the back of the divan. "You will leave soon?"

"The army rides within the week," he said, avoiding her eyes.

"To look for Frederick?"

"Frederick? He is just a small man of Vienna. His brother Charles is the great prize but we do not expect to flush him out. He will skulk in his castle in Germany."

"The preparations go well?"

"Ibrahim plans for thirty cannon to pummel the walls, provided the mud does not lay claim to them again on the journey north."

She placed her hand on top of his. "You will truly be the greatest of all the Sultans, my son! The gypsies prophesied as much when you were born!"

"I have done my best," Suleiman said. He answered the pressure of her hand and was shocked by how frail she was, he could feel every bone and every knuckle, there was no flesh on her at all. He was suddenly afraid; he could not imagine coming to the Harem and not finding her here.

"I have heard whispers," she said.

"From where?"

"A little bird flies through my window every morning and sings to me. This morning he told me that the army is going to leave here without a general."

Suleiman tried to pull his hand away but the withered leaf of a hand was suddenly as strong and powerful as a man's. "Of course they will have a general, the very best."

"The best general in Stamboul is sitting right here with me. So the whispers are not true? You are going to lead your army into the Lands of War, as every Osmanli Sultan before you has done?"

"They do not need me. Ibrahim is my seraskier and he will manage the campaign just as well as if I am there." His mother fell silent. After what seemed like an eternity it was Suleiman who broke: "Who told you about this?"

She ignored his question in favor of her own: "When were you going to tell me?" she snapped. " After they had gone? How long did you think you could keep this from me?"

Suleiman jumped to his feet. "I decide matters of war, no one else!"

The Valide stared him down. "Do not ever again shout at your mother here in the Harem," she said.

He sat down again, white-faced.

After a moment, she said: "There are some things that no Sultan, however great, may decide on his own. You are first of all a Muslim and you must surrender to the will of God."

"I have had enough of these wars. It is pointless."

"It is your duty to the Osmanlis and to God!"

"Which I have always, until now, put above all else."

"Until now!" The old woman's eyes were suddenly hard. "It's her, isn't it? She has done this to you."

Suleiman turned away from her, stared instead over the roofs of the palace at the painted wooden houses that piled down the hill to the blue waters of the Horn. Suddenly the view did not look quite as pretty.

Someone had put her up to this, he thought. Whoever it was knew she was the only woman or man in the world who might speak to him like this.

"Down there in the bazaar they say she has bewitched you."

"So I am told. If I find any man repeat this calumny I will cut out his tongue and make him eat it."

"Then half the city would be mute, son."

"I make sure there is bread on their tables and meat enough for every one of them. They live under my protection, safe from the ravages of the armies that enslave half of Europe. I have given them Rhodes, Belgrade and Hungary. What more do they want from me?"

"They want their Sultan."

"They have him!"

"They do not! They have a Greek slave to listen to their complaints in the Divan and a Greek slave to lead their armies against the infidel. The only one who has the Sultan's ear and the Sultan's love is a Russian girl!"

"There are other things to life other than the petty quarreling in the Divan and the endless, pointless spilling of blood! I tell you how I shall become the greatest of all Osmanli sultans, it will be by giving the people laws and mosques and schools. I want to build not to destroy endlessly and for no good reason!"

"You have abdicated your power to Ibrahim and your manhood to a woman!" She took his hand again and held it tight. "Listen to me. I do not want you to be unhappy. Only you know what has passed between you and this woman. But you must remember also that you are a ghazi. Do not grow too fond of the ways of the Harem. Its purpose was to make us strong and to create sons; it was not intended for indolence and indulgence."

"No, it is the law that makes us strong, the kanun and the sheri'a."

"Suleiman, my whole life has been for you and for your Sultanate. I have been so proud of you. You are not cruel the way your father was cruel, and that has been your strength. But it has also been your weakness. I have seen it with Gülbehar  and with Ibrahim, and now with Hürrem . You must learn to stand alone."

"If I am alone, then what is left for me?"

"The world is what is left for you, the empire of the Osmanlis. Your grandfather's grandfather rode out of the desert so that you might live in a palace. Stamboul is not yours by right. It is a sacred trust and you must earn it by your devotion to God and to your people."

"But I have earned it, not only for my lifetime but every generation to follow. I did it with my kanunis, by giving this city and this empire written laws. I send my armies against Christendom because that is what I am fated to do, so what does it matter if I ride with them or I do not, as long as they go? After all this, there must be something left for Suleiman."

"Everything is left for you! The palaces, the finest Harem in the world, what - do you think you live like a beggar? Your ancestors lived in tents and ate from the saddle of a horse. You have grown soft!"

Suleiman gritted his teeth. "They do not need me in Vienna!"

"Of course they do! Now take back your authority before it is taken from you!"

"Taken from me? You mean Ibrahim? He would never turn against me …"

"What about Hürrem ?"

"What about her? She is just a woman!"

Too late he realized what he had said. His mother smiled bitterly. "Yes, just a woman. And what do you think I am, do you think I cannot read her better than you? You have allowed her to twist you to her own ends. Do you think I do not know this game?"

"What do you want from me?"

"I want you to be Sultan! You have hundreds of women to choose from here in this palace, why do you choose just one?"

"Because … because I can be myself when I am with her. Not the Sultan … not the Possessor of Men's Necks … just myself."

"And what does she want - for you to be yourself or for her to be the next Valide?"

"Insha'Allah! Please, give me peace. I love her, let it be."

"I cannot let it be, Suleiman. If you wanted peace then you should have been born a fisherman or a goatherd. You are a Sultan and your odalisques and your Cyprian wine and your pages do not come without a price. They are there to serve the Sultan and in return the Sultan must serve them. I fear for you. You have the soul of a poet but your Father's temper. It is a dangerous mix. You may one day be the greatest of all the Osmanlis or you may destroy us all."

"It is time I made my own decisions."

"Then let them be yours and not your wife's."

"You mean let them be your decisions - don't you?"

"Do your duty, Suleiman. Or you will be damned in this world and the next."

# CHAPTER 44

The great bazaar had been built in the time of Mehmet Fatih, Suleiman's grandfather. The riches of the empire were crammed into its tiny shops along the warren of stone alleyways; gold and silver, brocades and silk, crimson rugs from Damascus and peacock blue silk carpets from Baghdad. Outside the gates hawkers grilled corn cobs on charcoal braziers, fanning the flames with turkey wings and brushing ineffectually at the small, persistent black flies. Other hawkers sold tripe flavored with garlic or warm almond cream sprinkled with cinnamon.

Suleiman marveled at it all, lost in his own city.

But even among the tumult he recognized the order his ancestors had imposed. Everyone knew their place; the Turks wore white turbans, the Greeks" turbans were blue though their boots were black; the Jews had yellow turbans, as did the Armenians, but their boots were a startling crimson.

A spice merchant had been nailed to the door of his shop by his ears. The sign that hung around his neck said that he had been convicted of giving false measures. One of the crowd spat in his face and Suleiman did the same. He felt no pity for him; it was the law and it had been made to protect the people.

His mother was right, he had lived in palaces too long and he had grown soft. The smell of filth and offal made him gag and the gabble of voices hurt his ears. These were the people that came with their petitions to the Divan. He had seen them every day, begging his clemency or his judgment or his justice on their knees but he had never seen for himself how they lived in their own world.

Night fell quickly. A crescent moon rose above the roofs of the bedesten.

It was the first time in his entire life that he had not been surrounded by a bodyguard. Yet he felt safe here, what enemy would recognize him in these rags? Besides even if he were not the Sultan he would be safe; the yeniceris patrolled the streets of his city every night, and any act of violence was treated as an insult against Islam itself and punished accordingly.

The Valide would have apoplexy of she knew what he had done. But what better way was there to discover if this so-called gossip was true?

He strolled through the vaulted bazaar, lit now by a thousand lamps, delayed at the stall of a spice merchant, looking over the sacks of sesame seeds, aloe, saffron and liquorice root as if deliberating over a purchase. The vendor was involved in a heated debate with one of his customers; Suleiman heard the name Hürrem and stopped to listen.

" … since Selim was born he has not even looked at another woman! " the merchant said. He was a hook-nosed Greek with bad teeth and a sparse beard. He hawked abundantly onto the cobbles next to his stall, the expectorate narrowly missing Suleiman's sleeve.

"That is not possible," a customer said. By his white turban, Suleiman knew he was a Turk like himself. "He has a harem with three hundred of the most beautiful women in the Empire! No man could resist such a treasure for seven years!"

"Unless he is bewitched!" the Greek shouted and hawked again. It seemed he was incapable of talking above a whisper.

"You talk out of your ass so often your tongue should be at the other end."

"They say she is not a woman at all, she is a foul spirit, a djinn, from the forests of Wallachia." Hawk - spit.

"Well, there you are, everyone knows she is not form Wallachia, she is Russian. And if she is an evil spirit, like you say, why is Suleiman the greatest Sultan we have ever had? Look at what he has conquered - Belgrade, Rhodes, Buda-Pesth! Why two summers ago he was at the gates of Vienna itself!"

The merchant threw his hands in the air. "Exactly! Why did we not take Vienna when it was there for the asking? The witch made it rain right through summer so our cannon were bogged and useless." He hawked and spat on the floor of his shop with such violence that even the Greek took a step back. Suleiman thought of the saying that Ibrahim had taught him: It takes ten Turks to defeat one Jew in an argument, and ten Jews to defeat one Greek. "They say he cannot even pass his water without receiving her permission first."

"If anyone has him in their power it is Ibrahim!"

"Ibrahim is a great soldier." Hawk. "We need a strong Vizier." Spit. Spit again. "Especially when our Sultan has moon eyes for one of his slave girls. It will lead to no good! When a Sultan ignores his concubines it means some other woman has him by the thick member and she will lead him around like a donkey with reins!" He turned to Suleiman. "What is it you want?"

What I want is to take a sword and lop off your ugly head, Suleiman thought. Then I would hang it on the gates of the Sublime Porte and invite it to spit one more time. Instead he said: "I want nothing here. There is drool on your cinnamon."

He was pleased to hear the Turk laughing from inside the shop.

But the insults and calumnies he had heard echoed in his mind as he stumbled on through the bazaar. What Ibrahim and his mother had told him was true. His people were turning against him over her.

Bewitched!

Was there to be no hour of the day, no day of the week, no season of the year when he would be allowed to have his own life?

Very well, he would return to the Harem. He would show them he was master of his own house. He would do his duty and then perhaps they would give him some peace.

# CHAPTER 45

There was a protocol for choosing a girl.

There is a protocol for everything, Suleiman thought sourly as the iron-studded gates swung open. As he rode in the Kislar Aghasi was waiting to greet him, in a long-sleeved ceremonial pelisse and white sugarloaf turban. A hundred girls, pearls and jewels glittering in the sun, waited in the shaded area of the courtyard. They were fidgeting, nervous.

Any other man would tremble with anticipation, he thought. Why do I just feel this cold terror? Why is my Harem the most difficult place for me to be?

The great iron door creaked shut behind him and he dismounted. How long since he had done this? Before he became Sultan, before Gülbehar . The girls" eyes were hooded, none would dare look at him directly, yet he felt each one of them imploring him. A whole lifetime could turn on such moments, or so they believed.

The Kislar Aghasi touched his forehead to the cobblestones. "Great Lord."

"You are to be complimented," Suleiman told him, keeping to the protocols. "They are all quite exquisite."

"Thank you, my Lord."

The Kislar Aghasi moved into step behind him. Suleiman breathed in the scent of his women, jasmine and orange. Silks and satins shimmered, cheeks blushed pink, courting him. He bowed and greeted each one of the girls and as he did so the Kislar Aghasi whispered their names.

Why do I not drink from this fountain until I burst? he wondered. Other men would. Ibrahim tells me he has a different woman every night, sometimes two. He continued along the line, wondering which one he would choose. They are all so beautiful that even beauty itself becomes meaningless, he thought. This one, for instance. She might have been fashioned from alabaster by a master sculptor. Such perfection was intimidating.

"What is your name?" he said to her.

The girl murmured a response but her voice was so soft he did not hear what she said. He turned to the Kislar Aghasi. "What did she say?"

For some reason his Chief Eunuch hesitated. Perhaps she was new. "Julia," he said at last.

"Julia," Suleiman repeated. He looked at the girl a second time. Perfection indeed. He took a green handkerchief from the sleeve of his robe and draped it over her shoulder to indicate that he had made his choice. It was one Hürrem had embroidered for him herself. He knew she would be watching, unseen, and he hoped he had made his point.

"I shall walk in the garden now," he said to the Kislar Aghasi, who was staring at the girl with an expression he could not quite fathom. These eunuchs were strange creatures.

He walked on, out of the courtyard, to stroll among the peacocks and ostriches, and admire the view.

***

Hürrem turned from the window. Her fingers closed around the nearest object to hand, a silver candlestick that stood on a low table by the divan. She flung it across the room, splintering the blue Iznik tiles on the wall. Muomi ducked away, out of range.

Hürrem stood stock still, the muscles working in her jaw. "I have to stop this," she said.

"He is the Sultan," Muomi said. "How can you stop him?"

"Who is she?"

"I don't know her name, she's new. She came here from Algiers, she was taken from a Venetian galley that was captured by corsairs."

"Tell me how I can prevent this."

"My Lady ..."

Hürrem grabbed the gold ring that hung from Muomi's right ear and tugged down hard. Muomi screamed and fell to her knees. "Tell me how prevent it!"

"You're hurting me!"

"I want you to go to the apothecary and make me one of your potions."

"Please ... stop!"

Hürrem released her.

Muomi doubled over, clutching her ear. "If you kill her he will only choose another. If she dies just like Mustapha's servants, it will make them suspicious."

"What then? There has to be a way."

Muomi looked up at her, her eyes glittering. "Don't ever hurt me again."

"Just tell me what to do." She swallowed hard. "Please."

" There may be another way." Muomi straightened, still holding her ear. Hürrem had made it bleed. "Can you sup with him tonight?"

"Suleiman will not come to me now. He will not know how to face me."

"Then you have to find a way to persuade him. I am sure, for you, it will not really be that difficult."

"What is your plan?"

"There is a mixture … it can take away a man's passion. If he does not have her, then he cannot fall in love with her."

Hürrem allowed herself a tight smile. "Excellent. Can you get what you need?"

"I believe there is an apothecary in the bazaar who has what I need."

"Then I will send one of the pages to get it for you straight away." After it was arranged, Hürrem settled herself back on the divan. As Muomi was leaving she called her back. "Fetch the Kislar Aghasi for me," she said. "Tell him I need to talk with him urgently."

\*\*\*

Julia was taken first to the Keeper of the Baths. She was shaved and every part of her examined minutely for hair. Then the gedicli bathed her in water scented with jasmine and orange and her hair was shampooed with henna. Afterwards another girl coated her entire body with a mixture of warm rice flour and oil. Heated water steamed in pots beside her to keep the mud pack warm and supple.

When the Kislar Aghasi arrived, he found her sitting naked on the edge of the marble while several gedicli fussed around her, each one of them focused on a limb, or an ear, or an eye and the only sound was the rustle of their linen chemises.

Julia looked blank and slightly dazed. She let them prod and prime her, paint the nails of her toes, slip aloe under her tongue to sweeten her breath, darken her eyelids with kohl. Another knelt to dye her pubis with henna, in the traditional manner. Julia did not co-operate, nor did she resist. She might as well have been a child's doll.

I wonder what she is thinking? Abbas thought. Is she back in Venice, on her loggia with her needlepoint, watching the gondoliers on the Grand Canal? Does she sometimes sit with me under the purple canopy, does she ever think of me - or is that only my vanity wishing it so?

\*\*\*

Hürrem had a handkerchief bunched in her fist, and she twisted it around and around her fingers. Her eyes were red and swollen. Abbas almost felt sorry for her.

He executed a temennah, his right hand touching his heart, his lips and forehead. "My Lady, you wished to see me."

"What am I to do, Abbas?"

"My lady?"

"The Lord of Life has chosen to spend the night with another of his houris."

"It is his right, my Lady. You should not upset yourself. You are still second kadin. Nothing can change that."

Hürrem dabbed at her eyes. "What is her name?"

Abbas hesitated, suddenly alarmed. "As I said, my Lady, you should not upset yourself over trifles."

"I did not ask your advice, Abbas, I asked you her name."

She is like a small child, he thought; she seems to cry but her tears are actually rage. I cannot pretend I do not know who the gözde is, for I know the name of every girl in here. If I do not tell her, I will make an enemy of the second most powerful woman in the Harem. Besides, she could easily find out from someone else. "Her name is Julia. A very dull girl. Italian. She can barely speak a word of our language and though she has a pretty face she is spectacularly stupid. You can rest easy."

Hürrem tossed the handkerchief on the floor. Ah, I see we are done with that charade, he thought. When she spoke her voice was icy. "Do not presume to tell me when I may rest and when I may not. In fact, Kislar Aghasi, remember your place and do not advise me on anything. All you need to do is answer my questions."

"Yes, My Lady."

"I wish to see the Lord of Life. Could he perhaps sup with me tonight?"

"I do not think that is possible. When a Sultan chooses a girl ..."

"Again, I did not ask your opinion!" Her voice was like a whip crack "How many times must I tell you? You presume too much, Kislar Aghasi!"

"A thousand apologies."

"As I said, I wish to see the Lord of Life. Tonight. I did not ask if it were possible. I only meant that you should arrange it for me. He is still in the saraya, visiting with the Valide, is that not correct?"

"As you say, My Lady ..."

"Then arrange for him to dine with me tonight. Tell him I am contrite for those things I have said to him most recently and I wish to make my peace."

"But it may not be possible to-"

A long sigh, that reminded him of a snake rising to strike. "Abbas, do you remember what happened to the last Kiaya of the Robes? Perhaps you were not part of our Harem family then?"

His mouth was suddenly very dry. "I am not sure I follow you."

She stood up and walked up to him. "Yes you do, Abbas. Even if you were not here, no doubt someone has told you the story. The old fool who did your job before you would certainly have remembered and passed it on. This woman had the temerity to cross me. She kicked me, when I was one of her charges in the sewing room. Do you know what I did to her?"

"You had her leg cut off."

"Indeed. Imagine it, what it must be like when the  brings down his axe. They say they heard her screams in Üsküdar. What do you think it's like for her now, living like a cripple in the provinces? Yet the poor woman did not offend me near as much as you offend me now."

 "I meant no offence ..."

"I do not want your contrition, or your excuses. Tonight the Sultan may sleep with another, but do you know whose pillow he will share tomorrow? When a woman has a man between her legs, Abbas, she has his undivided attention. So I suggest you remember what happened to the Kiaya and make sure the Lord of Life sups with me tonight."

"Yes, my Lady."

Abbas was dismissed.

He came out sweating and leaned against the wall, panting for breath as if he had just run up three flights of stairs. How he hated himself for his weakness. Why was his life yet so important to him that he should give in to her whims like this? But they would not kill me, he thought. That is not their way. How can you enjoy someone's suffering when they are dead. Even though Hürrem  does not see her old Kiaya, she still likes to think on how she still tortures her, far away in Diyabakir.

So, all right, tonight he would be her puppet. But let her harm Julia and the worm would turn.

# CHAPTER 46

"She wants to dine with me? Tonight?"

"I think she believes you are punishing her. She wishes to show her contrition."

"This is my Harem. Does she not understand what that means?" Suleiman fidgeted. "No, Kislar Aghasi, it is impossible."

"Perhaps if you explained this to her yourself. She has become accustomed to your exclusive use of her, I am afraid. To ignore her now would be only to accentuate her suffering."

"You explain it to her. You seem to have a better understanding of her moods."

Abbas could smell his own sweat. *I cannot push him too hard or he will have the guards throw me out and perhaps put me to the bastinado. But if I do not leave here with his agreement to this excruciating arrangement, I shall forfeit one of my feet to Hürrem 's temper. How miserable is my life?*

"My Lord, a few kind words from you at supper would perhaps save you a lengthy speech at breakfast."

Suleiman sighed. "Do you really think so, Kislar Aghasi?"

"I am convinced of it."

Suleiman drummed his fingers on the back of the divan. "How do you know so much about women?"

"I spend every day amongst hundreds of them. I have almost begun to think like one."

Suleiman raised an eyebrow at that. "Oh, very well. But tell her I cannot stay long."

*God be praised,* Abbas thought, *I have that witch off my back.* "I know she will greatly appreciate your gesture, my Lord."

"I hope so, Kislar Aghasi. I hope so."

# CHAPTER 47

"I prepared the meal myself," Hürrem said.

Suleiman surveyed the feast; vine leaves stuffed with milk-fed lamb, small pieces of spit-roasted chicken, shish ketabi, revani cakes, halwa and sherbets. Suleiman picked at the food. Guilt had taken away his appetite and that only made him angrier with her; she had no right to make him feel this way in his own Harem.

"You do not like it?" she said.

"I do not feel hungry."

"You must eat something," she said and picked up one of the pieces of chicken and put it in his mouth. "Muomi brought me some new spices to try."

He studied her face. She had been crying, that was obvious, and her cheerfulness now was so evidently forced.

"Shall I make a shadow play?" she asked him.

"Not now."

"What about some music. Shall I fetch my viol?"

He shook his head and pushed his plate away.

She pushed it back. "Please eat, my Lord."

"I told you, I am not hungry!"

"Have I given you offence?"

"There is no offence. I am not hungry and there is an end to it."

"There are times I have been presumptuous in your presence. In my passion for you I have forgotten my place. I wish to acknowledge my fault." Hürrem now dropped her mask of conviviality. She stared at her hands and looked thoroughly miserable.

Suleiman wanted to reach out and comfort her but that would not do, he could not let her see that his pain was as great as hers. She should understand that as much as he loved her, he had a duty to Islam and the Osmanlis, and she had a duty to him. Duty was a hard lesson to learn and it was as well that she learned it now.

"It has pleased me to make you my sanctuary from time to time, but you would do well to remember that I am still your seigneur and I will not abide jealousy from you." He stood up. Without warning Hürrem crawled across the carpets and kissed his feet. Suleiman was shocked. He had not wanted to humiliate her like this.

"Hürrem ," he whispered, "I am bound by my duty. You must understand this."

He left her lying there on the carpet. He told himself he had taught her a hard lesson. He hoped that this time she would remember it.

\*\*\*

"After he had gone Muomi entered and knelt to retrieve the dishes on the table.

"He hardly touched his food," Hürrem said. "Will it be enough?"

"It only takes a little," Muomi said. "The only thing standing in his bedroom tonight will be the two guards at the door."

\*\*\*

Abbas did not recognize her.

They had dressed her in a rose-pink silk chemise with blue harem pantaloons and a headdress glittering with emeralds, diamonds and opals. Her face was concealed beneath a bead-fringed yashmak. All that was visible was her eyes, and they had been completely ringed with kohl. Her wrists and ankles were dripping with gold.

Corpo di Dio, Abbas thought. It is like they hung the entire contents of the Treasury on her.

As she rose to her feet, a gedicli held out a heavy cloak for her to put on. Once she was dressed in it the broad hood and long sleeves hid her completely, so that not even a finger was visible.

He escorted her down the winding passageways to a narrow door. A coach waited for her in the cobblestone courtyard. They climbed in and set off in silence. The last time you were alone with me like this, he thought, I pulled back your veil and asked you to run away to Spain with me.

"Are you frightened?" he said.

"Yes."

"Don't be. The Sultan is a gentle man, he means you no harm."

She was shaking somewhere inside the mountain of brocade and jewels. "What must I do?" she murmured and he heard the panic in her voice.

"Have you ever lain with a man?"

"No, never!"

"Never? But you were on your way to meet your husband when you were captured."

"He never touched me the whole time we were married."

Corpo di Dio! There was no God! If he was, then he was a sadist and a tyrant! Why else would He bring together a virgin and the eunuch who loved her unless it was for sport?

So how could he help her, even now? "You must simply do everything he says. If it is your first time, it may hurt a little, but the depilatory hurts more, so they tell me. Be agreeable and try at all costs to please him. You know what to do when I leave you alone with him?"

"The Kiaya has told me many times. I remembered it exactly the first time."

"I am sure you did."

"Why did he choose me?"

"Because you are the most beautiful woman in the world," he heard himself say, and thought he had given himself away and, mortified, he kept his silence afterwards. The carriage drove through the gates of the Sublime Porte.

\*\*\*

Suleiman lay on the bed in a simple white robe. His turban, though, was magnificent, the plume of a white egret fastened to it with a cluster of white diamonds and rubies. The room was fragrant with the frankincense burning in the brass censers that hung from the ceiling.

Abbas touched his head to the carpet three times. "Great Lord."

"Kislar Aghasi," Suleiman said, as was the protocol, "I have mislaid my handkerchief. Do you know who has it?"

"Yes my Lord. I will have her bring it to you."

Abbas raised his great bulk from the floor and took long enough about it. Suleiman sensed there was something amiss with his Chief Black Eunuch. He was sweating heavily though it was not a hot night and his eyes had a frozen look about them. He had seen that look sometimes after a battle in men who had endured too much. He hoped the Kislar Aghasi was not sickening, he would be a hard man to replace.

Abbas went to the door and ushered in a small, cloaked figure. He removed her ferijde and whispered something to her. He pushed her forward and then hovered anxiously by the door.

"Go," Suleiman said to him.

The door shut softly and they were alone.

The girl took out the handkerchief he had placed across her shoulder that morning, fell to her knees and crawled on all fours to the bed. She lifted the coverlet, raised it to her forehead and to her lips, and crept up the bed, exactly as the Kiaya of the Baths had told her to do.

Suleiman closed his eyes and wished with all his soul that he were with Hürrem .

# CHAPTER 48

Suleiman rose naked from the bed, staring accusingly at the girl who lay curled on her side beside him. The candlelight cast long shadows over the hills and valleys of her body. She was ... perfect. Too perfect perhaps, that was the trouble.

He threw on a silk robe and went to the open window. A yellow moon sat fat and low over the Asian shore. A witching moon.

She was beautiful, this Venetian. Her body was like satin to the touch, a paradise for the eyes, yet he had been unable to raise any passion for her. He had no appetite tonight at all. I might as well have been ... Abbas!

Something ... someone ... has made a eunuch of the Sultan of the Osmanlis! Fear and rage and confusion tumbled over inside him. This had never happened to him before, and it could never be allowed to happen again. The girl watched him from the bed, doe-eyed. Could it really be that she did not know what was wrong? She had not uttered a word the whole time. Perhaps what Abbas said was right, she was stupid as an ox, and could not speak a word of Turkish anyway.

But one day she would learn, if she stayed long enough. And what would she say about him then, when the other Harem girls what it was like to lie with the Sultan?

The trouble was, she was not like his Hürrem . She had no tricks, there were no soft moans and feathery touches to encourage him. She had just laid there, and offered him her beauty, as if that was a precious currency in his Harem.

He wondered if any woman could stir him again now after Hürrem . What if it was witchery? Better to be mesmerized by Hürrem  than humiliated by a Gaiour.

He could not let this get out, could not let her giggle to her fellow odalisques that the Lord of Life and the Possessor of Men's Necks had been unable to bull her.

He went to the door and threw it open. "Kislar Aghasi!" The halberdiers standing guard at the door jerked with fright. "Where is the Chief Black Eunuch?" he shouted at them. One of them ran off to find him.

Suleiman slammed the door behind him and went back to the bed. He picked up the girl's clothes and flung them at her. "Get dressed!"

A few moments later Abbas appeared in the doorway, his eyes wide with fright. Suleiman pointed to the Italian. "Get her out of here!"

"She does not please you, my Lord?"

"GET HER OUT!" He grabbed Julia's arm - she had on only her harem pants and a silk chemise - and dragged her across the carpets and hurled her through the door. Then he snatched a yataghan from one of the halberdier's belts and went back inside, slamming the door behind him. He held the point of the blade to the Kislar Aphasias chin. A thin trickle of blood oozed and ran down his neck.

"She is to speak to no one when she leaves here. No one, do you understand? And if she is alive tomorrow morning your head will be feeding the crows on the Gate of Felicity. Do you understand me?"

Abbas could not speak. He nodded.

"Now get out!"

***

Abbas stumbled through the cloisters of the Topkapi Saraya, a sealed parchment clutched in his hand. He found the Aga of the Messengers, whispered his instructions and slipped something into his palm as added incentive to complete the task quickly. He had to get this message across the Bosphorus to Ludovici now. Immediately. Did he understand?

Yes, Kislar Aghasi.

Julia was locked up in a cell below the Ortakapi. It was nearly midnight which meant that by the time Ludovici received the missive he would have less than five hours to make his preparations. It might not be enough time.

I will defy him, Abbas thought, defy the Sultan. What will they do to me for that? But if I do not arrange her execution she will die anyway, they will give some other slave the job and he will make sure it is done promptly and well. This is her best chance, her only chance.

"Julia," he muttered as he ran back to the palace, "Julia, what have you done?"

# CHAPTER 49

Just before dawn Abbas led Julia through the gate at the Bosphorus wall, and down the stone steps to the water's edge. Something made him look up. He saw a flock of white birds that the Stamboulis called the Damned Souls wheeling in the sky above them. The strange thing about these birds was that they never made any sound; even the beat of their wings was silent. No one ever saw them roosting or feeding; they just seemed to drift over the black waters night and day. It was said they contained the souls of the houris who had been drowned in the waters below.

This was the traditional way for a Sultan to be rid of his brother's wives when he assumed the throne, or to punish a girl who had somehow found a way to get pregnant by one of the white eunuchs. The mud at the bottom of the harbor must be thick with the whitening bones of former wives and odalisques.

Now you, Julia.

She had been crying all night and the kohl had run down her cheeks, making her look like a djinn. Her braids hung in a tangle round her face. She wore only her chemise and harem pants and she hugged her arms to her chest, shivering in the cold of the morning. He could see the gooseflesh on her.

"Where are we going?" she asked him.

He had two of the bostanji-bashi's men with him, they were there to report that the job had been done correctly. He intended to give them no cause for doubts. "You will not be returning to the Eski Saraya," he said. He took her arm and pulled her down the bank to the waiting caïque.

"What's happening?"

"Just do as you are told."

He slung her into the boat. She looked down then and saw the sack. She must have realized by now, Abbas thought. He took a silver cord from the folds of his pelisse and tied her hands behind her.

"Please, no," she whispered.

He put her feet in the sack and tugged it up around her hips. There was a pile of smooth stones in the stern and he placed them in the bottom of the sack. Then he lifted it over her head and knotted it with rope.

He threw her on her back. "Don't struggle until you hit the water," he whispered to her in Italian. "It will be all right. Trust me."

Then he stepped out of the caïque and joined the two bostanji in the other boat.

*** 

They rowed past the promontory of Seraglio Point and the sombre sea walls of the palace, towing the caïque to a spot roughly midway between the peninsula and the Asian side. It was still dark but he knew dawn could not be far off. They had to do this now. Mist swirled over the water.

The bostanji decked their oars and they drifted with the current. Abbas looked at the tiny boat drifting behind them, illuminated by the lantern at the stern. The shapeless bundle was still struggling in the sack so that the boat rocked gently in the water.

"Take the lines," Abbas said. The bostanji picked up the two ropes that trailed over the stern and twisted them, so that the caïque began to roll and then take water. Finally it listed to starboard and capsized. There was a splash as the sack tumbled into the water; a rash of bubbles floated on the surface and then was gone.

The bostanji cut the ropes. Abbas sat slumped in the bow and let the two assassins row him back to Seraglio Point. Then they heard a splash behind them. The bostanji looked over their shoulders.

"A fishing boat," he said to them.

"They're out early in the fog."

"You want to go back?" he said to them casually and held his breath.

Then they heard nets going into the water. It was too misty anyway, he could see them thinking, they risked a collision. And besides, what was the point now? They shrugged and kept rowing. The morning kept her secrets.

*** 

Julia gasped as she hit the water, the stones in the sack dragging her feet first to the bottom. She knew it was pointless to struggle; she had resolved to suck in the water straight away, get it over with quickly; but as soon as she felt the caïque capsize she had instinctively breathed in a lungful of air and held it.

She struggled with the ropes behind her back, and to her astonishment, they fell away.

She fell fast through the water and it felt as if someone had pierced her ears with two hot needles. She tried not to scream against the pain and lose her last breath of air. She tore at the sack and the ropes that the Kislar Aghasi had tied around it fell away.

She struck out blindly, that one last breath of air carrying her up, as her chest pumped in agony. As she broke the surface she tried to take another breath but her mouth and nose was full of water and she started to choke. She paddled furiously at the water but felt herself going under. Then a hand reached out for her but she was too exhausted to keep herself afloat any longer and everything went black.

# CHAPTER 50

The carumasali glided silently through the water. Abbas had told him in the letter to look for his riding lights in the darkness and hope for the best. There would be no other boats trying to navigate Seraglio Point at that time of night.

The mist that clung to the water had made it both easier and harder; harder to for him to see them, but easier because they could not see him. They did not even dare breathe, every small sound carried over the flat water as if they were in a church.

Only the creak of timber and lines.

Then he saw it, a light blinking close by, and the helmsman pulled the tiller hard over. They could not come too close, not until they knew she was in the water.

He didn't care about the woman, for God's sake, he hardly knew her. But he knew what this meant to Abbas. It was his hope of redemption. And in some strange way it was his hope also.

They all heard the splash, and for a moment he saw the caïque silhouetted against the mist, and then she was gone. The assassins dropped their oars in the water.

He heard Abbas say something to the men with him.

Then she came up, right beside them, gasping. At that moment the helmsman lit a lantern and shouted a command to his fellow, who hoisted the nets over the other side, making as much noise as he could about it. Abbas knelt down and reached out a hand for her, and dragged her to the side. The sailor let go of the nets and ran over to help him pull her onboard.

She lay there, blue and still. He thought she was dead and started to shake her only thing he could think of do. She vomited water on the deck.

Her face was a mess of kohl and paint. She looked pitiful, but at least she was breathing. She was cold and he wrapped her in a blanket. Hardly anything to stir a man to risk his entire life, he thought. Just a small thin girl, ringing wet. He held her to warm her up and wondered if she would still be alive when they made the shore.

\*\*\*

A fresh breeze ruffled the Bosphorus, the cries of the muezzin calling the faithful to prayer. The tower of the Divan rose through the mist, sunlight glinting off the spire. A beautiful morning to die.

Did I do enough? He wondered. What if the knot he had tied in the sack was too tight, what if she did not get out in time? What if Ludovici did not find her in the fog?

A messenger arrived and placed a scroll in his hands. He broke the seal and read it through quickly. It was from Ludovici. The goods had arrived safely and were in good order. He would put them in the warehouse until he was ready to ship them on.

He swayed on his feet, put a hand out to steady himself against the sill.

"Is the Kislar Aghasi unwell?" one the pages asked him.

Abbas nodded. "The Kislar Aghasi is quite well," he said and took the letter to the fire and burned it.

\*\*\*

The Valide was restless and could not sleep. She roamed her apartments picking up vases and studying them, running her hands over the ceramics and the silks of the divans, as if trying to imprint each on her memory, so that she might remember it.

I can hardly remember a time when I was not here, she thought. I cannot even recall the day they came for me.

She went out to the terrace. It was cool, and there was a yellow stain to the sky over the Asian side. The sun would rise soon. I wonder if I will see it set, she thought.

"Are you all right, Crown of Veiled Heads," one of her maid servants asked her.

"I have to go away for a while," she said. She felt suddenly light headed. The strength went out of her and she wondered if any of it had been really worth all the trouble. No one will remember me when I am gone. At least I have given the Osmanlis a fine Sultan.

The room began to spin and she staggered. She heard her gedicli scream as she toppled to the floor. Oh this won't do, she thought. There's no dignity in this.

\*\*\*

She had been propped up on pillows, while her servants hovered. Look at her, like a dried out husk. She was lost all in the bedclothes. No one ever looked so old as when they were dying. There was no artifice to support her now. Her gedicli had applied kohl to her eyes and put a little taplock on her head but it had only made her look even more ghastly. The Kislar Aghasi was there. He looked terrified, as well he might.

"Is she dying?" she asked him.

" My Lady, she cannot move or talk. She sleeps most of the time. Who knows when Almighty God will call her home?"

"She cannot talk?"

He shook his head.

"She he has no way of communicating with us?"

"We put a pen in her hand but she is unable to use it. The fingers on her left hand twitch a little, that is all. "

"Can she understand what is said to her?"

"I don't know. It appears so. She slips in and out of this world."

Hürrem  smiled. "You see how quickly the world turns, Kislar Aghasi. Just the other night you were ready to defy me."

"I should never defy you My Lady."

"No, you never should. It would be unwise. In future mind your manners better. Your life is in my hands now."

"Of course."

"Where is the Sultan?"

"He has just left. He is most distressed."

Hürrem  went to the  bed. "You are sure she cannot speak? I would like to say goodbye to her."

"She has had an apoplexy. It has taken away all her powers."

Hürrem  stared at the old lady. "I want everyone out of the room," she said to Abbas.

"My lady?"

He thinks I am going to put a pillow over her head, he thought. Look at her. I don't need to.

"The law says that the Kislar Aghasi and her gedicli should stay with her at all times."

"Kislar Aghasi, do you remember what I just said to you?"

He rapped out a short command to the maidservants and ushered them out of the door. He hesitated.

"You too, Kislar Aghasi."

He went out, no doubt praying that the Valide was still alive when he came back in.

***

Hürrem bent over the bed. "They tell me you cannot speak," she said to her. Saliva had pooled on her cheek and against the pillow, but her eyes were bright. "That's it, open your eyes. Look at me. It's me, Hürrem ."

Yes, she understands me well enough, Hürrem thought.

"I am going to tell you a secret." She moved closer so that her lips were close to the old woman's ear. "Mustapha will never be Sultan. I promise you. Do you remember the time he fell ill and no one ever knew who poisoned him? I will tell you who did that. It was me. I found a way then and I shall do it again but next time I shall not fail. I am going to be the next Valide. And when I am I shall destroy your son and even in Paradise you will not find rest. What do you think of that?"

The old lady tried to move. Hürrem laughed at her. "You didn't suspect. Perhaps you are not as clever as you thought you were. Kislar Aghasi!"

The Chief Black Eunuch rushed in. He must have been standing with his ear to the door. Never mind, he could not have heard her and would not dare say a word even if he had.

"What is wrong with her? I think she is having another seizure."

There was froth on the old woman's lips and she was writhing as if she was trying to get off the bed. Abbas called for the gedicli and they tried to hold her down.

"What is happening?" Hürrem said.

"I don't know, I am not a physician, My Lady."

"She looks like she is trying to say something," Hürrem said. "Does it look that way to you Kislar Aghasi? Something has upset her a great deal. I hope it was nothing I said to her. She looks like a fish flopping about in the bottom of the boat. It's unseemly. Tell your girls to try and do something will you?"

"They are doing their best."

"You should send another message to the Lord of Life. He should be here if he finds it distressing or not. I do not think she is long for this world."

"I shall do so at once."

"I hope he gets here before she dies. It would be a shame for him to miss it."

She gave the old woman's hand a last reassuring squeeze and went out.

# CHAPTER 51

"It was him wasn't it?" She stood at the water's edge staring at the lights flickering on in the palace. She was wrapped in a fur cloak but she could not stop shivering.

"Yes," Ludovici said.

"What happened to him? It was my father, wasn't it?"

"Abbas got a letter. Lucia gave it to me and said it came from you. I had no cause to think otherwise. So in one respect I was the instrument of his downfall. He was lured to the Ponte Antico and taken to a ship in the harbor …" His voice trailed off.

"How did he not die after what they did to him?"

"He was lucky or unlucky depending on how you see it. I have been told by those who know about these things that there is a high mortality rate for those who are razored in this way. I cannot imagine what he has been through."

"So my father did this to him?"

"It seems so."

" And yet he still loves me?"

"It was hardly your fault, madam. You were innocent of this and yes it seems he has carried his love for you even here to this place."

"How long did you know about this?"

" He has been here in the Harem for five years, I have been in Pera for three. But he only came to visit me when you arrived in the Harem. He asked me for help in getting you out but at the time he had no plan on how to do it. When I received his message I had only a few hours to act. Because of my business I was able to procure a small caramusali and the two Greeks I brought with me this morning to help rescue you."

"I need to see him again."

"I don't think he wants that."

"But I have to. I did not even recognize him. That must have been excruciating for him."

" Yes, I cannot imagine what that was like for him. But I cannot command him to come back here. I imagine that he does not want to see you, after what has been done to him. They tell me the excessive weight is something to do with ... the operation, if we might call it that."

"And the scar on his face?"

"He tells me that was something that happened in the struggle. It became infected afterwards and that is why he looks as he does."

Julia hung her head. "He was such a beautiful boy."

"He still is."

She smiled at that. "What will they do him when they find out he has tricked the Sultan?"

"Knowing Abbas, they will not find out."

"I hope not. And it was brave of you, also. to do what you did for me."

"I did it for him. And the courage - I think the courage was all his. You know, in Venice, I always scoffed at him. I vowed that I should never fall in love with any woman. I thought it fanciful and weak and I tried many times to dissuade him from his pursuit of you."

"You were right to do it. It would have saved him so much pain."

"No, I was wrong."

"How can you say that? Look at him now!"

"Don't pity him, he would hate that. And there is no need to pity him. No matter what they did to him, they could not take away his courage or his honor. He honored you tonight and in doing so he has scolded me for my petty life. For all the women I have, I have never loved like he has. I am ... envious of him. He knows more than I will ever know about what it is to live."

\*\*\*

Few slept soundly in the Eski Saraya. Sirhane lay on her side, her pillow wet with tears. Cehangir moaned and tossed in his bed, haunted by nightmares. Meanwhile Suleiman knelt distraught beside his mother's bed and when she died he uttered a small cry. Ibrahim thought he heard something, as he paced the terrace of his palace near the Hippodrome. Gülbehar thought she heard it, too.

It sounded like a ghost, or a warning. Mustapha shivered, as if a ghost had touched him. A shadow passed across the moon. He stopped to listen, but there was only silence. Perhaps it was just an owl, he thought.

Abbas stood at the window of his tiny cell and looked across the Golden Horn to Galata. "I promise you I will love you forever," he said.

If you love her until next week I will give you two gold ducats.

I feel sorry for you, Ludovici. You feel nothing inside. But one day you will, life will seek you out and make you feel again. As for me, I shall find the greatest part of me in loving truly.

She was safe tonight, sleeping sound in Pera. Oh I may not be a man any more but tonight I shall sleep sound in mine. Antonio Gonzaga robbed me of a lifetime in your arms, he thought. But unlike him at least I shall die a good man and there are not many complete men who can say that.

He took out the small velvet pouch that had arrived that afternoon from the Venetian quarter, sent by messenger. He opened the drawstring and emptied the contents into his palm.

Two gold ducats. For the first time since he arrived at the Harem he smiled.

# CHAPTER 52

There was snow on the gate of the Ba'ab-i-Humayun when Suleiman returned from the Lands of War. He rode stiffly, deaf to the cheers of the yeniceris and the enthusiastic crowds that lined the Divan Yolu to welcome him back.

Where was the glory? Suleiman thought. This time they had not even got as far as Vienna. Ibrahim had been stalled for over a month by a tiny garrison of soldiers at Guns, and the campaign that was to take Austria and lure the Holy Roman Emperor into a decisive battle petered out into a series of cavalry raids and retribution between his generals over who was to blame for the fiasco.

He returned in mourning. The Valide, his mother, was dead. Though he mourned her, a part of him felt strangely liberated. Even as he said his prayers for her he felt the burden lifting from his shoulders. There was no one who could scourge him with duty now.

The European campaign had been an exercise in futility; the interlude with the Italian houri had been a disaster. It was abundantly clear to him now who was his wisest counselor, both on the battlefield and in bed. She was the only one he could really trust.

He had been away far too long.

Hürrem , bewitch me again.

# PART 5

## THE PASSAGE OF DUST

# CHAPTER 53

## Topkapi Saraya, Stamboul 1535

When should I kill my sons? Suleiman wondered.

Do I have it in me to do it?

My father did, that was his legacy and his endowment to me. Should I be less of a father to Mustapha?

Yes, he is the shahzade, the chosen. But if he attains to the throne he will have to kill off all other aspirants if he is to sleep easy in his bed. Selim will not be a loss. But what of poor little Çehangir? The boy can hurt no one. He is crippled and his sweet nature will be no threat to anyone. Would you toss him to the chief high executioner to strangle?

And Hürrem, my sweet Hürrem; what will happen to her? Mustapha's mother will have her thrown in the Bosphorus the moment he takes the throne. Gülbehar nearly took off her face once in the Harem. They say that now she grows fat and lazy in Manisa and rails about my little russelana all the time and calls her a witch.

Not much mercy there.

So what shall I do? Shall I kill them or leave the problem to my oldest son after I am dead? How will Almighty God judge me for my cowardice?

And if I do kill them, when should I do it?

And what about their mother, the only woman I ever truly loved?

*\*\*\**

On the other side of the Bosphorus, Ludovici Gambetto sent his concubine scurrying from the room, preferring his own company tonight. He stood on the terrazzo and stared at Julia Gonzaga's window. There was no light on; he imagined she was asleep.

He remembered how he had pulled her from the water that morning three years ago. The first time he had touched her she was cold as marble. She had remained that way ever since; beautiful, cold and lifeless.

He had brought her back here to the palazzo, wrapped in blankets, hidden her from everyone. Soon afterwards she had fallen ill with a fever and he thought she would not survive. How cruel that would have been for Abbas, who had risked a terrible death to save her. But she had lived, though for months afterwards she barely spoke.

Ever since she had dressed and behaved as a widow, grieving for the Sultan's Chief Black Eunuch. In Venice, their encounters had been perhaps no more than an adventure; after learning what he had done for her, and how much he had lost in loving her, he suspected she had now fallen in love with him too.

Well, too late, for either of them. She has passed from one gilded prison to the next, he thought. Abbas's punishment for trying to steal her from her father was to be castrated by cutthroats at her father's hire and sold as a slave; his further punishment was to have her captured by corsairs and be her gaoler in Suleiman's pretty prison there on the other side of the Horn. And now here she was confined once more; untouched, unwed, but at least unharmed.

What was he to do with her? He had preserved her life here among the gardens and gilt rooms of his palazzo in the Venetian quarter. He supposed at first he had hoped she might grow to like him a little and take him into her confidence, but in all this time she had only ever treated him with the forbearing respect, as if he were a kindly gaoler. He even wondered if her experiences at the hands of the corsairs and the Turke had turned her mind.

Nothing I can do, he thought, for my best friend, trapped over the water in the Sultan's harem" or for this remote and enchanting woman. But I will somehow find a way to make this right, for all of us.

# CHAPTER 54

## The Eski Saraya

A gediçli ushered her through the apartment. Güzül was impressed, despite herself. Hürrem now had her own garden with a marble fountain and an aviary with nightingales, canaries and some birds she had never seen before, large hook-nosed creatures with feathers of red, green and royal blue. It was whispered in the bedesten that she had even been presented with a bed from Amoy in China, made from ivory, and inlaid with sandalwood and large pieces of pink coral. It was supposed to have cost more than ninety thousand scudi, a fortune in itself.

Hürrem lay face down on a slab of marble, which was warmed from below by the palace boilers, while Muomi massaged her neck and shoulders. Her private hammam, Güzül noted, was as large as the Grand Vizier's audience chamber.

She executed a ceremonial sala'am on the floor, and waited on her knees for Hürrem to acknowledge her presence.

Hürrem blinked open one eye. "Ah, Güzül."

"Would my lady honour me so as to examine my poor wares?"

Hürrem assented with a slight movement of her head. Güzül bent down and unknotted the green silk handkerchief that she carried in her arms and spread the assortment of ribbons and lace trinkets in front of her, repositioning each one so that it might catch the morning sun to better advantage.

She still retains her slim body, Güzül noted. She looks like a cat, sleek and self satisfied. Her eyes were half closed in torpor. You would not think she has had five babies. By all accounts she had a wet nurse for all of them and lost all attachment to them after the cord was cut.

The moist strands of red-gold hair clung to her cheeks. It was as if the green eyes were watching her through stalks of dry grass, a predator lying in wait.

"So how is your mistress?" Hürrem asked her.

Güzül felt the blood drain from her face. "Mistress, my Lady?"

"Rose of Spring."

Güzül avoided the terrible green eyes. She rearranged the baubles on the carpet in front of her. "My Lady is mistaken."

"My lady is never mistaken," Hürrem said, and yawned. "You are Gülbehar's creature. You come to Stamboul to bring messages for her and spy on the Harem. These trinkets you sell are just a ruse, are they not?"

Güzül said nothing. She waited.

"Don't be afraid. All I want is a little information from you. This is the only merchandise that you have that I am interested in."

Hürrem scratched the calf of one leg with the big toe of the other. She stretched and Güzül watched the muscles of her buttocks tense; they were still small and hard like a boy's. *While Gülbehar grows fat and lazy on sweetmeats in Manisa, Hürrem starves herself and drinks from some secret fountain of eternal youth. Or perhaps it is the potions this Muomi makes for her.*

"For instance, can you tell me who is my lady Gülbehar's friend in the court?"

Güzül knew she was trembling. It was impossible to stop it.

"Look at it this way. While it is true that you serve the woman who might one day become the mother of the next Sultan, that is tomorrow and you might not live that long. Tonight I shall be whispering to the Sultan in the quiet moments and if I choose, I might tell him that a certain gypsy peddler came to the Harem and called his favourite kadin a witch, to her face, and insulted her beyond all imagining."

Güzül put out a hand to steady herself. "My Lady?"

"The choice is yours. Think about it for a moment."

Hürrem closed her eyes and surrendered to Muomi's attentions. Güzül felt faint. *How long has this witch known about me? They said she could read minds.*

"Ibrahim," she murmured, as if by speaking his name in a whisper she could pretend she had not said it at all.

"Ah, the Chief Vizier," Hürrem said. "Who else could it be? But I wanted to hear it from your lips. He has never liked me. He is like a jealous lover, is that not so, Güzül?"

Güzül could not find her voice.

"You have a choice to make, old woman. You cannot serve two mistresses while you have only one life."

"My Lady, I will do anything …"

"Don't make the bargain before you know what it is. Come now, you have been a hawker all your life, you should know better than that."

"What would you have me do?"

"Over there, on the table, is a small stoppered bottle. There is a small amount of liquid inside it. I want you to put it in your robe and take it with you to Manisa. Then you must find a way to pour the contents into Mustapha's drink. Do you think you could do that, Güzül?"

Güzül groaned.

"A difficult choice, I understand. But before you rise from your knees, you will have made it. You or Mustapha. If it is you, I shall make sure your death is not swift. Three days hanging by a steel hook in the bostanji -bashi's yard should not be overlong. So, what is it to be?"

"It is impossible, my Lady, the food tasters sample everything ..."

"Ah, I see. You are stalling now, thinking that the Chief Vizier will save you. It is true that he also has the Sultan's ear. But there are other parts of the Sultan that are more desirable to possess and whoever holds them leaves him open to the greater persuasion. Who would you gamble on, in your situation?"

"My Lady, please, anything else ..."

"There is nothing else. What do you decide?"

She means it, Güzül thought. What am I to her? I have heard the Chief High Executioner can be very creative in his methods. They say three days in considered a quick death if he really puts his mind to it. "I will do what I can, my Lady."

"No, not quite good enough. You will do this for me or you will die. Do we understand each other?"

"But ..."

"It is a simple bargain, Güzül. I shall not be there to hear your screams and I shall sleep soundly in my bed."

Güzül watched as a string of saliva spilled from her mouth onto the carpet. God help me in my sorrow!

"Thank you for showing me your trinkets, but I am adequately provided for."

Güzül gathered up her jewels with trembling fingers and wrapped them inside a large handkerchief, carefully knotting the corners. Then she went to the marble table and picked up the pretty blue and white Iznik bottle. She left the room a much older woman than she was when she entered.

Hürrem closed her eyes and groaned softly as Muomi worked her strong hands into her neck muscles. I will have to settle with the Grand Vizier very soon, she thought. He wants Suleiman for his own.

But he is mine. I will share him with no one.

\*\*\*

The Divan was a long rectangular room, with low sofas round the walls. A wickerwork grilled window bulged from the end wall, hung with a curtain of black taffeta. It was known as "the dangerous window" for this was the place the Sultan might come to listen secretly to the proceedings of the Divan.

It meant that when the pashas came to report to him at the end of the day, they could hold back nothing for they could not know whether he had listened at the window that day or not.

Today he watched as Ibrahim listened to an Armenian trader's long complaint of some minor usury against a Jewish merchant. He wondered at his Vizier's endless capacity for detail. Thank God for men like him, he thought.

How far we ghazis have come! My ancestors spent their lives on the great plains of Anatolia, carrying everything with them and sleeping in goat-hide tents. Now the sons of Osman live in palaces, pray in the great church of the Aya Sofia that the Christians built and where the Emperor Justinian had prayed. Now he, their greatest son, was rebuilding this great city that stood at the gateway of Europe and Asia. He dreamed of a marble city that would establish Muslim civilization for all of time.

It was the task that God had intended for him. But fifteen years now he had been Sultan and he was tired of destruction; tired of jihad, tired of the endless wars demanded by his generals and his soldiers, tired of seeing bodies piled like windrows in the moats of enemy forts.

Let his Vizier guard the Empire from now on. Instead of warring he would give his people a civilization that would last a thousand years. He would rebuild Stamboul to the glory of Islam, give the Turks laws that would guarantee them peace and order, and bring these restless nomads home.

That was where greatness lay.

# CHAPTER 55

## Topkapi Saraya

To dine with Suleiman in his private apartments was a privilege that had been granted to no other man, but Ibrahim no longer anticipated the honour as he once did. Suleiman had become a tiresome companion, talking endlessly about the plans he had made with his builder, Sinan, for some new mosque. It seemed to him that his Sultan had forgotten that the lifeblood of the Empire was conquest. Why should he have to remind him of this? When a warrior forgot to saddle his horse and sharpen his sword, he became the prey and not the hunter.

After the killerji-bashi had removed the plates Ibrahim filled two crystal goblets with Cyprian wine and began to read aloud from the history of Alexander. He recited his march into Persia, the defeat of the Persian king Darius at Gaugamela, and the capture of Babylon.

Ibrahim paused in his reading and looked up at Suleiman. "We must go to Babylon too, my Lord."

Suleiman nodded. They had received news in the Divan just that day; the Persian Shah Tamasp had recaptured Babylon and killed or captured his entire garrison. As Defender of the Faith Suleiman could not ignore such a challenge to his authority.

Tamasp was a Shi'a, a heretic, who protected the rebel mullahs and allowed them to preach their ungodly doctrine in Mesopotamia and even into Armenia. They dared preach the infallibility of their own imams who in turn claimed a mystical interpretation of the Qu'ran. They offended him as no Gaiour ever could. After all, the only sin of a Christian was ignorance.

To have them now preaching their evil in the holy city of Baghdad was not to be borne.

"Why so solemn, my Lord?"

Suleiman sighed. "Must we always be rushing to the gates, Ibrahim? We subdue one attack, there is the sound of trumpets from another wall."

"It is the way of it for emperors and kings. It is what you were born for." How is it that I understand it so much better than he does?

"There is more to Empire than fighting wars. I want to leave behind something that will endure after the dust of armies has vanished over the horizon."

"There will always be armies, my Lord. Always." And thank God for it. What was a man if he did not have a saddle under him and the smell of leather and dust in his nostrils? Suleiman was getting too soft, too fond of his Harem.

No, too fond of Hürrem.

"I am tired of it Ibrahim."

"My Lord a man cannot be Sultan and live his life without conflict. He must subdue others or be subdued himself. It can never be otherwise."

"Then we are no better than dogs in the street."

"It was Mohammed who urged us to jihad, my Lord. When we go to the Lands of War we take the green banner of Islam with us."

"Mohammed, Ibrahim? What do you care for Islam?"

"It is my religion, my Lord."

"Religion is a convenience for you. You use it to justify what you love to do, which is go to war. Don't you think I know that, old friend?"

Yes all right, religion is for hypocrites and dusty old scholars, Ibrahim thought. But if you know this about me why do you entrust me with so much? "I am a faithful soldier of Islam."

"You are a good soldier and a loyal Vizier. That is enough for me. The rest is between you and God."

"You mock me, my Lord."

"You mock all of us."

No, you're wrong. I don't mock you. You I love like a brother. You enrage me but those things that anger me about you are also what I love. I love you for your gentleness and I love you because you need me. I have laid my dreams at your feet and you have allowed me to live every one of them.

"In a few days we will ride together under the green banner once more. The cool wind will blow away all your misgivings."

"No, Ibrahim, I did not wish to go to Vienna three years ago, and I was persuaded. Time proved me right in my estimations. For five months I watched our cannon sinking deeper into the mud under the walls of a fortress whose name even now I cannot remember. The Roman Emperor did not come to fight us as I said he would not. This time I will not be swayed. You will take my army to Persia alone."

Ibrahim stared at the floor in stony silence.

"Is this such a terrible burden? Other men would weep at such an honour."

"A Sultan's place is with his army."

"Do not lecture me on my duty!" And then, more gently: "Can you crush this Shah Tamasp and rid me of this meddlesome mosquito?"

"Of course."

"Then do it, Ibrahim. From now on, you will be my guardian at the gate."

"I wish that you would not do this."

"I have decided."

Ibrahim hesitated. It was time he was told; he had delayed the news long enough. "My Lord there is a matter you should know of ... a messenger came to me today from Manisa. There has been an attempt on the life of your son, Mustapha."

A sharp intake of breath. "Who brought you this news?"

"It was one of Gülbehar's couriers, my Lord. There is no mistake."

"What happened?"

"He sat down to dine with the captain of his personal bodyguard. The man drank some wine and fell ill abruptly. He died in agony an hour later."

"And Mustapha?"

"He had not yet drunk from his cup, praise be to God."

"Who did this?"

"There is no proof," Ibrahim said.

"That means you know. Who was it, Ibrahim?"

He avoided Suleiman's eyes. Let us see if he is so blind that he cannot see what stares the rest of us in the face. Suleiman reached over and grabbed his wrist. Ibrahim winced, he had forgotten how strong he was. "You are wrong," Suleiman hissed.

"My Lord, who else could it be?"

"It is another of Gülbehar's fantasies! Bring me one shred of proof!"

"My Lord, you have given her too much power! How often do I see you now? We no longer hunt, we eat together like this but rarely, she occupies your every waking minute."

"I see," Suleiman said. "So you are jealous."

"I am afraid of what is happening to you. The Suleiman I knew would never let his army go to battle without him."

"The Suleiman you knew was a boy who simply did what his father did. I am my own man now."

Ibrahim knew he had already pushed too far, but he could not hold his tongue any longer. He heard the blood drumming in his ears. "She wants Mustapha dead so one of her sons will be Sultan!"

Suleiman did not answer for a long time. When he did, his voice was devoid of emotion. "You have been my friend a long time, Ibrahim. Do not make me hate you."

"My Lord ..."

" ... Go now. I must think."

Ibrahim rose to his feet and left the room. Damn her! Perhaps he had already left it too late. If Suleiman's mother, the Valide, was still alive, she would have known how to bring him back from the edge. But there were no more restraints on his character now.

\*\*\*

The Enderun was the inner school of the palace, where the princes were groomed for lives of leadership along with the cream of the devshirme. Aside from the princes, whose blood had been diluted by generations of concubines, none of the other boys were Turks. The young Christian slaves who were brought there were taught that they no longer possessed any family, any country, or any future outside of the Sultan.

They learned the Qu'ran in Turkish, Arabic and Persian; they were trained in pike and lance throwing as well as music, embroidery and the care and training of falcons and dogs. They were taught good manners, leatherwork and weapon making as well as manicuring, haircutting and turban dressing.

Their lives were strictly regulated; they had a bath daily, and a manicure and pedicure every week. They were given a fresh handkerchief each day and a haircut once a month. Discipline was strict. The white eunuchs who were charged with their education looked for all the world to Selim like mummified old women.

Graduates of the Enderun learned not only how to become soldiers but were taught also all the principles of statecraft and courtly behaviour. For six years they would not leave the palace, undergoing a constant process of culling. The best would be inducted into the Palace system, as treasury clerks or masters of the wardrobe and might become pashas or governors in time. Others would become officers in the Spahis of the Porte, the Imperial Cavalry.

Only Selim and Bayezid and Çehangir attended the Enderun through hereditary right and not through merit, a distinction that was only painless for Bayezid, whose easy going charm and proficiency on horseback had earned him the respect and affection of his tutors and classmates.

For Selim, every day was a nightmare. He longed for the day when power would disguise his shortcomings. His only consolation for life's disfavour was Çehangir. He was seven years younger, a hunchback and a cripple. If God had been cruel to Selim He had been entirely vicious to Çehangir.

His crippled brother had been sent to the Enderun when he was eight years old. For amusement Selim had taken to following him across the courtyard every morning, trailing one leg, shoulder hunched, head bowed, imitating his curious lopsided walk. It won him some grudging laughter from his classmates and finding a softer target was the best means of deflecting ridicule from himself. Besides, Çehangir never complained. How could he? He already knew he was an embarrassment.

One day Bayezid saw him doing it. He was aping Çehangir as he went across the yard, lapping up the laughter from his audience, when suddenly everyone went quiet. Someone tripped him up and he found himself lying on his back, his younger brother standing over him, fists clenched.

Bayezid cuffed him smartly across the face. "That's our brother! What do you think you're doing?"

Selim scrambled to his feet, aware that every eye was on him. His cheeks burned with humiliation. He could not let his younger brother best him. He charged.

Bayezid stepped easily aside and tripped him again, throwing him headlong on the hard cobblestones. Selim yelled in pain. He thought he had broken his knee. He lay there sobbing.

"If I see you mocking our little brother again I'll break your head!" Bayezid hissed.

The other boys moved away, whispering and laughing, this time at him. After a while the pain eased and he sat up. He could barely straighten his leg and his elbow was bleeding. He wiped the bitter tears from his eyes.

The courtyard was empty now; only Çehangir remained., He shuffled over and offered Selim his hand. Selim ignored him and got to his feet by himself. He turned his back on him and limped away.

\*\*\*

Mohammed Dürgün had heard what they called him: The Man Who Never Smiled.

Yet there was nothing remarkable, or even fearsome, about him. He looked like any one of the hundred clerks in the palace.

He did not look up as Mohammed entered. He stared at the document on the table in front of him.

"You are Muhammad Dürgün?"

"I am."

"You are from Kirklareli?"

"Yes."

"Your father served at Mohaçs and the siege of Buda-Pesth?"

"He did." Mohammed hesitated, unsure what to do or say next. He hoped that what he had heard about this man was true or he had come all this way for nothing. "He died last year, from the pestilence."

"If so, then by law the lands return to the Sultan." Rüstem Defterdar took a quill from the desk and made a notation on the parchment in front of him.

"Is there ..." He paused not knowing how to say it. He rode two days to get here, just to try and save the lands Selim the Grim had given his father after the siege of Belgrade. "Is there not some way?"

Rüstem paused. "Your father's name was Hakim Dürgün?"

"Yes."

"According to my records you are mistaken. He is not dead. It says here he still lives. He should return to the Treasury the equivalent of one asper per sheep per year. Do you have any questions?"

"No, Defterdar."

"Then that is all."

He left the Defterdar's office, stunned at the simplicity of what had just happened. The Fatih's laws strictly forbade any fiefdom passing from father to son. Yet in the few moments he had been with the Defterdar, he had become the owner of his father's land - for a price. His father had been taxed at one asper per two head of sheep. Rüstem had doubled the tax in order to mislay the record of his father's death. Mohammed knew where that extra money would go.

Still, it was worth it.

He only wished Rüstem had looked up. He would have liked to have seen the colour of his eyes.

# CHAPTER 56

A path of coloured pebbles wound through the dappled shadows under the black cypress trees to a six-sided kiosk behind the Gate of Felicity. It dominated the selamlik gardens. The marble dazzled the eyes; even the windows were fretted with gold. The walls were inlaid with a faience of feathery leaves inhabited by fearsome chillins, their eyes set with rubies and majolica stones. The floor had been so carefully crafted by Suleiman's artisans that it appeared to be made from a single piece of rock crystal, instead of thousands.

A garland of honeysuckle dripped from the trellis. It was a paradise within a paradise.

Suleiman rested on a gold-embroidered mattress watching the sunlight dance from the damascened lantern hanging from the cupola above him. Hürrem lay beside him. He should have been at ease here but all he could think about was the news from Baghdad. Duty, he heard his mother whisper. Duty.

But where was his duty? To his yeniçeris or to his people? Going to war was like feeding raw meat to the dogs. Could his duty not rather be in laying the foundations for the future?

From the moment he had settled on the throne all eyes had turned to Mustapha to judge if he was capable of the succession. From the very moment of making you Sultan they are preparing you for death.

Hürrem reached up and stroked his cheek. "You are frowning again. What are you thinking about?"

"About Mustapha."

The smile flickered, like wind brushing a flame. "What is wrong, my lord?"

"I have distressing news. Someone tried to poison my son."

She stared back at him, eyes wide and candid. "He is all right?"

"Praise be to God, yes."

"Who did this?"

"We don't know." He watched her, looking for some clue. "Ibrahim accuses you."

"Of course he does. He thinks all the evil in the world comes through me."

"He thinks you want one of your sons to be Sultan."

"Well of course I do! Do you think Gülbehar will be gentle with me when Mustapha sits on the throne? Do you think I want all my boys throttled and end up there in the Horn, tied in a sack? I pray every day that God will be merciful and spare us. But Ibrahim flatters me if he thinks that I have the power, here in your Harem, to harm a great prince five days ride from Stamboul. And for all that I fear Mustapha, I could not harm him. He is your son and I could not cause you such pain. I would rather die first."

Suleiman said nothing.

Hürrem snatched the ceremonial dagger from the scabbard at his waist. She held it against the soft flesh of her wrist. The rubies studded in the handle glittered in the yellow afternoon sun.

"If you believe it of me, tell me to open my veins and I will do it. I would rather die than have you suspect it me of such a crime. If there is even a grain of doubt, say the word and I will save your bostanji  from blunting his sword."

Suleiman hesitated. He wanted to believe, with every fibre of his being he wanted to ...

Hürrem slashed downwards and blood spurted onto the pure white of her chemise and down her arm. Suleiman wrenched the dagger from her hand before she could cut herself again. "Hürrem!"

"No, I don't want to live anymore! Let me do it!"

He ripped the rich brocade of his own pelisse to bind the wound. Hürrem struggled in his arm, crying hysterically. He held her tight, rocking her in his arms, startled by what she had done. She would have bled to death if I had not stopped her! I wish Ibrahim had been here to see this. His pages ran to assist him and he carried her, still weeping and bleeding, back to the palace.

\*\*\*

By the flickering light of the candle Muomi carefully unwound the brocade around Hürrem's wrist and examined the wound. Hürrem watched her, her face shining with sweat.

"Is it bad?"

"The blade missed the main vein, my lady. If you had cut there, it would have been much worse." She redressed the wound with a poultice of herbs and put on a fresh linen bandage. "You must have cut very carefully."

Hürrem smiled weakly. I think I got carried away in the moment," she said. "But it was the only thing I could think of to do to convince him."

# CHAPTER 57

Hürrem smiled as the Kislar Aghasi - the Chief Black Eunuch - was ushered into her presence. Abbas knew that could be a good thing or a bad thing. The fact that she was laughing might mean anything. He imagined she would be in excellent spirits the day she ordered his execution.

Since the death of Hafise Sultan, Suleiman's mother, Hürrem had assumed the position of Valide. It meant that he was now her chief servant, and subject to her caprices. It was an impossible position. She had the ear of the Sultan while he was captain of three hundred increasingly restive odalisques, a harem in name only. Girls complained to him on a daily basis that they had cobwebs growing between their legs.

He executed the three ceremonial sala'ams that were required and allowed two pages to help him back to his feet. Hürrem watched this performance with amusement.

"My Abbas," she murmured.

"Your servant, Veil of Crowned Heads."

Hürrem dismissed the pages with an almost imperceptible nod of the head. The fountains that bubbled from the golden spigots on the walls would disguise their conversation from eavesdroppers. Abbas experienced a shiver of dread. He never enjoyed Hürrem's secrets.

"You're trembling. Is something the matter?"

"I am simply overcome in the presence of your beauty."

Hürrem threw back her head and laughed aloud. "Abbas, you are pathetic."

What is the point of being otherwise, he thought, since I am no longer a man and for some reason I do not wish to die.

"You suspect that the palace executioner is standing behind you with his cord."

Abbas felt sweat erupt on his face. He did not dare turn around and look for himself but now he could not get the thought out of his mind. It was just like this witch to do something like that.

"Poor Abbas. There is no bostanji . Look for yourself."

He stared at her.

"I mean it. Go on, look."

He did as he was told. The chamber was empty. Relieved he turned around to face her again, smiling, hating her with such intensity that he felt his teeth ache. She is killing me, this woman. She wishes me never to have peace again.

"The information you gave me about Güzül was true. I compliment you." She leaned forward, resting her chin on her hand. "As the Lord of Life seems to have little use for his Harem, you are largely redundant, are you not, Abbas?"

"As My Lady says." What was this leading up to?

"Since the death of Hafise Sultan, may God bless her and keep her in Paradise, your main function has been heading my household, Our fortunes seem to be interwoven."

"I am much blessed."

"Yes you are. But am I blessed with an obedient servant?"

"Veil of Crowned Heads, I live to serve you."

"Perhaps."

Abbas felt dread settle in his chest like cold lead.

"Do you remember Julia Gonzaga?"

Abbas swayed slightly on his feet. "One of the Harem girls perhaps?"

Hürrem laughed again.

"Ah, I remember now. She did not please the Lord of Life. She sleeps in the Bosphorus."

"She sleeps in Pera, with the Gaiour s."

Oh well, that's it, she knows. It was as if something had snapped inside him. All the tension went out of him. If she knows, she knows. I am at her mercy now, damn her.

"Why did you do it, Abbas?"

You think I would tell you the truth, and allow you to mock the only thing of dignity I still cling to? "She paid me."

"You defied the Sultan for money?"

"Wouldn't you?"

Hürrem clapped her hands, delighted with this answer. "Ah I like it so much better when you are honest with me and do not pretend to be servile. You are a snake pretending to be a sheep. I like it when you show your fangs."

"Am I to die?"

"Do you want to die, Abbas?"

"A part of me wants to die."

"I would not try to stop you. But you know the punishment for disobeying the Sultan in this way. They hang you on a sharpened spike and leave you to turn black in the sun. I am still not sure where they insert the hook but they tell me the effect is not pleasant. They say it can take three days to die, sometimes longer."

"Please, my Lady."

"I do not expect you to beg, Abbas. You know that is not my way."

"What is it you want?"

"Your obedience. That is all. Your obedience until the day I die."

Abbas stared at the rug at his feet. "I am already a slave. It does not matter to me who the master is."

"Then you will find me someone who can bring me Ibrahim's head?"

The very notion took his breath away. "Ibrahim?"

"You think escaping the Sultan's bright shiny hook is worth nothing? I will not trade your three days of mortal agony lightly, my Abbas."

Oh I would like to take a whip to you, little ziadi, little witch, and whip you till you lie begging at my feet.

But that is never going to happen. Until then I must make the best I can of my life. "I will help you," he said.

\*\*\*

Abbas sat on the sleeping mattress he had unrolled from its niche in the wall, a white cat curled on his lap. He believed, as Mohammad had, that cats had souls like men and he spoke to it as he would another man.

"What can I do, little Ziadi? She has held a mirror up to my face and I have looked into it and I see nothing there. Once I thought I had courage. But it one kind of courage to risk death, quite another to embrace it, even after all I have suffered in this life."

The cat purred and the big green eyes blinked slowly in the darkness.

"If she wishes to destroy Ibrahim, then I will help her. What does it matter to me now? I will give the Laughing One her perfect foil; the Man Who Never Smiles."

# CHAPTER 58

They lay on the divan, in the candlelight, the crescent moon framed by the pen window.

"Stay here forever," Hürrem whispered.

"He smiled. "And what would happen to the Osmanlis if I did?"

"The Empire would crumble into dust. I don't care."

"Sometimes…" He left the sentence unfinished. "There have never been enough hours, Hürrem."

"Will there be another war drum and another campaign this year?"

"The Shah of Persia has become impudent. It is time to swat the mosquito."

Hürrem frowned, petulant as a little girl. He picked up her hand and studied the linen bandage around her wrist.

"Will you go with them?"

"All the way to Persia for one troublesome insect? I shall leave that to Ibrahim."

Hürrem put her arms around his neck. "You really mean it this time? What about the Roman Emperor, Charles?"

"The Pope has called for an alliance against us. He wants Naples and Venice to join with him to secure the Mediterranean. Ibrahim is delighted, of course. He would fight all year long if he could."

"So we will fight two wars this summer?"

"No, it will be years before they agree on who will lead their crusade and when, if at all. Ibrahim says the Christians could not agree on which direction the sun comes up. They will have to wait for another time."

"He is sure of that?"

"No one is always sure what a Gaiour might do next. Five years ago Charles sacked Rome, and they call him the Roman Emperor. Such men have no honour. Who can tell what they will do? But I trust Ibrahim's judgment."

"My Lord, forgive my impudence but last night I had a dream. I dreamed you treated with the King of Naples and the Doge of Venice for peace. You offered them sanctions and a treaty in return for securing the ocean against Charles. You said that if they did not agree, it would give your admirals an excuse to raid their coasts all summer long. Do you think that a fine dream?"

Suleiman threw back his head and roared. Such a calculating mind was wasted on a woman. She would have made a fine Vizier. Though perhaps it was not wasted at all; not while she spoke only to him. "One day I will make you my Grand Vizier," he said.

"Perhaps you should. I will have Ibrahim as my scribe."

"He would die first." He grew serious. "Do not mock him. Without Ibrahim we would not have this time together. He is the only one who can help me shoulder the burden."

Hürrem stroked his beard, watched the play of thoughts on his face. She chewed on her bottom lip, a sure sign that she had something else on her mind.

"What is it little russelana?"

"It is nothing."

"Tell me."

She looked up into his face. "This Ibrahim. Do you not worry sometimes that .. that he might ... abuse... his power?"

"Ibrahim? Of course not."

"There are such rumours in the Harem. Because I never know the truth, I worry for you."

"What rumours?"

"I do not wish to speak against Ibrahim. I know he doesn't like me, but that is not the reason."

"But what rumours?" he repeated.

"That he mocks Islam and consorts with Gaiours. That when he meets with ambassadors he calls himself Sultan."

He laughed. "Women's fantasies!"

"All right, I'm sorry. I should not repeat the stories I hear. You're right it is almost always vicious nonsense."

"Ibrahim is rash and boastful but he would never betray me."

"Do you forgive me?"

"What is there to forgive?"

She got to her feet. Her hair, hands and feet had been dyed with henna and there were thick circles of kohl around her eyes. It was her plan, for that day at least, to be like any of the scores of houris in the Harem.

Without warning she performed the three conventional sala'ams expected from any odalisque brought to his bed for the first time. Then she unfastened the pearl buttons of the silk gömlek. Her nipples had been painted with hashish, a favourite trick of the Harem girls. When he suckled her breasts he would swallow some of the drug and it would enhance his climax later.

Bare to the waist she dropped to her knees and approached the divan like a common slave. His breath caught in his throat. Just when he thought he knew all her tricks she surprised him. This was like their first night all over again.

She kissed his feet in the traditional act of humility. He gasped as her fingers loosened his robes for her ministrations.

She is my Harem, he thought. She is like a thousand women.

The black deaf mutes who guarded the doorway could not hear his moans. But a peacock, rustling among the tulips beneath the window looked up startled. The Sultan's sighs of pleasure intermingled with murmuring of water from the fountains until the moon edged below the branches of the plane trees and the flames on the candles guttered and died.

*\*\**

The city was a vast mosaic of colour, below the long fingers of the minarets and the gleaming cupolas of the mosques. The Kanun of the Fatih proscribed that all houses should be painted for the religion of their inhabitants; so there were clusters of grey houses where the Armenians lived, ghettoes of yellow for the Jews, while Turks themselves had red.

It made the Defterdar's house easier to find. It was painted black, to signify a member of the Sultan's Court.

Abbas rarely ventured into the crowded alleys of Stamboul, and he assured his anonymity now with a black ferijde . Rüstem's house had a private courtyard at the back. A page ushered him inside. Rüstem was seated in a kiosk at the rear. A marble fountain murmured nearby.

Rüstem executed a brief temenna and indicated that Abbas should sit opposite him on the carpet. A page brought sherbets and laid a silver platter of pastries between them.

"I have come at the request of the lady Hürrem," Abbas said.

Rüstem showed not a flicker of interest.

"It seems that you have a common interest."

"What might that be?"

"Yourselves."

Ah, a reaction. Not much, just a lifting of the eyes, a muscle working in the cheek. But something at least.

"Explain yourself, Kislar Aghasi."

Abbas knew that Rüstem was corrupt, of course, but had kept his silence. In the Harem one did not spend a valuable currency like information too freely. It was hoarded, carefully, in case one needed to lift the mortgage over one's own head at a future time.

As Defterdar, Rüstem was responsible for collecting taxes from the timariots, the feudal cavalrymen given small fiefdoms in return for their service in wars. On their death it was supposed to return to the Sultan. It was one of the basic tenets of the Osmanli system; only the Sultan could accrue hereditary wealth.

Well, that was supposed to be how it worked.

Abbas leaned forward: "The Veil of Crowned heads has asked me to tell you about a man named Hakim Dürgün. It seems that last year he died of the pestilence. Yet he still farms his timar near Adrianople. A remarkably diligent ghost, do you not agree?"

"Remarkable. I will look into it."

"You should also look into the case of another timariot in Rumelia who died four years ago. About the time you became treasurer, in fact. Since then he has taxed the farmers on his land eight aspers per sheep. And yet you have done nothing about this avaricious spirit. Is it because you are afraid of the dead or because his ghost passes you two aspers per sheep for yourself?"

"How do you know so much about ghosts?"

"Wherever there is a black man, I have a pair of ears. And there is not a palace or a treasury in the entire kingdom that does not have a supposedly deaf mute who hears everything."

Rüstem selected a pastry and chewed slowly. "What is it you want? A cut of the business?"

Abbas admired his calm. "Nothing so common. Please. I have not come here to line my own pockets. The Lady Hürrem sent me."

"She does not need money."

"Of course not."

"A favour then?"

"More than a favour. I think we are talking about an alliance."

For the first time he raised his eyes and looked directly at Abbas. They were November eyes, Abbas thought. Not cold, just grey and empty. "That would be an interesting arrangement. Does she realize that Ibrahim is my patron?"

"Of course. You did not think I would keep it from her?"

"I think you only tell anyone what they need to know and no more."

"I understand you are to accompany the Vizier on the campaign in the east."

"What interest could the second kadin possibly have in a military expedition to Persia?"

"None. Her interest is Ibrahim."

Rüstem frowned. "What does she want from him?"

"She is concerned for him. She worries that if he has become too besotted with his own power. His boasting is already the scandal of the court and the bazaars."

Why should she be concerned about it? I have heard she does not care for him overmuch but surely his arrogance cannot touch her in there."

"Her reasons are not your affair. But it seems the Vizier is heading for a fall, and she would like it very much if you hurried his downfall along. She would like evidence of his treachery."

"He is hardly a traitor."

"It does not matter to my mistress if he is or he isn't. Just that you collect evidence of it."

Rüstem selected another pastry while he thought this over. "That might be difficult to do."

"Not too difficult, I hope. Or one night, when the Sultan is wrapped in the embrace of his second kadin., she will whisper to him how you have embezzled taxes from the timariots and corrupted the fiefs."

Rüstem did not look afraid. All that registered was a frown of disappointment, as if he had been outmanoeuvred at chess. "And what reward should I hope for, should I prove a resourceful ally?"

Abbas was surprised by the question. "Your life?"

"If we are bargaining, Kislar Aghasi, as you say we are, then I should like to counter offer. Tell her that should I give her Ibrahim, I would like to enter into a more permanent arrangement with her. We might be very good for each other."

Abbas grunted in surprise. "I will tell her," he said.

The Man Who Never Smiled almost did. But he restrained himself at the last.

Later, as he made his way back to the palace, Abbas passed a dead horse that had been left in the gutter. The dogs had been at work on it and had dragged its entrails out through a hole they had torn in its stomach. Try never to fall, he reminded himself. Once your belly is supposed, even for a moment, they will rip out your guts without a second thought.

# CHAPTER 59

## Galata

Galata was built on one of Stamboul's seven hills, just across the Horn from Seraglio Point. It was dominated by the Galata Kulesi, a round tower built by the Genoese as part of the city's fortifications. Tiny houses and shops clustered at its foot, next to the harbor, and this was where the Jewish and Genoese commission agents kept their homes. Berbers and Red Sea Arabs had warehouses here also, and filled them with spices, ivory, silks, glass and pearls. There were even small shops where wine and arak were served.

The smell of fish and salt from the Bosphorus overlaid the dank urban stink.

Ludovici also kept a house in the quarter, although no one ever lived in it. Its purpose was a safe house where he might receive his spies and pay baksheesh to palace officials. Endless comings and goings at his palazzo in Pera by government pashas might excite too much comment.

The house was painted yellow, the colour of the Jews. It was sparsely finished. Most of the rooms were empty; the only room that was furnished was an upstairs audience chamber; there was a low cedar table and some cushions scattered about a rich Persian silk carpet. They belied the humble surroundings.

It had taken four servants to ease Abbas" enormous bulk to the floor. He now concentrated his attention on the pastries piled on the silver plate in front of him. When they were gone he dipped his fingers daintily into a silver bowl proffered by another of Ludovici"s servants. He belched politely into a silk handkerchief.

He came once a month now, disguised in his black ferijde. Ludovici had tried at first to speak to him as he did in the old days, but the Abbas he had once known was gone. Aside from discussing politics he seemed to gain no pleasure from his visits, though he provided invaluable insights into the workings of the Topkapi. He never took baksheesh for his information. Ludovici wondered why he still came.

There could only be one reason.

"How is Julia?" he said, breaking the silence. It was always his first question.

"She is well."

"Business is good?"

"Thanks to your help."

Abbas nodded. That side of things did not interest him overmuch. "You know she cannot stay in Stamboul much longer. It is no longer safe here. Not even in the Comunità Magnifica."

"What has happened?"

"I cannot tell you that."

"But Abbas …"

"Please. Get her out of Stamboul. As soon as you can."

"Where could she go?"

"It doesn't matter as long as it is not Stamboul. I have done all I can to protect her, but the situation is impossible now. Do you understand?"

"I will do what I can."

Abbas gripped his arm with one massive fist. "No, that is not good enough. You have to get her out! Now!"

"All right," Ludovici said. What on earth could this be? "Has someone found out about her?"

"Just promise me that you will get her out of Stamboul."

Ludovici frowned. "I promise," he said. "But „,"

"Let us go to other business," Abbas said and would talk no more about it.

## The Hippodrome

Suleiman sat on a pure white Cappadocian horse, watching his march through the Atmeydani. Ferries were waiting to take them across to Üsküdar and Asia. Behind him, veiled and hidden behind a lattice grill, he could feel Hürrem watching him. The knowledge of her presence helped still his nagging doubts.

The Hippodrome shook to the rumble of supply wagons and siege engines. Choking clouds of dust swept across the square whipped up by the horse's hoofs and the iron spiked shoes of his infantry.

Ibrahim appeared through the haze, resplendent in a white cloak. "Your blessing on our endeavour, my Lord. Would that you were with us!"

"You must defend Baghdad against the devil."

"I will crush the Shah as you have commanded me!" He reined in his horse to review the army at Suleiman's side.

First came the azabs; irregular infantry, criminals and jailbirds and cutthroats come to fight for loot or else die and go straight to Paradise. They had nothing to lose and were sent in first at every charge; "moat fillers", Ibrahim called them.

The regular cavalry - the Spahis of the Porte - thundered by, their horses caparisoned in gold and silver cloth, saddles studded with jewels, their conical helmets and burnished steel chain mail gleaming. They were spectacular in purple, royal blue and scarlet according to rank and regiment.

Next came the yeniçeris , enormous Bird of Paradise plumes waving in the wind like a moving forest, blue skirted cloaks swinging with every stride, muskets slung over their shoulders. The huge copper cauldrons that served as each regiment's standard went with them. A white banner emblazoned with the flaming sword of Mohammed fluttered in the wind, embroidered with gold text from the Qu'ran.

Next came the dervishes, naked except for green aprons fringed with ebony beads, wearing towering hats of brown camelhair, chanting from the Qu'ran. Madcaps rode up and down the lines, long hair straggling from under their leopard skin caps, horses festooned with feathers. They were the crazy scouts, the religious fanatics who carried out the suicide raids no one else would attempt.

At the rear came the Divan, judges in green turbans, viziers on horseback glittering with jewels. With them came the camels bearing a sacred fragment of the holy Ka'aba, lumbering under the brilliant green folds of the standard of Islam. A metal sanchak Qu'ran, in miniature and inscribed in bronze, jangled at the top of the standard.

Finally there were the supply wagons, camels bowed under the weight of powder and lead, rumbling bronze siege cannon.

I should be with them, Suleiman thought.

"I will bring you back the Shah's head!" Ibrahim shouted.

What was it Hürrem had said? Do you not worry sometimes that he might abuse his power?

"We must regain Baghdad. As Defender of the Faith, I am sworn to protect it!" He felt a stirring of unease. I have put all my faith in you, Ibrahim. God grant that I have not trusted you too much.

### Pera

Julia was sitting on the terrazzo. Ludovici stopped on the steps on the way from the garden to admire her. Abbas was right, he thought. She is so beautiful. If only I could make her feel about me the way she felt about him.

She is mine, but only because she has no choice. She is virtually a prisoner. She cannot leave my protection for fear of her life; having once been a concubine she may not return to Venice, for they would treat her like a whore. Serena would send her away to a convent.

There is nowhere else for her to go.

She looked up from her book. Ovid. So remote, like an angel carved from ice. She saw him watching her. "Ludovici," she said. He was wearing a rust-coloured kaftan, like a Turk. "You enjoy playing the renegade, don't you?"

"It has nothing to do with it. It's cooler in such hot weather."

"What is wrong? You look worried about something."

"We must talk," he said to her.

She fixed him with those ice blue eyes. A vision, as Abbas had once described her.

He sat down, fidgeted, wondered how to start. Finally: "Julia, you have been here under my protection for almost three years."

"And I have always been grateful to you for all you do for me."

"Are you happy here?"

"Happy? What is happiness?"

He shrugged. Well, I don't know, he thought. Meat and wine on the table, a silk doublet, a woman to warm the bed. "You should be married."

"I am married. If Serena is still alive."

"I don't know if he is. You said he was sick the last you heard of him. He was an old man when you married him. I could make enquiries, find out."

"I don't really care about him." She picked up her book.

He spread his hands in a gesture of helplessness. Their conversations always went this way. It was as if she had been scooped hollow with a spoon. She was broken. How to find repair?

He felt like a father with a disgraced and unmarriageable daughter. What was he going to do about this?

"What is wrong?" she said. "You are staring." He looked away, flustered. I wonder what she thinks about all the time? What goes on behind those ice blue eyes? Perhaps she read his mind, for she said, unexpectedly: "Do you ever see him?"

"Yes, sometimes."

"Does he ever ask after me?"

"Always."

Her eyes glistened. "Poor Abbas."

He reached across the table and took her hand. It was warm. "I want you to be happy," he said.

"You have kept me safe. Isn't that enough?"

\*\*\*

The door was slightly ajar and the flickering candlelight danced on the marble floor. Ludovici paused in the shadows, deafened by his own heartbeat. His mouth went dry.

He pushed open the door. Julia sat at her dressing table, combing out her hair. The silk of her nightgown shimmered in the light. A small cross glimmered between her breasts. She saw him in the mirror and froze. She set down the brush. "Ludovici?"

He imagined bunching her gown in his fists and tearing it side. "Goodnight, Julia," he said and gently shut the door.

# CHAPTER 60

## Azerbaijan

Rüstem had already calculated that, provided he did not commit himself too soon, he could profit from the Kislar Aghasi, regardless of how the dice fell. It was plain that there would soon be a confrontation between the Harem and the Divan; it was politic then to have a foot in both camps.

He would therefore encourage Ibrahim in his ambition. If he emerged triumphant, he would be there at his side. If he failed he would seek his reward from the witch, the ziadi Hürrem.

\*\*\*

It was a long march through the lonely steppes of Anatolia. The army trailed a cloud of dust that spiralled a hundred feet into the air. The jackals fled in their wake.

The Sultan's horde; an endless column winding into the wilderness east and west, mile after mile, the akinji scouting ahead, camel trains and heavy guns creaking over rutted roads far behind, the column stretching from horizon to flat horizon. A summer passed as they made their way east, finally arriving at the feet of the great mountains of Asia and the cool still waters of Lake Van.

Finally they glimpsed the blue-tiled domes of Tabriz, glittering in the sun. Ibrahim hurried on after the Shah, but the Persian would not fight, would not risk his cavalry against artillery and instead chose to slip away into the mountains of Sultania.

By the time Ibrahim realized his pursuit was useless, the first chill of autumn was in the air.

\*\*\*

Ibrahim's standard of six horsetails - only the Sultan had more - was jammed into the hard earth. The tent whipped in the wind. Razor-backed mountains rose against a mottled sky.

When Rüstem entered the Grand Vizier's tent, copper braziers had already been lit against the chill. And this was yet summer. What must winter be like in this place?

Ibrahim brooded on a throne of ivory and ebony wood. Rüstem touched his forehead to the carpet in salute.

"Rüstem? Should you not be guarding the camel train and the silks?" He noted the hard edge to the Vizier's voice. He was in a dangerous mood. The frustrations of the past weeks had begun to tell, as the quick, decisive victory he had counted on did not come.

"I thought I might be of service to you, my Lord."

"To help count the money?"

"In the matter of the Shah, my Lord."

Ibrahim flushed with anger. "The Shah!" Rüstem had never seen the Vizier lose his icy calm. He wants this victory too badly, he thought, and that will disturb his judgment. "The Shah is no better than a jackal! He runs away from us then doubles back to sniff at our spoor and snap at our heels."

"Our scouts have still not located his army?"

"These are his mountains. He knows every valley, every ridge."

"Perhaps there is a way to flush him out."

Ibrahim seemed desperate. "How?"

"If you offer him a treaty ..."

"Never ! I have vowed to crush him!"

"You are not treating with a European nobleman, my Lord. The Shah is just a jackal, as you have said. There would be no dishonour in using an offer to treat simply as a means to draw him close enough to strike."

Ibrahim brooded on this. Then: "What do you suggest?"

"If we can get a message to him ..."

"How can we do that?"

"I am sure the Sufavids are watching us, even as we speak. Any lone messenger travelling east will be intercepted. They will find us - we do not have to find them."

"They will cut off his ears and nose and send them back in a leather pouch!"

"They might. But then again - perhaps the Shah does not wish to spend every summer skulking in the mountains. He cannot make war on us forever."

Ibrahim got up and paced the tent. Outside, the sky had turned lead grey. Rain clouds swept towards them with the swiftness of charging cavalry.

Rüstem watched Ibrahim think it through. He held his breath. This was the moment; if Ibrahim took the bait, his fortune was assured. Ibrahim would raise him up or he would lift himself up on the Grand Vizier's corpse. Either way, he would not be a clerk for ever.

"Let me take the message to him."

Ibrahim gaped at him. "You, Rüstem?"

"I will coax the jackal from his lair."

"When does a defterdar become an ambassador?"

"When he has ambition."

Ibrahim nodded his understanding. "What is your plan?"

"A sealed message from you, my Lord, offering him Tabriz and Azerbaijan in return for the holy city of Baghdad. We respect his borders to the east."

"He will never believe we would strike such a bargain."

"I can persuade him, if I have him face to face. And you have a duplicate of Suleiman's tugra, his personal seal. It is affixed to the offer, he must believe it is genuine."

"Supposing he listens to you. What then?"

"We bring him and his escort to the plain under flag of truce and we massacre them like the dogs they are."

The rainstorm was overhead now and broke like a volley of cannon fire, thundering onto the hard ground and slapping violently on the roof of the tent. The flares in the brazier flared in a gust of wind. "He will never believe it."

"Let me try. Perhaps he has heard of the alliance the Pope wants to bring against us. I will convince him we are more concerned for our borders to the west and wish to be rid of him."

Rüstem knew that Ibrahim had promised the Sultan the Shah's head; and after Vienna he could not afford another failure, not with the ziadi Hürrem whispering against him. He needed this victory.

"All right, Rüstem. If you can bring him to me, your reward will be beyond your wildest dreams."

Rüstem bowed. And you only know the half of it! he thought.

# CHAPTER 61

Shah Tamasp regarded the miserable creature in front of him. The man had been brought to the camp blindfold and in chains by two of his scouts. He lay face down in the dirt at the entrance to his pavilion, two scimitars pressed into the flesh of his neck, while the Shah read the contents of the missive he had brought with him.

The Shah showed the letter to his mullah, who passed it to one of his generals. They shook their heads. What trickery had the Suleiman's Vizier devised now? The Shah snatched it back and read the letter a third time. He was a young man, thin as a whip with cruel eyes. When he spoke his voice was high and sibilant as a girl's. "What is your name, messenger?"

The wretch raised his face a few inches from the ground. "Rüstem, my Lord." There was a trickle of blood on his lips.

"What is your rank in Suleiman's army?"

"Defterdar, my Lord."

"A treasury clerk? When do the Osmanlis send their money counters as couriers?"

"The Grand Vizier trusts me."

The Shah frowned. Well, this was odd. "So Ibrahim is persuaded to sue for peace. Is this what his Sultan wants, also?"

"Ibrahim has the confidence of the Lord of the Two Worlds. He has his tugra."

"Yes, I see that."

"He has given him leave to make treaties in his name."

"Defterdar Rüstem, can you tell me why your so-called Lord of the Two Worlds does not lead his army against us himself, as his father did?"

"He has tired of war, my Lord. He wishes for peace."

So it was true, then. Suleiman was weak. The offer was reasonable. Too reasonable? But if it were real, he could present his mullahs with a great political victory. They could not hold Baghdad in the face of the Osmanli armies. When Ibrahim grew tired of chasing him through the mountains, he could take Tabriz and the Holy City and return to Stamboul. And then they would have to do this all again next year.

Yes, perhaps this clerk is telling the truth. Rome worries them more than Baghdad.

And yet.

"Such a treaty might be possible, messenger Rüstem. But we must meet at a place of my choosing, with only bodyguards in attendance."

"You doubt Ibrahim's honour?"

The Shah smiled. "Of course. He's a Turke."

"Greek," Rüstem corrected him.

"Well there you are then."

He nodded at the two guards, who dragged him roughly to his feet. "If he agrees to my conditions, tell him I accept his offer. Go in peace, Defterdar Rüstem."

The guards dragged him away. The Shah watched them put him on his horse, still chained and blindfolded. They led him through the rows of tents toward the south. He wondered again about Suleiman. An Osmanli who wanted peace? A lie or the first sign of weakness? Well, as God wills.

The wind was cool today, but winter was still a long way off. The Osmanli army would not be going home just yet. He would have to wait and see.

***

"If you follow the spur, it will lead you to the valley where your friends are camped," the Persian said and ripped the blindfold from Rüstem's face. The other rider unlocked his chains.

Rüstem blinked in the sunlight. One of his guards, a bearded ruffian in a battered conical helmet, tugged at his beard. "Next time we meet, perhaps the Shah will let me wet my word on your liver."

Rüstem ignored the insult and took the reins of his horse. He had no time for Persians, his was a greater game. The gamble had paid off. A simple thing now to conclude this business.

Poor Ibrahim. He was far too fond of the grand gesture to be a truly great Vizier. Greatness required calculation and planning. Someone with the ability to see opportunity in danger.

Someone like himself.

The two Persians galloped away and he was left alone on the high steppe. He allowed himself a small smile. Then he rode back down the spur towards the camp. He rode like a clerk, but he had the heart of a bandit.

# CHAPTER 62

Ibrahim's face betrayed both amusement and wonder. One finger tapped a tattoo on the arm of his throne. The silk tent flapped in the wind as it buffeted and sighed.

"So you found the Shah?"

"Yes, My Lord."

"You astonish me, Rüstem. I thought never to see you alive again. They kept you blindfold, no doubt."

"Indeed."

"They treated you well?"

"Passably."

His robe was torn and filthy. There was blood and matted dirt in his beard. Had he suffered? The pale grey eyes betrayed nothing.

"Your lip is cut."

"It is nothing."

Ibrahim roared with laughter. "And I thought we might never see you again! What a loss you would have been to the world of poetry and good conversation!"

"I think not, my Lord," Rüstem said, seriously.

Ibrahim shook his head. He sometimes entertained a fantasy in which he scooped off the top of Rüstem's skull with his sword, like an egg. When he peered inside there was no brain, just an abacus. "So what does the Shah say to our offer of treaty?"

"He has refused it, my Lord."

Ibrahim's face darkened, but the smile stayed doggedly in place. "He does not trust us, Rüstem?"

"It was the authority of the letter he mistrusted."

"The authority …?"

"He said he could not treat with you."

The smile vanished. "Why not?"

"He said you were only a soldier, and that he could only accept such an offer as genuine if it were signed by the Sultan, not the Sultan's clerk."

Ibrahim stood up. He clenched his fists to stop the trembling in his hands. Then he grabbed Rüstem and threw him across the tent. Rüstem lay on his side, looking neither frightened or really all that surprised.

Ibrahim drew the killiç from the jewelled sheath at his waist and raised it, double-handed, above his head, then brought it down, with all his strength, on the back of the throne, sending splinters of ivory and wood spinning across the tent. "The Sultan's clerk? Is it the Sultan's clerk who sits every day in the Divan and administers the Empire? Is it the Sultan's clerk who leads his armies into battle for him while he pleasures himself in his Harem? The Sultan? I AM THE SULTAN!"

"He spoke in ignorance, my Lord."

"Does he think the Sultans sends clerks into battle? Does he, Rüstem?"

"I only repeat his words. He said he could not treat with any but the Sultan of the Osmanlis.."

"How long must I endure this? The Sultan has entrusted to me his kingdoms, his armies, his power, everything! The making of war or the granting of peace are in my hand. Does the Shah know who it was called for the army to come here? It was I - not the Sultan! I take the burden and yet he calls me the Sultan's clerk!"

"But my Lord -"

Ibrahim held the killiç in front of Rüstem's eyes, turning it slowly so that the light pooled and shivered on the blade. "When we take him, we take him alive."

"First we must lure him out. If we convey to the Lord of Life a message …"

"No! I swore I would bring him back his head! Should I now rush to him with entreaties for his aid?"

"… Then perhaps there is another way?"

"Another way?"

"All the Empire knows how greatly the Sultan has honoured and trusted you. Perhaps you should impress this upon the Shah. You must show him that you have the authority to make such a treaty."

"How?"

"You must extend the offer again. Only this time you must sign it as the Sultan."

Ibrahim stared at him. Did this lunatic realize what he was saying? "That is impossible."

"What else may we do, my Lord? Except chase him around the mountains until winter comes."

"I may do many things, Rüstem, but I cannot assume the title of Sultan."

"Who will know once it is done? You may bury the document with the Shah."

He has a point, Ibrahim thought. Unthinkable!

And yet …

Why not? I am Sultan in everything but name. He has trusted me with his Divan and his armies; if he did not wish me to invoke his power, why would he give me so much?

"I cannot do it," he said.

"In that case let us hurry on and take back Baghdad but he will take it back as soon as we are gone. But you promised the Sultan his head and this is the only way to lure him out."

Ibrahim closed his eyes. Rüstem was right. How could he return to Suleiman without this victory? The Austrians had humiliated them at Güns; now the Shah taunted him from the mountains. And until their Asian border was secure again they could not take their armies against the Roman Emperor in Europe. His destiny was in the Green Apple, not here in this wilderness. It was Rome that would carve his name alongside Alexander's in history. If he must take a hammer to swat this mosquito, then so be it.

He told Rüstem to get up and fetch a quill and parchment.

\*\*\*

To the Shah Tamasp of Persia, greetings and health, may prosperity and glory signal your days. From sundry verbal communications we have cognizance of your desire for peace, and by the grace of the Most High, whose power be forever exalted! we ourselves have no desire to make war on our brothers in Islam. We therefore make it known that should you give up the holy city of Baghdad and all territories you have conquered by force of arms, we shall cede to you Tabriz, and the lands known as Azerbaijan, should you pay tribute each year of one thousand gold ducats. Night and day our horse is saddled to ride and meet with you to conclude our peace.

Written in the year of the Hejira, 941.

Ibrahim. Seraskier Sultan.

# CHAPTER 63

Seraskier Sultan!

Rüstem reined in his horse on the ridge overlooking the Osmanli camp. The smoke from the morning campfires drifted upwards, throwing gauze over the distant panorama of the mountains. From here he could see the scarlet tent of the Grand Vizier, his standard with the six horsetails limp in the still of the morning.

Seraskier Sultan!

Rüstem turned and rode away towards the north. He spurred his horse beyond the first ridge, then wheeled around and galloped west. When he did not return Ibrahim would assume the Shah's men had murdered him. By the time he gave him up for lost he would be in Stamboul.

Seraskier Sultan!

### Topkapi Saraya

Suleiman crumpled the letter in his fist, his face ugly with grief.

The pashas and muftis and generals who surrounded him all fell silent. They tried to look miserable, but they didn't fool anyone. He knew what they were all thinking. The vain boastful Greek had finally written his own death warrant!

Rüstem Pasha stood in the centre of the Divan, waiting his turn to speak. There was no scent of perfume on him now. He stank of horse. He claimed to have ridden for three weeks from the borderlands of Azerbaijan to bring his news.

I would rather your horse had fallen and broken your neck, Suleiman thought.

"You wrote this at his command?" he said finally.

"Yes, great lord. He bid me take it to the Shah Tamasp. He affixed your seal."

Suleiman knew he was trapped. Ibrahim, I could have forgiven you anything, but not this! If Rüstem had come to me privately with this, I could perhaps have found some way to excuse you. But now he has made it public and presented me with your treachery in front of everyone. There is nothing I can do for you.

What have you done?

"Why did you not do as he commanded and take this to the Shah?"

"My Lord, I know my duty. I could not allow such treachery to take place. I am your loyal servant."

You pathetic little worm! Suleiman thought. How dare you speak to me of treachery! Ibrahim has served me faithfully for more than a quarter of a century, he is my boyhood friend, he was my Seraskier, now my Vizier. How do you know this was really treachery? How can you be so certain?

"The Sultan owes you a great debt, Defterdar Rüstem," he forced himself to say. He stared at the crumpled parchment in his fist. "How does the campaign progress?"

"Since Tabriz, Ibrahim Pasha trails the Shah through the mountains but our only glimpse of him has been the dung of his horses. The Agas urge Ibrahim to Baghdad but he ignores their counsel. He says he is the only one capable of achieving victory. He says it has always been so."

A sigh passed around the chamber. How dare Rüstem say such things! Suleiman wondered. He repeats these calumnies in front of everyone as if they were figures from a balance sheet.

"What of the morale of my army?"

"They all ask for your presence to lead them. Without you they believe they cannot achieve victory. Even the yeniçeris believe Ibrahim will only lead them further into the mountains, to disaster."

Suleiman watched the dust filtering through the shafts of yellow sunlight. The passage of dust; the passage of life, the passage of all reputations.

Behind him, high on the wall, was the dangerous window. There was no one there this morning to witness Ibrahim's fall of grace, but Suleiman wished with all his heart that he was up there now, that he could watch someone else make the terrible decision that he knew must finally be made.

# CHAPTER 64

## The Eski Saraya

Suleiman removed his turban and ran a hand over the smooth skin of his scalp to the single scalplock at the base of his skull, the legacy of his ghazi forefathers. He closed his eyes. He felt the weight of his royalty more keenly today than any time in the fifteen years since he had taken his throne.

She entered silently through a velvet curtain and knelt at his feet. For once she had no smile to greet him. She kissed his hand and rested it against his cheek.

"You knew?"

"Yes, my Lord."

"How?"

"Whispers in the Harem."

"How is it the Harem know everything that happens even before I do?"

"When I came through the curtain and saw your face I knew the whispers must be true."

He stroked her hair and his face softened. "What am I to do?"

"May I see the letter, my Lord?"

He still held it crumpled in his fist. She took it from his fingers and unfolded it. It was barely legible, badly creased and the sweat from his hand had smudged the ink. But she could still read the signature.

Seraskier Sultan.

Oh Rüstem, she thought. Abbas chose well. You have a rare genius for intrigue.

"He sues for peace with the Shah under your name," she said.

"It is madness. What could have possessed him to do such a thing?"

"Is this Defterdar Rüstem to be trusted?"

"He is just a clerk. In his misguided way he thinks he does well by me. The treason is there written beneath my own seal. Seraskier Sultan! There is no circumstance, no provocation, under which any man might call himself Sultan other than me. To do so is rebellion. He knows it."

"But he is your friend."

"Yes, my friend, and much more than a friend. It only makes this even more unforgiveable."

"Do not act too rashly, my Lord."

He shook his head. "You may be the only one today who speaks for him. Suddenly he has enemies I did not even dream of. They have swarmed from every crevice in the Palace walls to denounce him."

Yes, I will speak for him, she thought, and when his head is rotting on the palace walls, you will remember that I did. There is nothing anyone can do to save him so I may not fear overstating my case. "You must go to him."

He nodded. "The longer I delay, the more damage this shall do to me. I cannot ignore this, but I cannot bring myself to harm him, little russelana. It would be like cutting out my own heart."

"If he is indeed your friend, there must be some way you can excuse him."

He snatched the letter from her hand. "There is no way! What excuse can there be?" He jumped to his feet and went to the candle. He held it to the flame, twisting it in the flames, watching it burn.

"Here, it is ashes now. He will tell me of this letter with his own lips when I arrive. If he is truly my friend he will not try to hide this from me." He crushed the ashes with his boot.

Hürrem stood up and wrapped her arms around him. She pulled his head to her breast and felt him cry in her arms.

"Hürrem," he said, "what would I do without you?"

"Shh," she murmured and stroked his head, despising his weakness more than she had ever done.

# CHAPTER 65

The last hot days of august, the time of year when only the poor were left behind to swelter in the furnace of the city. No time to start a campaign, so hot in Europe and so dangerously close to winter in Asia. The prospect of the long, crushing ride across Anatolia depressed him deeply.

He would cross the Bosphorus with three hundred cavalry and rode to Üsküdar and then head east across the baked plains towards Asia. There would be a full cycle of the moon before he reached his destination, a month of choking dust and aching muscles. Yet he did not wish ever to arrive.

Sultan Seraskier!

\*\*\*

He followed the trail of Alexander through orchards of figs and olives, fields of cotton and wheat. They passed through Konia where he stooped to honour the tomb of Jalal-ud-din Rumi, the founder of the Dervish order. From Konia they roasted under the desert sun. The only other life they saw was the black tents of nomads and the baked walls of the caravanserais built as sanctuary for the camel trains from Samarkand and Medina.

They passed through Edessa, the birthplace of Abraham, where old men sat in the shadow of the fortress and tossed chickpeas into a pool of sacred carp. From there they rode up into the mountains, and the air turned suddenly cool and the brown steppe gave way to bare rock and tumbling ravines. The wind savaged men and horses like a whip. Wild storms appeared from nowhere. It was a place only goats and sheep and the Kurds could survive.

And the Shah.

They rode twelve hours a day, stopping only when their horses were too exhausted to continue. They reached Azerbaijan.

The scouts rode ahead to find the camp. Finally, one afternoon they reached the crest of a ridge and saw the army spread out on the plateau in front of them. Exhausted beyond all measure Suleiman wanted to throw himself on the ground and weep. Instead he drew himself taller in the saddle and rode down the slope to greet the wild cheering of his troops.

\*\*\*

The tents had been erected in crisp lines, according to division and regiment. Holes had been dug at regular intervals as latrines. Horses had been corralled, siege engines, supply wagons and cannon drawn up in strict order.

The camp was silent, for no fighting, gambling or drinking was tolerated. But when the men of the askeri recognized the Sultan's standard of seven horsetails and saw the bearded figure with his green robes and snow white turban the hush erupted into wild cheering.

Word spread quickly. Suleiman had returned to lead them! He would guide them through these mountains and to victory!

He reined in his horse before the scarlet silk tent with the six horsetail standard. Ibrahim emerged and quickly executed a ceremonial sala'am on the ground in front of him.

"My lord," he said.

Where is the boyish grin now? he wondered. Where is the young man who would rush to embrace me whenever we had been too long apart? Look at this petulant scowl.

"Do you have the head of the Shah for me?" he said.

Ibrahim took a long time to reply. "Not yet, my Lord," he said.

"Then we will remove to Baghdad. The Sultan shall lead his army now."

# CHAPTER 66

"It is good you are here, my Lord. But the reason for your arrival distresses me. Do you no longer trust me as your Vizier?"

They were sitting on the thick carpets in Suleiman's pavilion. The coals in the copper brazier glowed, fanned by a sudden draught. Suleiman was tired, the journey had exhausted him. He could barely think. And he was cold. He pulled his ermine lined robe tighter around his shoulders.

"A Sultan's place is at the head of his army, as you never cease to remind me."

"Is that the only reason, my Lord?"

"As protector of the Faith I am obliged to defend Baghdad, not have my army chase phantoms through the wilderness."

"Once we defeat the Shah, Baghdad is ours anyway."

Suleiman searched Ibrahim's face for the truth. Any moment, he thought, he will confess to me what he has done and why. There can be no secrets between us, he would not allow it.

"Perhaps we should treat with him," Suleiman said, testing him.

"And what should we offer him?" Ibrahim said.

"What do you think?""

"Nothing. Except perhaps a rope for his neck."

Suleiman shook his head. "He is as elusive as our Holy Roman Emperor. Perhaps we will never bring either of them to battle. It is more important that we do our duty and be patient. We defend the Faith."

"The Faith!"

It was clear Ibrahim regretted this blasphemy the moment it was spoken. "It is the reason for my army, Ibrahim, there can be no other. The jihad is only for God." The horses were growing restless outside, he could hear them stamping their hoofs, unsettled by the wind. "Tomorrow we march on

Baghdad. We will retake the city and if necessary we will winter there. The mountains are no place for an army."

"As you command." Ibrahim stared at the coals in the fire, his lips compressed in a thin line. "Why did you do this to me?"

Suleiman almost throttled him. After your treachery, you dare question my actions? "I am tired. I must sleep. Leave me now."

"But My Lord ..."

"Leave."

It had been their tradition to sleep in the same pavilion when they were on campaign. But this time Ibrahim did not protest his banishment. He rose to his feet, made his sala'am and left.

*\*\**

During the night a blizzard swept down from the mountains. Suleiman woke to the sound of horses and camels screaming in the storm. A gust of wind shook his pavilion so violently he thought it must rip in two. He threw on his fur robe and went outside.

Curtains of driving sleet obliterated everything and he had to shield his face with his hands to protect himself from the stinging slap of the ice. Torches flared for a moment and were instantly extinguished by the wind.

His pages trembled with terror. Even one of his bodyguard fell on his knees. "May God protect us!" he screamed. "It is the Persian magicians!"

"It's just a storm!" Suleiman roared. "Get up, man!"

Damn Ibrahim, he thought. Damn him for his treachery and his stupidity. Damn him!

*\*\**

Dawn, and the entire valley blanketed in white. Ibrahim staggered through the drifts, stunned. Tents sagged under the weight of the snow. The frozen leg of a camel protruded from a drift.

A terrible hush had fallen across the valley. An eerie light poked through the black anvils of cloud. Whole regiments had been buried in the drifts, tents torn away by the force of the wind. Pieces of canvas flapped on broken poles.

Ibrahim heard what he thought was the moan of the wind but the wind had died away now. He realized it was the cries of men trapped under the snow mingled with the cries of dying horses. "God help me in my sorrow," he murmured. He had never tasted defeat before but he knew it now, in full measure. Instead of blood, there was snow.

Men staggered dazed and snow blind through a landscape none could recognize from the night before. Some clawed at the snow to release a comrade or hauled on the rope of a camel half buried under a snow bank. The rest turned their eyes toward the jaws of the pass, dreading the arrival of Persian horsemen against the dawn. They were helpless if they should come now.

"Ibrahim!"

Suleiman stood above him on the slope, and he recognized on his face the same berserk fury he had seen once before - at Rhodes, when he had called for his chief high executioner to kill his Grand Vizier.

But now I am the Vizier ...

"What have you done?"

Ibrahim spread his hands helplessly. Who knew there could be snow in summer?

"If the Persians come now, we will all die here!" Suleiman came closer, so that the pages and solaks around them could not hear what he said next. "I sometimes wondered if you and I were not born to the wrong families. It seems that I was wrong."

He turned away and plunged through the thigh-deep snow towards the wreckage of the camp. They must reorganize quickly, Ibrahim realized, and make their retreat. But that was no longer his responsibility. The Sultan was in command again now and he would issue the orders of the day.

# CHAPTER 67

## Galata

Each time Abbas shifted his weight the silk of the kaftan rustled like dry leaves. His face shone in the light of the candle. "These are dangerous days," he said. "You have made sure she is safe? She is out of Stamboul?"

"Yes," he said and met his eyes. "She is gone."

Abbas grunted, satisfied.

"Abbas ... do you still love her?"

"There is no past tense of love," he said.

"But you hardly knew her."

"That is true. And yet they say you know all you need to know of any man or woman in the first instant that you meet. I have never yet encountered a villain who did not make my stomach queasy or my skin itch at our first greeting. On every occasion that I met a friend for the first time it was like I knew them for a lifetime already. Like you, Ludovici. I picked you as a stalwart from the moment I first saw you and you have never let me down. Even now, when I am changed beyond all recognition. So I knew her from the first. You love in a moment or not at all."

It was true, Ludovici thought. He had felt the same about Abbas, even though he was a Moor and a Muslim and he himself was a Christian and the son of a togato. He had told himself they had become friends because they were both exiles; he because he was a bastard and Abbas because he was a foreigner. But it had been more than that. They were, he supposed, like souls.

That had never occurred to him.

"Do you still have eunuchs in your household, Ludovici?"

"I have a harem of my own," he said, as if that explained everything.

Abbas said nothing but there was reproach in his silence.

"They are treated well."

A raised eyebrow, but nothing else.

"Do you ever think about the old days, Abbas, about Venice?"

"Sometimes. Yet it seems like another lifetime."

"Do you ever wish you had done things differently?"

"A man's fate is written on his forehead by God at the time of his birth, and this was mine. I could not have done differently, as a cloud cannot decide which way it will travel through the sky. Its direction is guided by God's wind, and so was mine."

"Then on the day of Judgment God will have no right to judge you for your sins. Instead He should ask your pardon."

"That is blasphemy, Ludovici, and I shall not listen to it." He clapped his hands to signal to his mutes that he was ready to leave. "One last question. Did you ever take Julia into your harem?"

The question took him off guard. "But she is not a concubine. She is a Christian woman of high birth."

"Yes, but did you do it? Did you make her your houri?"

"No. I did not."

A smile. What was it? Gratitude? "Good," Abbas said. "I am glad."

He got to his feet and prepared to leave. "And if I had?" Ludovici asked him.

"But you didn't," Abbas said. "So why ask?"

\*\*\*

When Ludovici returned to Pera he went to his study and stood at the window, looking over the Horn, thinking. He shouted instructions to Hyacinth to fetch Julia. The eunuch shuffled away along the corridor. Ludovici sat down at his oak desk by the window and waited.

She entered silently, heralded by the rustling of her long skirts on the marble. "You wanted to see me?"

Ludovici stood up and offered her a chair. "Please. Sit down."

She did so, and he pulled up a chair next to her.

"Is something wrong, Ludovici?"

He had to tell her. He had lied to Abbas, he couldn't lie to her as well. "Abbas wants you to leave here. He says it is dangerous for you."

"Do you think someone at the Harem has found out I am alive?"

"Perhaps. I don't see how."

"Did he tell you?"

"He just said it was dangerous for you to remain."

"But ... where should I go?"

"I don't know. I can send you back to Italy, to a convent perhaps."

She shook her head. "Why should he think I would prefer that to being a concubine. Though perhaps the evening entertainments would be different."

The remark shocked him. He turned away and stared at the twilight gathering over the Horn.

"Do I have a choice?"

"I'm not your gaoler."

"Then unless you have some other plan, I should rather stay here."

"At least you would have company."

"Nuns?"

"You can't stay here forever."

"You need me to go?"

"No, but … you have no one …"

"I had no one when I lived my father. The only time I had … anyone … was when I was the Sultan's whore."

He took a deep breath. He might as well say it. Wasn't this what was on his mind from the start? "What do you think of me, Julia?"

"What do I … what do you mean?"

"Come now, you have lived with me in this house for three years. You must have formed an opinion."

"You are a kind and decent man. I am very grateful to you. You saved my life and gave me sanctuary here."

Ludovici felt his heart sink. For some reason he would rather she hated him. "I made enquiries in the Comunità and with the bailo. Your husband, Serena, is dead."

She took a deep breath. "When?"

"Three weeks ago on Cyprus. I learned the news today."

"So I am a widow?"

He nodded.

"Well. It changes nothing though, does it?"

"Perhaps it does." He turned away from the window. "Marry me."

She stared at him, astonished. "But you have many women," she said. "Why would you want to marry me? How could it possibly serve you?"

"Isn't it enough that I do?"

Julia got to her feet, then sat down again. It was the first time he had seen her anything except serene.

"I have told Hyacinth to get rid of my concubines. They will all be married off to wealthy Turkish husbands. It is you that I want."

"Ludovici, stop. What is it that you are looking for? The girl that your friend saw in the church in Venice. She doesn't exist anymore. Perhaps she never did. If you were to marry me, what would you expect?"

I should not have asked her, he thought. I am betraying Abbas. I am taking full advantage of her situation. She is right to ask me; yes, what is it that I want?

"You want me to come to your bed?"

"I am afraid I am enchanted. Just as Abbas was."

"And look what happened to him." She touched his hand but withdrew before he could take it. "You must understand. I don't feel anything anymore. I walk into a room and I watch myself from the corner. I cannot explain it. I might look pretty in your bed but I fear I will make a very poor companion. And if it's a lover that you want, it might be better to have me as your mistress for a short time. Then you might more easily discard me, for I am sure you will be very disappointed."

"I shall never discard you."

"No, I don't believe you would. Listen, Ludovici, you are Sultan here. Put your handkerchief on my shoulder, and I will come. Just let me stay."

"It's dangerous, you understand? I will look into things, see if there is somewhere else you can go."

She stood up to go, then hesitated. "Why have you never asked me this before? I know you wanted to. I could see it in your eyes."

"Because of Abbas."

She kissed him on the forehead. Her perfume made him ache. After she had gone he sat for a long time moving, thinking about all she had said. Was it true that she felt nothing anymore? That was perhaps not so surprising after all she had been through. But she had agreed to be his mistress. Isn't this what he had dreamed about for three years?

"Abbas, forgive me," he muttered. But forgive him for what exactly? If it was her love he wanted then she was as unattainable as she ever was for his friend, the Kislar Aghasi.

## Mesopotamia

Baghdad had been built from the same stones as the ancient city of Babylon. It straddled the Tigris and the Euphrates, palm trees framing the domes and minarets. Suleiman stared at the walls, motionless on his white Arab stallion, watching the siege engines and cannon rumble into position and breathed a prayer of thanks. The crisis was past.

The Persians had not attacked that morning in the mountains, through grace of God. His presence had galvanized the army, and by that evening they had reorganized and begun the long slow retreat from the mountains that might have buried them.

The Empire of Mohammad, the army of Islam, would have been destroyed, thanks to my Seraskier Sultan! True Believer or not, he has a duty to me and his ambition blinded him to it.

Ibrahim rode towards him, the rubies and emeralds embroidered on his saddle glittering in the sun. He grinned as if the horrors of the last week were just a bad dream to be dismissed with the dawn.

"Why so solemn my Lord?"

"Why? Because you should have stood at these gates two months ago. Because a week ago you almost led my army to ruin!"

Ibrahim shrugged, as if it were a minor offence. "Your generals itched for a long campaign, and we have given them one. That old bear at the head of the yeniçeris is still melting the snow out of his boots!"

"You may laugh, Ibrahim but this was our objective. Babylon! We did not come here to placate the Aga nor find the Shah. We were here to chase away dogs from a holy place!"

Ibrahim grew sullen. "You said you wanted the dog's head."

"No, I did not say that. You did." He squeezed the flanks of his horse with his knees and trotted ahead, leaving Ibrahim alone on the plain.

# CHAPTER 68

## Stamboul, 1535

Early spring but snow still clung to the roofs of the kiosks in the Topkapi, fell in minor avalanches from the dome of the Aya Sofia and froze the fountains in the courtyards of the Eski Saraya. Only Hürrem and the Kislar Aghasi himself were allowed the fur-lined kaftans of rank; the odalisques and servants were obliged to freeze as they made their way along the icy cloisters. Inside the Palace, all the shutters and doors tightly closed against the cold, the stale aroma of incense and charcoal and hashish mingled with each other to create a suffocating fug. Hürrem had her servants spray her apartments with orange blossom and rosewater to relieve it.

The fall of Baghdad and the passing of the long winter months had not stilled the gossip about the Suleiman and his Seraskier Sultan; if anything the anticipation of the army's return had intensified it. News came infrequently, couriers riding day and night for twenty, even thirty days to bring news.

It was the scandal of the whole city, of course, how Ibrahim had defied the sultan even to the point of assuming his title. This scandalous development was not intended to go beyond the Divan but how could you keep secrets in a city like this? Rüstem had made sure everyone in the city knew of it within days.

Merchants spat and cursed the Greek's name in all the bazaars. The statues in front of his palace in the Aytmedani had even been defaced one night. All Stamboul had hated him for years, resenting his power over the Sultan and the way he flaunted his wealth. No one was surprised or dismayed that he had finally gone too far.

Or had he? Only one man still tolerated his excesses.

Many times Hürrem assumed that Ibrahim was already dead, strangled in his tent by the bostanji  or hung on a gibbet in a Baghdad square. He could have been mouldering in his grave for weeks by the time any chaush might arrive with the news. But the long winter was almost over and Ibrahim still lived. Like some terrible spirit it seemed he could not die.

How far could he goad the Sultan before he finally did something about it?

Now Abbas settled himself on his knees to deliver the latest news: "A courtier has arrived at the palace my lady. Suleiman will be back in Stamboul in the next few days."

"With Ibrahim?"

"Yes, My Lady." I do not believe this, Hürrem thought. What does it take? One day his Vizier will put a dagger through Suleiman's heart and he will reach up and kiss him on the lips.

"There is other news," Abbas said,

"Tell me."

"The Shah attacked the rearguard of the army on its return through Azerbaijan. Four generals were lost, eight hundred yeniçeris surrendered."

"Who was Seraskier?"

"Ibrahim. The Sultan had ridden ahead with his bodyguard."

Well, some good news at least. "It seems the Greek's golden touch has deserted him."

"Yes, my Lady."

"It is not the outcome we all prayed for yet that is no fault of yours, Kislar Aghasi. You have done well."

"Thank you."

"Rüstem, too. He shows a great talent. I am sure we will find a use for him again in the near future. You should convey him my thanks and assure him he will be amply rewarded."

"I will tell him."

Abbas executed a temenna, eager to be out of the room. It was not just the overpowering heat from the charcoal braziers and the cloying smell of perfume. He felt physically ill at what he had done. He had no love for Ibrahim, or any of them. But he felt base and discredited by it. Still, if his toadying had bought her time to get out of Stamboul, then it had been worth it.

"By the way, have you seen Julia?" Hürrem said, just as he reached the door.

"No, my Lady."

"I am curious, that is all. I have been wondering about what you told me. How much could a simple slave girl pay you that would be worth risking your neck?"

She knows. "I took pity on her also."

"Ah, pity was it? My good, brave Abbas."

"As you say."

"She is mistress now to Ludovici Gambetto, one of the Venetian merchants on Pera. Did you know?"

The room started to spin. "Yes, My Lady, I knew," he said, and hoped that she believed him.

"I hope she pleases him more than she pleases the Sultan."

"I hope so too."

"Thank you, Abbas."

He returned to his cell, fire burning in his heart. Mistress? You told me you had sent her out of Stamboul and instead you have her in your bed. Ludovici, what have you done? You lied to me, you lied!

# CHAPTER 69

Suleiman looked suddenly old. Yet there was no physical change since the last time she had seen him. There was no more gray in his beard, his back was still as straight. Of course, his skin had been burnished by the long winter in the desert and mountains, and that had made the lines on his face more pronounced. But it was not that; he just looked drained, as if all the juice had been squeezed out of him.

He sat in front of a low table, his hands clenched into fists in his lap. His homecoming had been muted; she had welcomed him home in her apartments in the Eski Saraya, they had shared a meal though Suleiman had eaten hardly anything. Instead of ravishing her, as she had expected, he had fallen asleep on the divan. Now awake again, he seem scarcely more refreshed than before.

"What is wrong, my Lord?"

"You know what is wrong. All Stamboul knows what is wrong. What may I do, little russelana?"

"What happened in Persia? You confronted him about the letter?"

"I waited for his confession, but it did not come. He acts as if nothing has happened. What should I do now? Bring Rüstem before him?"

"May he find excuse that way?"

Suleiman shook his head. "I wanted only his free admission. I could not bear to debate it with him and have to listen to his lies. The letter was signed under my seal. What could he say that would pardon him?"

"And yet?"

"And yet I love him, Hürrem. Not as I love you, but ..."

You must execute him, Hürrem thought. Otherwise we are all in danger. Ibrahim is not stupid. If you give him time, he will make a move against you,

258

he knows it is his only hope. How can you still hesitate? "You might exile him, as you did Achmed Pasha."

"Achmed Pasha used his place of exile as a base for revolt. Do I dare take the same risk with Ibrahim, who is a far better general than he ever was?"

Of course you cannot, Hürrem thought. I am relieved you have at least thought that part of it through. "He has been your friend for so long, my Lord. I know you love him like a brother. Do not ask me for my counsel in this."

"Yet who else may I trust?"

She stroked his cheek. "But he was the greatest of your Viziers."

"Yes but now his ambition and his greed have outreached him., On our return from Baghdad he allowed the beys of Cairo and Syria to camp in a valley, with no escape. As commander he should have been watchful for an attack at our rear. Instead he was more concerned to ensure the safety of the bales of Persian silk he had looted. He allowed the Shah's cavalry to inflict the greatest defeat my army has ever suffered. Instead of celebrating our victory at Baghdad we are mourning the loss of almost a thousand good men. All thanks to … Seraskier Sultan!"

Hürrem held his hands in hers. "He is guilty of negligence in his command, through his own self interest. He has done the unthinkable, and assumed the name of Sultan. My Lord, I feel your pain, but what else can you do?"

The sun set behind the roofs of the old palace. "He comes to dine with me tonight alone at the Topkapi Saraya."

Hürrem put her head on his shoulder. Incredible! What does it take to lose your loyalty? "What will you tell him, my Lord?"

"I do not know. I never thought this day would come. "I cannot end his life, Hürrem, I cannot. I have given my word."

"My Lord?"

"I made a vow when I made him Vizier - I swore to it before God - that while I lived he need not fear me. He has my oath on that."

They sat in silence. Long shadows crept across the carpet. Pages crept into the room to light candles and oil lamps. "Must he die?" Hürrem whispered.

"The law says he must."

"Then there is a way, though I hesitate even to whisper it. But if it ceases your torment …"

"Tell me."

"You have sworn not to put him to death while you are living. Then let the order be carried out while you are asleep. The muftis say that while a man sleeps he does not truly live. It is like a small death. So you can fulfil the law, your duty to the throne and to Islam, and still not violate your oath."

Suleiman said nothing for a very long time.

"So be it," he said at last.

# CHAPTER 70

The flickering light of the lamps was reflected in the rubies inlaid in the censers. They reminded Ibrahim of the camp fires in the valley of Sultania the night before the snowstorm. As if he wished to be reminded of that! He ran a finger around the rim of his jade cup, staring into the blood red wine. "We have given a lashing to the Persian dogs," he said. "They will be licking their wounds for as very long time."

"The campaign was not well advised," Suleiman said. "We were almost drawn into a trap. As it was, the final battle went to the Shah. He will be celebrating now, despite our victories at Baghdad and Tabriz."

"There will be other summers."

"To what purpose?"

Ibrahim's anger was sudden. "We have an empire that rivals that of Alexander the Great. Why should we engage in this moping? We have Baghdad, the Shah has the snow and the rocks!"

"We lost many good men for no reason. The Defterdar Rüstem, for example."

Ibrahim felt the blood drain from his face. Why would Suleiman bring up Rüstem? Was he dead? On the contrary his spies had whispered to him that he was still alive, had been seen in Manisa.

Rüstem!

If it was true the enormity of this betrayal took his breath away. In other circumstance he might have applauded such sleight of hand. "What do you know about my clerks?" Ibrahim said, unable to meet his eyes.

"Only that this one was murdered by the Shah engaging in some secret diplomacy of yours. Did he volunteer for his mission or did you order him to go?"

"He volunteered, He seemed very eager."

"And what was his purpose?"

"I attempted to lure the Shah out of the mountains. That was my only intention. I attempted a minor deception." It sounds as if I am pleading, Ibrahim thought. Well perhaps I am. He must realize I meant no harm against him.

"It seems you failed."

Ibrahim tried to read Suleiman's eyes. God help me in my sorrow! He does not believe me!

"I tried everything to finish the Shah for you. If I went too far, it was only my enthusiasm for victory that was my fault." There, it was said now; a plea for forgiveness, without confessing the sin. What if Suleiman only suspected? What if Rüstem really were dead right now, eating shit in the devil's latrines?

Unless Hürrem had some hand in this.

"Well, it is done now," Suleiman said.

"There will be other victories, my Lord. Like Rhodes and Mohacs. Do you remember how close we came to giving up then? If we can endure the black times, God is sure to reward us."

"It was your counsel that prevailed at Rhodes, Ibrahim."

"I am glad you remember. Remember too that I only wish to serve you."

"And you have served me well, many times. But victory in itself means nothing unless it serves Islam. Perhaps we have both forgotten that."

"Every victory furthers Islam."

"Does it? You must know the mind of Mohammed before you can speak for him."

Ibrahim swallowed his anger. As Suleiman had just admitted to him, he would not have prevailed at Rhode or at Mohacs without him. "I was not born to Mohammed," he said carefully. "I still have much to learn."

"It is too late for that. I do not think anyone can teach you anything now." If he had smiled as he said that Ibrahim might have smiled along with him. But Suleiman did not smile.

"Shall we go hunting in Adrianople again this summer?" Ibrahim said.

"Perhaps. Only God knows the future."

"I could fly the falcons for you again. Like the old days."

Suleiman did not reply.

"Do you remember the time that boar rushed my horse from the thicket on the Marantza River? You saved my life then."

"You stood and faced it even though you were unarmed. You looked as if you were not afraid of anything."

Yes, because the boar only had razor-sharp tusks, Ibrahim thought. Not a palace full of mutes with bowstrings. "I was not afraid because you were there to protect me."

"I cannot always be there. We must all face death alone some time."

No, he could not mean it! I am your Vizier, Suleiman! Your Seraskier, your friend! I have eaten at your table, slept in your tent through endless campaigns! "The only thing I fear is the way death comes. You swore to me once that you would never condemn me. I could not bear the dishonour of dying that way."

"I remember my oath, and I will never break it."

Ibrahim stared at him in confusion. What then? What is he planning? "My Lord, I am just a man, and I have made many mistakes. There is something I must confess-"

Suleiman put up his hand to still him. "You do not have to plead your case with me Ibrahim."

"But my lord-"

"There is no need to say more. I am tired. We will talk again tomorrow."

\*\*\*

Suleiman rose to his feet. His head felt like lead. The drugged wine had affected him more than it seemed to have affected Ibrahim. He just wanted to sleep, longed only for this ordeal to be over.

"The pages will prepare your bed. Sleep well, my friend."

Ibrahim rose to embrace him. "Sleep well, my Lord."

Suleiman embraced him, then pushed him away and went into his private chamber, locking the door behind him.

\*\*\*

Hürrem rose from the bed and hurried over to him. He was gray. I must not let him change his mind, she thought.

She was naked except for rose damask trousers and a single pearl fastened around her waist. He did not even seem to notice.

I will make him notice, she thought. I will make him drunk with wine and drunk with me and when he has had a surfeit of both, he will sleep. When he wakes it will all be over.

"My Lord ..."

"He all but begged me for his life."

She laid her head on his chest.

"I cannot stand this! Hold me little russelana."

She took him over to the bed. "Drink this," she whispered, and offered him a goblet of wine.

"It will help me sleep?"

You should be unconscious already! she thought. He took the goblet and swallowed it in one draught. He allowed her to undress him then, something she had never let him do before. He sat on the bed, head bowed, and then she laid him down.

She lay on top of him, her small breasts brushing his chest. She wriggled against him. He did not respond. She kissed his chest, his belly, his …

He twisted away from her and sat up. He made for the door.

"My Lord!"

"I cannot …"

She thought he would break then, even tried to throw open the door, then remembered it was locked. He sank to his haunches, his hands across his stomach as if he had been stabbed. Hürrem refilled the goblet with more of the drugged wine and hurried across the room with it. She held the cup to his lips and he gulped it with the desperation of a man dying of thirst. "Do not let it happen while I am awake, russelana. I must not break my oath! Let it not happen while I am awake!"

She cradled his head between her breasts, cooing to him as if he were a baby. "Sleep, my Lord. Sleep …"

After a while she felt his head grow heavy. She lay on the floor beside him and held him while he twitched and muttered in his sleep. She prayed for the bostanji to hurry up and do their work.

# CHAPTER 71

Ibrahim paced the room, ignoring the bed the pages had made up for him, fighting the heaviness in his limbs and the numbing tiredness that had all but overwhelmed him. He walked into the wall. The wine! Suleiman had drugged him!

No, he would not do that! Never!

He must stay awake. He would not let them find him sleeping. He must stay awake! He was Ibrahim, Vizier to the Magnificent. He could not die at the Sultan's hand. He had his prince's word, his oath before God.

So why had the pages locked the door behind them?

He felt dizzy and leaned against the wall. If I sit down I will sleep. It must have been the wine! This cannot be happening.

He heard footsteps in the corridor outside and a noise that sounded like the yelp of a dog. The deaf-mutes! The bostanji ! A key creaked in the lock and the handle began to turn.

God help me in my sorrow!

The door swung open.

There were five of them, all Nubians. The bostanji "s assassins were eunuchs prepared for their unique assignments by further alterations to their physique; their eardrums had been  pierced with needles and their tongues had been cut out. This way they could not succumb to the pleas of their victims or tell anyone what they had done.

Ibrahim took out his dagger and staggered to the door that separated his room from the Sultan's. He hammered on it with his fists. "My Lord!"

The bostanji edged towards him.

"My Lord! Suleiman! Please! Stop this!"

***

Suleiman jerked awake. "What was that?"

Someone was hammering on the door. Ibrahim! Ibrahim needed his help!

Hürrem covered his ears with her hands and cradled his head against her breasts. She started to sing, to drown out the shouts from the next room. Ibrahim is dying, he thought, and yet I am still awake.

"While I yet live ..."

He heard a scream. I have broken my oath. I have murdered my friend.

***

Each of the five bostanji  held a silken bowstring, the ritual instrument of execution for those of high position or with royal blood. It was a silk bowstring that had dispatched Suleiman's own uncles, cousins and nephews.

Ibrahim held the dagger in front of him and turned to face them.

The first of them grinned and moved in, as if he had not even seen the knife, perhaps overconfident of his ability to evade it. As he lunged Ibrahim sidestepped him easily and the knife flashed up and out.

The assassin stared at him in surprise. Blood spurted rhythmically from his neck and up the wall. He out his hands to his throat in a vain attempt to staunch the flow and fell to his knees.

Ibrahim backed against the wall, as the other bostanji  fanned out across the room, more wary now. Their comrade died, noisily.

They signalled to each other with deft, almost imperceptible hand signals. He tensed, ready.

When they moved again it was quickly and in unison; Ibrahim struck out in a broad arc in front of his body and leaped back. One of them moaned, a deep mournful sigh from deep within his chest. Blood poured from a gash in his arm.

His assassins moved in again. Ibrahim slashed again, and one of them fell, but Ibrahim's shout of defiance was cut off as a bowstring closed around his throat. The other two went to grab him and he slashed again, and saw another of them reel back, clutching at his face.

But then the other had hold of his arm and had twisted it behind him, trying to break his grip on the knife. The bowstring tightened around his throat.

Most men clawed at the bowstring; it was instinctive, he had been told. Instead Ibrahim used his free hand to plunge two splayed fingers into the eyes of the second attacker. The man screamed his grip loosened just enough for him to twist his dagger arm free, the blade slicing through the man's hands and arms as he pulled it free.

He turned it in his hand and stabbed behind him. He felt a rush of warmth on his back and the noose around his throat loosened. He stabbed

265

twice more, but the second time the dagger was torn from his grip. It had jammed between the bostanji "s ribs as he fell and it would not pull free.

Another bowstring closed around his throat. His attacker was one he had already wounded; he could feel the blood dripping from the man's arm and down his neck. He tried to twist around but the assassin jerked backwards with the noose, pulling him off balance.

He put his hands to his throat, and in that moment when his reflexes took over from his warrior's training he knew he was lost. He tried to slide his fingers under the bowstring, but it was drawn taut, biting deep into the flesh of his throat. His chest spasmed and he kicked out in panic, all reason gone. Bright flashes of light exploded in front of his eyes.

He tried to scream Suleiman's name, but no sound came. He could no longer control his limbs. Black shadows closed in from all sides.

## The Hippodrome

Güzül hurried along the Atmeydani under the imposing red walls of Ibrahim's palace. A messenger had brought an urgent summons to her house in the Jewish quarter a few minutes before. Ibrahim wanted to see her immediately.

She was ushered through the gates by the guards. She hurried across the courtyard to the stairs that led to the pasha's hall of audience. She kept her head down, lifting the skirts of her ferijde as she ran, taking care not to slip on the thin film of ice on the cobblestones.

She was halfway up the stair when she was aware of the figure watching her from the shadows. He wore a fur-lined green pelisse and white sugarloaf turban. The Kislar Aghasi! She stared at him in confusion.

"Ibrahim is dead," Abbas said. His voice was flat. He sounded sad, if anything; or reluctant.

Güzül turned and looked behind her. Two bostanji stood at the foot of the stairs, their killiç drawn.

"It is at the order of the Lady Hürrem," Abbas said. "Go with God." He turned away, his duty done, with no particular desire to see the bostanji complete their work.

## Topkapi Saraya

Suleiman watched from a window high above the Third Court as Ibrahim's body was loaded onto the back of a horse. A blanket of black velvet had been laid on the horse's back, and a special ointment had been put in its eyes to make it weep. A bostanji led the horse away. He would be taken to Galata and buried in an unmarked grave.

The two dead bostanji had been dragged from the room. None of them had escaped injury. One had lost an eye, another his nose. There were dark splashes of blood up the four walls. It looked as if two small armies had gone to war in there.

"He fought well," Suleiman said. His face was white. He was trembling.

"Please my Lord," Hürrem said. "Do not torment yourself. Your orders were just. You could not do other than what you did."

"Oh my russelana," he said. He clung to her.

After all, she thought with some relief, he can cling to no one else now.

# PART 6

## THIS WOMAN HÜRREM

# CHAPTER 72

Suleiman watched Mustapha spur his Arab to the crest of the hill. Its long, silky tail stood straight in pureblood fashion. He has grown into a handsome young man, he thought. A fine prince. Already he has four sons of his own from his harem. Twenty six years old already; the same age that he had ridden from Manisa to take the throne.

The awkward, bowed figure of Çehangir followed, the hooded gyrfalcon on his outstretched arm. Suleiman had been surprised and gratified at the friendship that had developed between Mustapha and Çehangir in the past weeks. The young prince had taken his less well favoured brother under his wing, had showed him how to hunt with the falcons and spent hours with him in the Place of Arrows, showing endless patience. They were the most unlikely of half-brothers, he supposed. Çehangir now followed him round like a puppy, spent hours watching him ride at the çerit.

He urged his own horse to the rise to join them there, so they could watch the archers and their dogs sweeping through the marsh below, flushing out prey.

Çehangir rode down the slope and released his gyrfalcon, as Mustapha had shown him. It swept into the air with a piercing cry.

"Look at him," Mustapha said proudly. "He tries hard to overcome what God has willed."

"Promise me you will never harm him," Suleiman said.

"Harm him? Why would I do that?"

"When the throne is yours. You know the law."

"I am not my grandfather."

"Yet it is your right, if you wish it."

"Then I give you my word - I shall not harm him, or any of my brothers."

I wish I could believe you, Suleiman thought, but will you feel the same when your life and your throne is threatened? The Fatih's murderous blood is in my veins and in yours. "What you do after I am gone and in Paradise is with you and with God. But spare Çehangir."

"None of them need fear me, my Lord. That bloody custom ended with my grandfather."

"You may feel differently in time."

"If they do not raise their hands against me, I shall not harm them."

"You are not children any longer. Selim and Bayezid are men now, like you."

"The decision will be theirs. If they take arms against me, I shall act. That is the way of princes. The throne shall be mine, in time. But you may tell them what I said. I don't want their blood on my hands."

How can you be sure what you will do when the whispers start? he thought. How can any of us be sure? He thought of Ibrahim. When was there a day when he did not? "As long as you do not harm Çehangir," he repeated.

The gyrfalcon swooped on its quarry and the dogs bayed and sprang forward and the archers let out a whoop of triumph. Çehangir turned and grinned at Mustapha, such a good pupil. Another life ended on a beautiful spring morning.

## The Eski Saraya

The shadows retreated across Asia toward the cold dark of Europe. Sunlight inched through the cloisters and dark gardens, dissolving the mist that curled around the roofs. A spider, clinging to its beaded web, was outlined against a lemon sky; an owl tolled the watch song of the dawn.

The muezzin called the city to prayer. "Allahu akbar! La illaha illa"llah ..."

Hürrem stood at the lattice window, shrouded in a fur pelisse. Her hair hung loose about her shoulders, unkempt and unbraided. She shivered in the cold, staring at the minarets of the Aya Sofia, flashing like the tips of lances as they broke through the morning mist.

I am a heartbeat away from oblivion, she thought. If Mustapha should live, my sons will be murdered or imprisoned, I will be banished to some lonely place in Anatolia with only the jackals and goats for company.

She called for Muomi to come and perform her toilet. She sat in front of the mirror and watched her comb out her hair. She felt as if she were staring over the edge of a cliff.

"Stop," she said.

She leaned closer to the glass. She withdrew her hand from her pelisse and ran her fingers through her hair, saw the terrible truth confirmed. A grey hair.

You cannot deny me any longer, the mirror said. The tiny lines at the corner of your eyes will grow deeper until you can no longer disguise them with kohl and this first gray hair will soon be followed by others.

And what will happen when he sees you growing old? Will the Lord of Life still be yours to command then? Will he still overlook the paradise of willing, ambitious little houris eager to use their transient charms to replace you in his bed? Even now there may be another Hürrem scheming to exile you, as you did to Gülbehar.

She snatched the ivory handled brush from Muomi and smashed into the mirror, splintering her reflection into shards.

"Get Abbas! Get him now!"

\*\*\*

"How is Julia?" she said.

Abbas felt himself falling yet again towards a black pit. She would never let him be, this witch. She would torment him with this until death. Damn Ludovici.

"I trust she is well?

"How did you find out about her?"

"I cannot tell you that. A woman has to have some secrets." She sat on the divan, her legs tucked beneath her, her body curled into the fur of the long green pelisse. "Oh Abbas, you should not be frightened of me! I am your friend. If I intended to denounce you to the Lord of Life, I would have done it long ago."

"I live only to serve my Sultan and the Crown of Veiled Heads. I am thankful for your pardon, though I shall surely answer for all my sins before God."

Hürrem clapped her hands in delight. "What a fine speech! You have become the perfect diplomat, Abbas. You are a credit to all eunuchs everywhere."

How I would like to rip out your evil tongue and keep it in a jar! "And you are a credit to all women everywhere, My Lady"

Hürrem cocked her head to one side, and her tongue traversed her upper lip. She stood up, letting the pelisse fall away from her shoulders. She was naked underneath.

Abbas gritted his teeth and lowered his eyes to the floor.

"What is the matter, am I too ugly to look at?"

"No, My Lady, your loveliness dazzles me," he said, trying to maintain control of his own voice. Nearly twenty years in the Harem have done you little harm, he thought. You know your body can still stir a man, even an incomplete one like me. A wet nurse for every infant and I have never seen you touch a sweetbread, though they lie around in here like apples in an

273

orchard. But why are you doing this to me? Why would you flaunt yourself at a eunuch?

"They tell me you were razored after puberty. How old were you, Abbas?"

"Seventeen years old, My Lady."

"Did you have any knowledge of women before then?"

"Some."

"Not many survive such an operation at that age, do they? You were one of the lucky ones."

"I should hardly call it luck," he said before he could check himself.

She reached up and stroked his cheek. He could smell her perfume, oranges and jasmine. "Poor Abbas, do you still sometimes feel desire then?"

He lowered his eyes to her body. O Great God, help me in my sorrow! She knew the answer to that, of course. Even in his hatred he longed to caress her breast. The look in his eyes had already betrayed him, he knew.

"Do you still think about Julia?"

He felt as if he were choking. "No, My Lady."

"I can have your unbiased opinion then. Do you think I am still as lovely as the other girls in the Harem?"

She turned around slowly on the tips of her toes. This woman is mad, he thought. Mad, dangerous and depraved in the soul. "Lovelier," he said.

Her eyes glittered. "Isn't it strange? A naked woman is powerless before a real man. Yet with you I am quite safe. It creates a bond between us, doesn't it?"

"We are all tied by bonds of service."

"Exactly. And you have to give yours service to me. Because of Julia."

Just tell me what you want and leave me in peace, he thought. "You only have to name your desire and it is done."

"My desire? My desire is that you burn down the Harem. I want this place utterly destroyed. You can do that little thing for me, can you not, Abbas?"

\*\*\*

Their time at the Enderun was almost finished. Soon they would be sent out to the provinces and take up governorships, as their father had done. Selim could not wait for the day to come. But there were scores to settle before he left.

His tutors, for instance. One of them, Hakim, had singled him out for special treatment the whole time he was there. He even beat him when he could not recite his Qu'ran, though he would never beat Bayezid. Once he even put him to the bastinado; it was a simple enough device, stocks secured the feet and the soles were beaten with long sticks. Even five years later Selim could still remember the pain. He had shrieked like a baby at each blow and Hakim only ceased the beating when Selim had begged, through his tears, for him to stop. He had been unable to walk for a week and it was a month before the scars healed.

And he had not forgotten how his little brother had humiliated him in front of everyone in the courtyard. Perhaps, he thought, there is a way that I might let them both remember their days at the Enderun as fondly as I do.

There was a playing field below the walls of the Second Court where all the boys practiced at çerit; the tutors called it a game but it was more like a mock battle. They used horses with short necks and strong bodies, bred for their speed and their ability to check quickly. Riders armed with javelins three and a half feet long would manoeuvre in two teams of twelve around an open field and hurl their weapons at each other's heads. The side with the most hits at the end of the "game" was declared the winner.

There were frequent injuries; sometimes boys were killed. Selim dreaded it as much as Bayezid excelled at it.

Although they were on opposite teams - Bayezid rode for the Blues, the Sultan's favoured team (of course) and Selim for the Greens - he knew any attempt to injure Bayezid was doomed. He was just too good a rider. Selim would only expose himself to risk. His usual tactic anyway was to hang back and try and preserve his own skin.

The solution was surprisingly simple. He found Bayezid's horse one day before a game and sawed halfway through the saddle strap with a serrated knife.

Tents had been pitched round the field and crowds of yeniçeris clustered round to watch. Selim knew the Sultan would probably be watching also from the walls overlooking the field. Well they won't be able to cheer their young hero today, Selim thought. I'd like to see Hakim's face when our young hero is trampled under the hoofs.

The two teams circled each other, the thunder of the horses echoing from the palace walls. Clouds of dust drifted across the field. Bayezid broke and charged first, as he always did. Two of the Greens split from the group and headed towards him at full tilt. Selim checked his own horse to the flank.

As the riders closed he heard a shout and saw one of the riders fall. The horses thundered over the top of him. He lay face down in the dust.

Immediately the two Greens dropped their javelins and leaped from their horses.

"It's Bayezid!" someone shouted. "He's hurt!"

Selim walked his mount through the settling clouds of dust. Bayezid was still lying there, face down, he had not moved. There was a satisfying smudge of blood on his turban. Selim tried to look concerned.

"Is he dead?" he asked, hopefully.

\*\*\*

But Bayezid did not die. The lump on his head was impressive and he limped badly for many weeks afterwards and could not ride in the çerit, but he did not die. When it was discovered that the fault was with his saddle harness Hakim was put to the bastinado for negligence and exiled to Bitlis.

Not the perfect revenge, but it would do. I may be slow to learn certain lessons, Hakim, but I am not slow in everything.

# CHAPTER 73

The Sirocco originates in the Sahara, its hot breath scalding Tripoli and Algiers and the ruins of Carthage before heading across the Mediterranean towards Europe. By the time it reaches the distant shores across the ocean thunderheads have banked to the stars behind it. Everything wilts.

On the night he had chosen to execute Hürrem's latest caprice, it rushed through the narrow streets of Stamboul like a gale, bending the branches of the cypress trees in the palace gardens, whipping the red and green flags of the palace into a frenzy, piling froth on the distant shores of the Bosphorus. Its stinking breath was oppressive.

Perfect weather, Abbas thought.

He had delayed four nights before judging the wind at its peak. The Palace was in darkness when he set off with two bostanji through a little-used gate in the southern wall. The three eunuchs were gone for less than an hour but when they returned an orange stain was already creeping up the horizon and over the roofs of the cramped wooden houses in a false dawn.

As soon as they were back inside the saraya Abbas found the bostanji - bashi and slipped an emerald ring into his palm. He used sign language to indicate that the two men who had accompanied him on his errand that night should not live to see the morning.

Then he returned to his cell and waited, wondering what other crimes he might yet commit in the name of love.

*\*\**

The booming of the tambours echoed through the dark streets. The Palace woke to the cries of: "Yanghinvar! Fire!"

Abbas ran from his cell. He could hear women screaming from one of the upstairs dormitories. In the courtyard below two guards had drawn their yataghans in confusion - idiots, he thought impatiently. Couldn't they smell the smoke?

He did not hesitate; after all, he had had days to rehearse each move and Hürrem had made it quite clear what his first duty should be. He rousted two of his pages from their beds and rattled off the list of instructions he had memorized: prepare the coaches; get all the women downstairs into the courtyard; send six other pages to the dressmaker and bring all of Lady Hürrem's possessions down to safety.

Naturally she could not leave anything behind of hers. Not even if the whole city roasted.

Then he ran puffing up the stairs to her apartments.

*** 

He was astonished at her appearance. She must have been grooming herself all night, he decided. She had on a stunning emerald-green kaftan of alternating crescent and stars over a white chemise emblazoned with rumi scrollwork in gold thread. Her hair was plaited with tiny emeralds and pearls and her yashmak was in place. Muomi stood beside her, holding a ferijde of violet silk.

So this is what one wears to a fire! She was perfumed, of course, for she would not present herself to the Sultan after an inferno reeking of smoke.

"What took you so long, my Aga?" she hissed. "Did you want me to cook in my bed?"

"They have just sounded the alarm, My Lady," he gasped. He was panting from the exertion of climbing two flights of stairs.

"Why did you need to wait for the alarm? You already knew the city was alight."

Abbas lurched to the window and groaned aloud. God help me in my sorrow, I had not meant for half of Stamboul to be swallowed up by the conflagration. The wind had fanned the flames into a firestorm and the wooden buildings on the hill below were being gobbled up in moments. The fire was rolling towards them like a wave.

He watched a house catch light, flare and then cave in, sending a shower of sparks into the night sky. All in a matter of moments! People rushed up the alley, carrying all they could on their backs, tripping over each other in panic. The mass of people looked like a river flooding through a chasm, a torrent of torches and wide-eyed oxen, blindfolded rearing horses and unveiled women.

God forgive me, Abbas thought. I never imagined anything like this.

A red hot cinder was hurled towards him on the wind and caught his cheek. He howled and jumped back. "We must hurry!" he shouted.

"I have been waiting to hurry for hours," Hürrem said, as if she were late for a formal entertainment at the Hippodrome.

Muomi helped her into her cloak, drawing the cazeta over her face to preserve her anonymity and her dignity. Then she put on her own hooded cloak and Abbas led them out of the apartment and down the stairs.

He had thought they would have more time. Even with all my preparations I may still be too late, he thought. The coaches were waiting on the cobblestones. "Get ... inside!" he shouted, gasping for breath. "Quickly!"

The two shrouded figures pushed past him and into the first coach. He shut the door behind them. A hand snaked out from behind the taffeta curtain and grasped his own. The hooded figure leaned towards him and for a moment he thought she was about to whisper her thanks.

"Leave behind anything of mine," she hissed, her face invisible behind the cazeta, "anything at all - and it will be your head!"

## Topkapi Saraya

Abbas slumped to his knees to execute his sala'am at the feet of the Lord of Life. He rested his forehead on the carpet a little longer than was necessary and was afterwards unable to rise to his feet once more. His pelisse reeked of wood smoke and his face and turban were smeared with grime.

Suleiman watched him, creased with anguish.

"A thousand pardons my Lord," Abbas gasped.

"Does my servant need the physician?"

"I am merely fatigued." Two pages finally helped him back to his feet.

"There has been a fire at the Eski Saraya?" Suleiman was impatient for the Kislar Aghasi to tell his story and leave. Where was Hürrem?

"The entire palace was in flames when I left. However all the women are safe."

"Hürrem?"

"She waits outside the door. I guarded her life as I might that of your most ..." He staggered and recovered. " ... precious treasure."

"We are in your debt," Suleiman said. Just depart and let me see Hürrem! He was not dressed for audience with slaves. He had been abruptly woken from his sleep and wore only a kaftan and fez. "There were no injuries?"

"I fear a number of my pages and guards were burned in the fire ... as they were attempting to recover some of my Lady's jewels and clothes from her apartment."

"The palace is destroyed?"

"My last vision of it ... it was totally engulfed in flame."

"I commend you Abbas, for your efforts. Send in the Lady Hürrem and the rest. We shall speak again in the morning."

"My Lord," he said and slumped again to the ground to perform a final sala'am. Suleiman thought that he had fallen unconscious but with one final effort he raised his great bulk from the floor and staggered from the room.

A few moments later a figure swathed in violet silk appeared and almost immediately fell to the ground, this time from exhaustion not because of any ceremonial. Suleiman leaped from his divan and rushed across the room to help her. "Hürrem, are you all right?" He threw back the cazeta. Her face was pale and her eyes red from crying. "My little russelana, are you hurt?"

She shook her head. He felt her tremble in his arms like a small bird. "They shouldn't have gone back in there just for a few trinkets," she said. "I told them not to."

"Who?"

"Those poor servants ... it was just some silks and bracelets ... not worth a life."

He felt her heartbeat as he held her and thanked God for it. "When the messenger told me about the fire and I saw the glow above the saraya ...I do not know what I would have done if anything happened to my russelana ..."

"It was terrible. It was the smell of smoke that woke me. I thought I was going to die."

He buried his face in her neck and gratitude swiftly transformed into desire. He wanted to reclaim his possession of her over death. He hooked his fingers into the neck of her chemise and tore it down its full length. "Until the coaches came I thought you were gone," he said.

"It was kismet," she said.

"Russelana," he said and felt his voice catch in his throat. He rolled between her legs and took her, there on the carpets, sobbing with relief. Where would he be without her?

***

Suleiman does not look quite as well disposed to the mercies of the Great God this morning, Abbas thought. He looks, perhaps, even a little sour. "You must accommodate Hürrem and the other women in the Palace here until other arrangements can be made," Suleiman said.

"It poses a problem, my Lord," Abbas said.

"I do not wish to hear of problems."

"I would not burden you with such trivialities, but it requires your special permission."

"To set aside one corner of the Palace for my haremlik? How difficult can it be to find rooms for a few women and their servants?"

Abbas stared at him, appalled. Could it be that the Lord of Life was ignorant of the true size of his Harem - and in particular, Hürrem's private arrangements? "My Lord, my Lady Hürrem's retinue alone is a large one, as befitting the favoured kadin of the Lord of Life."

Suleiman shifted irritably on the divan. "How large?"

"She has herself thirty pages and slaves ..."

"Thirty!"

" ... and one hundred and three ladies in waiting ..."

"What?"

" ... and of course there is her purveyor and her dressmaker. It means a total of one hundred and thirty seven people, including myself."

"Abbas!"

"Add to that number the one hundred and nine girls who still remain in my Lord's Harem, plus perhaps an equal number of pages and hand maidens ..."

Suleiman tugged at his beard. He looked alarmed. "My private quarters will be totally over run."

"Until other arrangements are made." Abbs tried not to gloat. Oh, she's really got you this time.

Suleiman sighed. "Very well."

"My Lord?"

"There is nothing else to be done. The Harem must be housed somewhere. Take whatever rooms you need, I will authorize it. In the meantime I shall summon my architect, Sinan. We shall have to set to work on a new saraya for the Harem immediately."

# CHAPTER 74

There are lines around her eyes, Selim thought. I never noticed them before. But then how often have I seen her in the last twelve months? He kissed her hand and Bayezid did the same. Then they stood back, their arms crossed on their breasts as they had been taught to do in the Enderun.

Muomi stood behind her, always there, at her shoulder. How he hated her. Black and sullen and malevolent. She's a witch.

"You've grown into a fine boy, Bayezid. Your tutors say you are a fine horseman and athlete."

"Thank you, Mother."

"But you must try harder at your studies. Even when you leave the Enderun, you should never stop learning. If you are ever to become Sultan you will need more than your skill with a javelin and a horse."

"I will do my best."

Don't waste your breath, Selim thought. He ignores everything you say. My brother's handsome head is as hollow as a drum.

"And you Selim ..." Hürrem sighed. "They say you are too fond of sweetbreads."

"I study hard."

"Really? Your tutors say they have to pound every lesson into your head with their knuckles."

Yes, they do, and don't think I will ever forget it. "I will do my best, Mother," he said, testing the defence his brother had used.

"Your best is not good enough. You are my firstborn. You are the one on whom the hopes of the Osmanlis rest if anything should ever happen to Mustapha."

Is that entirely true. Mother? I have seen the way you look at my little brother. I think your hopes reside elsewhere. It's never been a secret who your favourite is. But then, he's everyone's favourite, the tutors especially. Everyone except Suleiman. He dotes on my idiot brother Çehangir now that Mehmet is dead. So unlike Mehmet to get sick. Until he died he had done everything right.

But things were changing at last. Now he had a chance to get away from the palace, away from the shadow of Bayezid. When he took up his governorship in Konya, Bayezid would be on the other side of Anatolia, at Amasya. If Fortune were kind he would fall of his horse one day playing çerit.

"You must write to me often," Hürrem said.

"We will, Mother," Bayezid said, for both of them.

I will curse you every dawn and evening in my prayers, Selim thought.

"My hopes rest in you," Hürrem said to Bayezid. Then she turned to Selim with a beatific smile. "Oh Selim, you are the shape of a watermelon!"

\*\*\*

The shape of a watermelon.

Selim often wondered who it was he hated the most; himself for not being more like Suleiman or Bayezid, because he was. While he was white and fat, Bayezid was olive and lean and handsome. It was one of life's cruel jokes; two brothers born under the same roof, one with personality and strength and talent, the other without talent at all. He imagined God had a similar sense of humour to his mother.

But now as he said his goodbyes to his mother he remembered again the fragility of his position. When his father died - tomorrow, in thirty years, but someday - the fight for the succession would begin. Mustapha was shahzade, and he guessed that even his noble soul would not shrink from having all of Hürrem's sons eliminated to protect his throne.

If by some great fortune Mustapha were already dead, then the throne should be Selim's. But he did not imagine for an instant that Bayezid would let him have it. One of them would have to die. The Fatih's law allowed for a Sultan to kill all his brothers and their children to protect his succession and the stability of the empire. Would the yeniçeris support him against his brilliant warrior brother? Unlikely.

A grim future.

"Go in peace," Hürrem said to Bayezid and Selim.

Peace! As if there was any peace to be head for a son of Suleiman; let alone a watermelon like me.

\*\*\*

Hürrem stared at the vaulted ceiling. A germ of an idea had insinuated itself into her mind.

Selim ...

Thanks be to God, Selim did not look so much like his real father, the former Chief White Eunuch. Though who would remember him anyway? Those dangerous days in the court of the Eski Saraya were long past and lived on only now in Selim.

When he was born she had not been sure who the father was, yet by the time he was grown and it should have been plain to everyone, Çehangir had come along to cast doubt on everything. Who would have believed the Lord of Life could have sired a hunchback cripple? So then why not a fat, pasty-faced and surly youth with no real talent except for nursing slights?

He was no ghazi, and no Sultan, just as Suleiman's mother had said.

It was obvious to her which of her boys would succeed if there was a contest for the throne between them, which one should have her blessings and her encouragement. Bayezid would make a fine Sultan, if it came to it, almost as good as Mustapha.

And then another idea presented itself in all its panoramic and glorious perversity and she laughed aloud.

# CHAPTER 75

## The Bosphorus, off Çamlica

They escaped the hot August night on the slick still waters of the Bosphorus. A black and gold caïque was always in readiness for them at Seraglio Point and Suleiman sailed into the Horn with Hürrem, accompanied only by three deaf-mute bostanji to man the tiller and oars. They drifted with the current a stone's throw from the shore. Torches burned at prow and stern.

There was a cabin at the stern hung with black velvet curtains to assure their privacy. Hürrem peered out, saw the dark cedar-grown cemeteries of Çamlica slide past in the darkness.

Suleiman seemed once again preoccupied. He had changed so much since Ibrahim's death. He seldom laughed anymore. He had dismissed all the musicians from the seraglio and had their instruments burned. He never even asked her to play for him now; he said the music of the viol reminded him too much of Ibrahim.

He had learned to punish himself in small ways. He sent his favourite green and white Chinese porcelain back to the treasure house at Yedikule and ate instead from earthenware. He had drunk not one drop of wine since his Vizier's death.

He spent more time now with his architect than he did with her. "I have consulted with Sinan," he said, predictably. "He has drawn some plans I would like you to see."

"You are going to build a mosque in my honour?"

"It is not holy to joke that way."

"I am sorry, My lord. I thought you liked me to be a little wicked sometimes."

"This is a serious matter and requires your attention. I have asked him to design a new palace on the ruins of the old Eski Saraya."

What is this obsession with building, she thought. Once he was merely the Sultan by God-given right; but since Ibrahim he has found this need to justify himself.

"I would like you to study his plans and give them your approval."

Hürrem pouted. "Is it so terrible for you, having me here in the palace?"

"You know that is not the case. There is simply no room for the Harem at the Topkapi. It is impossible."

"Of course there is room. Why not have Sinan put his talents to use in the Fourth Court? A man could gallop through there all day and not reach Seraglio Point."

"A wild exaggeration. Besides, there are other considerations."

"Tell me them."

"Considerations of state."

"It all sounds so pompous."

"The Harem simply cannot be part of the royal palace. It has always been separate."

"It is a large harem, my Lord. Do you still hunger for the other girls?"

"Of course not."

"Then perhaps if you no longer require them, you could order the Kislar Aghasi to find them husbands. Then it would be only me and my household that you would need house here."

"What you are asking is unthinkable. Sinan has been commissioned. There is an end to it."

Hürrem realized she had gone too far. She should not push him. She had not really expected that he would agree. She nuzzled closer, resting her head on his chest. There were better ways to get what she wanted. "I am sorry of I gave you offense, my Lord. It is just that I would so hate to be parted from you again."

"Hürrem sometimes you forget yourself."

She nestled closer. "Do you love me, my Sultan?"

"I love you more than my life."

"More than Gülbehar?"

"Gülbehar! I have not thought about her for months."

"Yet she is first kadin."

"It is the law."

"But you love me more?"

"What more do you want from me? I have sent Gülbehar away. The only time I ever visited the old Harem was to see you. I love you more than I have loved any woman."

"So will you make me your queen one day?"

Suleiman said nothing for a long time, seemingly dazzled by the impertinence of such a suggestion. Then he started to laugh.

"What are you laughing at?"

"Don't look so angry, little russelana."

"Tell me why you are laughing at me!"

"It's impossible!"

"Impossible to think of me as anything other than a slave?"

"Of course. The Sultan may never marry."

"It is part of the Sheri'at?"

"There is nothing written."

"It is not in the kanuni?"

He shook his head.

"Then why not?"

Suleiman tried to pat her cheek but she twisted away. "No Sultan has married since Bayezid the First," he said.

"You are greater than him. You are greater than any Sultan there has ever been."

"There are good reasons for this."

"Dead men make the rules for you? You are the Kanuni, the Lawgiver. That's what they call you isn't it? You. You make the laws not ghosts from the past."

He sighed. "I will tell you a story about our history and the very first Bayezid of the Oslamlis. He was a Sultan long before we came here to Stamboul. He married a Serbian princess, a very beautiful woman; her name was Despina. At the time we were struggling with the Mongols for control of Anatolia. Bayezid met Tamerlane in battle at Angora and was defeated. It was a terrible defeat; Bayezid was captured and so was Despina. Tamerlane wanted to humiliate us so he forced Despina to wait naked on him and his generals at table. It was the darkest moment in our history. The shame of it still burns in every ghazi. Our weakness, you see, is our women. Since then no Sultan has ever married, so that we can never be weak that way again."

"That was long ago. Your people were nomads then. Now you are lord of the world's greatest empire. Who will ever take me prisoner my Lord?"

Suleiman sighed. "What you ask is impossible."

"There are no more Tamerlanes. The whole world quakes at your feet …"

"Let us talk no more about it."

"But my Lor-"

"We talk no more about it!"

She fell to her knees on the floor of the barge and kissed his hand. "Forgive me, My Lord. My passion for you sometimes drowns the voice of reason."

He sighed and lifted her from the floor onto his lap. He had a look of weary forbearance, as if he were admonishing a child. Sometimes you are impertinent and rash. Now I want you to give me your opinion on Sinan's plans. Let that be an end to it. You are fortunate that I indulge you even this much."

"Yes, my Lord," she whispered and lowered her eyes.

After she had gushed appropriately at the wonder of Sinan's designs, she let Suleiman unfasten the pearl buttons of her chemise and then toss aside her sheer silk pantaloons. The night was warm. The moans of the Sultan's pleasures drifted across the oily black water. The owls in the cemetery at Çamlica added to the symphony of the night.

I will not go leave here, Hürrem thought. There is a way to persuade you and I will find it.

# CHAPTER 76

The Sultan's personal quarters - the selamlik - were separated from the Harem by a single door. It led from his bedroom onto a cloister and then to a maze of courts and dormitories that had once belonged to the pages and eunuchs of his own retinue.

It had become known inside the palace as the Golden Road for it led directly to Hürrem's apartments; and it was along this cloister that Abbas hurried now, the sleeves and hem of his pelisse trailing the cobblestones, his cheeks puffing with exertion. He paused before going up the steps to the first floor apartment, getting his breath.

When Hürrem finally received him, he was still panting from his exertions. He dabbed at the oily slick of perspiration on his forehead with a silk handkerchief.

"Well?" Hürrem said.

"The Lord of Life commands your presence in his bedchamber, My Lady."

"I see," Hürrem said. "I am sorry, Abbas, but you must inform him that I cannot come." The Kislar Aghasi gaped at her. "Close your mouth, Abbas, the flies are getting in."

"You … cannot come? Was that what you said, My Lady?"

"Yes, that is correct. I am unable to attend him."

This was the moment Abbas had dreaded. His fortune was inseparable from hers, and now she had quite plainly gone mad. Finally. God help me in my sorrow.

***

Suleiman lay sprawled on the divan, apparently calm. But his eyes were pinpoints. "She refuses me?"

Abbas felt an oily bead of sweat trickle down his spine. His handkerchief was already sodden. "She said, My Lord, that her life was at your command but that she might not come and lie with you without offending God and His sacred laws.."

"She lectures me on the Sheri'at now?" Suleiman was still for a long time; when he jumped to his feet the movement was so sudden and so unexpected that Abbas involuntarily took a step back. Suleiman stamped to the bed, tore off the silk coverlet and tore it in half. "She cannot defy me! Me!"

"She says she wishes no offence. She says she heard it from the sheyhülislam's lips. He says that being free she may not yield to you what, as a bondswoman, she could give without offence to God."

"Abu Sa'ad told her this?"

"Yes, that was what he said. Abu Sa'ad." Let that pompous and self righteous old fool feel the torch on his skin for a change. Let him explain this mess, in the name of God.

Suleiman drew his killiç from the scabbard by his bed. He looked at the blade then at Abbas. Abbas felt a hot trickle running down his leg. Lately he had found this happening more and more when he was under stress. It was the result of the castration, he knew, another indignity to pile upon the ones he already suffered.

Suleiman plunged the sword into the mattress. "Abu Sa'ad," he said.

"It was his fetwa that started this," Abbas said.

"We must consult him then, since he knows God's mind better than I."

Suleiman stormed out of the room. Abbas whispered a silent prayer and followed.

*** 

Any other man would have quaked at being roused from his bed to face the Lord of Life, the King of Kings, the Possessor of Men's Necks and bear the brunt of his towering rage. But the sheyhülislam feared only God and knew with unwavering conviction the heart and mind of the Infinite. He looked surprisingly calm.

There were only three men in the vast audience chamber; Suleiman, Abbas and Abu Sa'ad. The guards who had fetched the mufti from his bed now waited beyond the door.

Suleiman glowered at the cleric from his throne, hunched and seething. "I need a fetwa," he said.

Abu Sa'ad bowed his head.

"It concerns the Hasseki Hürrem - the Favoured Laughing One. You know that I have released her from my kullar, my slave family? She is now a free woman."

"So she has told me," he said.

"As a free woman may she still lie with me in accordance with God's holy law?"

Abu Sa'ad had the answer to this question ready, as it was the very same question Hürrem had sought his opinion on earlier that day. The answer remained immutable, no matter who was asking it. "Even if you laid with her a thousand nights as a bondswoman, it would be a mortal sin before God now that she is free. It would put her soul in mortal danger."

Suleiman looked as if he would like to strangle him. "How might she resolve this problem?"

"She may only lie with you now without stain if she is your wife."

The Sultan seemed to have discovered something in his mouth that was to his distaste and was considering whether to spit it out. What would happen now? Abbas wondered. Since Hürrem refused his bed and Suleiman could not possibly give her marriage, there seemed no help for it. The Sultan would go back to his Harem for comfort and Hürrem would be banished.

I imagine he will get rid of me too, Abbas thought.

"Get out," Suleiman said. "Both of you."

\*\*\*

Such a beautiful room, Suleiman thought. Such a vast room. How long had men laboured over this faience on the walls? And these rich crimson and blue carpets! They still bore the impressions of his Kislar Aghasi's knees. He closed his eyes and listened to the murmuring of the fountains. There was frankincense in the censers. So perfect here. If only a man's surroundings were enough to make him happy.

Today I would be no more or less miserable in a hovel, he thought. In the end it is only the heart that makes us happy. Now it comes down to a simple choice: give her marriage or give her up.

The ceremonial throne was uncomfortable but he did not have the energy or inclination to move from it. His limbs felt frozen. He sat there for hours, staring into the vaulted cupola above him, wondering what his life would be without her.

He was not alone through his despair; tradition, duty and fear sat beside him through his vigil, arguing back and forth like wives at the fish market. They all had an opinion and expressed it as forcefully as the sheyhülislam. He wished he did not have to listen to their carping but not one of them would go away and leave him be.

***

The Fourth Court of the Topkapi Saraya was a miniature forest of old pines and twisted cypress swarming up the slopes of Seraglio Point. On one side it overlooked the training fields of the çerit and the crumbling Byzantine monasteries that now served as stables; on the other was the sparkling blue of the Golden Horn. Suleiman liked to walk here sometimes, to admire the view, to watch the cavalry training.

Today he walked head down, oblivious to everything but the tumbling confusion in his mind.

Give her marriage or give her up.

How could he give her up? He could see her now, walking beside him, braided red-gold hair stirred by the wind. She was laughing and he imagined he felt the solace of her simple wisdom: "You are the Kanuni, the Legislator. You are not bound by history, any restraint imposed on you is placed there by you yourself. You are bound only by the Sheri'at. My Lord, don't look so solemn! Is it really so terrible that you should finally choose to do what you have already done in your heart?"

"You make this marriage sound so simple," he said aloud. "It is our traditions that tie us to our ancestors. Ever since Tamerlane-"

"Do you really think what happened to Despina could ever happen to me? Shall any of your enemies even see the walls of Stamboul? Who is there that can defeat your army in battle?"

Suleiman climbed The Hill That Made The Camel Scream, to the very highest point of the court. From there he could look south to the islands of the Marmara; beyond lay the Mediterranean and his colonies in Egypt, Barbary and Algeria. If he looked east across the wind-whipped Bosphorus he could see Asia where the caravan roads led to Syria, Azerbaijan and Armenia. Below him the harbor was fringed with the masts of galleys belonging to Dragut, his admiral, who had turned the Mediterranean into a Turkish lake and just beyond lay Galata and the warehouses and palaces of the Venetians, the Genoese and the Greeks, who all paid him tribute. Look north and he could make out the Gaiour  palaces at Pera; behind them was Rumelia, Bosnia. Wallachia, Transylvania, all fiefdoms of the Osmanlis.

Such an Empire.

"What king is there now who may conquer you and make me wait naked at his table?" he heard her say. "Your Empire spans Europe and Asia and Africa. Even the Holy Roman Emperor refuses to face you in battle. Who is you are afraid of? Shah Tamasp?"

"They are all dust at my feet."

"So which king is it that makes you tremble so that he can make you give me up ... one who loves you so?"

She took him by the hand; at least he imagined that she did.

292

"You are the most powerful man in the world and yet you dare not do what you most desire. You are ruled by your own fear."

Her eyes filled with tears. The fancy was so real that he reached out to touch her. But there was no one, just the wind. He realized that if he gave her up that was all there would ever be walking beside him; no one. He might sleep with the most beautiful women in the entire Empire but without her he would be alone again to shoulder the terrible burdens of the Empire and God. She was his conscience, his consolation, his counsel, his advocate and his ease. She was his friend.

She was the Vizier who could not betray him, as Ibrahim had done; she was his Harem, a thousand women in one, balm for his spirit as well as his body.

"I cannot give her up," he said, and the decision was made. He would do the unthinkable because the alternative was unbearable.

\*\*\*

When Abbas was summoned once more into the presence of the second kadin, he braced himself for every possibility except the one that presented itself. She was, he noted, in high spirits and wasted no time with pleasantries. "How would you like to be rid of your girls, Abbas?" she asked him.

"My Lady?"

"The Sultan no longer has need of his harem. His concubines are to be married off. You are to start making arrangements immediately."

Abbas could not hide his astonishment. A Sultan without a harem? "I compliment his judgment."

"You compliment mine," she laughed.

"I shall proceed as you command."

"Do you not wish to know why, Kislar Aghasi?"

"It is not for me to question the decisions of the Mighty."

"Abbas, you are indeed a treasure! I shall tell you anyway, since you will hear of it soon enough. The Lord of Life is to dispense with his Harem because soon he is to take a Queen!"

Abbas blinked at her. "A Queen, My Lady?"

"You are looking at the future wife of the Sultan of the Osmanlis, Abbas." She laughed again. "Are you not awed by the splendour of such a sight?"

"As you say," Abbas agreed. Impossible, he thought. Impossible! Suleiman would never go through with it!

\*\*\*

On the occasion of the marriage of Suleiman to the Hasseki Hürrem - the Favoured Laughing One as she was now known inside the court - Stamboul

293

witnessed the greatest celebration it had ever seen. Bread and olives were distributed to the poor; cheese, fruit and rose-leaf jam to the middle classes. The main streets were festooned with the scarlet flags of the Osmanlis and the green standards of Islam.

There was a public procession of wedding gifts; hundreds of camels laden with carpets, furniture, gold and silver vases, as well as a hundred and sixty more eunuchs to enter the service of the Lady Hürrem. Wrestlers, archers, jugglers and tumblers performed in the Hippodrome day and night.

In another procession a huge loaf of bread, the size of a room, was dragged through the streets on a raft by ten oxen while the city's master bakers threw hot loaves covered in sesame and fennel seeds to the crowd.

Lions, panthers and leopards were paraded in the Aytmedani. Thousands of people lined the arena, and those who could not get in climbed trees for a better view. The Sultan's slaves showered fruit or money or silk among the spectators. The arrival of giraffes elicited gasps of astonishment.

Meanwhile, in the seraglio, Hürrem became queen in a simple ceremony witnessed only by herself, Suleiman and Abu Sa'ad. Suleiman touched Hürrem's hand and whispered: "This woman Hürrem I make my wife. All that belongs to her shall be her property."

Finally, she was Queen of the Osmanlis. It was her most perfect day.

Just one man threw a shadow over the celebration. He dogged her wedding as he had haunted her footsteps for the last seventeen years.

Mustapha.

Now twenty six years old, he waited his moment in Manisa. I am Queen now, Hürrem thought. I am safe from other women. Now there is only one man to fear. All of this means nothing while he yet lives.

\*\*\*

A raised platform had been erected in the Hippodrome and from there Suleiman watched the entertainments on a throne of lapus lazuli, his sons either side of him.

Selim fidgeted on the carpets at his father's feet. He was hungry. A feast had been prepared at the Palace; venison, guinea fowl, imam biyalti - fruit soup with real ice - snow flavoured with honey, amber and musk. His stomach growled.

Below them, in the arena, a lioness was tearing the innards from a boar with casual sweeps of its paws while her partner yawned without interest. Selim giggled at the boar's kicking and squealing. It was on its back, turning the dust pink. The lioness circled, still watchful of its tusks.

Something made Selim turn around. Through the screen behind his father's throne he saw a pair of green eyes watching him through the gilded lattice. Mother, he thought.

He turned away again but felt her eyes still on him. How did she manage all this? He wondered. How did she ever get my father to marry her? To have such a powerful mother was both a consolation and a terror. If she could bend the Sultan to her will, she could do anything.

So what does she want from me?

The lioness had finished toying with the boar. It was shuddering, lying on its flank, still alive, as the lioness bent her head to tear free the first chunk of meat. Normally such things excited his appetite. But suddenly he was not hungry any more.

He looked around again but the eyes were gone.

# PART 7

## PARADISE ON EARTH

# CHAPTER 79

## Pera

The carriage clattered to a halt in the courtyard below her window. A black eunuch jumped down to settle the horses while another opened the door. The windows were covered in black taffeta so she could not make out their visitor. She was only mildly curious. Ludovici often entertained visitors during the day, usually other merchants from the Comunità Magnifica.

A figure emerged from the coach, head and face invisible beneath the hood of a cloak and her black cazeta. Not a finger or toe was visible so she realized it must be a woman.

A few moments later Hyacinth tapped on her door to announce a guest. She gaped as the woman entered, removing the hood of her ferijde .

"Sirhane!"

\*\*\*

She had changed hardly at all. She was perhaps a little thinner; otherwise it was as if the last six years had not happened. They were back in the seraglio again, the Sultan's odalisques, best friends and at the end, for a short time, Julia remembered with a blush - lovers.

The Syrian looked glorious, as she always did. She wore an entari of green Bursa brocade, open in front and joined at the waist by three pearl buttons. Beneath it she was all snow-white silk, shimmering to her ankles. Rubies glinted on her fingers and in her hair. There was a pearl at her waist. Julia was dressed in sombre black after the Venetian fashion. She felt drab beside her.

She clung to her like a schoolgirl. "I never thought I would ever see you again," she said, laughing. "Tell me everything!"

"You are looking at a respectable married woman," Sirhane said.

"How did you get out of the Harem?"

"It was all arranged by the Kislar Aghasi. Suleiman is disposing of all his women …"

"It's not true!"

"Hürrem has persuaded him that he no longer needs his Harem! Abbas arranged for me to marry an Aga in the Spahis of the Porte. His name is Abdul Sahine Pasha. He is a big brute of a man with a beard and his member is as thick as my wrist!"

Julia clapped her hand to her mouth.

"I don't mind. He treats me well enough. I think he prefers the boys, I don't know. He is not so bad. I could even grow to love him, if he were not a man." She rested her head on Julia's shoulder. "I have missed you so! Perhaps it is wicked to say so, but while you were there I was happy in the Harem. Happier than I was any time in my life."

"So was I, Sirhane."

"I truly thought you were dead."

"How did you find out I was still alive?"

"It was on the morning that I was to leave the Harem. The Kislar Aghasi came to me and told me you had not drowned after all. He said you were here in Pera, married to a Venetian."

"Abbas told you?"

"I thought the Sultan had put you in a sack and tossed you in the Bosphorus! For six years I mourned you. I still cannot believe it is you!" She threw her arms around Julia's neck and kissed her. "What happened? How did you survive?"

"It's a long story," Julia said, wondering if it would ever be safe to tell her.

"And to marry a gentleman from the Comunità!"

"We are not married and he is more pirate than Venetian gentleman. Still, look at us, whoever would have thought that we would have come this far!"

***

The sun dipped below the seven hills, and the calls of the muezzin rose from the dusky, dusty city. Light pooled like liquid gold on the Horn as the silhouettes of the cypress trees faded into the gloom below the walls of the seraglio. Julia and Sirhane sat on the terrazzo, talking in whispers.

"Is it really true?" Julia said. "Suleiman has married off his entire Harem?"

"Yes. There is no more honey in the honeypot. All that remains is Hürrem and her household. The Laughing One has a hundred slaves in waiting now, so she has plenty to laugh about. She comes and goes whenever she likes, thirty eunuchs trail along in her wake wherever she goes."

"If a snake can survive so long among vipers, it deserves to grow long."

"The Kislar Aghasi told me she was the reason the Sultan ordered you drowned."

Abbas, Julia thought. She wished she deserved his devotion. If only there was a way she could help him as he had helped her.

How did you escape?" Sirhane said.

Should I tell her? Julia thought. She did not want to endanger Abbas, but Sirhane must have already guessed. She told her everything. "So that is what happened. What hand Hürrem had in it I do not know. But anyway I am alive now, so I try to forget about it."

Sirhane looked disappointed. "Poor Abbas."

"I try not to think about it. He may look like a monster, Sirhane, but he has a heart like a mountain. He is the bravest and most devoted man I have ever known or even heard of."

"How he must suffer."

"That is perhaps why he contrives to always look so fearsome. To disguise it."

"And that witch of Suleiman's. You should try to be more hateful. It is not becoming for a woman not to be spiteful."

Julia shook her head. "What Hürrem does cannot affect me now."

"Then you are the only one in all the Empire who is not intimidated by her. Foreign ambassadors include gifts for her as well as the Sultan now. They even send her letters to try and sway her opinion. The viziers, muftis and Agas pay her tribute through the Kislar Aghasi. Even my husband does it. He says she is more powerful than Ibrahim ever was."

Julia smiled. "Poor Suleiman."

Sirhane curled her legs beneath her, curling into the divan like a pampered kitten. "What was he like?"

Julia was reluctant to talk about it.

"Tell me!" Sirhane urged her.

"He hardly said a word. He took off my clothes and then he lay on top of me."

"And it's not big?"

"No."

"Only they say it's really huge."

"Sirhane …" Julia spread her hands helplessly, amazed as she always had been to be discussing such things so shamelessly with her. "He lay on top of me and he made some noises. Then he rolled off again. Nothing happened." She remembered how Ludovici had made love to her that first time. Until then she had not realized why Suleiman had been so angry with her.

"The Sultan is impotent?"

Julia grabbed her wrist, alarmed. "If you ever say those words again outside this room we will all be killed!"

"The best gossip I ever had and I cannot tell anyone!"

"It will mean our heads!"

"I know. You don't have to shout." She pouted. "… What is it like with Ludovici?"

Julia hesitated. "Not the way it was with us."

Sirhane seemed pleased with this answer. She watched the lamps flickering to life in the old city as the echoes of the muezzin faded into the gathering violet dusk. A stillness settled over the city. "I must go," she said.

"So soon?"

"I should not be here at all. If Abdul ever found out, I might end up in a sack myself."

\*\*\*

Julia watched Sirhane get back inside her anonymous black carriage. I did not escape the Harem, she thought. I brought it here with me. It was both my captivity and my liberation. It plunged my soul into mortal sin and brought my body to life. Now Sirhane has come back into my life, the Harem will rule me again.

Would they become lovers again? Sirhane called it adultery without consequence. Was it a sin to love another woman that way?

She saw a slight movement of the black taffeta curtains and knew Sirhane was watching her also. She waved, though she knew she could not see her. Then the carriage clattered away through the gates and the loneliness returned.

# CHAPTER 80

Fate had been kind to Ludovici Gambetto.

Almost.

He had powerful and influential friends at the Sublime Porte and his business had prospered beyond all imagining. Fortune had also delivered him a beautiful mistress from a noble Venetian family.

Yet within these silver caskets were slivers of real pain. His good fortune was founded on his best friend's anguish; Julia belonged to him only because she could not belong to anyone else.

Even after eight years he was still not reconciled to the fact that his oldest friend now lived in the Sultan's palace as a eunuch and a slave. And then there was Julia; useless currency to anyone but him and the source of endless self-recrimination also. He had lied to Abbas and kept her here in Stamboul despite his friend's entreaties to get her out of the city, and out of the Osmanli empire. Abbas had never spoken a word to him about it but he guessed that he knew about the deception. He could still see it in his eyes every time they met. The guilt of his own duplicity gnawed at him.

If only it had all been worth it; if only she could love him a little.

A part of him - the part that was still Venetian - said that it did not matter. She was his, she was beautiful, his to bed and enjoy whenever he chose. What else could he want?

But the renegade in him was not happy with this. What was it that he wanted then? He wanted her to feel the same for him as he felt for her. He wanted her devotion. Perhaps he was more like Abbas than he ever knew.

He had built a new palazzo on the heights of Pera, dressed Julia in the finest velvets and put rubies and diamonds on her fingers. No one saw them, of course, for she was never allowed to be seen. The colony knew he kept an Italian mistress, and he had heard her identity was the source of much gossip.

It amused him to hear the names they came up with. One of them was a former mistress of the Pope himself. It didn't matter; they would never invite him to their houses anyway.

\*\*\*

He stood on the terrazzo and watched her. She was down in the garden, reading. The summer flowers were still in bloom, and the air heavy with the scent form the umbrella pines. He went down the marble steps to join her. She looked up. "You look pleased with yourself," she said.

"No, I cannot take the credit." He sat down beside her. On the harbor the caïques criss-crossed the bright water, the violet silhouettes of the mosques silhouetted against the shore.

"What has happened?"

"I have heard whispers form the Porte. They say Rüstem Pasha is to marry the Sultan's daughter."

"Mihrmah?"

"That's the whisper."

"Then he will almost certainly be the next Vizier."

"Yes."

"That pleases you?"

"If I were on the side of the angels, it would not. But I am only a humble merchant and I cannot afford to be on God's side in this. I have not really been on the side of Heaven since I left Venice. Perhaps not even there. That is why I have all this."

"That is a blasphemy, Ludovici. And I still do not understand."

"Suleiman's Vizier, Lütfi Pasha, is too difficult to do business with. He is too honest."

"A fatal flaw in a Vizier."

He smiled. "Indeed. Rüstem on the other hand would sell his own mother for ten per cent commission. For fifteen, his grandmother and his canary."

"He will be excellent to your purposes, then."

"I am sure he will be a great success."

"And therefore you can send more caramusalis through the Dardanelles without fear of inspection. But what made Suleiman choose Rüstem for such a wonderful match?"

"His charm and good looks?"

But Julia had already worked it out. "Hürrem!"

"Yes that is what they are saying in the bazaars. Time will tell. Though what he has done to deserve her patronage I can only imagine." He studied her. Something different about her today, a bloom in her cheeks that had not been there before. "You had a visitor yesterday," he said.

She could not meet his eyes. "Is that wrong?"

"Who was it?"

"A girl. She was an odalisque at the seraglio, as I was."

"You were friends there? But how did she know …?"

"Abbas."

"He told her?" He sat up straighter. "Abbas told her about you?"

"He wanted her to know that I was safe."

"Nothing is ever safe. Now that someone else knows about you, you are even less safe."

She threw down her book. "You pin me to the wall like a butterfly. Sometimes I would rather be dead!"

Ludovici was shocked to silence. Julia seemed to regret her outburst almost at once. "I am sorry. I know there is nothing you can do. It is not your fault."

Ludovici hung his head. "No, what you say is correct. I have no right. I have kept you locked away like this for my own selfish … " He reached for her hand. "I have been thinking about this lately. I have a vineyard in Cyprus. You could go there and live under another name. You would not have to live like a prisoner there."

"You could give me another name but someone there would recognize me. When they knew what had happened to me, they would treat me like a whore." She drew herself up. "I would rather stay here."

He shook his head. This was unexpected. "But why?"

"I like it here. I do not wish to go to Cyprus."

I should just put her on a boat and make her go, he thought. That is what Abbas would have me do. Was she finally starting to feel something for him or was there some other reason? He never knew what went on behind those angel's eyes.

Ludovici lapsed to silence as he contemplated the best way to tell her his next piece of news. "There is something you should know," he said finally.

"Is it bad news?"

"I don't know what you will think of it. It's about politics."

"Politics?"

"Julia, you will remember that I told you, two years ago Suleiman's navy defeated the our Republic's fleet at Prevezzo."

"Yes, I remember."

"Venice is a city built on the sea and for the sea. It needs command of the ocean to survive. Suleiman is slowly choking it to death. The only Venetians who have welcomed this state of affairs are men like me, here in Pera. We can charge a lot more for our wheat.

"How does this affect me?"

"There is a legation arriving soon from Venice. They have come to see the Sultan, to sue for peace." He hesitated. "Your father heads the legation," he said.

She turned white. "My father? He is coming here to Stamboul?"

"He is expected any day."

"Will he come here?"

"I doubt that. The Comunità consider me little better than a pirate."

"You did not imagine that I would wish to see him?"

"No, I did not think so. But I thought you should know."

She closed her eyes. "What about Abbas?"

Do you want me to inform him of this?"

"Why would you not?"

"Abbas has become a powerful man. Ambassadors to the Sublime Porte have been thrown into the dungeons at Yedikule before now. Your father could be in danger."

Her eyes glittered with venom. "You do not think I would wish to protect him after what he did? Yes, I should like Abbas to know, very much. In fact, I should like to tell him myself."

Ludovici had not expected that. A meeting between Julia and Abbas? But he supposed it was about time. "I will see if I can arrange it," he said.

# CHAPTER 81

## Galata

The carriage was just an oblong box on wheels, painted with flowers and fruit, no different from a hundred others in the city. It clattered through the filthy alley and stopped outside an anonymous two storey house painted yellow, like all the others in this predominantly Jewish quarter. A page opened the door and Julia stepped out.

She, also, was anonymous beneath her ferijde , the long sleeved cloak worn by all Turkish women in the street. It was black silk, the only clue to her station in life; poor women wore alpaca, while women of the court wore lilac or rose silk. She wore two veils; the gauzy yashmak that covered her face nose and mouth and then over that a black cazeta that fell from her head to her waist, with just a square cut hole for her eyes.

She hurried into the house, leaving her pages to wait by the coach.

Abbas.

He was even more obese than when she had known him as the Kislar Aghasi in the Harem and unrecognisable as the beautiful boy who had courted her in Venice. He was sweating, even though it was still early morning and not yet warm. He dabbed at the pillows of fat bunched under his chin with a silk handkerchief. Sweat stained the edges of his huge white turban.

She tried to reconcile her memory of the passionate, bronzed boy on the gondola with this nightmarish creature with one white vacant eyeball and bloated face. This ugly falsetto eunuch who had grimaced with outrage at their very first meeting inside the Harem and whispered such strange endearments as she waited to die one early morning by the Bosphorus was the same boy who wanted to her to run away with him when she lived in Venice.

This was still her Abbas.

He looked up and stared at her in astonishment. "Who are you?" he said. But she guessed that he already knew. He tried to struggle to his feet and clapped his hands for his pages to come and assist him.

After they had him back on his feet he sent them outside. "Julia," he breathed.

She lifted the cazeta, let it fall behind her, like a cape. Then she unpinned the yashmak. "Hello Abbas."

He covered his face with his hands and turned his back to her. "You should not have come," he moaned.

"I had to see you once more."

"I told Ludovici I never wanted to see you again. Why do you wish to humiliate me like this?"

"Please, Abbas ..."

"If you knew the pain you cause me, you would not have done this!"

She felt like a fool. How did she think this meeting could go otherwise? "Abbas ... ?"

"Why did you come here? Why did Ludovici allow this?"

"Please turn around."

"So you can gaze on my beauty?"

"Abbas, I do not care how you look. I have always loved you and I still do."

"Stop it!"

"Turn around. Please."

When he turned back to her his face was mottled and his one good eye stared at her with grief and with outage. "Go away! What good can this do now? My love for you has cost me everything! Just let me forget, for pity's sake!"

"Abbas, I never had the chance to thank you ... you saved my life."

"I did because I loved you. You do not need to thank me. How will you return my love? With your kisses? Will you take me to your bed? Shall we become lovers at last?"

Julia took a step towards him to try and comfort him but he held out a hand to stop her. "Don't," he said.

"Abbas ..."

"Can you even imagine what it is like for me? There is no release for me, ever. I want to love and be loved, but that can never happen. I am a slave and even less than a slave. There is no hell after death, Julia, it is here, it is now and it is where I reside every day and every night." His rage spent he slumped against the wall. "Please, just go."

"All right. But first there is something I have to tell you. I did not come here to torment you."

"Tell me then and go in peace."

"It is about my father."

"Gonzaga?"

"He is coming here to Stamboul."

"Coming here? How do you know this?"

"Ludovici was informed yesterday by the bailo. La Serenissima is dispatching a peace legation to the Porte and my father will be the ambassador."

Abbas slipped further down the wall until he sat on his haunches on the carpet. "So the devil approaches Paradise," he said.

There was nothing else to say. Julia desperately wanted to comfort him. She knelt down beside him and he did not protest as she leaned forward and gently kissed his cheek. "I am sorry," she whispered. "I do love you, Abbas."

"I love you, too," he said.

She started to weep. He patted her head, gently. "It's all right. Don't."

She got up, replaced the yashmak and the cazeta. She was still crying. Now that she had started, she could not stop.

After she had gone Abbas stayed crouched against the wall, his kaftan skewed around his knees. He heard the clatter of the carriage wheels on the cobblestones as she left. After a while the shadows slanted across the room, and he watched dust motes drift through the chevrons of light that angled through the slats in the window.

He drew his knees up to his chest and curled on the floor. Just before evening his pages came, helped him to his feet and half-carried him downstairs to the carriage. Then they took him home, to Hürrem.

## Pera

Antonio Gonzaga watched the Kubbealti Tower at the Topkapi Palace rise like a miniature campanile from the skyline as they sailed past the battlement walls on Seraglio Point.

"So that is the home of Il Signore Turco?" he said.

"We must treat warily with him," the bailo said.

Gonzaga snorted with contempt. The bailo was more Turke than Venetian now himself, he thought. The man has gone native.

He despised the Comunità. All these merchants lived in Turkish palaces and lived in Turkish gowns. What was more disturbing they spoke of the Sultan and the Divan as if they were more important than the Doge and the Consiglio.

"We should take care not to provoke him," the bail went on. "The Mediterranean is now, after all, just a Turkish lake."

"Do not disturb yourself, bailo. One day the Lion of Venice will consume all its enemies. Until then, I shall do as you suggest and play the lamb. But I

shall not grovel to him. Our setbacks are only temporary. Do not forget that.
"

# CHAPTER 82

The Ambassador of the Illustrious Signory of Venice made the short trip across the Golden Horn in the royal caïque. When he reached Seraglio Point, two pashas and forty heralds escorted him and his delegation the rest of the way to the Ba'ab i-Humayün, the gate of the Majestic One.

Gonzaga tried to appear indifferent to the great arch of white marble and the contents of its mitred niches. The decapitated heads had ripened in the sun and there were more heads piled like cannonballs at the main gate. A group of urchins were playing with them.

Gonzaga put a scented handkerchief to his nose.

The arch was a full fifteen paces long and when they emerged from it they entered the first court of the Topkapi Palace, the courtyard of the yeniçeris . The court was full of people; servants carrying trays of hot rolls,; a page being carried on a litter to the Infirmary; a troop of blue coated yeniçeris on the march, their Bird of Paradise plumes of the veterans cascading almost to their knees. Yet he was struck by the hush, after the tumult of the street outside. In here no one spoke above a whisper.

The Ortakapi, the gateway to the second court, was flanked by two octagonal towers with conical tops, like candle snuffers. There was a huge iron door and Suleiman's tugra - his personal seal - hung above it on a brass shield. There were yet more heads blackening on spikes on the wall above.

Gonzaga was ordered to dismount.

"We must go on foot the rest of the way," his interpreter told him.

Gonzaga reluctantly complied.

There was a waiting room leading off from the gatehouse. While Gonzaga cooled his heels in a sparsely furnished cell the interpreter passed the time by pointing out a cistern used for drowning and the beheading block. The Chief

High Executioner, he said with some pride, could process up to fifty heads a day.

Gonzaga thanked him for this information and settled down to wait.

Three hours later he was escorted through the gate to the Second Court.

\*\*\*

How dare they can make him wait like this! He was so furious at the insult to his person and to La Serenissima that he did not spare a glance for the fountains or the box hedges or even at the gazelles that grazed on the lawns. He stamped between the honour guard of yeniçeris lining the pathway to the Divan, head down, his retinue hurrying behind him.

He was aware of the silence though. The only thing to be heard was the sigh of the wind in the trees.

He was escorted into the Divan.

This, however, was impressive. He had never witnessed such a riot of colour. Despite himself he stared in awe at the brilliance and variety of the costumes before him; the Grand Vizier in bright green; the muftis of religion in dark blue; the grand ulemas in violet; the court chamberlain in scarlet. Ostrich plumes waved like a forest, jewels flashed in turbans and from scimitars. There were silks and velvets and satins.

And the aromas! Hundreds of dishes of foods were set out on the silver tables; guinea fowl, pigeon, goose, lamb, chicken. The Ambassador of the Illustrious Signory of Venice looked around for the chairs. Instead he was made to squat on the carpets with the rest of the company to eat his lunch.

"When may I see the Sultan?" he hissed at his interpreter, an unhappy looking man who was sweating profusely.

"Very soon!" the man whispered back. "But we must be silent for the meal!"

As the interpreter had suggested the meal was eaten in total silence. Pages leaned over their shoulders and squirted rosewater into their goblets with unswerving accuracy from goatskins slung over their backs. Attendants in red silk robes moved silently to and from the kitchen. Just a raised finger was enough to have a servant hurry over to fulfil any request. Pastries, figs, dates, watermelon and rahat lokum were served as dessert.

Still, not a word spoken.

In fact the solemnity of the occasion was not broken until the meal was completed and the assembled dignitaries rose to their feet. At that point the slaves descended on the plates and scrambled for the remains of the food like a pack of dogs. It only confirmed what Gonzaga had suspected all along.

Big show. Nice clothes. But just heathen beneath it all.

\*\*\*

The Ba"ab-i-Sa"adet, the Gate of Felicity, guarded the selamlik, the Sultan's inner sanctum The double gate was surmounted by an ornamented canopy flanked by sixteen columns of porphyry and guarded, by Gonzaga's calculation, by at least thirty eunuchs. They wore vests of gold brocade and each had his curved yataghan drawn, each razor sharp edge flashing in the sun.

Gonzaga was given a gold cloth to put over his clothes so that he would be fit to present to the Sultan. The Chief of Standard then came to receive his gifts.

Four Parmesan cheeses.

The interpreter did not comment on this bounty. He was made to wait while this treasure was presented to the Lord of Life.

Suddenly two chamberlains grabbed him by the neck and arms, pinioning him. They forced him to his knees to kiss the portal and then dragged him across a gloomy courtyard, between another double line of guards, and into the Audience Hall, the Arzodarsi. They ignored his protests. They could not understand his Italian anyway.

His impression of the Lord of Life was fleeting; a white turban adorned with a huge egret feather, three diamond tiaras and a ruby the size of a hazelnut, a gown of white satin ablaze with even more rubies. He had a beard and a proud nose.

A throne, fashioned form beaten gold, stood in one corner of the hall like a four poster bed surrounded by a carpet of green satin. It was so vast that the Sultan's feet did not touch the ground. Pearls and rubies hung from silk tassels on the canopy.

Gonzaga was even afforded a glimpse of his own august person, on his knees, held down by two black slaves, in the reflection of a gilt Vicenzan mirror. He was by now almost inarticulate with rage. While he fought for words, the Vizier, standing at Suleiman's right shoulder, turned to his interpreter. "Has the dog been fed?"

"The infidel is fed and now craves to lick the dust beneath His Majesty's throne."

"Bring him here, then."

Gonzaga was compelled into the act of sala'am by the chamberlains. He was then dragged into the middle of the chamber where they again forced his head onto the floor. Approaching the throne they pressed his forehead to the carpets a third time.

"The dog has brought tribute?" the Vizier asked.

"Four cheeses, Great lord."

"Store them in the Treasury with the other gifts."

The Ambassador of the Illustrious Signory of Venice was then dragged backwards to the door. Yet again his face was introduced to the carpet, and he was then propelled from the Arzodarsi into the forecourt, where the chamberlains released him.

Gonzaga was incandescent with rage. "What … what is the meaning … you humiliate me this way … I have not addressed the Sultan!"

"You may not address the Lord of Life directly," the interpreter said. "Now we go to the Divan. You may put your entreaties to the Vizier and the Council."

"What?"

"It is not possible to speak directly with the Sultan."

"Then why did you bring me here?"

His interpreter looked absolutely terrified. "Please, this way, My Lord," he said. "You will speak to the Vizier now and he will take your message personally to the Lord of Life. Please don't shout. You'll get me into trouble."

Gonzaga could not believe his ears. He turned on his heel and stalked away, his interpreter scurrying after him.

# CHAPTER 83

## Pera

"We come here in peace and they spit on us! How dare they treat us this way!"

It was two days since the Ambassador of the Illustrious Signory of Venice had been honoured with an audience with the Sultan of the Osmanlis and he was still shaken. Ludovici poured him wine from the crystal decanter to soothe his nerves.

"That is the protocol," Ludovici said. "All ambassadors are treated alike, ever since Murad the First was assassinated by a Serbian noble."

"I was not even given the opportunity to speak to him in person! Who does he think he is?"

"He is the Lord of Life, the Emperor of the Two Worlds, Maker of Kings and Possessor Men's Necks - that's who he thinks he is, your Excellency. Besides, all decisions on foreign policy are taken by the Vizier for Suleiman to ratify. He never conducts negotiations directly. It would be too demeaning."

"Demeaning!"

They were in the drawing room of Ludovici"s palazzo. He saw Gonzaga cast a critical gaze over the long table of polished chestnut and carved chairs upholstered with crimson damask. Gilt Vicenzan mirrors hung on the walls. Yes, Ludovici thought, impressed aren't you? Not bad for a bastard.

He had not expected to ever entertain a Consigliotore here, and he supposed that Gonzaga had not expected to find himself here either. But politics made for strange bedfellows. "You must understand," he said, "their whole system is built around a rigid hierarchy. To their mind the Sultan has no equal anywhere in the world. Not even the Pope - or the Doge."

Gonzaga snorted with derision.

"The Sultan is the only one in this whole Empire who attains his position by virtue of his birth," Ludovici continued. "All others rise by their own abilities. They do not even have to be born a Muslim. The last Vizier, Ibrahim, was the son of a Greek fisherman. A Christian. They have a system called the devshirme. They take men and women from all over the Empire and train them to be part of the kullar, which is what they call the Sultan's slave family. Those with real ability can rise to pre-eminence. Those with more brawn than brain are conscripted into the yeniçeris , which is their soldier elite. And they are elite; full time professionals and the reason they have conquered half of Europe. As for the women, the mother of the Sultan might start life as the daughter of a Circassian peasant farmer. The system is eminently fair and eternally surprising."

"I understand the point you are making, but perhaps your admiration for them is tempered by your own bitterness."

Ludovici bowed his head to concede the point. "It is true, in the Republic men such as myself must go abroad to find their own measure. However, even an impartial judge would see that their system is not only fair but it also promotes peace inside the society. For instance, although the Turk fights the infidel -as he calls us - with all the means at his disposal, nowhere else in the world can a man practice his religion as freely as he may inside the Osmanli empire. Even when they made war on you - on us - we in Pera were allowed to practice our Catholic rites in peace. Down there in Galata you will find Jews, Muslims, Christians all working side by side. In Rome they are still putting Lutherans to the stake."

"Is that why you asked me here Ludovici? To list the Sultan's virtues? Perhaps you will convert to Islam yourself?"

"I remain a loyal subject of La Serenissima. But I have lived here a long time, your Excellency, I understand their ways."

"Thank you for the lecture. It has been most instructive."

"That was not my purpose in inviting you here."

"You said you had a proposal for me." Gonzaga finished his wine and helped himself to more.

"I understand your negotiations with the Vizier did not go well."

"The impertinent little man wants us to pay tribute and cede the island of Cyprus! He will want the San Marco as his summer palace next!"

"Can we refuse his demands?"

"Ever since Prevezzo Suleiman has us by the throat, as you well know. Without uninterrupted trading routes our republic will sink into the Adriatic. Thanks to your enlightened Turk!"

"There might be another way to settle this, Excellency."

"I'm listening."

"As I think you know my activities do not always align with the strictest reading of the law."

"You're a pirate."

"Not quite. But I have made some unusual allegiances in the course of my business. They might now be of some use to La Serenissima."

"How?"

"It is true that I admire the Turk, but I love my country more. Perhaps you should abandon your negotiations with the Sultan. I might instead be able to arrange a meeting for you with the Turkish admiral, Dragut."

"Dragut?"

"Now he really is a pirate, for sale to the highest border. Ecco, if Venice must pay tribute for use of the sea lanes I am sure Dragut would not be quite as unreasonable in his demands as the Vizier."

Gonzaga drained his glass. "You think he would do this?"

"Dragut is not one of the kullar. He's a freebooter. Make him the right offer and he'll switch sides. What's it worth to you?"

"So you can do this?"

"Of course."

Gonzaga smiled. "Well my renegade merchant, perhaps you could be of service to the Republic after all."

"I am so glad you think so," Ludovici said.

***

Julia watched the conversation from the shadows at the top of the stairs. Her father! Yet it was like looking at a total stranger. He looked grayer and smaller than she remembered. Almost twelve years since she had seen him, but his voice still put a chill through her. It brought back memories of silent, gloomy meals, black, dusty Bibles and of course, Abbas screaming in the hold of a privateer.

She searched in her soul for some ghost of filial affection but found nothing. She felt instead a deep kinship for Ludovici, as he handed yet another goblet of wine to the man who had destroyed his best friend and crushed the spirit of the woman he loved.

# CHAPTER 84

## Stamboul

Sirhane now had her own hammam. Her husband lived in some luxury, befitting a man of high rank. She had sent a message to Julia, inviting her to visit with her at his palazzo. "Let's bath together," she said, when she had shrugged off her ferijde . "Like the old days!"

Now Julia sat naked on the edge of the bath while Sirhane held a stone jar of scented oil and splashed some on her hands. She massaged it into Julia's shoulders.

"Does Ludovici know you are here?" she asked her.

"No. I haven't told him."

"No one needs to know." Julia groaned as Sirhane's thumbs found a sore spot. "You're tense. Are you worried about being here?"

Julia shook her head. "Do you remember your father?"

"My Father? Of course."

"How old were you when you were taken away?"

"Fifteen."

"Did you cry?"

"For a week. Why?"

"Tell me what happened."

"We were farmers. My father had sheep and a few goats. Also we grew seeds and a little grain. He was a kind man, but he was very old when I left. He is probably dead now. My mother, too. I had ten brothers and sisters. I miss them all. But what good is it to brood about it? If I were still with them I would be in a field driving a plough or picking sunflowers."

"But your father, did you love him?"

Sirhane seemed perplexed by the question. "Of course." She squeezed hard on Julia's neck muscles. "I suppose so. Julia, what is wrong?"

"Sirhane, I fear for my soul."

"Your soul?"

"There is something evil in, I feel it."

Sirhane laughed, then realized that Julia was serious. She wrapped her arms around her shoulders and hugged her. "What is it? First you ask me about my father, then you tell me you are evil ..."

"There is so much about myself I do not understand. Why can't I love a man? Why do I prefer your company to my husband's?"

Sirhane stiffened. "It's not wrong."

"Of course it is."

"We harm no one. A woman cannot violate another woman."

"It would do harm, if he knew. I know he loves me, I know he wants me to love him. I betray him every time I see you."

"Julia, what is all this about?"

She sighed and rested her head on Sirhane's shoulder. The gauze wrap felt rough against her cheek. She allowed Sirhane to cradle her.

"If you knew something terrible was about to happen to someone and you did nothing to prevent it ... is that wrong?"

"I don't know."

"What do you think?"

Sirhane ran a hand across the frieze of Iznik ceramic on the walls, feeling the condensation cool on her hand. It was emblazoned with a verse from the Qu'ran in white and blue script. "Every soul will taste death. We test you with both good and evil as a trial. And you will be returned to us." "It depends," Sirhane answered carefully. "Has this person done anything wrong?"

"Yes ... oh, yes."

"And is his punishment ratified by law?"

Julia did not answer and Sirhane did not press her., Instead she said: "What will happen if you keep your silence?"

"Someone will die."

"And if you do not?"

"A person will has caused great suffering will go unpunished."

"Then if it were me, I would keep my silence. But there is more to it than that, isn't there? Who is this person? Do you love him?" Is it Ludovici? she thought. Is it me?

"I should love him, but I cannot. That is why there is something bad in me."

You are talking in riddles. There is nothing bad in you, Julia. You are kind and you are gentle."

"You're wrong," Julia said. She lay her head on Sirhane's lap. Sirhane stroked her hair. It was never spoken of again.

## Pera

Gonzaga informed only the bailo of his meeting with Dragut. Ludovici had impressed on him that the fewer who knew about it in advance the better. He omitted Ludovici''s role in the arrangements. Gonzaga was prepared to protect him while he was still of possible future use.

A messenger arrived that afternoon at the bailo's residence with a sealed missive for Gonzaga. It informed him that Dragut would be on the galleot Barbarossa, moored in the harbor at Galata. Gonzaga was to meet him there at midnight and he was to come alone.

That night he left Pera in a coach. The bailo wished him luck and waved him farewell. He disappeared down the hill towards the inky bowels of Galata.

# CHAPTER 85

A pink glow lit the sky from the nearby foundries. A carriage clattered out of one of the yokush, a violently steep alley that finished right there on the deserted waterfront. Abbas watched from the shadows as a man stepped out. The driver handed him a lighted lamp. He was wearing the robes and a bareta of a togato.

He passed close to the doorway where Abbas stood, and he saw his face clearly illuminated by the lamp. A decade rolled back. He was in the hold of a stinking privateer and he felt the terror overwhelm him yet again.

*\*\**

There had been three of them, a knifer and two assistants. It came back to him as if it were yesterday, scalded on his memory. He remembered the large raised birthmark on the knifer's temple, at the hairline; in the lamplight it looked like a large raisin. The knifer had a high pitched voice like a choirboy. He had laughed the whole time. It was almost as if he were playing some schoolboy prank.

They had tied a white bandage round his lower belly and thighs to slow the bleeding. This operation had taken a long time because he had kicked and struggled so fiercely. The knifer had sworn at him but they let him exhaust himself before they set to work. When he was finally subdued they bathed his penis and testicles with hot pepper water. He had screamed at the scalding pain and the knifer laughed again and told him he would rinse them in cold water as soon as they were off and cool them down for him.

Abbas had struggled with all the strength he possessed. But against three men, his hands tied behind his back, it had been useless. He sobbed and pleaded with them to name their price, anything, just don't do this!

That only made the knifer laugh even harder.

He screamed so loudly when they did it that his voice was hoarse for a week afterwards. Then they cauterized the wound with boiling pitch and he vomited and passed out.

When he came round they were still binding the wound using paper that had been saturated in cold water. They put a spigot in an opening in the bandages to restrict the flow of urine and blood.

He started screaming again but the screams seemed to come from outside himself. Another voice inside him was quite calm and told him not to worry, that he would soon bleed to death and then it would all be over.

The knifer's assistant dragged him to his feet and began to walk him around the hold. One circuit took in the blue lolling head of Julia's duenna, whom they had murdered earlier that night; another a pool of blood-stained bilge, a coil of tarred rope, some sacking, a broken winch cable. Then it began again.

They walked round and round the hold for hours. What horrified him was the way the two men talked to him continually, encouraging him, recalling other operations they had seen and telling him everything would be all right. You have to walk, they said, it stops you going into shock, and then you'll die. Come on, we'll help you. You're doing well. You're a brave one, a tough one, we'll get through this. It was as if they were friends come to rescue him instead of his tormentors.

What was even worse, he felt his hatred of them slipping away. He sobbed and thanked them when they finally eased him back onto the floor, half crazed with pain and barely conscious.

He had no idea how long he lay there. Someone lit a fire inside his body and he started to burn with fever. But they would not let him drink and his tongue swelled in his mouth until it almost choked him and his lips cracked and he could not speak.

One day the men came back into the hold and bent down to examine the wound. They removed the bandages and nodded to each other, apparently satisfied. When they released the spigot a flow of urine spurted across the hold like a fountain.

"Well done," one of them men said and patted him on the shoulder. "You're going to be all right."

All right? What was "all right"? A few weeks later they sold him in the market square at Algiers. From there he was brought to the seraglio, to suffer in glorious splendour, to live the rest of his days as a besilked freak.

He envied the other eunuchs. Most had never known sexual maturity. He was one of the few who had survived such an operation when it was done so late in life. As he grew accustomed to life in the Harem he watched the rest of his body change, turning soft, then running to fat. Food became his only pleasure.

And every day he cursed the name of Antonio Gonzaga.

\*\*\*

The memory passed in just a few seconds; soon he was alert again. He watched Gonzaga head towards the Barbarossa, lamp swinging. The galleot's outline was silhouetted by the glow from the arsenal at Top Hane. He looked back up the hill. Two men slipped into the shadows. Of course, he trusted that Gonzaga would not be so foolish as to come alone. Well, that did not matter. His own men would take care of that.

He moved out of the doorway and followed Gonzaga towards the Barbarossa.

## Pera

Julia knelt in her private chapel and stared at the wooden crucifix above the altar. She had come here to ask for forgiveness, to pray for absolution and the strength to fight her weakness. Instead she felt only anger.

What sort of God had allowed a boy like Abbas to suffer so much and a man like her father to prosper?

Her father's God.

She rose from her knees. She would find her solace elsewhere.

# CHAPTER 86

Gonzaga sensed that someone was behind him before he heard the footsteps. He turned and peered into the shadows.

"Che Xiè?"

No answer.

But there was someone there, he was sure of it. If it was one of Dragut's men, surely he would have shown himself? Perhaps it was one of his own men further along the wharf. He turned and hurried towards the gangway of the Barbarossa.

The galleot was deserted. The lamps that burned on the fore and main masts threw long shadows across the deck. There was no night watch and no sound from below.

He heard someone on the dock and spun around. Something was wrong. He drew his sword. Four shapes melted out of the shadows, blocking the way back. He composed himself. They must be Dragut's men.

"Which one of you is Dragut?" he said.

"Dragut is not here," a falsetto voice replied in faultless Venetian dialect.

"Where is he then? I demand to see him.""

"He is getting drunk in Üsküdar. Now drop your sword or we will be forced to take it from you."

Gonzaga heard the rasp of steel as swords were drawn from their scabbards. "Who are you?"

"Drop your sword. You don't know how to use it anyway. I assure you these men here are expert." He uttered a sob of fear and the blade clattered onto the cobbles at his feet. He shouted for his body guards. No answer. He dropped the oil lamp and ran.

Two more men appeared from the darkness and grabbed him before he had gone even five paces. They wrestled him to the ground. "Tie him up," the falsetto said.

His hands were pinioned behind his back and tied with rough hemp. He screamed again for help so they stuffed a foul rag in his mouth. One of the men lashed out with his boot, kicking him in the ribs, then rolled him over onto his back.

The falsetto picked up the oil lamp that he had dropped and came over. Gonzaga found himself staring at one of the ugliest men he had ever seen, a fat Moor with one eye, half his face mutilated by some ancient injury. In the lamp light he looked like a devil from hell.

"Antonio Gonzaga," he said. "Do you remember me?"

Remember him? His mind reeled. What was he talking about?

He squinted up at this apparition in panicked confusion. He was a Moor, yes, but not wharfside scum like the others. He wore a sable-lined pelisse, embroidered with pearls and silver and he had on soft yellow leather boots. There was a large round pearl in his ear. He crouched down, and removed the sodden rag from Gonzaga's mouth. "You really don't remember, do you?"

"Of course I don't remember you! I've never met you!"

"No, we never met. But you did know me, and I knew your daughter."

"My daughter's dead, she was murdered by pirates!"

"Perhaps."

"Who are you? Corpo di Dio, I have money. Do you want money? Tell me what you want."

"What do I want? I want you to remember, that's all. I want you to think about your daughter, the most beautiful woman I ever saw, that I ever will see. I want you to send your mind back twelve years, to the son of the Captain General of the Republic of Venice."

Gonzaga remembered then, and wet himself. The monster holding the lamp shook his head. "Yes, I did the same. It's terrifying knowing that you are utterly helpless, isn't it?" He stood up. "Take him aboard!"

Gonzaga screamed but one of the men quickly shoved the rag back in his mouth. They lifted him easily, hands and feet, and carried him onto the Barbarossa and down into the hold.

Perfect justice, Abbas thought.

Belowships, in a privateer in some filthy dock. That was how it all started for me.

# CHAPTER 87

Abbas hung the lamp on a hook fixed to one of the beams and leaned against the bulwark as the men deposited their whimpering cargo in a lapping pool of tar and seawater. His eyes were starting from their sockets and he was trying to say something through the gag.

Abbas waited until they were alone, then he said: "I will take the rag out of your mouth now. But if you scream, I shall replace it. Is that clear?"

Gonzaga nodded.

"There."

The words came bubbling out in a torrent. Like when they pulled that spigot out of me, he thought. " ... I didn't know what was done to you, I swear, I only ordered them to beat you, to discourage you, that's all, if I have wronged you I swear that I will make it up to you, I am a rich man, I have much I can offer you, I am a Consig-"

Abbas stuffed the gag back in his mouth. He's like a dog trying to vomit up its breakfast, he thought. Still I understand how he feels. It was like that for me once.

"I might have known that all I would hear from you is lies and vanities. What can you offer me, Consigliatore? Money? I have more than I shall ever need. The Sultan and his lady pay all my expenses. I have fine clothes and more diamond than even you could fit in your long pockets. No, what I desire is only what every man is granted at his birth. And you took it away. You cannot give it back."

Abbas drew a short killiç from the sash at his waist. He held it close to Gonzaga's face, turning it in his fist so that the blade caught the reflection of the lamp. "Look at this, Excellency. A simple instrument. You can cut bread with it or you can ruin a man's life. It depends on the intention. What is my intention, Excellency? Can you guess?"

He pulled up Gonzaga's robe, exposing his thighs and lower belly. He gripped Gonzaga's testicles in his fist, squeezing. Gonzaga's face suffused with blood as he tried to scream through the gag.

"Can you imagine what this is like? Did you imagine it when you ordered it done?"

Gonzaga shook his head violently. Abbas touched the knife to Gonzaga's flesh, drawing a thin line of blood. Gonzaga thrashed on the floor like a beached fish. Abbas jumped up and slumped against the bulwark, sweating. He put the knife back into the sash at his waist.

"No Consigliatore, I would not wish such a horror on even my worst enemy, and you are that, and more. I cannot do it, not even to you. I would never stain my own soul with such a sin."

Gonzaga curled his knees into his chest and rolled onto his side. He started to weep.

"I will show you the mercy you never showed to me. I will give you your life, such as it is worth. Every second that remains of it is yours to savour. In the morning Dragut sails for Algiers. I have instructed him to sell you in the market place in Algiers as a galley slave. When you are chained to a bench, awash in your own filth, working eighteen hours a day at the oars you can think about what you did to me and to your daughter. You will have plenty of time for reflection. Some men survive five years of it before their strength gives out." Abbas went to the companionway. "If only you had shown me such consideration! I would have thought it the greatest mercy compared to the future you chose for me! Go with God, Excellency."

He saluted the Ambassador of the Illustrious Signory of Venice then took the lamp from its hook and left Antonio Gonzaga to the darkness and his dreams.

### Pera

The moon had fallen below the seven hills when Ludovici returned. Julia was still awake. She sat by the window staring into the candle.

He put a hand on her shoulder. "It is done," he whispered.

He felt the answering pressure from her fingers but she did not reply. After a while he left here there and went to bed, knowing he would not sleep.

### The Topkapi Saraya

Abbas selected his own key from the hundreds on the key ring stuffed in his sash. The former Kapi Aga was the last of the white eunuchs to be given the responsibility of the keys. Now the Sultan only entrusted a complete rasé with the responsibility.

He slumped onto his cot. The cat jumped onto his lap, purring, and he petted her absently, his mind drawn inside, to the shadow play deep within his own mind. He removed his turban and put his head in his hands.

Revenge did not taste particularly sweet. It had left an emptiness inside him. What would he do with his suffering now that he could no longer dream of the sweet lure of vengeance? Now his score was settled he must live out the rest of his days knowing that this was really as good as it would ever be.

Nothing could change what had been done.

\*\*\*

The full moon shimmered on the cupolas and minarets of the Harem like a frost making the plane trees in the courtyards appeared ghostly. The eunuchs guarding the iron-studded doors stood like mahogany statues.

Far above them a woman stared across the Horn, imagining the waving grasses of the Georgian steppe; in the window below a eunuch looked over the Marmara Deniz and thought of the sun-dappled canals of Venice. Abbas and Hürrem both paced the night, souls eroded by loss and longing, each of them a tiny outpost of hell in one man's Paradise on earth.

# PART 8

## DANGEROUS WINDOW

# CHAPTER 88

### Topkapi Saraya, 1553

Suleiman had lived nearly fifty nine years and age gnawed at his bones. He spent more and more time now closeted with the sheyhülislam reading his Qu'ran.

He had gout, his elbow and knees occasionally becoming swollen and so tender he could not stand the slightest touch and these attacks sometimes lasted as long as a week. He had also developed an edema and had taken to wearing rouge to hide the sickly pallor of his skin. He ate little, usually just some baby goat washed down with iced sherbet.

Hürrem grew more afraid. Suleiman mortality reminded her of her own fragile tenure on life.

She had been patient for so long. Now she was afraid that time was no longer on her side. If something was to be done about Mustapha then it would have to be done very soon.

\*\*\*

For over a decade now the executioner's sword had been poised over his children's heads. There was nothing even the King of Kings could do to protect his own children after death because his own great grandfather, the Faith, conqueror of Stamboul, had made this bloody kanun:

The ulema have declared it allowable that whoever among my illustrious children and grandchildren may come to the throne should, for securing the peace of the world, order his brothers to be executed. Let them hereafter act accordingly.

As the years drew on Suleiman was troubled by his own mortality, and the gnawing of doubt. We will never be a great people, he thought, unless we put aside this savagery.

Hürrem, as always, had given voice to his innermost fears. "I am so afraid," she whispered to him one night as she lay in his arms.

"Afraid? Of what my russelana?"

"Not for me, for my sons." She laid her head on his bare, smooth chest. "My Lord, when you die - may that day never dawn! - my life shall longer be worth living so I fear nothing on my own account. But when Mustapha attains the throne the Kanun of the Fatih tells him he may execute all his brothers, even poor Çehangir .."

"We have gone beyond such barbarity."

"It is not Mustapha I fear. He has a good heart."

"What then?"

"When he comes green to the throne and discovers his own voice, he will be surrounded by those not as well disposed. We know Mustapha shall be Sultan but who will be his Vizier? Would a dried up prune like Lütfi Pasha show any compassion for poor Çehangir? Could even the astrologers in the House of Time foretell what plans the Aga of the yeniçeris might hatch against Selim, because he cannot ride? What traps might a jealous pasha lay for Bayezid because he is so able?"

Suleiman held her tighter. She was right, after his death she would be helpless, and so would his sons. Mustapha had given his word, and yet ...

He was relying on Mustapha's nobility. The boy was no butcher; he was as loyal as he was brave, there was no malice in him that he had ever discerned. His was the just hand for the banner of Mohammed. "Mustapha is a good man."

"His mother still lives, and she hates me."

Gülbehar! When he died she would become the new Valide Sultan, head of the Harem. How hard would she press Mustapha to invoke the Kanun of the Faith? "What would you have me do?"

"Never die."

He smiled in the dark. "We all die. It is God's path for us."

"Then I shall pray I have a voice in the Divan to protect me. Rüstem perhaps ..."

Yes, there was wisdom in that; Rüstem Pasha, his son in law would protect his wife and her brothers. He had proved his loyalty with Ibrahim. "I will think about it." "

They had said no more about it. But soon afterwards, when Lütfi Pasha died of the pestilence, Suleiman ignored the usual laws of succession and proclaimed his own son in law the new Grand Vizier.

The Man Who Never Smiled became the second most powerful man in the Osmanli empire.

\*\*\*

Abbas was ushered into the presence of the Vizier, executed his temenna and allowed his pages to lower his bulk to the carpet. The purple silk of his robe is as large as the royal tent, Rüstem thought. When he moves it's like a squadron of yeniçeris buggering each other under a blanket.

"May I extend my congratulations on your great fortune," Abbas greeted him. "God indeed smiles on you. To be Vizier of the greatest of all Osmanli sultans is a blessing almost too great to comprehend."

The Infinite had no hand in this, Rüstem thought. "All thanks and praise to Him."

"However my mistress has asked me to remind you that though God is great there are times when his Bounty - as His vengeance - may need prompting by earthly angels."

What a pretty tongue you have, Rüstem thought. "Tell your mistress I shall not forget her words and that I am exceedingly grateful for them."

"Well that is why I am here. To discuss the many ways you can prove your kind remembrance of her."

"Well, she wastes no time in calling in her favours," Rüstem thought. He clapped his hands and the pages scurried away to fetch sherbets and halwa while they settled to their discussion.

\*\*\*

"You have heard the whispers in the bazaar?" Abbas asked.

"The bazaaris do more than whisper, Abbas. They shout to each other in the bedestens how our Sultan has lost all appetite for war. What is there to be done? He finds glory now only in his rebuilding the city. He spends more times with his architects than his generals."

"We all worry that he is ignoring his duty to God, of course. But could there be those who seek to profit from it?"

Please, Rüstem thought, you and your mistress care as much for his duty to God as you do for the price of melons in the fruit market.

"You have heard these other rumours from the barracks?" Rüstem said.

"Everyone in Stamboul has heard them."

The trouble has started, as always, in Persia. Shah Tamasp was once again raiding their eastern border, torturing and killing the muftis and flaunting his Sufavid heresies, growing bolder all the time while Suleiman wrote poetry and dictated laws and planned mosques in his summer yalis in Adrianople and Çamlica.

Meanwhile his soldiers fretted behind the palace walls, hungry for action, growing more impatient day by day. All they talked of now was their adored Mustapha, waiting in the wings and sprouting the first gray in his beard. That one would not sit around drinking sherbet with his builders, they said. He would have taken us against the heretic Persian long ago. As soon as he takes the throne we will be on the march again, there will be more victories and more plunder.

But not everyone awaited the new sultanate quite as eagerly. It will be the end for Hürrem, Rüstem thought. And when she goes, I go as well.

From somewhere along the colonnaded gardens, a bell sounded the hour.

"What would the Lady Hürrem have me do?"

"Just remember where your loyalty lies."

Oh I shall never forget that, he thought. It lies where it always did. With myself. "I am loyal to my Sultan above all things."

"Against anyone who might seek to bring him down?"

"Of course."

"Then we rely on you to deal with this current threat to him."

There is no current threat, Rüstem thought, just the jabber of soldiers and eggplant vendors. But I see what you mean. This is our best opportunity to save our own necks. "Assure your mistress that I remain her husband's faithful servant," he said.

# CHAPTER 89

Suleiman lay with his head in her lap, his eyes closed. Insects murmured in the garden but in the Harem it was cool, almost chill. Almost midday but the sun had not yet penetrated the plane trees and only a weak yellow light filtered through the windows.

"You look tired, my Lord," Hürrem said.

"There is so much to do, little russelana, so much to do before I sleep."

"You should not work so hard."

But working hard is my duty, he thought. I have abrogated the day to day running of the Empire to Rüstem and the Divan so I can devote myself to the rebuilding of this city. Stamboul will be a worthier testimony to my reign than Rhodes, Mohacs or Buda-Pesth. When my grandfather conquered this city much of it was abandoned and derelict. Before I die it will have surpassed its former glory. I shall be able to shout: "Justinian, I have outdone thee!"

The focus of much of the building was the construction of imperial mosques for each one included a kulliye - a cluster of charitable institutions such as a hospital, a religious school, baths, a cemetery, a library, sometimes even a hospice and a soup kitchen. New quarters with new populations soon built up around them.

The Sehzade Camii was already finished, as was Mehmet's tomb, and the Selimiye Camii at Fener, honouring his father. Now he had commissioned Sinan to start work on the Suleimaniye, on the site of the old harem. It would be his masterpiece; the stone cupolas and minarets Sinan had imagined would dominate the Horn and the city of the Seven Hills for a thousand years.

He had also set himself the herculean task of drafting a complete legislature that would be the foundation of all future government. The thousands of kanuni that he was drafting would regulate the judgments of the Divans and give the Osmanlis, for the first time, a complete code of law.

He prayed to God for hours to finish the task he had set himself.

Hürrem stroked his cheek. "So deep in thought, my Lord?"

"I was thinking how quickly time slips by."

"Perhaps then you should not spend so much of it closeted with your scribes."

"I cannot rest until the work is finished. I cannot leave it to Mustapha, he is a great soldier and an able governor but he cannot apply himself to matters of law as I can. Besides other matters press on me. I must go to Persia. I cannot ignore the Shah's provocations any longer."

Hürrem frowned, pouting like a spoiled houri.

"Now what is wrong?" he said.

"Why send a professor to spank an errant child? Is Tamasp so great a king that he should warrant your individual attention?"

"There is no choice."

"Of course there is. Send Mustapha. The yeniçeris adore him; they will follow him anywhere."

A nerve in Suleiman's cheek twitched. "Why do you say that?"

"Have I offended you my Lord?"

"What whispers have you heard concerning Mustapha?"

"Nothing sinister my Lord. Indeed, I hear only good reports. They say he is a just good man, as you have always said. A great horseman, a brilliant commander."

"Too great perhaps," Suleiman murmured.

"Can a man be too great?"

"I thought you were afraid of him."

"You assured me I had nothing to fear. You know your son and I do not. I trust your word."

"I do not fear him as a Sultan when I am dead. Yet sometimes I fear him when I am still alive. I fear the yeniçeris ."

"They will never love him as they love you. You gave them Belgrade, you gave them Rhodes, you gave them Buda-Pesth."

"That was a long time ago. Many of the young recruits in the army now were not even alive when we took Rhodes."

"But you told me yourself that Mustapha is a just man, a good man. Do you think he would intrigue against you?"

Well do I? Suleiman wondered. It had been so long since he had seen him. He still thought of him as a lively bright-eyed boy, but he was a man now with grey in his beard. He was capable and he was ambitious; how could he not feel impatient?

But no, it was his own yeniçeris that kept him awake at night. They were the elite of the army; full time professionals who had made them masters of Europe and Asia. Most of the armies they fought against were made up of noblemen who had brought their peasants along with them as infantry. Whoever ruled the yeniçeris ruled the world.

They owed their allegiance to the same man; it was the Sultan who fed them each day and this was reflected in their battle standards - a soup kettle was emblazoned on all on their standards - and command structures. Their general was the Chorbaji-bashi - the Head Soup Ladler. His second command was the Ashçi-Bashi, or head cook. Each man had a spoon in a brass socket sewn in front of his cap.

Their ranks were replenished from the devshirme; recruits they were toughened with manual labour in the palace gardens or in the shipyards. They were taught unquestioning obedience to their generals and lived harsh celibate lives in Spartan barracks on poor pay; the only way they could hope to enrich themselves was by the plunder they took in battle. It was why the loved Selim the Grim so much; they were never short of loot in those days.

But it was also the yeniçeris who had forced his grandfather form the throne; and Suleiman had never forgotten how once, early in his reign, they had over turned their kettles outside their barracks as a symbol of revolt. Even though the rebellion had been quashed he had been forced to increase their wages. Even twenty years later he still glanced uneasily at their cook-kettles each Friday as he rode through their barracks in the First Court on the way to the mosque.

In theory they were his slaves; but with their constant demands for war and loot, and the continuing threat they posed to security, he wondered sometimes if he was not theirs.

He tried to explain this to Hürrem. "There have been times when I have gone to war just to satisfy them, even though I deemed it unwise. If they can rule me, perhaps they can rule him."

"How far is Manisa from Stamboul?"

"When my father died I rode here in five days to claim the throne."

"Then if you fear him, Lord, give Bayezid his seat. Send Mustapha east to Amasya or Karamania."

"Manisa is the traditional seat of the chosen shahzade. He will think I have abandoned him in favour of your son."

"He knows you cannot give him guarantees."

"I cannot do it to him."

"Then let us speak no more of it then. If Mustapha is a good and just man, what do you have to fear? He will not try to manipulate the yeniçeris against you."

Manipulate them against me? Could he do that? If he did, I would lose not only my sultanate, but everything I have worked all my life to build. I have dreamed of an Osmanli Empire outside of tents and warring. Soon my nomad tribesmen will have a capital boasting the finest architecture in the Orient. Literature, painting and music are flourishing. We have left behind the barbarity of the past; the peaceful succession from myself to Mustapha is to be proof of that.

The next day he spoke to Rüstem in private audience. He set his seal on a letter commanding Mustapha to leave Manisa and take his family and court to Amasya, in the east, twenty six days ride from Stamboul.

## Pera

Ludovici Gambetto knocked softly before entering Julia's bedroom. She was sitting up in the bed, waiting for him. He sat down on the edge of the bed and took her hand. There was something he wanted badly to say to her, but he could not find the right words.

While he hesitated she reached up and pulled out one of the hairs at his temple. "Gray hair!" she said.

He pulled away from her. "Nonsense!"

She was laughing. "At last! I thought you would never grow old!"

"I was in the kitchen. The cook threw flour at me."

"It's a gray hair. There must be others. Do you want me to look?"

"It is just a trick of the light."

"Well, I have them. Look!" She pulled back her widow's peak and pointed them out. "See. With my hair so black you cannot mistake them."

"You still look beautiful to me."

"Good," she said. She took his face in his hands and kissed him.

It was the first time she had ever done anything like that. It took his breath away. He let her pull him onto the bed. "Oh, Julia," he whispered.

\*\*\*

Afterwards he lay beside her while she slept, watching the gentle rise and fall of her breast in the candlelight. He traced the contours of her cheek with his fingers. She was just exquisite, a work of art; and until tonight, like a beautiful painting or a faience in one of Suleiman's mosques, that was all she had been to him. Something wonderful to look at, even when they were joined.

Tonight, something in her seemed to have shifted.

It was not that she was incapable of great emotion, of course. Her relationship with Sirhane, for instance. A few months ago the Syrian had left for Amasya with her husband, who had been appointed to the shahzade Mustapha's bodyguard. Julia had pretended to be ill; she did not eat for days nor did she leave her room.

He was not a fool.

He tried to understand; Sirhane had been the only real friend she had perhaps ever had. After all, with Abbas and Sirhane she had had a choice. He had been forced on her and she had been obliged to be grateful to him.

Another man might have felt betrayed, or furious, or both. But instead it gave Ludovici hope. Be patient, he told himself. One day she might feel this same way about you.

Her door had been locked to him for week, but he had not tried to force himself on her, and one night she had left the door to her bedroom open and he had gone in as if nothing had ever happened. You cannot make someone love you, he thought. You just have to give them the opportunity.

## Amasya

Clumps of cobalt forget-me-nots pushed through the patches of hard snow. Wild ducks rose from the grass, their wings whirring as they flapped away, panicked by their approach.

Mustapha turned his horse away from his escort and waited for Çehangir. Out here with only the wind for company he knew they would not be overheard.

"A fine day's hunting," he said.

Çehangir looked flushed and physically tired. "Yes, a wonderful day." They rode together for a short while in silence while Mustapha decided how to best broach the subject on his mind. "How is our father?" he said, finally.

"He suffers badly with the gout. It gives him a foul temper. I stay out of the way best I can."

"Does he seem troubled?"

Çehangir seemed ill at ease with the question. "I see him only rarely. I don't know."

"Does he speak to you of me?"

"Is something wrong between you?"

"Is there? I do not know."

"You are the shahzade," Çehangir said, as if this was the talisman to all his troubles.

"One can be shahzade for too long," he said. The sun had retreated behind the mountains and there was ice in the air.

"Suleiman loves you," Çehangir said.

Does he? Mustapha wondered. Then why did he send me out here? Why have I not seen him in so long?

He could smell snow on the wind. "We must hurry," he said. "The mountains are bitter here at night, even in spring."

Mustapha patted his half-brother on the shoulder and together they rode back to join their escort. He wondered what his half brother was not telling him. Or perhaps no one except the Hasseki Hürrem knew what Suleiman was thinking any more.

\*\*\*

The fortress was perched high in the mountains overlooking the Green River. In the courtyard the yeniçeri guards stood motionless in their leather winter cloaks. Torches set in the walls set their shadows dancing over the cobbles.

In a room high above them, a page in a turban of apricot silk set a silver jug of steaming black coffee on the low table beside Gülbehar's divan. She warmed herself by the charcoal brazier as she waited for her son.

He burst in, his face bronzed by the cold wind. He has been hunting, she thought, and has ridden hone in the dark, even though he knows the dangers of ice and swollen rivers this time of year.

He kissed her hand and settled on the divan beside her. Nearly forty years old now, and he still has the energy of a raw youth. Which is just as well because he will be an old man by the time he is Sultan. If only Suleiman would spend more time on the battlefield, in harm's way..

"How are you, Mother?"

"I am well. Here, I have had the kiaya fetch us coffee." She clapped her hands and one of her gediçli stepped forward and poured the coffee into two silver cups.

It was scalding and laced with honey. She disliked its bitter taste but she had heard that it was now the fashion in Stamboul to drink it. "So, now I hear Rüstem has reduced your allowance."

Mustapha grinned. "Does the shahzade have no secrets?"

"Not from his mother."

"Do not upset yourself. It is nothing."

"Nothing! It is an insult!"

"Her is trying to provoke me into doing something that would benefit him far more than it would benefit me. He will regret it when I am Sultan."

"If."

"Mother …"

"You trust your father too much. Look what he did to me." She immediately regretted saying that. It makes me sound like a bitter old woman, she thought. Perhaps that is what I am.

"He did nothing wrong. The heir's mother is always sent with him when he takes up his first governorship."

"Then why did he not send Hürrem to Manisa with Bayezid?" She put down her silver cup and the coffee spilled onto the tray. "How many more of these insults will you bear? He marries the witch, makes her queen, then exiles you to the mountains and gives her devil's spawn the shahzade's seat at Manisa. Now he turns his back while Rüstem makes you a pauper! If it is a goad, then accept it and let him deal with the consequences!"

"That would be foolish."

"Would it, son?" Her eyes filled with tears. A fine boy, the finest prince the Osmanlis would ever see, and they were conspiring to ruin him. And so handsome! You deserve to be Sultan, she thought.

"He is my father and he is my sultan. Any action against him would be a sin against Heaven."

"I am sure no such noble thoughts have crossed the mind of his new queen."

"In the matter of succession, Suleiman is the only judge."

"How naïve you are!"

"I know you do not trust her. Neither do I. But I put my trust in Suleiman."

Do not trust her? Gülbehar thought. I hate her so much it makes my bones ache. That day in the baths, I should have torn her apart with my bare hands. How I would like that opportunity again, she would get more than a few scratches.

"In time we will balance all injustice," he said. "I do not fear Bayezid and I certainly have nothing to fear from his roly-poly brother. Suleiman could exile me to Cathay and while I live the yeniçeris will not accept either of them over me."

"The yeniçeris are not as patient as you. They want you to do something about this now."

Mustapha shook his head. "That would be wrong."

"Suleiman's father did it."

"And "If I raise rebellion against him, what will happen when my own sons are of an age? We become no better than barbarians."

"Mustapha ..."

"No, I will not do it. One day the throne will come to me by right. I will wait. I will not offend my father and I will not offend God!"

### Sultanahmet, Stamboul

He has to die," Rüstem said.

Mihrmah blanched and lowered her eyes. "But he is the shahzade ..."

"Yes, Mihrmah and if he is ever Sultan what do you think will happen to us? I will tell you. The first thing he will do is put my head on a spike outside the Ba"ab-i-Sa"adet and then send you into exile with only hyenas for company. And what do you think will happen to your brothers?" Rüstem discussed it as if he were reciting the final moves of a chess game. She had never known anyone discuss death as dispassionately as her husband. "Your father made me Vizier thinking I could protect you and your family. But Mustapha hates me almost as much as he hates your mother."

Mihrmah turned her head away. Such a pretty day to be discussing murder! It was spring and a warm breeze was blowing from the south. Dolphins were playing near the shore in the Sea of Marmara. "But if we are found out in this ..."

"There is more risk in doing nothing."

"What shall I say to my father if he asks my opinion?"

"Tell him you live in mortal fear of the shahzade. That is what he will expect you to say anyway."

She watched him eat, mechanically and without relish. Really, bread and water and an abacus and he would be in Paradise. "Whose idea was this? Yours - or did it come from my mother?"

He smiled, and the effect was chilling. She knew what they called him, of course, but it was not true. She knew his secret; his two eye teeth were larger than the rest and when he smiled they betrayed him because they gave him the appearance of a wolf. That was the reason he never did it. "Does anything happen in Stamboul that she does not instigate?"

"And if we fail?"

"If we fail we have lost nothing for Mustapha is already our enemy. If we succeed we have power over the Sultan and the next!"

# CHAPTER 90

The Sultan's apartments, as the rest of the palace, served two functions; to display the wealth of the Osmanlis and to preserve their secrecy.

The wealth was quickly apparent; verses from the Qu'ran, in sülü script, circled the room, a faience of white on blue. The stained glass windows were masterpieces of emerald and crimson. Gilt Vicenzan mirrors hung on every wall and the bed was raised on a canopied platform, strewn with coverlets of gold brocade and crimson velvet. By the side of the bed was a golden ewer for washing the hands.

Awe-inspiring, even though no one ever saw this room except his eunuch slaves and Hürrem.

The compulsion for secrecy inspired the fountains that had been cut into the walls; golden spigots murmured perfumed water into marble urns, preventing whispered conversations being overheard; and then there were the sacnissi, little gazebos that jutted out from the walls where the Sultan could sit and observe the gardens without being seen himself.

But soon after Hürrem became queen a further refinement was introduced; a concealed doorway was carved into the wall behind one of the gilt mirrors. It opened onto a stairway that led directly to the apartments of the Lady Hürrem herself, so she could come and go without being seen.

It was from this doorway that Hürrem emerged one afternoon to find Suleiman pacing the room like a caged beast, even though his right knee was still swollen from another episode of gout.

"My Lord," she said and performed her sala'am.

Suleiman seemed to barely notice her. He was holding a piece of paper in his right hand and he waved it in her direction. "What do you make of this?"

"I cannot tell from this distance. But if you were to ask me, I should say that it is a piece of parchment."

"I am sorry, I forget myself." He hobbled toward her and helped her to her feet. "I can scarcely believe the evidence of my own eyes." He handed her the document. "Here, read this."

Hürrem read it quickly through. It was addressed to the Shah Tamasp; after a long soliloquy of greeting it made an offer of marriage for one of his daughters. It then went on to outline the benefits to both parties from such an arrangement.

It was signed under the tugra of the shahzade, Mustapha.

"It is a forgery," she said, though she conceded it was a very good one. Rüstem was to be commended. "It must be."

"You think so?"

"How can it be otherwise?"

Suleiman collapsed in despair on the divan. "Why would someone do this? Why?"

"It could be Rüstem," she said, and was immediately pleased with herself for pointing it out, for it was obvious by the look on his face that it was the first thing Suleiman had thought of too.

"Why Rüstem?" he said, and she supposed he was testing her, for any fool could work that out.

"When Mustapha is Sultan the first neck he will break will be your Vizier's. So he could have done this. But before you stick his head on a pike there are other culprits you might consider."

"Such as?"

"It would please the Holy Roman Emperor immensely if you were to fight with your own son. It would not even be beyond the Shah himself to arrange such a forgery."

"I hope you are right!" He gasped and held his knee. Hürrem stroked his temple with her long fingers. "What am I to do? What am I to believe?" he moaned.

"Why would Mustapha do such a thing anyway? The Shah is the sworn enemy of the Osmanlis. It makes no sense."

"There is a saying, Hürrem. "The enemy of my enemy is my friend." If Mustapha sees me as his enemy now, then an allegiance with Tamasp would make all the sense in the world."

"But he's a heretic!"

Suleiman sighed. "Perhaps you're right."

"Where did you get this, anyway?"

"From one of Rüstem's spies at Amasya. Rüstem has spies everywhere." Suleiman gave her a sad smile. "You are such a comfort to me. I live among snakes and vipers. Yours is the only voice of reason and moderation." He winced again.

"Shall I send the physician for your knee?"

"No just stay here by my side. That is greater medicine than any potion that fool can give me." After a while he closed his eyes and she thought he was asleep. But then he said: "I must ride east again with the army."

"My Lord, you are unwell, you must not!"

"We must finish with the Shah, there can be no peace while he is still conspiring against us in Asia. The yeniçeris , my generals, the ulema, they are all clamouring for me to do something about him. As Defender of the Faith I have no choice."

"Send Rüstem in your place."

"The yeniçeris  would riot. They expect me to lead them."

"I am just so afraid. You are unwell and the mountains in Persia are cold even in summer. You yourself have told me that a week in Azerbaijan is like an entire campaign in Hungary. I am being selfish, my Lord. I am terrified of losing you."

"No, I must go."

Hürrem knew she had to say something. You could really die there, she thought. Do not ignore this one hard truth when you have believed so many of my lies! "I know you do not fear any hardship, but by choosing another course you might serve a double purpose."

"Ah little russelana. I knew the way you were looking at me there must be some new plan in that pretty little head."

"Let Rüstem advance to Persia through Amasya. Sign orders telling Mustapha to accompany him on the campaign, with his own troops."

"Rüstem? Mustapha will feed him to his dogs."

"Not if he bears your seal. If he co-operates, especially when he hates your Vizier so much, you will know the document is a forgery and that Mustapha is loyal. If he doesn't …"

"I might go myself and divine Mustapha's loyalties."

"If Mustapha plans treason do you risk discovering his true ambitions in the middle of Amasya? You will have to then rely that the yeniçeris  will support you and not him. Remember how your grandfather lost his throne."

Suleiman sighed and brooded on this for an eternity. Finally he said: "Do you really think it will come to that?"

"I only counsel caution, my Lord." She knelt at his feet. "Please hear me on this. I love you with my life."

"I tell you, if I could give up my throne and still do my duty to God, then that is what I would do. I would willingly exchange my lot with any blacksmith in this city. Aside from you the sultanate has only brought me care beyond belief."

She rested her head on his lap. Who would want to be a blacksmith? He was losing his mind. There was only one problem with power, and that was how to keep it.

He let the letter slip from his fingers to the floor.

# CHAPTER 91

"How is Julia?" Abbas asked. They were always his first words. How is Julia. And Ludovici would always answer; She is well, my friend. She asks for your prayers and hopes that you are well also.

After their formalities Abbas lowered his head and concentrated on the business at hand: black market wheat.

The trade was the worst kept secret in the Osmanli Empire. There was active complicity from every Turkish nobleman with arable land; eighteen months previously even Rüstem had sailed his own roundships to Venice by way of Alexandria and had made a staggering profit on just one shipment.

Ever since the summer of 1548 Turkey had enjoyed five excellent wheat harvests, while Venice was starved for grain; the profits for the traders grew in proportion. Ludovici"s caramusalis sailed regularly to Rodosto on the Black Sea, ostensibly to load hides or wool. On the way they made clandestine calls to the port at Volos to take on wheat. On the return trip they were ignored by the Turkish warships that were supposed to enforce the embargo, but the privilege was expensive.

"Rüstem Pasha wants another thousand ducats a month," Abbas said.

"I can't afford that!"

"I'm sorry, old friend. But there is much baksheesh to pay. If it were just the Vizier …"

"If it were just the Vizier I suspect the price would still be a thousand. Is there no limit to his greed?"

"Apparently not."

"Tell him I refuse."

"Don't be rash, Ludovici. Even after the extra baksheesh you will still make a twofold profit on every kilo of grain unloaded in Venice. What do you pay here? Twelve aspers per kilo. Rüstem knows you are making thirty five in Italy."

"I have to make a profit."

"Those were his words also."

Ludovici sighed. There was nothing to be done. If you wanted to do business in the Empire you had to pay whatever the Vizier demanded. Everyone knew that.

They continued with their business; agreeing on routes for his ships, payments to minor officials in the provinces and the counting of the ducats that Ludovici had brought with him in a leather pouch. Finally it was done and Abbas relaxed. He helped himself to a little perfumed water - he never drank wine - and as usual began to gossip about activities inside the haremlik like an old woman at the supermarket.

He was Ludovici"s prime source of information on the moods and internal politics of the Sublime Porte. After Abbas had finished his tirade against the iniquities of the ziadi, as he referred to Hürrem, and the extent of the corruptions introduced by Rüstem pasha - of which he was now an integral part - he said, almost casually: "It is said that the shahzade is planning a revolt."

"Mustapha? Where did you hear that?"

Abbas shrugged. I heard he has arranged marriage with one of the daughters of the Shah Tamasp. He solicits his support in a rebellion against Suleiman."

"Suleiman knows about this?"

"You think you and I should know of something that was hidden from the Lord of Life?"

"This is disturbing news."

"You and your friends should send a delegation to treat with him. When he comes to the throne he may not be as well disposed to our business as Rüstem and you will miss our Vizier's avarice then. It may be as well to make an accommodation with the shahzade now. Have your money on both horses."

""Can Mustapha succeed?"

Abbas shrugged and the great dewlaps beneath his chin trembled. "He has the support of the yeniçeris ."

"Not if he allies with the Shah."

"That may be just a ploy to make Suleiman move against him."

Mustapha's popularity with the army had never been a secret but Ludovici had heard no word of sedition until now. But then he supposed every rebellion must have a beginning.

And if all this was true - and Abbas's information had always been accurate in the past - then he and his fellow traders in the Comunità should make their move now. When he came to the throne Mustapha might not be well disposed to the traders who had helped line his enemy Rüstem's pockets. He should indeed place a bet on both cards, the knave and the king.

"What about you, Abbas? What will you do?"

"I will accept the will of God." He clapped his hands - it was the movement of his hands that was the signal, not the sound - and the two deaf-mutes who accompanied him hurried to assist him to his feet, a feat not easily achieved.

Finally Abbas was ready to take his leave. "Go with God," he said.

"Go with God," Ludovici repeated.

Abbas hesitated at the door. "If anything happens to me, take care of Julia. I wish you would listen to me and get her out of this accursed city. If you really loved her, that is what you would do."

## Topkapi Saraya

"It is done?" Hürrem asked.

Abbas bowed his head. "I did as you asked me."

"Good." She smiled. "How is Julia?"

"Julia is well," he said, refusing to take the bait. "She asks for my prayers."

"What a loyal friend you are. Thank you. You may go, Abbas."

Abbas left, disgusted with her, disgusted with life. Disgusted with himself.

I am sorry, Ludovici, for using you this way. But I have done you no harm, I promise you, it is just a ploy, but it will not hurt you or Julia, or I would not have let this minx persuade me to do it.

\*\*\*

Poor Çehangir, Suleiman thought.

His deformity made it impossible for the poor boy to stand upright; he always looked like he had an invisible sack on his shoulders and was bowed under the weight of it. He could not ride a horse above a canter, could not aim a bow and arrow, could not even lift a sword.

A fine son for a ghazi. Yet of all of them, this was the one he loved best.

"You have seen Mustapha?"

Çehangir did not lift his eyes. He never does, Suleiman thought. He cowers in front of me like a stall keeper. "He is well, my Lord. He sends his greetings."

"His mother is well also?"

"Indeed, my Lord."

Suleiman felt dispirited. The boy looks as if I am about to send him to the executioner. "You look tired," he said.

"It was a rigorous journey."

"The hunting was good?"

"Yes, we hunted every day."

"Mustapha shows you great friendship." Why? He wondered. Because he loves you or does he want you to spy on me? What companionship could a man like Mustapha find in a cripple?

"I think he feels sorry for me," Çehangir said, as if he could read Suleiman's mind. He was startled by this candid admission. He was more acute than he credited.

"I am sure that is not the case," he said, but he brooded on this possibility for a moment and then said: "Did he speak of me?"

"He asked after your health."

Because he loves me or because he hopes me dead? How the Divan has poisoned my thinking! "Nothing else?"

Çehangir seemed to hesitate, then he shook his head.

"I am happy to see you safely returned."

Çehangir was eager to leave. He is as terrified of me as I was of my own father, Suleiman thought. This was the real legacy of the Osmanlis. We destroy our own children.

# CHAPTER 92

## Stamboul

Steam rose from the damp cobbles and the twitching flanks of the donkeys that trudged single file through the narrow twisting streets around the fruit markets. It was melon season and the hawkers had piled their fruits in pyramids on their stalls and on the ground, flecked and striped, green and golden. The smells assaulted the senses; ripe fruit, sewage, wood smoke.

The wooden houses overhung the street and the morning sun could not penetrate here. It was chill.

Suleiman forced his aching joints up the hill. He followed a hamal, one of the porters employed by the bazaar. The man was bent double, his hands almost at his ankles, boxes of figs roped in a huge tower on his back.

He had done this once before, leaving the palace anonymously to test the opinion in the street. He had decided it was time to do it again.

He stopped at one of the stalls and pretended to examine the peaches while he listened in on the hawker's conversation with his neighbour.

"They say the Sultan will ride east again, against the Shah," he heard him saying.

"He should have gone years ago! The Persian has mocked us enough. We have the greatest army in the world and he leaves them sitting around in their barracks!"

"Mustapha would not have let the Shah humiliate us like this," Suleiman said, goading them.

Both men looked at him warily. But the merchant could not help but take the bait. "Mustapha is a great warrior. He would have had the Shah's head mouldering on the gate long ago."

"Perhaps it is time for Mustapha to be our new Sultan," Suleiman said.

The men both looked at him as if he had gone mad. "Keep your voice down! The Sultan has spies everywhere!"

"I am not afraid of the Sultan," Suleiman said.

"He only says what everyone else is thinking," another man chimed in. "Suleiman is an old man. I was still drinking my mother's milk when he last won a great victory."

"Still, he has done many great things," the melon seller said. "He has built us fine mosques, to the glory of God and his navies rule the Mediterranean."

"What good is his navy when the Shah of Persia lives in the desert? I tell you, it is only a matter of time before Mustapha gets tired of talking to goats in Amasya and sweeps Suleiman from his throne. And everyone knows it!"

"Be still!" the merchant said to him and then turned to Suleiman. He looked angry and obviously suspected Suleiman for a spy. "If you want to buy some peaches let me see your money. If not stop bruising the fruit and go away and talk someone else's head off their shoulders."

Suleiman shrugged and walked away. He followed a donkey through the press, the wicker panniers on its flanks piled with cherries. The man's words still rang in his ears: "It is only a matter of time before Mustapha gets tired of talking to goats in Amasya and sweeps Suleiman from his throne! And everyone knows it!"

So everyone knew it, did they? Except him. Lost in thought he did not see the donkey lift its tail to defecate on the cobbles. Suddenly the Sultan of the Osmanlis, King of Kings, Lord of Life, Possess or Men's Necks, had shit on his shoes.

# CHAPTER 93

## Amasya

A month later Rüstem arrived below the cliffs on the Green River with a squadron of Spahis of the Porte and an oda of yeniçeris . He struck camp under the sombre walls of Mustapha's citadel, planted his four horsetail standard outside his tent, and waited.

Rüstem heard Mustapha's approach. Unlike the camps of Christian armies, the Turks maintained order and an iron silence. There was no drinking and no gambling and except when in battle, prayers were observed five times a day. Not even a single rider could approach the camp without him hearing it.

He heard the hoof beats first then an uproar, rolling like thunder through the lines, as if a skirmish of cavalry had broken through the lines. Rüstem went outside and waited.

There were no more than two dozen riders, all but one wearing the scarlet silk jackets of Spahi cavalry. Mustapha was the only one in white. There were heron's feathers in his turban, held by a diamond clasp that flashed in the morning sun so that Rüstem had to raise a hand to shield his eyes.

The yeniçeris  ran through the camp after him, blue coats flapping, letting loose a deafening ululation that echoed from the cliffs until the noise seemed to surround them on all sides. Now they milled around him and his escort, still whooping, happy to eat the dust of the Chosen. Mustapha did not acknowledge their acclaim. He kept his eyes fixed on the royal tent.

Rüstem had his bodyguards drawn upon either side. God help me in my sorrow! he thought. Dust drifted in an orange cloud over the Vizier and his generals. Rüstem spat grit from his mouth.

The shahzade dismounted and the cheers faded dramatically away. They waited; a savage, shuffling mass. He executed a swift temenna. "Where is my father?"

"He is unwell. He has appointed me as Seraskier for the campaign."

Rüstem tried to hide the play of emotion on his face. "How ill is he?"

"His physicians say his malady is not mortal. But he could not bear the rigors of a long campaign." Rüstem looked beyond Mustapha. Thousands of his men were watching this exchange, some just a few paces away. "I have never heard such loud cheers. Not even for the Sultan."

"They cheer me because I am his son."

"Of course. Let us withdraw inside. The dust has parched my throat."

Rüstem led the way inside his pavilion. Pages brought halwa and rosewater and then Rüstem produced a letter from inside his robe. He handed it, without comment, to Mustapha.

It was the letter offering marriage to the Shah's daughter, under Mustapha's tugra. "This is monstrous," Mustapha murmured.

"You deny it?"

"Deny that I would offer an alliance to an enemy of our Empire and of Islam? What do you think?"

"It bears your seal."

"It is a forgery, of course. Has my father seen this?"

"Of course."

"And what does he say?"

"I am not privy to his deliberations. What is your reply?"

"I smell your stink on this!" he said and threw the letter in Mustapha's lap.

"I am not your enemy, Mustapha. Those soldier outside are your enemy. They cheer too loud for you."

"I have never and will never say or do anything against my father. He knows that."

"He awaits your reply."

"He shall have it."

"First I have orders from the Sultan himself. You are to assemble your troops and accompany me on the campaign against the Persian heretics. Under my command."

"I shall do as he orders," Mustapha said with disgust and got to his feet. He left without speaking another word.

After he had gone Rüstem sent for the Aga of the yeniçeris. He was a fair haired wiry man, a Slav, the left side of his jaw gone where he had taken grapeshot during the siege of Rhodes. The Bird of Paradise plumes on his cap rustled as he performed his sala'am. He stood to receive his orders.

"You should prepare a squadron of your best men. Mustapha is to be taken from the Palace tonight and returned to Stamboul in chains."

The Aga hesitated. For a soldier trained from a child to unquestioning obedience, it was a startling reaction. Finally: "As you command," he said.

"The men should be ready at dawn. That is all."

The Aga was so easy to read. His true intentions lit his face like an illuminated page of the Qu'ran. This would be so simple. As simple as Hürrem had promised it would be.

## Topkapi Saraya

The Golden Road led from the Harem mosque past the Sultan's apartments and through the haremlik to a tower. Hürrem's silk kaftan rustled on the cobbles. She threw open a small door and followed a darkened staircase up to the Dangerous Window. When she got there, she sat down close to the taffeta curtain and peered through a small chink in the curtains. Through the latticework, she could just glimpse the marble pillars of the Divan. She could not see much, but she could hear everything.

"You are sure of this?" she heard a man say. It was Suleiman. He had returned to his duties in the Divan in Rüstem's absence.

"My information is utterly reliable." She did not recognize this other man; one of Rüstem's army of bureaucrats, no doubt.

"There is no chance that your spy has made a mistake?"

She heard the man cough with embarrassment. She imagined the Sultan's use of the word "spy" had distressed him. "I have my information from several sources. The Venetians in Pera are convinced that Mustapha is about to launch a rebellion. The bailo himself has sent a chaush in secret to Amasya with a letter. We do not know the contents, but we may surmise with some accuracy that they are making accommodations with him."

How satisfying, Hürrem thought, to hear one's own rumour repeated in the Hall of the Divan as a hard truth! Abbas had done his work well. For years she had given him little titbits of the truth to feed the Italians. Now they had swallowed the big lie whole.

Suleiman could not see the Lord of Life but she could imagine his face. It would be as if he were straining to break wind. She almost giggled aloud and put her knuckles into her mouth to restrain herself. I am brilliant, she thought.

"I still do not believe this," she heard him say.

"My Lord, my inform-"

"Enough! I do not want to hear any more about your spies!" Suleiman stamped out of the hall.

Hürrem hurried away as well. Her Sultan would surely summon her for his solace for this latest blow. She must be there to comfort him.

# CHAPTER 94

## Amasya

An angry murmur rose from the camp. Where was the discipline now? Rüstem thought. It was like the drone of bees disturbed by a foraging bear. The two solaks on guard outside the pavilion shuffled nervously at their posts.

The discharge of the harquebus sounded like cannon fire and the echo resounded from the cliffs long after the man had fallen, clutching his chest. The second drew his sword in a futile effort to defend himself and his post. There were more flashes, like sheet lightning, and he screamed and fell, clutching his face.

Their assailants rushed from the shadows. They paused to deliver the finishing blows to the two men thrashing in pain on the ground and then rushed inside the tent. Rüstem recognized only one of the men, the Aga with the scar on his face, though it was plain from their uniforms that they were all his yeniçeris.

Rüstem mounted his horse and turned to the captain of the spahis, who waited alongside on the ridge above the camp. "It seems we are faced with a rebellion."

"So it appears."

"It is fortunate I am not in my pavilion. I imagine those butchers are about to fire their harquebuses into my mattress."

On cue, there was a loud bang, followed by another.

"We must ride hard back to Stamboul and report this to the Sultan. Let us hurry, in case Mustapha comes after us." He spurred his horse and disappeared into the darkness with his escort. They circled the encampment and headed west.

\*\*\*

Gülbehar had been woken from her sleep with the news of the rebellion in Rüstem's camp. She sat shivering in her ermine robe, huddled around the glowing coals of a brazier. Sirhane entered and performed her sala'am. She looked dazed still from sleep and her hair was unkempt.

Her husband was Mustapha's equerry. She thinks she is a widow, Gülbehar thought, believes that is why I have summoned her.

"Your husband is safe," she said.

Sirhane's shoulders sagged with relief. "Thanks be to God …"

"But there is danger, for all of us now."

"We will leave Amasya?"

Gülbehar shook her head. "There is nowhere to run." She stared into the coals. "There was a rebellion at the royal camp tonight. The yeniçeris tried to murder Rüstem Pasha."

Sirhane gaped at her, not understanding.

"Mustapha did not incite them to this. If only he had, there would be no danger. But when Suleiman hears of this, he will certainly blame him for it. I need your help."

"My help?"

"If Suleiman moves against my son, he will move against his household too. Your husband will be executed, his property confiscated and you will be exiled. You will end your days as a beggar. Is that what you want?"

Sirhane shook her head.

"Your fortunes are tied to ours now. So you will have to act quickly. You remember the Kislar Aghasi, do you not?"

"A good man, as I remember him."

"I want you to go to Stamboul and find him." She leaned forward. "I want Hürrem dead. Offer him anything. Anything! If he can do this for me my son will become Sultan and Abbas may have anything he desires. Persuade him, Sirhane. For my sake - and for yours, persuade him to do it!"

# CHAPTER 95

## Topkapi Saraya

Suleiman was hunched on his throne, as if his chest had collapsed inwards and his chin and shoulders no longer had anything to support them. He stared at Rüstem without speaking. The only movement was the flaring of his nostrils as he breathed.

"It grieves my heart to bring you this news," Rüstem said. "I rode here in fear of my life. Yet it was not my life that I held so dear, but yours."

Suleiman moaned deep in his chest. "Did Mustapha order this?"

"I do not know, my Lord. The yeniçeris came in the middle of the night and killed my guards hoping to find me defenceless in my tent. I was forewarned and was thus able to escape."

"How many?"

"I do not know. But the Aga led them."

Suleiman shook his head.

"What about Mustapha? You met with him?"

"When he rode into camp the yeniçeris cheered him till they were hoarse. They shouted that he would lead their standards to the House of War. I heard many of them say you were now too old to lead them and that I was just a clerk with no skill as a general. They clamoured for the shahzade."

"You showed him the letter?"

"He said he was not answerable before any but God. And since I was not the Divine he had nothing to say to me. He also said ... he also said that I should write my final letters to my family. He said that the next time I saw Stamboul it would be from a pike on the Ba"ab-i-Sa"adet."

"Those were his words?"

"They were, my Lord."

The cry of anguish startled the Vizier as no sudden act of violence ever could. The Sultan threw back his head and wept.

He dismissed his Vizier. Rüstem hurried out of the audience hall, astonished and delighted that his lie had worked so well. It had been a great risk, of course, but he had always been confident that Hürrem knew her man.

\*\*\*

The summer garden was heavy with the scents of herbs and roses and the rhythm of the cicadas was hypnotic. It would be so easy just to lie here in Hürrem's arms and forget that the careful tapestry of the future that he had woven was unravelling in his hands.

Every law he had made, every foundation stone he had laid, every campaign he had fought had been with one intention; that one day he could pass the banner to Mustapha, knowing all he had achieved was in safe hands. Sedition would undo everything. The Osmanlis would return to the blood and barbarity of the past.

Perhaps the yeniçeris were right, perhaps he was too old to lead them. But the burden of the sultanate was his until death, that was the law, and to allow Mustapha to usurp it would be to bathe his grandchildren and their grandchildren in blood.

"Do not listen to any of them," Hürrem whispered. "Be proud that you have a son the yeniçeris love so dearly. You are his father. His sense of duty will stop him making use of this uncanny power he has over them."

"If you are wrong about this, you and your sons are in mortal danger."

"You yourself are the source of my esteem for him. Yes, it terrifies me if these reports are true. I would rather believe the yeniçeris acted alone without his knowledge. If they did not …"

They heard a great sigh above them and they both looked up, through the open shutters of the kiosk. The city's population of storks, who nested each year on the domes and roofs and minarets, had all taken to the air over Stamboul, flying south for their first reconnaissance ahead of the winter migration. Thousands of them trailed across the sky.

"Time is running out," he said. "Summer is nearly over. I must ride east with the army or I will lose the throne."

"What will you do?"

"I do not know. Who might guide me in this?"

"Abu Sa'ad, perhaps?"

Suleiman considered. "Perhaps," he said.

\*\*\*

Abu Sa'ad watched the Kislar Aghasi devour almost the entire tray of halwa the pages had put in front of him. He ate slowly and with great determination but with the utmost delicacy. He wore an expression of ecstasy on his face like a dervish when they first went into trance. When he had finished he washed down the honeyed cakes with a little iced sherbet.

He settled back on the cushions. "I have a message from the Lady Hürrem," he said.

"May God preserve her," Abu Sa'ad murmured.

"It seems she has found great comfort in the Faith."

"She has been most diligent in her studies of the Qu'ran."

"It now appears she wishes to glorify God in a way that will endure beyond mortal clay and preserve the Faith through the centuries."

"God shall smile upon her."

"She intends shortly to make over a great part of her personal fortune in the form of a waqf - that is, she will place it in trust, so that more mosques may be built and maintained in the city."

The mufti bowed his head in acknowledgment. "Her generosity becomes such a great lady."

"She says it is your inspiration that has persuaded her to do this. She says it is you that has led her to the one true faith and she sees, too, how you comforted the Sultan in his hours of trouble. She asks only that you continue to do your work with all wisdom."

It was some moments before the mullah understood what was required of him. He stroked his beard in thought. "The troubles in the East weigh heavily on the Lord of Life at the moment."

"Oh, were that his troubles were resolved!" Abbas said. "The Lady Hürrem has prayed night and day for God to help him resolve his heart ache. She would give anything to have these burdens lifted from her lord's shoulders."

"I shall give him what guidance I can."

"Good. My mistress will be most relieved to hear that."

After he had left, the sheyhülislam produced his tespi beads and murmured prayers of thanks and supplication. God was good, God was great. But to bring his teaching to the people and to build great mosques took money. For the greater glory of the divine a man must sometimes bend his soul a little to the winds of time.

# CHAPTER 96

## Stamboul

But the sheyhülislam was not the only one to receive a visit from Abbas that day. How did I ever manage when I kept the Sultan's harem as well? he thought. Now the girls are all long gone and there are still barely hours enough in my day.

"Sirhane," he said. "It has been a long time."

"Kislar Aghasi," she said. She kept herself covered now, even though he had seen her naked more times than her own mother.

He threw back the hood of his ferijde . "I received your message," he said. "What is you want with me?"

"Gülbehar sent me."

"I had anticipated that." He looked around the room, the gilded ceiling, the glazed floral tiles on the walls, the pink shadow of the Aya Sofia looming through the fretted wooden grills that covered the windows. "So this is the palace of the Abdul Sahine Pasha."

"He is equerry to the shahzade now."

"He grows in wealth and fortune."

"Is it good fortune to live in the house of a condemned man, Kislar Aghasi?"

Abbas shrugged. "There is nothing I can do about it."

"Gülbehar said that there is. She says I can offer you anything - anything."

"She is generous. In that case - what about my manhood. That is my asking price for any favour. I will not settle for less."

"Abbas ..."

"I have amassed wealth and power beyond any dream I had when I was a youth. But it is all useless to me. Do you understand? So what is it that Rose of Spring thinks she can offer me? And what is it that she believes I can do for her?"

Sirhane lowered her eyes. "Does Suleiman know of Julia?" she said, her voice barely a whisper.

The room started to spin. Was there nothing left to believe in? "You were her friend."

"You know what is at stake."

"What is it in this whole world that is worth doing what you have just suggested? I was the one who told you about her. I understand that you would betray me, but would you betray your best friend also?"

"Very soon a woman will die. Perhaps Hürrem, perhaps Julia. You decide."

"Hürrem?"

"You are the only one who can save us from her now."

"Hürrem is dust. Like every tyrant she will have her day and then she will die. You would sully your very soul just for these brief moments you have here on earth?"

"It is a good bargain, Abbas. The death of a witch for the life of the woman you once loved."

"She told you?"

"She told me everything, about how you courted her secretly in Venice, how you wanted her to escape with you to Spain. She still loves you, Abbas. She said you were the bravest man in the world."

"And you would still betray her to that witch? I thought you loved her."

"We all love ourselves more, Abbas."

"They have cut off my manhood but they did not cut out my heart. For the first time in many a year there is someone I feel sorry for. You make me want to vomit."

He wished he could see her face. The chador shook. Was she trembling or weeping? "Do it or she dies, Abbas. Spare me your pretty speech."

Abbas signalled to his pages to help him rise. He spat at her feet. "Very well, I will do it," he said and left.

\*\*\*

She looks radiant, Abbas thought. She never looks as young and as lovely as when she is planning an execution. It rejuvenates her. The green velvet taplock had been pinned at a jaunty angle on her head and she wore a kaftan of pistachio velvet bordered with ermine. Pearls glistened in the insteps of her ship-ship.

So this is my day to die, Abbas thought. Well, I have delayed it long enough. Now that it is decided I feel curiously free, even light-headed. I am glad you are happy also, My Lady. I should have hated to have cut out your little black heart when you were as sick of the world as I am.

"Have you done as I asked?" she said.

"I have spoken to the mufti, as you commanded. He is fully aware of what is required of him."

"My good, faithful Abbas."

"As you say, My Lady."

"And what shall be your reward?"

Oh so you are going to toy with me. I had hoped you would. I have had twenty five years of impotence. Tonight I shall be a man again. "What reward should you like to honour me with, My Lady?"

"Your pick of the Harem perhaps?"

Abbas smiled, acknowledging her mordant wit. "My lady is too kind."

Perhaps she divined the change in him for her eyes were suddenly hard. "You look pleased with yourself, Abbas. Perhaps you would like to share the joke with your mistress?"

Abbas took a step towards her and his hand strayed to the jewelled dagger in the sash at his waist. Hürrem lowered her eyes, understanding his intention immediately. The guards positioned around the room were too far away, too somnolent at this routine audience, to save her now.

He smiled. As soon as she screams, he thought, I will do it.

But Hürrem did not scream. "Ah my Abbas. At last." She seemed almost … excited.

"I have waited for this moment for so long," he whispered.

"And what has stopped you?"

What has stopped me? The answer is simple. Julia. But also, I am afraid to die. Not afraid of pain - God knows I have known enough of that - and not even in love with any part of my life. I am just afraid of what is after this. I believe it does not end here, but how will God judge all I have done?

"Are you not afraid for Julia Gonzaga?" she said.

Abbas felt his fist tighten on the warm ivory. Do it now! Something screamed inside him. Do it now before the witch finds a way to weaken your resolve. "Julia?"

"On my death there is a letter I have placed in safe keeping, to be delivered to my Sultan. He will be most disappointed to discover that she still lives in Pera and is perhaps the source of rumours about his failings in the Harem."

Abbas felt the palace crashing about his shoulders. He froze. What if it was true? He was trapped. He could not kill her and he could not withdraw.

Hürrem laughed. "I would swear that your black face has almost gone quite pale!"

Abbas swayed on his feet. Use the dagger on yourself, he thought.

"You think I am going to punish you?" she said.

Her eyes were aglow with pleasure. What kind of a woman was this? "I shall kill myself first," he said.

"My dear Abbas, why would you do that?"

"You have tormented me for the last time!"

She leaned closer. "Take your hand away from that crude instrument. Do you think I am angry because you want to kill me? Of course you do! It's only natural. Besides half Stamboul wants me dead. But you have just proved to me that no matter how much you hate me you could never harm me. It makes you the most trusted and obedient servant that I have."

Do it anyway, the voice inside him screamed. Do it!

Abbas slumped to his knees. "I am so weak," he said.

"Yes," she said, "but so very useful!"

## Topkapi Saraya

"I have a problem that I seek your advice on. A case was brought to me in the Divan that has perplexed me greatly. I have decided to come to you for your ruling under the holy laws of the Qu'ran."

Suleiman paused to collect his thoughts.

"A merchant of good position has three sons. One of them, the eldest, he favours above all the others. He has always trusted him with good salary and good favour. When he dies, the business and all his wealth will be his. However one day he discovers that his son is plotting to kill him and take over his business. He cannot wait for his own father to die. The merchant has discovered all these things beyond doubt. What should that merchant do, and what sentence should lawfully be pronounced under the Sheri'at?"

Abu Sa'ad did not blink. "The Qu'ran is clear in such matters. The servant must die."

Suleiman gave a long sigh. "And if that servant's name was Mustapha, the shahzade?"

"Death," Abu Sa'ad said.

Two days later Suleiman mounted his horse by the fountain in the Third Court and left his palace with his household regiments, bound for the east. Orders had already been sent to the Agas at Amasya to bring their troops south for the march on Erzerum. Another chaush was sent with further orders for Bayezid to come from Manisa and administer government at the Topkapi in his absence.

Suleiman knew he must hurry to reassert his authority over the army. But first he must talk to Selim.

# CHAPTER 97

## Konia

The city stood in a vast and dusty wheat bowl on the Anatolian steppe, a mecca to the Osmanlis, for it was home to the monastery that contained the bones of Jalal -ud-din Rumi, the founder of the dervish order. It was also the governmental seat of Karamania, where Selim was apprenticed as second prince in succession to throne.

Suleiman had heard rumours, whispered in the corridors of the palace and the bedesten of the city, that Hürrem's oldest son was a drunkard. The lumpish awkward youth had now become a figure of fun.

Now, as he looked into his son's face, he knew the rumours were true. His complexion was inflamed from too much wine, the broken capillaries on his cheeks and nose like a crimson spider web. Suleiman closed his eyes and thought, for the hundredth time: this cannot be the future of the Osmanlis! Can I really give up Mustapha for this?

Selim did not notice Suleiman's mood. He was engaged in his own personal diatribe. " … of course Mustapha hates me, should he come to the throne I have no doubt his first act will be to send his bostanji to murder me. Can you imagine what it is like to live like this? I have no friend in all the world but you."

You whine like a peasant, Suleiman thought. "You have heard the calumny against Mustapha?"

"I do not doubt a word of it.,"

Of course not, Suleiman thought. But then, yours is scarcely an objective point of view. "We shall settle this at Aktepe. I have a question for you: if I were to hand Mustapha to the bostanji , you would be next to bear the yoke of the Osmanlis. Do you think you can bear such a burden, Selim?"

Selim beamed. "I am your son! I was born to it." But the smile soon vanished. "But if I am next, why did you give Manisa to Bayezid?"

"It was expedient to do so."

"If I am to be shahzade I should be there."

God help me in my sorrow! He is like a recalcitrant child! "All is not settled yet. We are talking of Mustapha's life here. I am only asking whether you think you can bear my burdens. I have not promised them to you."

Selim grew sulky. "Yes, father."

He could hardly credit that this was a son of his, named after the rampaging warrior that was his own father. Yet he supposed he himself was not the butcher his own father had been. Why should we think our children will become shadows of ourselves?

Perhaps it was his own fault for not paying him enough attention when he was a child. He had dedicated the future to Mustapha, and now it was too late to undo what had already been done. Selim had grown without direction and was lost to him.

"So what are you going to do?" Selim asked him.

"I don't know," Suleiman sighed. "I really don't know."

## Pera

Julia could barely contain her impatience. She watched from the window as the coach clattered to a halt in the courtyard and a figure in a purple ferijde stepped out and hurried inside. It was so long since she had seen her. She was trembling like a girl.

Hyacinth escorted Sirhane into the room. As soon as they were alone Julia threw her arms around her and hugged her until Sirhane protested and pulled away to catch her breath.

Julia tore the cazeta from her face. "Take this off, I have to see you."

Sirhane tore off her ferijde , then took her hand and led her to the divan. "I have missed you so," she whispered.

"Look at you! You still defy the years, Julia."

If only I could say the same, Julia thought. You look so gaunt and tired. There were dark circles under Sirhane's eyes. "Are you well?" she asked her.

"A little tired from the journey, that is all."

"It's been so long. When your messenger came I could not believe that you were really here in Stamboul."

Sirhane smiled weakly. "It is a long way from Amasya."

"Tell me all your news! What brings you here?"

"Abdul sent me away. There has been trouble."

"Trouble? Is he all right?"

"Yes but … he felt it was too dangerous for me to stay. There has been so much trouble."

"Are things really that bad?"

"You have not heard?"

"Only what Ludovici tells me. He says that Mustapha tried to make an alliance with Shahn Tamasp."

"That was Rüstem's doing. But now there is much worse. The yeniçeris tried to murder the Grand Vizier in his camp on the Green River. Everyone blames Mustapha."

"Murder Rüstem?"

"He escaped of course and now the Sultan thinks Mustapha wants to take away his throne, as his own father did. What can we do? My husband is loyal to the shahzade. If there should be a war …"

"War? Is there anything we can do? If you need to hide …"

"Hide from the Sultan? When he is king of half the world?" Sirhane threw her arms around her neck and wept. "I am so sorry."

"What for?"

But Sirhane did not answer her. Julia felt her trembling. Her crying seemed to go on forever, but finally Sirhane pulled away. "I would never hurt you," she said.

"I know that."

Sirhane caressed her cheek. "Just remember that, please. I would never really hurt you."

"I don't understand. Sirhane, you must tell me what has happened. There something else, isn't there?"

Sirhane shook her head. "Just hold me," she said. "I'll tell you later. Not now."

***

But Sirhane did not tell her. Instead they went together to the hammam and bathed, like the old days. But it was not like the old days; in the Harem Sirhane was always talking, always laughing, and she responded to Julia's merest touch. Today she was remote, lost inside her own head, and the muscles in her neck and shoulders were taut as bowstrings.

"You are so tense," Julia said.

"Of course. Do you wonder at it?"

Julia poured a little more sandalwood oil onto her hands and rubbed it into her neck and shoulders.

"How is Ludovici?" Sirhane asked her, breaking a long silence.

"He prospers."

"Is he still as attentive as he always was?"

"Yes, he has never grown tired of me, though I wonder that he has not sent me away long ago. Lately I have even felt …"

"Felt what?"

"I have grown fond of him."

"Well that is natural. I feel the same way for my husband."

"He still treats you well?"

"He has another wife now, an Armenian. She is eighteen and very beautiful. She was selected for him at the last devshirme."

Julia did not know what to say.

"He still comes to my bed once a week. But of course he spends most of his nights with her. I miss him then. I never thought I would. Do you ever miss Ludovici when he is away?"

"I miss you," Julia said.

"Perhaps you should learn to love him more than you do." Sirhane twisted around. "You are right, I am too tense. Come, I will attend to you instead."

Julia ached for Sirhane's touch but when she oiled her, she did it with the reserve of a gediçli. Finally Julia took her hand and brought it to her breast. But Sirhane pushed her away and whispered, "Not yet."

Instead they went back to the bath and lounged in the water, Sirhane filling the silence with idle chatter about life in Amasya and inconsequential memories of her life in the Harem. And it was all forced, and false. Suddenly they were strangers and Julia had no idea what was now between them or why.

Finally they ran out of things to say to each other and Sirhane said she must go. As she was leaving Julia took her by the arm. "You still have not told me the real reason you came to Stamboul. Please, don't go like this. There was a time we had no secrets from each other."

Sirhane summoned a smile. "I told you, I am worried about what is happening in Amasya. Don't you understand, Julia? By the time the first snows arrive I could be a widow, exiled to the Persian border. What do you want me to do, laugh about it?" Sirhane pulled away and put on her ferijde .

"Will come again?"

"Of course." Sirhane kissed her lightly on the lips and then pulled the cazeta over her face. "Goodbye Julia," she said and there was a dreadful finality to it.

## Anatolia

Suleiman rejoined his army on the plains at Aktepe.

The yeniçeris were silent as he rode among them. Yet how you cheer Mustapha, he thought. He posted the seven horsetails standard outside the royal tent and sent for his chaush, told him to ride to the fortress and summon Mustapha to his presence at once.

Then he waited, prowling the tent, cornered and afraid.

# CHAPTER 98

"For pity's sake you must not go!"

Mustapha took his mother's hand. She snatched it away, angry at this condescension.

"The Sultan commands my presence. If I refuse he will take it as rebellion."

"And if you go he will accuse you of it anyway and who will there be to protect you?"

"It is my chance to speak up against the lies said against me."

"If he wanted answers, why did he not come here and ask you himself? Why did he go first to Konia?"

"I don't know. I will ask him."

Gülbehar jumped to her feet, turning away to hide the tears of frustration that came all too readily these days. "Let them accuse you of what they want! There is no proof!"

Mustapha wondered if she should tell her about the letter and his conversation with Rüstem. He decided against it. "The yeniçeris already laud me as their leader. Where can I be safer than among them?"

"Here! You will be safer here, in your fortress, far away from Suleiman and Rüstem!"

"I must above all things obey my father. He has summoned me, I will go."

"And what if only his bostanji are waiting?"

"He gave me my life. He has the right to take it back."

"No! He has no right! I gave you that life also, I suckled you at my breast and raised you from an infant! He has no right to take you from me!" Gülbehar doubled over, sobbing. Mustapha leaped up to stop her from falling. He cradled her in his arms and led her to the divan.

He rocked her in his arms.

Finally he whispered. "I have to go."

Gülbehar gripped his arms, as if she could squeeze his defiance out of him. "Take the sultanate. You have waited long enough. You have only to say the word and the yeniçeris will rise with you. There is no need for bloodshed. Your own grandfather removed Bayezid from the throne and exiled him. It is within the law."

"It is against the law of Heaven. Suleiman taught me that."

"Of course he did!"

"I cannot do it. It is impossible. I would rather die than dishonour my name before all the princes of the world and stain my soul before God."

Nothing would move him on this, she knew. They had had this same argument now for years. The minx had won. She could imagine her sprawled on her divan, laughing. Life was so simple if you believed in nothing but your own preservation.

"My honour is worth more than any empire this world may give me. What sort of king shall I be if I give up my very soul to attain it? I shall rule without shame or I shall not rule at all."

"You are a fool."

"You know you do not mean that," Mustapha said.

"You let her win so easily!"

He pretended not to hear her. "He will not harm me, Mother. He is a man of honour, as I am."

No, she thought. He is not a man of honour, he is a man of law. They are spurs of quite different metal.

"I will leave at dawn."

"Very well," Gülbehar whispered. " Go with God." She let him kiss her hand. Her eyes followed him to the door, believing she would never see him again.

When he had gone there were no more tears to weep. She sat by the window, watching the stars wheel across the face of the earth to new tomorrows, helpless in her prison, defeated by her own destiny, and her son's..

## Aktepe

The camp was in silence.

The smoke of damp fir wood clung to the air. Water carts creaked between the rows of tents, sheep scurried in choking clouds of dust to the butchers" tents. A group of blue-jacketed yeniçeris played fortune dice by a charcoal brazier.

When they saw Mustapha they jumped to their feet and crowded around his horse, as they had done at Amasya. Word quickly spread through the camp; the shahzade had come to lead them against the Persians! The shouts became a roar and carried through the camp to Suleiman's pavilion. He was in consultation with Rüstem and when they heard it they both fell silent and listened.

"Padishah, Padishah! Emperor!"

"Here comes the ghost of my father," Suleiman murmured.

The cheering continued for a long time, long after Mustapha had disappeared inside the pavilion he erected close to Suleiman's, waiting for the summons to appear and make his case against his accusers.

But that night his accusers came to Suleiman first. The ghost of his Selim appeared at the foot of his bed. He held out his hands and in them he held the heads of his entire family, like so many bushel of apples.

"Here, my son," he said. "Here is your future."

# CHAPTER 99

Dawn.

All the previous afternoon and evening Mustapha had received the salutes of his generals in his tent, and now the camp was once again silent. The muezzin called the army to prayers; thousands of turbans were drawn up in rows, bobbing against a mauve sky.

When Mustapha finished his prayers he made himself ready. He dressed all in white, as a token of innocence and put his letters of farewell inside his robe close to his bosom, as was customary for any Turk when facing danger.

He mounted his Arab stallion and prepared to ride the few yards separating his tent from his father's pavilion, as demanded by tradition. His Aga and his equerry, Abdul Sahine, accompanied him.

Mustapha knew the entire army was watching him. They all knew what was about to take place and why he had been summoned. Would they reconcile or would Mustapha stake his claim to the throne?

Mustapha slid down from his saddle and removed the dagger at his waist. He handed it to Abdul Sahine. He saluted the solak guards who stood outside and went unarmed to his father.

With this the yeniçeris went back to their duties in orderly silence but not one of them had a mind for it. They all prepared to hail a new Sultan before sunset.

\*\*\*

The pavilion was enormous, divided into rooms by walls of billowing gold silk. The entrance had peacock blue and ruby red carpets and there were divans against each wall. A small silver topped table stood in the centre.

"Father?"

Mustapha pushed aside a curtain and stepped into the Audience Chamber. Empty. The tent whipped in the wind with a sound like a whip crack.

Not quite empty. A black bostanji stepped from the shadows behind him. And another. Three more came from behind the curtain in front of him. One held a silken bowstring.

He saw a shadow move behind the silk. "Father?"

The bostanji moved swiftly, barefoot. Mustapha was not afraid, just angry. He dodged the eunuch and stepped into the centre of the room. "Father, listen to me first! Let me face my accusers before you condemn me! This is not just!"

Outside he heard the rasp of steel, followed by shouting. He realized his Aga and Abdul Sahine were being attacked. His only chance was to slip past the bostanji. A prince could only be dispatched with a bowstring, his blood could not be spilled on the ground. If he could get back out of the pavilion, no one else could harm him. If he could reach the yeniçeris he would be safe.

But he would not demean himself that way. He had never run away from a fight before, he would not run now. "Father, listen to me!"

The bostanji-bashi tried to throw the silken noose over his head but Mustapha read his attention and squirmed away. He barrelled into one of the others and wrestled him to the ground. Another came from him but he jumped back and the man's impetus sent him sprawling across the silver table.

"Father, I never once betrayed you! Why do you betray me now! Come out and speak to me!"

"Will you never dispatch that which I bid you!" Suleiman wailed from behind the curtain.

But the deaf-mutes could not hear him. Mustapha was his only audience. "Call off your idiot assassins and let us speak like men! I am innocent! You stain your honour before the Empire and before God!"

"Get it done!" Suleiman moaned.

"Father, listen to what I'm saying!"

\*\*\*

Suleiman put his hands over his ears and closed his eyes, willing it to be over. No, no, no! There could be no excuse for treason! The evidence was clear. Mustapha might try to mesmerize him with his candied words but he had seen and heard reason enough.

If I let him speak, he will sway me. Then as soon as I am compliant again he will rally the yeniçeris to him, as they had rallied to his grandfather. I will not let you take my throne, Mustapha. I have still so much to do.

Yet you were my first son, the hopes of my youth.

All my dreams lay with you.

Now all my dreams rest with Selim.

He tore aside the curtain. "NO!" he shouted. "Stop!"

Too late.

Mustapha lay at his feet, eyes open, the bowstring around his neck. Suleiman closed his eyes and turned away. He signalled to the mutes: "Wrap him in the carpet and throw him outside the tent."

He stood alone in the middle of the pavilion and waited. A soft moan, like the rushing of wind, passed through the camp. It rose to a keening of despair as the yeniçeris approached the tent and saw what had become of their champion.

There, he thought, there is your shahzade now! See what you have done. This is your doing, not mine! You wanted blood, all of you. Now you have it.

# CHAPTER 100

"Give us Rüstem's head or we'll come and take it!"

Strange how even now he seems so unruffled, Suleiman thought. I believe he is already calculating odds, measuring risk. The yeniçeris swarm around my tent baying for his blood and it is like there are stone walls three feet thick between him and that mob, not just a few strips of gold and purple silk.

"They blame you, Rüstem," Suleiman said.

"My lord, Mustapha was his own undoing."

The tumult was deafening. The entire complement of yeniçeris, led by their Aga, milled at the entrance, their killiç drawn. All that held them back was two solaks and the sanctity of the Osmanlis.

Yet if just one man should have the courage to stare down centuries of awe, he thought, then the tide would sweep them all up and swallow them.

"They want a scapegoat," Suleiman said. "Since they do not dare lay a hand on their Sultan, they have decided that you will do."

Was there a flicker of uncertainty in Rüstem's grey eyes? I might do it, too, he thought and wondered at himself. Now I have done the worst thing I could imagine, I believe I am capable of anything.

"Have you dispatched a chaush for Amasya, my lord?"

Suleiman was impressed. Even facing death Rüstem kept a practical turn of mind. "Yes. His wife and sons will shortly follow him to Paradise."

"Then we have nothing further to fear from him."

"Not from Mustapha, no." Suleiman had to shout to raise his voice above the shouts of the soldiers outside. "Do you not fear the yeniçeris, Rüstem?"

"They will do as you command."

"Will they? They were ready to put Mustapha on the throne at breakfast."

"But now it is midday and Mustapha is dead. The yeniçeris are like dogs. They just need a master."

"And raw meat."

"Indeed. Feed them and point them an enemy and they will follow."

Suleiman tore aside the silk curtain at the entrance and went out to face them. Immediately they fell silent.

He looked around at the thousands of faces, hands on his hips. How they hated him right now. And how he hated them. He would have had all of their heads on the gate at the Topkapi if he had his way. They were the ones responsible for killing his son.

The Aga broke the crackling silence. "We want Rüstem."

"Rüstem will be replaced. The gold seal of Grand Vizier will go to Ahmed, the second vizier. But you will not harm him. He is under my protection."

"He took our Mustapha from us!"

"I took Mustapha from you!" He stared them down. He would have this Aga's neck when things simmered down, he promised himself. The man was an ingrate. "I took Mustapha. I, your Sultan. And you shall bear it, and you shall do as I command now! Tomorrow we march on the Sufavids. There will be booty and women. If you want blood, let it be Persian blood."

"We want Rüstem," the Aga said, stubbornly.

"If you want him you must kill me first," Suleiman said and drew the jewelled killiç from the scabbard at his waist. "Who will be first to raise his sword against his Sultan?"

They backed down, though it took considerably longer than he thought it would. But one by one the yeniçeris turned their backs and went back to the camp. Finally only Suleiman and the Aga remained. "Rüstem told me to arrest him," he hissed. "Did he tell you that?"

"You possess the written order, in Rüstem's hand?"

The Aga shook his head.

"Then I do not believe you. It was just what I expected you would say."

The Aga turned and walked away. Suleiman went back inside. He threw everyone out and spent the next hour breaking every piece of furniture he could find.

## Amasya

The missive was written in white ink on black paper. Gülbehar did not need to read it to know what it said; she had known from the moment she saw the Sultan's chaush dismount in the courtyard. No, she thought, I knew before then; her son's fate had been sealed the moment he rode out of the gates.

She refused to accept the letter. She spat in the chaush's face, cursing him and his sons for eternity and tried to rake his face with her nails. Her maidservants restrained her and the man fled, his face pale, the kadin's wails of grief ringing in his ears.

## Stamboul

Sirhane knew Mustapha and her husband were dead the moment she saw the heavy set Sudanese step from the shadows. A castrato, and deaf-mute. A monster more than a man, their knives and needles had excised all sentiment and mercy out of him.

There was no point in pleading for her life. Just let it be quick.

His tongueless mouth made a strange yelping sound as he came towards her. She knew he would only leave when she was dead, with her head in the leather pouch that hung from the sash at his waist for precisely this purpose.

"Abbas sent you, didn't he?" she said. "He thinks I am still a threat to Julia. But I would never have done it, it was a bluff, I would never have betrayed her, never. I hope she will know that. I don't mind dying but I don't want her ever to hate me." She closed her eyes and kept her hands to her sides. There was no point in fighting him, it would only prolong the agony.

The bostanji looped the cord around her neck. He lifted her effortlessly from the floor, the corded muscles in his arms bulging, and quickly and efficiently choked the life out of her.

# CHAPTER 101

### Pera

Julia locked her door and stayed in her bedchamber for three days. Sometimes, in the evenings, Ludovici heard her crying through the door. He tapped on the door at mealtimes, more in hope than expectation, but she would not come out.

So he ate his meals alone, the clink of his spoon in his soup bowl echoing around the vaulted dining room. He stared at her empty chair and told himself he was a fool, for he would never have what he wanted from her.

When she finally reappeared for breakfast on the fourth morning, her face looked like a death's head and there were dark circles under her eyes. He stood up as she entered the room. She slumped into the high-backed mahogany chair at the end of the table.

"Are you all right?"

She thought she had not heard him. But then she said: "Do you love me Ludovici?"

"You know I do."

"Then find out who gave the order to do this."

"What good would that do?"

"Please. Can you do it? Ask Abbas. He will know."

"It was the Sultan. Who else would it be?"

"Why would he kill her? Her husband yes, but why her?"

Why does she want to know? he thought. In the Empire, execution was just the way. Whoever ordered it, they were beyond her power and his. The arrival of a death chaush was like fate, he thought; it often could not be foreseen or prevented.

"But he said: "I will see what I can do.""

377

## Galata

Abbas shook his head. "There is nothing she can do about it, Ludovici."

"I told her that, but I said I would try and find out anyway."

"You have given your word before and broken it. It would be easy to do it again. For instance, once you promised me you would send her away from here."

Ludovici stared at the carpet. He shrugged; what could he say? "I love her."

"Then you are a fool as well as a liar."

"If any other man said that to me-"

"You have placed my life in danger countless times through the years because you did not get her out of Stamboul when I asked you to. And now you are angry because I confront you with it? Did you think it was a trifle? Did you think I would ever forget it?"

"Love made a fool of you once."

"No, it made me a eunuch of me, it did not make me a liar." He looked up. "Don't look at me like that. If you are going to draw your knife, then do it. But otherwise we have known each other too long for such dramatics."

They fell silent.

"How does she look these days?" Abbas said, finally.

"She ages with much grace."

"She is still beautiful?"

"She is no longer sixteen. There is a little silver in her hair. But yes, she is still beautiful."

"I picked the fruit but you tasted it. Do you know how much I hated you for that?"

Ludovici nodded. "Yes, of course."

Abbas sighed and hung his head. "You asked me if I could find out who sent the assassin for Sirhane. I already know."

"Was it the Sultan or his witch?"

"It was neither the Grand Seigneur nor his lady. It was me."

"You?"

"She had threatened me that she would betray Julia's identity to the Lord of Life, tell him how his orders had been betrayed. Suleiman is not a man who forgives or forgets. He cannot afford to. I did as you would have done to protect her."

Ludovici sagged. "Oh, Abbas."

"You may tell her this or keep it from her, as you see fit."

"Sirhane was the only real friend she had. This will go hard with her. I think it is better if she does not know."

"She was much more than a friend. But I suspect you already knew this. They had been lovers in the Harem. It is not uncommon in there, you know. And they remained lovers ever since."

Ludovici nodded. "I know."

"And you still love her?"

"It's not really a choice."

"You see? You should have taken her far away when I told you to."

"I'm sorry, Abbas. I should not have lied to you."

Abbas selected a piece of halwa, then tossed it back onto the tray, all appetite gone. "It doesn't matter, old friend. I should understand you better than I understand anyone. What's done is done now. In the end we both loved and lost. Did we not?"

## Outside Tabriz

The chaush galloped towards the Sultan's silk pavilion. He had ridden day and night from Stamboul. He reined in beside the seven horsetail standard and jumped down, throwing the reins at the Sultan's equerry. He was ushered into the presence of the Lord of Life by the solaks and there prostrated himself on the ground.

The message he carried was handed to Rüstem Pasha who read it to the Lord of Life: Çehangir had been found dead at the Topkapi Saraya. He had hanged himself.

Suleiman's cry of anguish was heard around the entire camp. It echoed from the surrounding mountains, sending a shiver down the spine of the most seasoned of his soldiers. But when they heard what had happened none of them wept for him. It seemed to many of them that God's retribution had been surprisingly swift.

## Pera

They sat together in the gathering gloom; the renegade in the silk robe; the slave girl in the black vesture. They watched the sun until it disappeared below the rim of the earth and the world turned gray. Turkish galleots and Greek caramusalis were silhouetted against the pearly waters of the Horn.

"I do not believe it," Julia said. "The Sultan did not do this."

Ludovici had shrunk form telling her the truth; how could he? Had she not suffered enough without learning that her best friend had been about to betray her and the other had murdered her for it. Please Julia, he thought, just grieve and let it go.

"You must have loved her very much."

"She was my friend." She sighed. "She said I should learn to love you more."

"Do you think you ever could?"

"I don't know, Ludovici. I don't know anything anymore." She got up and went to bed.

# CHAPTER 102

## Topkapi Saraya, 1558

*By the grace of the Most High, whose power be forever exalted! By the sacred miracles of Mohammed, may the blessing of God be upon him! To thee who art Sultan of Sultans, the sovereign of sovereigns, the shadow of God upon the earth, Lord of the White Sea and the Black Sea, of Rumelia and Anatolia, of Karamania, of the Land of Rum, of Diabekir, of Kurdistan, of Azerbaijan, of Persia, of Damascus, of Aleppo, of Cairo, of Mecca, of Medina, of Jerusalem, of all Arabia, of Yemen, and of many other lands that my noble forefathers and my glorious ancestors (may God light upon their tombs!) conquered by the force of their arms, and which my august majesty has made subject to my flaming sword, and my victorious blade, Sultan Suleiman Kahn, son of Sultan Selim Khan. Father.*

*In sundry verbal and written communications I have appealed to my Lord for intercession against those who have sought to spread calumny against me. God knows I have never sought favour for myself, unlike others, who curry popularity with the ulema and the soldiery to raise themselves in esteem and rival our own blessed father. I am powerless against their conspiracy, I who have never sought but to serve you. All I have is your love, and that of my gracious Mother. My fate is totally in your hands. Yet because I do not try to sway the yeniçeris and swagger on my horse I am at the mercy of those who conspire against me. I know I could never outshine the great light that you have thrown upon the world.*

*I worry greatly for your safety, my Lord. Reports reach me daily that my own brother has been seen in the Porte, heavily disguised, talking with the yeniçeris in their barracks and spreading sedition and revolt. I pray that these reports are untrue for there is no rest for me knowing that my great Lord is in peril ...*

Suleiman tossed the letter aside. He looked grey and shrivelled on his throne of beaten gold, sunken between the two golden lions on either side, as if he were their prey. Rüstem waited patiently.

381

"He pleads with me like a woman!"

"He fears Bayezid."

"As he should. Bayezid is a lion. A true ghazi!"

"As you say, My Lord."

"And what do your spies tell you of Selim? He still drinks too much?"

"He spends all his time at the table or the chase."

"And he wants me to protect him from Bayezid!"

"When the time comes, my Lord, Bayezid will take the throne from him."

"When I am dead, let God be the judge." Suleiman closed his eyes. "I had hoped to bring an end to bloodshed over the succession when Mustapha … but it has only made it more certain. Do you know the saying, Rüstem? What has been will be. My father murdered for his throne, and it seems my sons will do the same. I don't understand why they want it so badly. I never did. My only regret was that my father did not live longer. The mantle of the ghazis is like a flaming yoke. It has already cost me two of my sons. Why did Çehangir hang himself, do you think? Out of grief for his stepbrother - or because he was terrified of me?"

Rüstem knew the Sultan did not expect him to answer and kept silent. Finally Suleiman indicated the letter that lay on the carpet between them. "Is there truth in anything Selim claims? Has Bayezid been to Stamboul?"

"My spies have heard nothing of this." If I do not know of it, then it has not happened, Rüstem thought. Yet there was a seed of truth in everything that Selim had said; Bayezid had indeed inherited Mustapha's role as champion of the yeniçeris. But that was as it should be; a Sultan could not take the throne without their support. Suleiman's only concern was that Bayezid might become too impatient, as Mustapha had.

Or at least; as it seemed he had done.

"Who should it be, Rüstem? Selim is oldest. The throne should be his. He is the shahzade."

"Bayezid is the only choice."

Suleiman nodded. Rüstem did not understand his seigneur's dilemma; I might be ill, and old, but I know what is sound and what is not, and the succession is something any fool could calculate on an abacus. Suleiman had smudged too many of his decisions with sentiment. If the mantle is like a flaming yoke, he thought, it is because he does not think clearly.

"Bayezid has no great love for you, Rüstem."

"I shall not be here to fear him, my Lord."

"But should that not be the case, then I charge you with your last mission. When I am dead you must send a chaush on a speedy horse to Manisa to advise the shahzade, Selim, and to tell him to make haste to the city." He paused, wincing at the gout in his knee. "Then you are to send another chaush to Bayezid, on an even faster horse, and tell him the throne belongs to the better man. In return Bayezid will no doubt spare you his displeasure when he is Padishah."

"It will be done as you command," Rüstem said.

***

It was decided then, Suleiman thought. Let God choose. He had done all he could. He had written the laws that would safeguard the future conduct of the Empire. Perhaps with these kanuni, the Osmanlis could survive another warrior, or even a sot, should it come to that.

Yet he feared that his true legacy would be two sons squabbling over his Empire like vultures picking at the eyes of a body not yet dead. God help me in my sorrow.

# CHAPTER 103

## Pera

Ludovici was sitting alone in the great hall, staring at the logs burning in the grate. Julia came to stand behind him, and rested her hand on his shoulder.

"You look troubled."

"I was thinking about what is going to happen when Suleiman is no longer Sultan."

"You think he is going to die?"

"He is old and he sick. He has ruled at the Grande Porte now for thirty eight years. No man lives forever. Even the Shadow of God Upon the Earth has to die sometime."

"I suppose you will miss him."

Ludovici smiled. "They could make one of their camels Sultan for all that I care. But change makes me nervous. A businessman cannot thrive in uncertainty. I need always to know who to bribe and how much."

"Who will succeed him?"

"I imagine the Lady Hürrem will have a large say in that."

"Perhaps she will proclaim herself Sultan."

"I doubt that even she could not manipulate that outcome. No, it must be Bayezid. How could it ever be Selim? The man is a complete debauch. He would make an excellent Bey of Algiers - but Sultan? Even I would not wish that upon the Turks." A log broke and tumbled in the grate. "I would it wish upon the Venetians though."

"And Rüstem Pasha?"

"Bayezid would rather drown in boiling pitch than have him as his Vizier. Besides, he is growing old too. Soon everything will change. A new sultan, a new vizier. For a while the Turks might even enforce the law and my business will be seriously disrupted."

The wind howled and rattled the windows. "I am sure you will continue to prosper somehow, my dear Ludovici."

"Perhaps, but the Divan is a nest of vipers and you can never be quite sure which hatchling is going to thrive."

## Topkapi Saraya

Frost glittered on the domes of the Palace as the . sun rose in a cold blue sky. Hürrem sniffed the north wind for scent of the steppe. She shivered and drew her ermine robe closer about her shoulders. She could never seem to get warm these days, even hunched over a blazing fire.

She nestled her feet beneath the tandir, the pan of lighted charcoal underneath the square tin-topped table in front of her.

She stared through the lattice window, imagining the steppe somewhere beyond the violet horizon. She closed her eyes and her spirit drifted free of the old woman dozing at the window, flew free across the waters and over the caravansaraya at Üsküdar. Üsküdar! Yes, she remembered it, there was a stone han with a central fountain. She had arrived there thirty five years before as a copper haired girl with venom on her tongue and defiance in her eyes. Look at her! She should have ended up as bait for the fish in the Bosphorus. How did such a wilful minx ever become the Valide?

But that girl was far behind her now, lost on the horizon. She flew north and below her was the Kara Deniz, the Black Sea, dotted with the tiny specks of the caramusalis. Soon she broached the coast and below her was a tribe of Krim Tatar, the grass lands dotted with their tent wagons. She swooped down and jumped on the back of one of the broad-shouldered horses and rode splashing through the reed-grown islands of the Father Dnieper. Ahead she saw a city of tents and horses and heard gypsy flutes. She waved and her mother looked up from the goat she was milking and waved back.

"My Lady!"

Hürrem woke with a start. Muomi was staring at her and shaking her arm. "What is it?"

"You were shouting, My Lady. Is everything all right?"

"Shouting?"

"Were you asleep?"

"Yes, asleep," she said, disappointed to be back here again, inside the Harem.

"Are you all right?"

"Of course I am all right. Go away."

Muomi shrugged and left the room.

After she had gone Hürrem felt a tear course down her cheek. She was only ever happy in her dreams now. Why did that black witch have to wake her and drag her back here to this prison?

What was the use? It had brought her no joy, this struggle for eminence over other women. There had been relief when Suleiman had first chosen her, and a certain satisfaction at outwitting Gülbehar - a minor achievement that, God knows. But never real happiness. Perhaps that was because women were not really her enemy, men were.

And then there was Suleiman; she hated him as much now as she had the day he first chose her, thirty five years before. No, before that; she hated him from the very first day of her enslavement in the devshirme, led from her village with shackles on her wrist. That venom still resided there, deep in her soul, a bitter green poison undiluted by time.

But it was not memory that had brought on this black mood. It was the nightingale.

It had been a present from Suleiman. He had given it to her on the day of their wedding, its cage crafted from cedar and studded with onyx and pearl. It had sung to her every day since; but this morning she had found it on the bottom of its cage, stiff and cold. She had removed it gently, cupping it in the palms of her hands, and stared into its unblinking eye.

As she held it, the bird sang to her for the final time. My life is your life, it sang. You have lived out your days just like me, in your own gilded cage, and the Sultan has admired you and enjoyed you and marvelled at your voice and at your beauty. But one day soon, just like me your cold eye will stare at the dawn and it will be over. Your time will have passed. The cage door will never open. Your song will be gone and you will be forgotten.

Well, old she might be, but she still had time to bring down one final curse on the house of the Osmanlis. She would yet have her revenge, a sweet justice she could savour from her tomb for decades, perhaps centuries, to come.

The answer was simple; the Osmanlis wanted Bayezid. More, they needed him, and left to their own devices Bayezid would surely overcome his indigent brother in the race for the throne. He was the strong one, the leader, the ghazi. Selim, for all she knew, was the son of a white eunuch.

So she would give them Selim.

Muomi rushed into the room and seeing Hürrem awake fell reluctantly to her knees. "My Lady, I thought I heard you shouting again."

"I wasn't shouting, I was laughing."

"Laughing, My Lady?"

"Yes, laughing. I feel suddenly warm again. Take the tandir and put it by the door. I think there is spring in the air."

***

The Suleimaniye mosque rose from the city like a mountain of gray marble, one man's prayer for God's mercy, fashioned in perfect symmetry. Other new buildings swarmed at its feet; soup kitchens, hospitals, public baths, a caravansaraya, a library, a medresse, schools and gardens. There were four universities also with the best professors of theology and law in all the empire. It had cost seven hundred thousand ducats, a king's ransom, and it had absolved a Sultan's guilt for the murder of his son.

Perhaps.

Suleiman admired it from the latticed windows of Hürrem's apartments, his hand on her shoulders. "It is magnificent, my Lord. In a thousand years men will look at it and regret they were not born in an age such as ours."

"I hope so, little russelana," Suleiman murmured. He held her tighter. She felt frail; he could feel the shape of her bones through the seraser brocade and it frightened him. She had been ill so often lately.

She wore a green taplock as she had the day he had first seen her in the courtyard, but it was a mocking echo of her youth. Beneath the kohl and henna and powder her skin was like parchment. Her hair was no longer gold; it was milky white at the roots and all Muomi's dyes could not replicate the burnished gold of her youth.

He clung to her as if he could protect her from death by his will alone. He loved her more now than he had ever done; his physical passion had been replaced by a feeling of ease and intimacy that he had shared with no one else. How could he live without her now?

"It is a wonderful achievement, My Lord." Her attention was still focused on the Suleimaniye.

"One day we will lie there side by side," he said and thought: let that day not come for many years!

"So I shall return to the hill where I was first imprisoned?"

"Not a prison," he corrected her, "just the old Eski Saraya." He felt her tremble. "Are you well, my russelana?"

"I have lost a little appetite."

"Shall I have my physician send you an elixir?"

"Muomi tends to me, my Lord. It is just the cold. I shall feel better as soon as Spring comes."

The north wind, the tramontana, howled like a djinn outside and Suleiman shivered inside his sable-lined robe. "You must take better care."

"Do not concern yourself my Lord. A few aches are to be expected when we grow older." She turned from the window. "Will you help me to the divan, my Lord?"

Suleiman waved away her gediçli and helped her across the room, shocked at how light she felt against his arm. He positioned her feet below the tandir, supporting her back gently with cushions.

"Thank you, my Lord. Please don't look so concerned. It is just a slight chill." A gediçli threw a quilt over her knees. When she had settled herself, she said: "My Lord, I would talk with you soon about the succession. I know it has been on your mind. They are my sons, and I know their hearts."

Suleiman took her hand. "Russelana, Selim is a loving son but he could never be a great Sultan. Bayezid is the ghazi."

"He will be popular with the yeniçeris at least."

"Without the yeniçeris, a Sultan cannot rule."

"The yeniçeris ! For whom you have nothing but contempt."

"There are times when a Sultan must use his sword, even if he despises war."

"But Bayezid knows nothing else. He would spend his whole life in the saddle if he could. My Lord, I do not say this to condemn him, only to give you pause. Selim is the oldest. He may not be a warrior like his brother but he may prove a true knight in the Divan. As you have said, it is the law and not the sword that will ensure the future of the Osmanlis."

"Selim is a debauch and a drunkard. He rarely attends his own Divan in Manisa. Why should we think that will change when he becomes padishah?"

"If Bayezid takes the throne, Selim will die."

"Let God decide it then."

Hürrem bowed her head. "I do not contend with your wisdom. I shall pray for both my sons."

He embraced her, a terrible ache in his chest. Unlike her to talk of politics and then concede so easily. Was she really as frail as she looked? Please do not leave me, russelana! I cannot live without you now. I have murdered my best friend and executed my son but I have never betrayed my love for you. It is the one thing that I know in my heart has been true and good.

Do not leave me russelana; please do not leave me.

# CHAPTER 104

### Topkapi Saraya

Only Muomi was with her when she fell.

Hürrem had ventured onto the balcony of her apartment very early that morning. Muomi heard her singing, an old song she had learned from her father, or so she said. It was cold and Muomi went to bring her back inside. Hürrem cried out just as she reached her and fell in her arms. Hürrem's handmaidens ran to assist her but by the time they laid her on the divan she was already unconscious, her breathing ragged in her chest.

### Galata

Ludovici received an urgent summons to meet Abbas at the Jewish house. He hurried to meet him there but for the first time in their entire acquaintance, Abbas was late.

When he finally arrived, there was no particular sign of an emergency. After the usual pleasantries he examined the pastries on the silver plate in front of him and selected one, ate it, then belched daintily into a silk handkerchief he produced from the abundant folds of his robe.

"I received your message," Ludovici said. "You said it was important."

"You have lived with Muslims all these years and still you have not learned the simple art of patience."

"And probably never shall."

"Yes, Ludovici, the matter is urgent, but urgent in hours not in minutes. I hoped to savour our meeting today. It will probably be our last."

"Why, what has happened?"

"The Lady Hürrem, the Laughing One, is dying."

"You are sure? It's not just another of her stratagems?"

"She has been suffering her malady for many months now. This morning she collapsed and they have taken her to her bed. She has the smell of death about her. I know it well. There is no mistaking it."

"But how does this affect me, Abbas?"

"It is Julia! You must send her away from Stamboul. Now! In the sight of God I swear she lives under the sword while she is in this city. I know you have land in Cyprus. Take her there with you."

"But her offence was nearly thirty years ago! Suleiman must have forgotten about her by now. I will not give up everything I have built here to run from shadows."

"He may have forgotten but once he knows she is still alive he will be bound by pride and by duty to punish both her and me. Do you think he will hesitate to give such an order? He will send his chaush for her into the Comunità Magnifica if he has to. He is hardly afraid of the bailo of Venice."

"Why would she do this?"

"To stop me murdering her. I would have done it, too! Hürrem has put everything down in her own hand and she has sworn that it will be delivered to the Grand Vizier upon her death, regardless of the cause." He reached over and took Ludovici''s arm. "Have you not had enough? You can retire from affairs a rich man now. Does your money matter so much to you? You must choose - your precious ships and warehouses - or Julia." Abbas coughed, a wet, hacking sound coming from his chest. He brought the handkerchief to his lips and when he took it away Ludovici noticed a watery red stain. "I beg your pardon. Someday this cough troubles me more than others."

Ludovici nodded. "All right, I will do as you ask. But you must do one favour for me."

"If it is within my power."

"My caramusalis may enter or leave the Dardanelles as they wish. They are never searched. My baksheesh to Rüstem is handsome payment for this privilege. Any passengers I wished to take on board would be guaranteed safe passage." Now it was his turn; he put a hand on his old friend's shoulder. "You come too. If Hürrem betrays Julia to Suleiman she betrays you as well. Get away from here now. Come with me and Julia to Cyprus. At least you can live out your last few years in peace."

"Peace? Does such a thing exist?"

"Please, Abbas. Tomorrow at dawn, at Galata. One of my caramusalis will be there, you will see the Venetian lion flying from its stern - but it will fly upside down. The captain will have his orders. Just get on board and hurry below out of sight."

"I will think it over."

"No! I do not want you to think! I want you to promise me that you will be there. As much as you wish for Julia's safety, I wish for yours."

"Thank you," he murmured. He coughed again. He clapped his hands and immediately the deaf-mutes were at his side, lifting him to his feet. When it was done he clung to them, wheezing from the effort.

"Promise me," Ludovici repeated. "Tomorrow at dawn."

"Very well," Abbas said.

"I will not say goodbye. We will see each other in the morning. Yes?"

Abbas forced a smile. "The start of a new day." He went downstairs and Ludovici watched him get into his carriage. He hesitated, halfway inside and looked up at the widow. "Ludovici," he called up. "If I am not there, say goodbye to Julia for me!" And then he was gone.

Topkapi Saraya

"Muomi," Hürrem whispered. The gediçli put her ear close to Hürrem's lips to catch the words.

"Yes, My Lady."

"Revenge."

"Yes, My Lady."

"I am dying now ... but afterwards Suleiman ... will come to you."

"What am I to tell him?"

"Whatever hurts him ... the most."

Muomi smiled. "Yes, My Lady."

# CHAPTER 105

## Pera

Julia had never seen Ludovici like this. He seemed defeated. He stroked his gold and silver beard, slumped in his chair.

She waited patiently for him to speak. What could be wrong? she wondered. And then she decided: it must be Abbas, and it was bad news.

"I am sending you away," he said suddenly.

"My Lord?"

"I should have done this years ago. It is for your own safety."

She was overcome by a wave of indignation. Was she still just another man's pawn, to be pushed around the Mediterranean at whim? "How can I be in danger?"

"The Sultan may soon know you are here."

"But surely that was all years ag-"

"Abbas is certain of it. It is not forgotten. Shortly the Grand Vizier will know of it and Suleiman will be forced to act. These people do not forget disobedience, Julia. Ever."

"Where do you want me to go?"

"I have estates at Cyprus. You will be looked after."

Julia imagined another lonely villa, some vines, a few servants, perhaps a few books and embroidery to occupy her. A monastery for all purposes. A monastery with wine. The prospect was intolerable.

She realized she would miss him if she went. She would miss his warmth beside her in the bed, his strength, the certainty of his friendship. I do not want to be without him now, she thought. At very last he has become a choice, and not a fact of life. "You wish me to leave you?" she said.

"No, that is the last thing that I want."

"Very well, then. I shall not go."

"You do not understand-"

"I understand perfectly. I just do not wish to leave you."

He stared at her, bewildered. "Why?"

"Perhaps I have grown fond of you." Her lips creased to a tight, sad smile. "Is that so hard to believe?"

"Yes it is. At least I never expected to hear it from you."

"If you will come with me, then I will go. If you will not, then I will stay here. I am decided."

"I could make you go."

"No, you wouldn't do that. It's not in your nature."

\*\*\*

Ludovici stood up and went to the window. Corpo di Dio! He had waited so long for her passion that this one moment of calm acceptance had taken him completely by surprise. He did not know what to say or do. He had been resigned to finally giving up something he thought he could never have. Now this.

"I do not know what to say."

Her skirts rustled on the marble as she came to stand behind him. "What will you do?"

"Do you mean what you say?" he asked her.

"Of course. I should have said it to you long ago."

"Then I shall join you in Cyprus. I will leave the running of my business in the hands of my undermerchant. I will let him cheat me shamelessly in my absence while I shall grow grapes and turn brown and wrinkled in the sun." He smiled. "Perhaps the Venetian renegade has proved his point to the Republic. I should like to be happy instead of just rich."

He remembered her as the first time he had seen her with Abbas, in the church of Santa Maria dei Miracoli. The vision in velvet, as Abbas had once described her. She was no longer an angel, was flawed by age and by sin. But he loved her, as always had done. And finally she wanted him back. That would always be enough.

He would like to have kissed her, but instead he reached out for her hand and felt her fingers entwine with his. He had never been as happy in his whole life.

# CHAPTER 106

Abdullah Ali Osman, Suleiman's private physician, was an unhappy man. Suleiman surveyed him from the divan, his face ferocious with despair.

"You must prescribe for her. If she dies, I shall make you responsible. You will enjoy an uninterrupted view of the next sunrise from the walls of the Ba'ab-i-Humayün."

Ali Osman touched his forehead to the rug. "As you say, my Lord." *God help me in my sorrow!*

A little while later a guard of eunuchs, their yataghans drawn, escorted him through the oak and iron gate into the silent sanctuary of the Harem. They passed hushed and cloistered courtyards and climbed a flight of narrow steps to the apartment of the Hasseki Hürrem.

He did not even spare a glance at the blue and white Ming vases or the gilt mirrors or the jewelled censers that hung from the vaulted dome like fruit. Fear had turned his eyes inward. *O that God had spared him to be alive in another time, when the Sultan did not love his women so much!*

A double line of eunuchs lined the pathway so that he could see nothing beyond them, but he knew she was there; her presence, the hush that surrounded her, dominated the room. The guards who had accompanied him from the Hall of Audience stopped and allowed him to walk ahead.

Nothing was said and he wondered what he should do.

Suddenly a hand appeared from behind the human barrier, pale and limp, the wrist supported by the plump ebony fingers of another eunuch. Probably the Kislar Aghasi, he decided. This was all he would be allowed to examine.

He took the hand reverently for he understood that he was the only other whole man, aside from the Sultan himself, who had ever been allowed to touch her since she had entered the Harem. It was an old woman's hand now, of course, with liver blotches, and the skin was flaccid. Nothing to excite the desire.

He felt for the pulsing of the blood, gauged the temperature of the skin that would tell him a little of her internal organs. He pinched the nails, testing for the quickness of the blood.

Her heart beats very slowly, he thought. Her body cools in readiness for death.

He must hurry, prepare an elixir to revive her organs and her vital humours. He had no wish to watch the sunrise from the main gate, no matter how splendid the view.

***

"Has the old fool gone?" Hürrem whispered.

"Yes, he is gone," Abbas said. The guards filed out of the room and they were left alone. Strange how much he had hated her yet now he admired the courage with which she faced her death. If only he had the same strength.

"I would not trust him … to pare my toenails."

"No, My Lady."

The whites of her eyes were no longer white; they were stained with yellow and sunken deep into her head. No elixir in the world is going to save her now, Abbas decided.

Her lips cracked into a smile. "So you are going to see me … dead, after all my Abbas. That … must please you."

"Indeed it does."

"Your candour is so refreshing … they all tell me I am … going to recover."

"I should say they are greatly mistaken."

Hürrem turned her eyes on him, slowly and painfully. "I have one more … errand for you."

"I hardly think you are in a position to command me anymore, My Lady."

"You want the … letter?"

Abbas controlled himself with difficulty. "Make your peace with God. The affairs of the world will soon no longer concern you."

She laughed; her laughter degenerated into a fit of coughing that left her desperately weak for a long time. But finally, when she recovered she said: "You are right, my Abbas. Muomi … has the letter. She … has my command upon my death … to deliver it to … you."

"There really was such a letter?"

"Of course. I never make … empty threats."

"Who was your spy?"

"Ludovici had a eunuch … Hyacinth. It's a pretty … name."

"Another eunuch?"

395

"A delicious … irony, don't you think? Don't look like that. I am not a … vindictive woman. Take the letter as my parting … gift. Go in peace … my Abbas."

Oh rot in hell, he thought.

He rose to leave. Tonight, he was sure, the witch would die. And at dawn he would be on a caramusali, gliding across the Marmara Deniz and finally, finally free.

She whispered: "Do you not hate them … these Turks?"

Had she really said that? He leaned closer to her, nose twitching at the stink of corruption. "My Lady?"

"What they have done .. to me. To you … Do you not … hate them?"

"My bones ache with it."

Hürrem closed her eyes. The effort of speaking was tiring her. "They have made me a … slave, and made you a … joke." Well, Abbas thought, even in death she does not choose delicacy over candour. "Do you not want … some measure … of vengeance?"

"What does my Lady foresee?"

"I foresee Selim … as the next Sultan."

"It will never happen."

"Who knows what will happen … Abbas? Perhaps you may still … be useful." She tried to moisten her lips with her tongue. They were cracked and a little watery blood seeped from them. "I have bequeathed you … to my son's service. Perhaps you can help me in this … my last endeavour."

She closed her eyes and in moments she was asleep. Abbas got up to leave but turned at the door and looked back. She looked such a fragile and pathetic figure. How could she ever have filled him with such dread?

And how, too, did he find himself in such sympathy with her, at this late hour? "I will help you," he said. "I will gladly do all that I can. This time you do not have to threaten me."

He went out, closing the door softly behind him.

# CHAPTER 107

### Marmara Sea

"Why didn't he come?" Julia said.

Ludovici leaned on the rail, watched the domes and spires of the great city fade into the violet haze of the morning, knowing he would never see them again. "I don't know. I never really understood his reasons for doing anything."

"But did he not promise?"

"He did, but then he implied that he might break it."

"Do you think he is still alive? You don't think she has killed him?"

"My sources inside the Porte will tell me soon enough. If they killed him then we were right not to delay. And if he is well and chose not come …well nothing will change his mind once it is made up."

The water shimmered with pools of gold as the sun rose in the sky. The caramusali reached into the breeze bound for the Dardanelles. Julia remembered the last time she had been out here, that morning she first glimpsed the city that had imprisoned and liberated her. A lifetime ago!

"I shall pray for him," Julia said. She put her hand on his. The breeze was salt and clean. She said a silent farewell to past lovers and felt the past slough off her soul like an old and withered skin.

### Topkapi Saraya

Hürrem was dying.

It was obvious to him, from the moment he entered the room. She was propped up on pillows; Muomi had braided her hair with pearls and the green taplock had been pinned to her hair. She had dressed her in a kaftan of pure white silk. It was all an absurd parody of her youth and he wanted to cry aloud when he saw her. Was this some kind of cruel joke?

He barely recognized her. The flesh had fallen away from her bones. She looked like a skull with a tight covering of translucent skin, her body shrunken and tiny like a doll's.

Muomi and Abbas crouched by her bedside, their faces dark with dread.

"Russelana ..." he whispered.

The others moved back. Suleiman sat down on the edge of the bed and picked up her hand. It was as cold as marble. "Don't leave me," he whispered.

"I am free, Suleiman." Her voice had lost all gentleness; it sounded like metal on a rasp.

He brought her fingers to his lips and kissed them. "I love you."

Her mouth creased like a bow. "You fool."

There was a moment of stillness.

"Life has been ... cruel to you, Suleiman. But then you have ... deserved it."

Something inside him turned to ice. He wondered if he had heard her correctly. He bent lower over the bed. "What are you telling me?"

"I am telling you to ... go and stew ... in hell."

Suleiman stared at her, appalled. He dropped her hand as if she had told him she had the pestilence. He turned to the circle of faces around the bed. "Get out! Get out all of you!"

Muomi and the other gediçli hurried out. Only Abbas hesitated.

"Get out!" Suleiman repeated.

The door creaked shut behind him.

When he turned back Hürrem was grinning; yes grinning, he thought, for it could not be called a smile. Her lips were drawn back from her teeth in a death's head vision of triumph. "Little russelana ..."

"I am not ... your little russelana. I have never ... loved you. Every day of my life I have ... hated you ... hated you with all my soul."

Suleiman clutched at the fluted gold column of the canopy to steady himself. "You are sick. I shall pay no attention to anything you say."

"I was your prisoner so I could ... do nothing else, but submit ... to you. But oh, how I have ... despised you!"

Suleiman covered his ears. "I will not listen!"

"Have you ever wondered why Bayezid is such a ... great warrior? It is because .... he belongs to Ibrahim."

"No! That is impossible."

"You trusted him so much ... you never knew what he did ... after he returned from Egypt."

"No!"

"So you see this is my … waqf, my bequest to the Osmanlis. Choose Suleiman! Fat, stupid Selim … or the son of the … Greek! I curse you and I curse … every Sultan who follows you … until your Empire crumbles away … into memory and ruin."

"Stop it! PLEASE!"

"How I hate you …"

"NOOOOOOO!" He took her by the shoulders and shook her. "You love me! Say it! You love me!"

He looked into her eyes and watched the light die there. A flicker, like a candle in a draught, and then darkness, He threw her back on the bed with all his force. She slumped onto her side.

"NO, IT IS NOT TRUE!"

He ripped the taplock off her head and the pearls that were braided into her whitened hair scattered on the marble floor. Her hair tore out from the roots and tangled in his fingers.

"Nooooooo …."

He picked up a stool and flung it at the Vicenzan mirror, saw his own image splinter into a thousand pieces. Then he ran from the room.

When Abbas found him he was curled up on the floor of his own bedchamber crying like an infant. His servants hung back, none of them knowing what to do. Abbas put him to bed.

He stayed there for three days crying and shouting at the phantoms that came to haunt him, and when he finally summoned Abbas it was to order that her apartments be locked and sealed so that he would never again have to go in any room where he had once heard her laughter or felt her embrace.

# PART 10

## GOD'S WIND

# CHAPTER 108

## Amasya, 1559

The two riders galloped towards each other at full tilt, the horse's hoofs drumming on the soft earth, the mud tossed into the air behind them in thick clumps. The first rider threw his spear and his opponent tried to slide out of the way on the lee side of his horse, but it struck him a glancing blow on his back. The mounted horsemen at the side of the arena cheered. The music of the drums and zounas became more urgent.

"Sssss," Bayezid whispered to calm his Arab, who was kicking with his forelegs, agitated by the music and the shouting of the riders around them.

"Another three points," Murad grinned, "another good day for the Blues."

"Soon we may be throwing real spears," Bayezid said. He took off again toward the centre of the arena and two riders from the Greens. As they closed Murad saw the first javelin, thrown too soon, pass harmlessly over his prince's shoulder as he ducked beneath the horse's head. Bayezid veered his Arab suddenly to the right and the other rider had to pull up sharply to avoid crashing into him.

Bayezid reined in his horse, which responded immediately. Before the other rider had realized what was happening he was behind him and his spear struck the Green between the shoulder blades. The man cried out in pain and slumped over his horse.

All around him the Blues stood in their stirrups and cheered.

Bayezid charged on, calling for another javelin from the pages darting between the horses. He grinned through his thick black beard at Murad. "What do you say, Murad?"

"I say we march today and cut ourselves a slice of barley pudding!"

Bayezid laughed. There was more whoops from the Blues as another of their team scored a direct hit with his spear and sent a Green tumbling from his horse with blood spurting from his head.

They were invincible that day. They could not lose.

\*\*\*

Bayezid found Gülbehar in the Harem garden, in the rose kiosk. The roses that gave it its name were in full flower, a blaze of rose and gold and pink.

She sat alone, the silence broken only by the steady click-click-click of the pearl tespi running through her fingers, her lips moving silently as she recited the prayers of Mohammed. Her face was hidden by her yashmak but the deep lines around her eyes betrayed her age. The years had not been kind to Rose of Spring. All that remained were the thorns.

She heard him enter but did not look up. "You look so much like my son," he said.

"I should like to be like him in every way."

"Not in every way, Bayezid, surely? My son is dead." She looked up for the first time. "So what brings you here to this old woman's garden?"

"I want your advice."

"My advice? I have spent my whole life in gardens like this one. What would I know of the world of princes?"

"I think you know a great deal." He paused, choosing his words carefully. "You know there is going to be war." Such a beautiful day, the air was redolent with the scent of roses. Too fine a day to be talking about bloodshed.

A gediçli poured Gülbehar a perfumed sherbet into a crystal glass. She sipped it.

"Because of Selim?"

"The troubles of the Osmanlis do not begin and end with Selim. The great grandsons of the men who followed the Fatih into battle now sit on their farms in Anatolia and are ruled by the great grandsons of the men that were conquered. The devshirme has burdened us with an army of bureaucrats, and a Bulgarian vizier forces them off their lands while he fills his own pockets with their taxes. Everything is baksheesh, baksheesh. A true Osmanli lives in the saddle of a horse not on a silk divan! He finds his power in the sword not in a bribe."

Gülbehar ran the tespi through her fingers, click-click-click. "Do you remember how they murdered my son? Do you remember what the yeniçeris said that day? Our hope is lost in Mustapha."

"I remember."

"We need another Mustapha and you are so much like him. You can ride, you can fight, you command respect wherever you go. I believe our hope might be reborn in you."

"If only Suleiman thought so."

"Suleiman was my lord for many years but truly I do not recognize the man he has become. Look at what he has done to you! He has shamed you and exiled you here to Amasya, as he did to my son. He has all but handed the throne to your idiot brother. This time we cannot blame it all on Hürrem."

"He knows what kind of man my brother is. It makes no sense."

"If you are Suleiman it makes every kind of sense."

"So what should I do?"

"It is Suleiman who has done it. He claims that what he does is for the Osmanlis but he's a liar. He just wants to hold on to his power and everyone who threatens it, he destroys. He pretends not to be a tyrant like his father, but he is worse. At least you knew where you were with Selim the Grim. He did not pretend to be something he wasn't."

"What are you telling me?"

"Selim is not your enemy. Your father is. Be careful of him Bayezid If you ride against anyone, let it be your father. Selim cannot hurt you. Your father will bury you and spit on your grave."

She held out her hand. Bayezid kissed it and took his leave.

Ride against Suleiman? he thought. No, that is unthinkable. Suleiman was just testing his mettle, that was all. He must know he could not let Selim remain at Manisa, just five days ride from the capital, while he lived like an exile a month's ride away. It was the Osmanli way and his father would understand that.

### Topkapi Saraya

Suleiman contemplated his grand vizier, motionless but for the steady tapping of his index finger on the golden arm of his throne. He was dressed magnificently; a kaftan lined with black sable, a crimson robe with gold tiger stripes, emeralds glittering in his turban and on his fingers. Yet he looked shrunken as if the pages had thrown an adult's clothes on a wizened little boy.

"It was the illness," Suleiman murmured.

Rüstem frowned. "My Lord?"

Suleiman jerked his head up as if suddenly aware of his presence. "Ah, Rüstem."

"I have come from the Divan, my Lord."

"The Divan," Suleiman repeated as if trying to remember what manner of thing that might be.

"I have bad news, my Lord."

"Bayezid?"

Rüstem nodded. It was disconcerting; one moment the Sultan seemed on the edge of madness, the next he was lucid and alert. He had been this way ever since Hürrem died.

"Has he answered the chaush?"

"He has."

"And what does he say?"

"His reply was short, my Lord." He produced the letter from the fold of his robes. He read the formal salutation, then: "He goes on to say just this, My Lord: "In everything I will obey the command of the Sultan, my father, except in all that lies between Selim and me.""

Suleiman uttered a small cry, like an animal caught in a trap. "She was very ill. She did not mean what she said."

"My Lord?"

"Why does he defy me?"

What else can he do? Rüstem thought. You virtually exiled him after Hürrem's death. "He raises an army at Angora," Rüstem said. "They say the veterans and the Turcomans are flooding to him. Meanwhile Selim has complained that he has received a woman's bonnet and apron from his brother as a gift."

"We must stop this. While I live they shall obey me!"

"There may yet be a way, my Lord."

"Tell me."

"Restore Bayezid to Kütahya. If not there, then Konia. Make some conciliation. But by assigning him to Amasya you give the succession to Selim."

"He must obey me!"

"If you insist on this we cannot avert a civil war."

"They are my sons! They will do as I say!"

"I fear we cannot persuade Bayezid to stay his hand, my Lord." He hesitated. "It was always my understanding that you wanted Bayezid as your successor."

"Then your understanding was at fault. You are getting old. The dropsy has addled your brain."

Rüstem touched his forehead to the carpet. "As you say."

"Tell Selim he is to proceed to Konia, to guard our southern route to Syria and Egypt. Send Mohammed Sokolli to protect him with a regiment of yeniçeris and thirty cannon. Meanwhile you shall command Pertew Pasha to go to Bayezid and try and persuade him to return without delay to the governorship of Amasya and extract from him a promise of fealty. My sons will not be allowed to drag this empire into war while I still sit on this throne."

"Yes, my Lord," Rüstem said. He rose slowly to his feet and hobbled from the room. Suleiman is mad! he thought, Hürrem's death had unhinged his mind. But he would do as the Sultan commanded. Let others worry about Suleiman's successor. He would be dead before then.

*** 

"You were ill," Suleiman said. "You did not mean what you were saying."

"There was a fever in my brain," Hürrem answered. "It was the devil who spoke."

"Bayezid is my son."

"Of course he is your son. I loved you with all my heart. Besides, I was close guarded in the Harem. Ibrahim could not have reached me in there. It was the Devil's lie."

"Yet he looks like Ibrahim," Suleiman said.

Suleiman reached out a hand to touch her but she was not there. Tears of grief and self pity welled up in his eyes. For thirty five years he had loved her, loved her more than anyone. He had given up his Harem for her and made her his queen. Of course she had loved him. It was the illness that made her say what she had right at the end.

Yet he could still hear her, as if she was in the room right now. He could see her lying on the bed, her face white, her voice jagged as metal. I have never loved you. Every day of my life I have hated you with all my soul."

"My little russelana, please …"

He opened his eyes, almost expecting to see her. But there were only the mutes, dumb to his grief, faces blank as stone.

Little russelana.

He remembered when he had first seen her, in the courtyard of the old Eski Saraya, that green taplock on her head and a childlike frown on her face as she worked the needle and thread. She was incapable of so much hate, he told himself. It was Satan speaking through her; she was already in Paradise when she damned him.

But how could he be really sure? It was the reason he had exiled Bayezid to Amasya and favoured Selim for the throne. Better a drunk than break the line forever with a traitor.

Even a traitor he had loved.

Hürrem, tell me you lied at the end; come back and tell you lied.

# CHAPTER 109

### Angora

In Spring Cappadocia is ablaze with wildflowers, the rain drawing a riot of colour from the sun-baked steps. Bayezid rode with his equerry, Murad, along a stream between ranks of tall, spindly poplars, fields of brilliant yellow rapeseed either side.

They reached the crest of the spur. His army was camped below under the towers of the Hisar fortress. Bayezid felt the warm flesh of his Arab quiver beneath him. The camp was at prayer; men were lined in rows, on their knees. Turbans bobbed in unison, thousands of them, row upon row upon row.

They had arrived in these past weeks from all over the plains; Kurds with broad scarlet sashes at their waists with woollen skull caps instead of turbans; Turkoman bandits in fur hats; black plumed Spahis who had deserted the Porte to come in search of the new Mustapha; and the dispossessed timariots in a motley selection of armour and conical helmets.

Now there were twenty thousand camped on the plain, a traditional ghazi army, the ancestors of the horsemen whose great grandfathers had conquered the steppes in the name of the Osmanlis.

Murad turned to Bayezid. "You lit a flame under the Empire. See how they flock to you. You are the future now."

"And I will not let them down," he said.

### Manisa

The shahzade Selim was in a black mood. Bayezid was amassing an army and still his father refused to make his move. Instead he had sent Sokolli and his cannon and a royal command to move on to Konia to face his brother. Was he not the Chosen? So why did his father still sit in his palace watching the sun move the shadows around the walls while "the new Mustapha" gathered strength at Angora, ready to murder him? Once again, he had been abandoned.

He emptied the crystal cup at his side and clapped his hands for his page to refill it.

Damn Bayezid. And damn Suleiman.

Perhaps they were plotting together. For all he knew Suleiman might even be at Amasya right now, feasting with him in the seraglio, or watching him show off to him at the çerit. Worse, his brother might be intriguing with the Aga of the yeniçeris to usurp the throne, as his grandfather had done.

He gulped down another draft of wine. Life was so unfair. His mother had never shown him any affection, and Suleiman had ignored him in favour of Mustapha and Çehangir. Perhaps he should have been born with a spine like a camel's hump, then he might have got a little attention.

He was assailed by a sudden wave of vertigo, as if he were on the edge of a black cliff; he clutched at the divan as an oily sweat broke out on his skin. They were all intriguing against him, weren't they? He was quite alone.

Even the wine would not shake this black mood tonight. He needed a distraction. "Abbas!"

His Kislar Aghasi stepped forward, bowing low. Ugly brute, Selim thought. Why did Hürrem insist he take him into his household after her death? Perhaps he was a spy. He should have this brute's head on a spike soon. He would think about it.

"My lord," Abbas murmured.

"I need some entertainment, Kislar Aghasi."

"What does my Lord wish?"

"Bring on the herd. The bull is pawing the ground."

"As you wish."

## Angora

The oil lamps had been lit in the campaign tent and his officers crowded in side by side with Turkoman and Kurdish bandits to stare at the charts he had unfolded on the carpet.

"Suleiman has ordered Prince Barley Pudding ..." a grunt of derisive laughter from the others for the nickname they had given Selim ... "to take his army and his household to Konia, to protect the land route to Syria. From us, I suppose he means. But we have no quarrel with Suleiman." Bayezid looked around at the hard, bearded faces. "We will ride south to confront Selim."

"He will run," someone suggested.

"Yes, my brother would like to run. But my father has sent him a backbone, in the form of a yeniçeri regiment and thirty cannon. It may be a harder fight than we expected."

"Thirty cannon will not stop us!"

"The cannon are not important, not even the yeniçeris. It is Selim. Once my brother is dead, the battle is won. It is as simple as that." He pointed to the map at his feet. "We will draw up our army here on the plain and wait. Sokolli has orders to keep us apart, not to attack. So he will draw up artillery in a defensive posture. We will give him the charge he expects to keep him occupied. Meanwhile we will leave a cavalry squadron here in the hills to the west. It will be small enough to pass unnoticed, a tiny dart just big enough to cut the vein in Prince Barley Pudding's neck. When he is dead we can break off the attack. Our work will be done. There will be no other shahzade then but me."

They all nodded. They were sure they would win.

### Manisa

There were three or four dozen girls, all of them naked. They were the most beautiful girls in the Empire, none older than twenty, some as young as twelve. They had been purchased in the outlying provinces or by Selim's special procurators at the market at the Place of the Burned Pillar, the same place where his mother had been sold.

Selim reeled into the hall, staggering from the effects of the wine.

They were all on all fours, breasts swaying as they moved about the thick rugs, a moving herd of coffee, alabaster and olive. Abbas, the Kislar Aghasi, snapped a short oxhide whip in the air above their heads like a cattle master to keep them moving.

Selim roared like a bull and started to strip off his clothes.

Abbas stepped back as Selim plunged in among the girls. Selim caught the back of one and tried to mount her. Abbas saw her grimace in pain.

Selim roared again. Finally he was inside her and began to thrust his hips violently. Then he pushed her away and crawled after another one, his great belly sagging on the ground. He caught a fair haired Armenian by her hips and she wriggled in distress.

No, don't do that, Abbas thought. He'll have you killed if you resist.

But Selim was too drunk to notice. He mounted her and his fingers cupped her breasts, squeezing so hard he made her scream. He liked that. He roared again and with a final thrust of his hips released her.

He clapped his hands and a page threaded his way through the girls with a cup of wine. Selim drained it in one draft and returned to his pleasures.

He mounted yet another girl, gripping her braids as if they were the reins of a horse. "Damn you, Bayezid! See, I shall impregnate a whole herd of women and my sons shall swarm over the throne like ants over a corpse!"

He released the girl and scuttled after yet another; but by now the wine had slowed him and he slumped forward on his face. He tried to struggle back to his knees. The girls cowered away along the walls but Abbas cracked the whip above their heads to force them back into the centre of the room.

Selim grunted and made after the nearest one. He caught her leg but she wriggled free and he toppled over onto his back, his belly heaving. He had already lost his erection to the wine, Abbas noted.

He made a final attempt to rise but his head fell back onto the carpets. He laughed again. "Damn you, Bayezid!" Within seconds he was snoring.

Abbas clapped his hands and the girls fled from the room. Four pages lifted the sleeping shahzade from the floor and carried him to his bedchamber. The prince of the Osmanlis, first son of the Magnificent, pretender to the throne of the greatest empire on earth, turned over and vomited copiously on the silk sheets.

# CHAPTER 110

## Konia

The dervishes had been fasting and praying for a month. Now, drunk with opium and faces ghost-white from talcum, they filed into the courtyard. The musicians sat in a circle, cross-legged on the hard stone. The flutes began to play, the soft wailing drifting upwards as a sliver of moon rose behind the dome of the türbesi. Torchlight threw long shadows on the walls of the monastery.

The drummers joined in, quickening the rhythm as the dancers began to spin, long skirts fanning out around their legs. They started their chant, saying prayers for the great ones.

The dancers inclined their heads to their right shoulders, their heavy garments giving off a low whistling moan, like the wind in the mountains.

Bayezid felt his own heartbeat speeding up in time with the music; still they whirled, until even the dancer's faces began to blur. But not one of them staggered, none of them fell.

The music ended without warning. The dancers fell prostrate to the floor, heads rolling on their shoulders, flecks of foam on their lips. They were in the trance.

He stepped into the circle and approached one of the dancers, a tall monk with a white beard and a brown face as wrinkled and hard as a walnut. They said he was one hundred and eleven years old. "Holy Man, can you see?" he said.

His eyes were open but his pupils were cold and glazed, like a dead fish. "I can see," the old man answered.

"Tell me what you see for the sons of Suleiman."

"If the one who is not the son of Suleiman becomes king, I see only misery and corruption and stink."

412

Bayezid crouched lower, trying to make out his words more clearly. The one who was not his son? "What of Bayezid?"

"I do not see him."

"Who do you see then?"

"A great wind that blows a curtain over everything. God's wind."

"What else?"

"There is nothing else. I see only the wind."

Bayezid stood up, frowning with disgust. All these monks only ever spoke in riddles. You could never get any sense out of any of them. He stamped away. Holy men? Holy wasters of time!

## Topkapi Saraya

Suleiman stared at the gediçli kneeling at the foot of his throne. Her tight curls were grizzled with gray but her eyes had lost none of their malevolence. For thirty five years she had been Hürrem's slave, and hardly worthy of his attention. Now he had summoned her here by express command. Muomi alone, he realized, could possess the remedy for his grief.

"You were the Lady Hürrem's handmaiden since she was first gözde. Yes?"

"Yes, My Lord."

"You knew her intimately?"

"I did."

"I wish then, to speak of intimate matters. There is no reason to fear," he added, " as long as you answer me truthfully, for I am your Sultan, and your allegiance is to me, not Hürrem. She rests now and is beyond mortal retribution."

"Yes, My Lord."

""I want you to think back, to your first years of service. Do you remember a man called Ibrahim who was my vizier for many years?"

"I remember, my Lord."

Suleiman leaned even closer so that now he was perched on the very edge of the throne. "Was it possible ... that the lady Hürrem ever received him in the Eski Saraya?"

Muomi raised her head and met his eyes. God help me in my sorrow, he thought. This woman is terrifying. She has Satan in her eyes.

"She received him once, my Lord."

He could not breathe.

"How?" he asked her finally.

"A bribe to the Kislar Aghasi, the captain of the Girls, before Abbas. The Lady Hürrem swore me to secrecy. She said I would die if I ever whispered a word of it."

She is lying, Suleiman thought.

413

She is lying.

She must be.

A lie, a lie, a lie.

"NO!" he screamed at her. He leaped from the throne and slapped her across the face. Muomi fell back, astonished that this frail old man still had the strength to hit so hard. She put a hand to her lips and it came away bloody.

"Bostanji !" Suleiman screamed and signalled to the deaf-mute who stood in attendance. The man stepped forward and drew the yataghan from his belt. With one movement he scythed Muomi's head from her shoulders. A fine pattern of blood sprayed over Suleiman's boots.

It was a lie.

It had to be.

# CHAPTER 111

## Konia

Wind.

It whipped at the pennons on the levelled lances and tore at the robes of the waiting horsemen. Bayezid sat immobile on his Arab stallion, his face partially hidden behind the nasal of the conical silver helmet. When he drew his damascened sword, thousands of his cavalry ranged behind him imitated his movement so the sounds of steel rasping on sharpened blades could be heard even over the howling of the wind.

Bayezid spurred his horse forward into a walk. The line of horsemen behind him followed.

Even at this distance he could see the mouths of the cannon on the other side of the plain. They would not fire on him, he was sure of it.

"Vvvvvt!" Bayezid whispered to his horse and it broke from its march into a canter.

Dust rose from the hoofs, a purple tail that spiralled from the plain like a trailing banner. Bayezid heard the ululation behind him as they gathered speed. The ground flashed past in a blur. Nothing could stand against this wall of lancers and the muscles of the Arab warhorses.

He brought his sword over his head and held it in front of his body, pointing towards the cannon. He ordered the charge.

He was sure Sokolli could not persuade his troopers to fire on their favourite son.

\*\*\*

Selim heard the drumming of the hoofs and felt the vibrations through the thick carpets strewn on the floor of his pavilion. He gripped the arms of his throne as if a chasm had opened up in the ground around him.

He clapped his hands and Abbas hurried to his side with the jug of wine. "Where is Sokolli?" Selim said.

"He is with the yeniçeris, my Lord."

Selim took the glass but his hands were shaking so badly he spilled most of it into his beard and down the front of his golden robe. Abbas refilled it. The last servant who had been too slow to refill the shahzade's goblet had lost both his hands at the wrist.

"Sokolli should be here with me," Selim said.

"With respect, it is better that he is with the gunners. Someone must direct them."

Selim badly needed to void his bowels. He drained his glass and rushed out of the tent.

\*\*\*

The horses had sensed the coming storm. They shook their tasselled heads and stamped their hoofs. Murad rode to the crest of the ridge and scanned the sky to the south. The horizon had disappeared. He watched the dust storm sweep across the Mevlevi monastery almost as if the dervishes had summoned it there.

"God's wind," Murad muttered. "It is headed straight for our cavalry. In a few minutes they will be blind."

He drew his killiç from his belt. It was time. There were two dozen riders waiting with him in the gully. He wheeled his horse to face them. "Now!" he barked.

\*\*\*

Muhammad Sokolli had expected trouble.

He had brought with him from Stamboul a hand-picked squadron of yeniçeris and solak guardsmen. They were veterans of the campaigns in Persia with Suleiman; a handful of them had even served as young men at Mohacs. They were loyal only to the Sultan.

He had taken the precaution of deploying them in a line behind the artillery. As he watched Bayezid's horde make the charge he thanked God for his foresight.

There were two banners of cloud drifting towards them; the cavalry from the front, the desert storm behind. He wondered which would arrive first.

"When I give the order you will fire!" he screamed over the rushing of the wind.

The yeniçeris looked at each other then at the advancing cavalry. Finally one of them found the courage to speak up: "We cannot fire on the shahzade!"

The horses came on.

"That is not the shahzade," Sokolli shouted at the man. "Selim is the shahzade, as decreed by your Sultan. Prepare to fire!"

Not a single trooper bent to the pyramid of musket balls beside their cannon pieces. "Long live Bayezid!" someone shouted.

Sokolli could see Bayezid now, in his green robes - a clever choice, Sokolli thought, the colour of Islam. The ground shook under their feet.

Sokolli drew his sword and turned to the soldiers waiting in line behind him. "Prepare to fire," he shouted. They rested their harquebuses on the forked sticks in their left hands and aimed at the gunners in front of them.

Sokolli turned back to the artillery troopers. "Fire or I will give them the order to shoot all of you."

Still they hesitated.

"Aim .." Sokolli said. Is their nerve going to hold, he wondered. Will they force me to fire? We will all die, if they do.

The cavalry were close now.

Suddenly one of the men picked up a cannon ball and heaved it into the mouth of his cannon. One by one the others did the same.

"Light the fuses," Sokolli said.

They lowered the trajectories, aiming at the onrushing horde.

*\*\**

Bayezid saw an orange blossoming of flame along the line of artillery, heard the howl of shot in the air. The earth erupted all around him. It was if God had taken an invisible scythe and raked it over their ranks. Suddenly he was riding alone.

They were gone! Almost every man riding with him in the first wave had disappeared. He saw a horse, wide-eyed with terror, trying to rise to its feet, dripping blood from its severed foreleg. Its rider lay in several dusty heaps beside it.

He turned in the saddle. The plain was littered with more little mounds, horses and men, some writhing, some lying quite still where they had fallen. The second wave came on. The ground erupted again and for a moment they, too, were lost behind a wall of flame and dirt.

Just a handful rode on through the cloud.

A third wave, a fourth.

They had to keep coming. He turned back to urge them on.

Now he heard the hiss of arrows in flight, the clang of musket balls and crossbow bolts hitting armour. The ground erupted again, and more horses were scythed away from their riders.

Bayezid raised his sword and stood in the stirrups so they could all see him. "Death to Selim!"

Another wave came, then another. His ragged army of bandits and horsemen did not waver. While the new Mustapha sat in the saddle, they were ready to die.

They would do it, he thought. Despite Sokolli's cannon, they would prevail.

\*\*\*

By the time Murad reached Selim's camp the storm had already rolled in, obscuring the horsetail standard outside the shahzade's tent. Where was he? They galloped in circles, hacking down the few guards who tried to stand in their way.

God's wind had obliterated everything.

Murad could not make out anything more than a few yards in front of him. "Where is he?" he screamed.

He could hear the rest of his raiding party but all sight of them was lost behind the stinging barrage of sand. He raised his arm to protect his face, did not see the man who ran from one of the tents and slashed the hamstrings of his Arab. The beast bucked and screamed and crashed onto its side.

The fall trapped him underneath his horse, jarring his killiç from his fist and winding him. He looked around desperately for his attacker. He glimpsed the blue jacket and gray cap of a yeniçeri. He fumbled for the spear in its sheath on the saddle and threw it.

His practice at the çerit had served him well. The spear took the trooper through his chest. The man fell back, choking and kicking.

The crippled Arab was scrabbling in the dust, trying to regain its feet. For a moment it lifted its weight and he was able to scramble clear. He crawled to the dying trooper and took his sword off him. His ankle was agony. He limped away, blinded by the storm.

\*\*\*

Murad heard a woman's screams. The dust cleared for just a moment and he saw veiled figures running from a silk pavilion, darting between the horses and the silhouettes of fighting men. Somehow they had found Selim's harem; Prince Barley Pudding could not be too far away. He limped towards them but then the dust closed around them again and everything was just shadow.

He was standing in front of a purple tent. There it was the horsetail standard! But where were the guards? Perhaps they had been lured away by the battle in front of the women's" tent. He tore open the entrance curtain and went in, dragging his injured leg behind him.

Bayezid, I will not let you down. You will be Sultan, I shall make sure of that.

He came face to face with an enormous Moor. He wore a kaftan of bright blue flowered silk. There were pointed ship-ship on his feet and a ruby glinted in his left ear. Although he dressed like a fop, he was one of the ugliest man Murad had ever seen in his life. His face had been scarred and only one eye remained. He was also obscenely fat, even for a eunuch. He gaped at Murad then fell prostrate on the floor in front of him.

"Please don't hurt me," he said. "I am just a harmless slave."

Murad snorted in disgust and burst through another silk curtain into the inner sanctum. Selim lay on his belly, arms and legs spreadeagled. Murad leaned his weight on his sword and rolled him over with his uninjured foot expecting to see him split open like an over ripe peach.

He heard the rustle of silk as the eunuch followed him in. "Is he dead?" Murad asked him.

"No, he is not dead, my Lord, only drunk. He fainted as soon as he heard the first cannon."

"Then he is fortunate. He will not feel my sword tickle his ribs."

Murad raised his killiç for the death blow. Suddenly he felt as if every nerve, every muscle had been numbed. The sword slipped from his fingers and fell onto the carpet. He did not understand what was happening.

He lay on his back, staring up at the eunuch. There was a jewel-handled dagger in the slave's hand and blood smeared down the blade. "I am sorry," Abbas said to him. "But I cannot let you kill him. I wish that I could."

Everything went black.

***

Bayezid turned his horse from the whipping blast of sand and rode back across the plain, his stallion picking its way through a litter of bleeding and moaning horses and men. How many have I lost today? he wondered.

Sokolli's cannon were silent. There was only the howl of the wind and the cries of the dying now. A horse nuzzled a fallen rider; the Turkoman tried to crawl towards him, both legs shot away, leaving a trail of gore in the dust. Bayezid jumped down and administered the merciful blow, sending the man to Paradise.

They were defeated. Their charge had been halted by a barrage of sand and grapeshot. It was God's wind. The monk was right, after all.

# CHAPTER 112

## Topkapi Saraya

Suleiman was propped on a divan in the Çinili Kiosk. The Judas trees were in blossom and the bay of Yenikapi was teeming with caïques, all piled high with eggplants cucumbers and melons they had ferried over from the Asian shore.

"You look ill, Vizier."

"Nothing that death will not cure," Rüstem said.

Suleiman shook his head. "I may be wrong but I suspect that even this late in your life you are developing a sense of humour, Rüstem Pasha."

"I do not think so, my Lord."

Suleiman shrugged. "There is no answer to my letter?"

"No, my lord. Yet that means nothing, in itself. Selim may have intercepted his messenger."

"Or he did not send a messenger. Perhaps he still defies me."

"Why do we draw our swords against him, my Lord? Is it wise?"

"Suddenly at this stage of your life you embrace a cause? I have trusted you all these years because you never let your heart stand in the way of reason. Indeed, I often wondered if you had a heart. Now you plead Bayezid's case? Are you in his employ now?"

"My Lord, I meant no offence."

"I am not offended. Speak openly."

"I just do not understand our strategy," he said while another part of him screamed: shut up! Why do you speak for Bayezid? He is no friend of yours! If he ever came to the throne his first act would be to exile you to Diyabakir! Be still!

"What is it that you do not understand?"

"The logic of it. Why destroy Bayezid? Mustapha went too far, he was a real threat to you. But if we crush Bayezid then the throne falls to Selim and Selim ..." He spread his hands in a gesture of despair.

"You will do my bidding in this."

"And yet," Rüstem persisted, "where is the offence? He rode against Selim, not against you. Would you want this great Empire to be entrusted to a weakling? Did Selim gain the victory at Konia? No, by the ninety nine holy names, he did not! It was the wind of the dervishes and the cannon of Mohammed Sokolli. Selim is not worthy. It makes no sense to me."

What djinn possessed me to speak like this? Rüstem thought. You know he will not change his mind, once it is set. There is only person who could ever manage that, and she is dead. So why provoke him? A whole lifetime you have kept your thoughts to yourself and now you are gabbling like a fishwife.

For one moment he thought Suleiman was even about to raise his finger to summon the bostanji . But instead he said softly: "I have decided that Bayezid is not shahzade. Selim is my firstborn. Enough."

Rüstem bowed his head. There is more to this, he thought, but after a lifetime of dealing in secrets I shall never know this one. He struggled to his feet and limped out of the chamber.

In his mind he turned the pages of his personal inventory: eight hundred and fifteen farms, seventeen hundred slaves, eight thousand turbans, six hundred illuminated copies of the Qu'ran, two million ducats ...

He was the richest man in the Empire, save the Sultan. He had proved himself a master of the game. The final book keeping of his life was confirmation of his mastery of life. Yet with death now beckoning with one skeletal finger, he struggled with the lingering suspicion that there was something that he had missed.

*** 

The great drum in the courtyard of the yeniçeris had not sounded for many years. It beat now, its echoes reverberating from the walls of the palace, hastening the last minute preparations. Suleiman mounted his horse by the fountain in the Third Court, wincing at the pain in his knees. Late that morning he led the army out.

They crossed the Bosphorus at Üsküdar, and by that afternoon the column wound through the Cyprus groves at Çamlica, forcing the heavy laden wheat carts off the dusty road. Runners jogged at Suleiman's stirrup; the plumes of his solak guardsmen bobbed behind him.

He tried to shut his mind to the rigours of the journey that lay ahead of him. At least twenty five days of hard riding to reach the fortress at Amasya; then a long campaign in the heat and dust, hunting down his own son like a wild boar. This is the civil war I did everything to avoid.

I am too old for endless days in this saddle, each step of the horse jars these old bones. I have made so many laws, he thought; but in the end the yeniçeris, the cavalry and the cannon were the only laws the Osmanlis really understood.

But he would not allow the line to be broken; if Bayezid would not bend to his will then he would be made to submit.

# CHAPTER 113

## Armenia

From Erzerum the Anatolian plateau rose into soaring snow-capped peaks and plunging valleys. Ranged along the mountain road were the shuffling remnants of the great army that he had assembled on the plains of Konia. Just a few thousand were left, most of them wounded, their horses lame and saddle sore. Most of the Kurds and Turkomans had melted away, back to their villages, to tend their sheep and angoras.

As Bayezid and his ragged climbed higher they were swallowed by gray clouds. The road snaked along a gorge, scree crumbling beneath the horse's hooves. The rock walls here had been polished by centuries of horses and donkeys who had hugged the cliffs to keep from falling into the chasm on the other side of the path.

The wind tore at robes, threatened at times to dislodge him from the saddle. The high passes were deserted save for the occasional lumbering brown bear. They passed a tarn, black and crusted with ice.

They were deep inside Armenia now. Lake Wan was a steel-grey mirror far behind them. A falcon wheeled over their heads, its cry piercing the rush of the wind.

The past few months were a jumble of skirmishes, all fought on the run. Bayezid had said goodbye to his wives at Konia, brought just his four young sons with him. They were guarded day and night by his personal guards. They were his treasure now, the prize around which he would gather a new army. While he and they still lived Suleiman could never rest, Selim could never rest.

They had to find some way to survive, to regroup. He would not throw himself on his father's mercy because he expected none. Look at what happened to Mustapha.

\*\*\*

The shepherd's hut had been built in the lee of the ridge. A trick of the eye made it appear as if it were floating among the mountains. Bayezid turned to his lieutenant. "We will camp here tonight. I shall make my headquarters in the hut there."

"Yes, My Lord," the man said and hurried away to relay the order.

The hut had been abandoned for the imminent winter. There were four stone walls with no shutters on the windows and no door. The floor was bare earth and the smell of animals was strong. A long way from the palace at Topkapi, he thought.

A rainbow arced across the valley, chasing a shower of rain through a rent in the clouds. The light had turned a sulphurous green, and a chill wind stirred the grass. Thunder echoed around the passes. What was he going to do? There was nowhere to run and his followers no longer had the numbers or the will to fight. He had to find a way to survive.

\*\*\*

Frozen rain poured in through the roof even after the storm had passed. The wind had wrecked many of the tents during the night. This morning a chill mist drifted down from the mountains, horses stamped against the dawn chill. Men stumbled through the camp wrapped in blankets silent as wraiths.

A jackal coughed somewhere close by.

Bayezid ate his breakfast without appetite, just campaign provisions; yoghurt laced with raw onions and salt, diluted with cold water and eaten with a little dry pita. Suddenly Bayezid heard shouts from the camp and he jumped to his feet, spilling his bowl, thinking that Suleiman's akinji raiders had found them. A rider, dressed in Persian light armour, had appeared suddenly on the ridge above them. Bayezid's battered army rose to their feet and glared up at him.

As he entered the camp he was disarmed by Bayezid's personal guard and led through the scowling ranks of Turks to Bayezid's tent. He received him sitting cross legged on the rich silk carpet that had been spread on the floor of the shepherd's hut.

The rider executed a formal sala'am. "I bring a message from the Shah Tamasp," he said.

Bayezid nodded and the lieutenant took the letter from the courier and brought it over. He read it quickly, then a second time, so that Bayezid had time to reflect on the astonishing offer that it contained. "The Shah offers us sanctuary?"

"Suleiman has never been a friend to Persia," the courier said. "When Sultan Bayezid ascends the throne, he hopes to find an ally at the Sublime Porte at last."

The wind gave an eerie moan as it gusted through the open windows of the yali. Ascend the throne! Bayezid thought. For now ascending the next ridge is as much as I can hope for. This offer is anathema, of course; yet it would give us a chance to draw breath without my father's cavalry sniping at our heels. We are cold and dispirited and defeated, there are more wounded with us than able men. What choice do I have?

"You will wait while I consider my reply," he said, but as the man was led away he already knew what his answer would be.

***

Suleiman looked up at the mountains. A heavy band of cloud clung to the peaks and high passes, weeping rain.

"He has gone," Sokolli said. "He has crossed the border into Persia."

"To the Shah?"

"He offered him sanctuary. My spies say Bayezid has taken a hundred of his men with him. The rest have gone back to their villages, They will not trouble us again."

Bayezid, you fool. While you remained in the Empire you had a chance. Did you not know my army was on the verge of revolt? Whole regiments of yeniçeris were refusing to march against you, patrols go out to search for you and return with their horses still fresh. I know they have searched no further than the nearest tree to sleep under. Only the akinji still fight, but they never care whose blood they spill.

If you had defied me one more month winter would have closed in and I would have been forced back to Stamboul. I would never have persuaded one of these men to come back and fight you again in the Spring. They loved you, they loved how you charged at their guns at Konia, loved how you fought on even when I brought my whole army against you. They love you every bit as much as they detest Selim.

The one thing they could not forgive is for an Osmanli to accept the mercy of a Persian. When you crossed the border you left behind everything they thought you were.

You fool. Even the yeniçeris will curse you now.

# CHAPTER 114

## Amasya, 1561

She did not perform her sala'am as she entered the room. But then she is an old woman now, he thought, not as concerned about the consequence of offending me. Strange that I loved her so much once; now it is like meeting a stranger.

"My Lord."

"It has been a long time," he said.

"As you say."

He sat down beside her on the divan. "Are you well?"

"As well as one can expect at this great age. And you, my Lord?"

"My legs swell and I ache all over."

Gülbehar fingered the tespi in her lap. "So what has brought you here then, so far from the comforts of the Porte?"

Time is cruel, Suleiman thought. Look what it has done to you, what it has done to both of us. It has robbed you of your beauty and me of my dreams. In the end we had no more control of our destinies than the leaves on the trees. "I wish to be reconciled," he said.

"I cannot believe that after all you did, what you did to my son, what you did to me, that you still expect my friendship and good favour. I am frankly astonished."

"I am still your lord and you are one of my kullar. You still have a duty to me."

"Am I then obliged to forgive you? Because, if that is what you are saying, then I must admit my failing. Once I would have done anything you bid me, my Lord, out of love, not duty. Now I do not care. I despise you."

"I could order your execution at this very moment if I chose! Age does not excuse your insults."

"Then do it. I am tired of your threats."

Suleiman rose to his feet. There was a blue and white porcelain vase in the corner of the room, the height of a man. Suleiman drew his killiç and smashed it with one blow. He stood among the shards and screamed: "I am your Lord!"

"You are my son's murderer!"

"I gave him life and he turned against me! What did he expect?"

"He was innocent. You are a butcher like your father!"

Suleiman placed the edge of the blade at her neck. She did not flinch, looked him straight in the eyes and waited. The pearl tespi clicked through her fingers.

Just like your father.

Be done with it, a voice said. You are the Sultan. How dare she speak against you, the Lord of Life, the King of Kings, the Possessor of Men's Necks? Women's necks too! Do it. Do it.

He lowered the sword.

"Enough" he said. He sent the sword clattering across the floor and stormed out of the room. Gülbehar returned to her prayers, the pearls clicking between her fingers while a gediçli brushed away the shards of broken porcelain.

Nothing can hurt me now.

### Shiraz, Persia

There was a nimbus around the moon. Below it, the Zagros mountains glinted in the moonlight, stark and alien and ice white. As if I had been exiled to the moon itself, he thought. He shivered in his fur pelisse.

He heard the ring of hooves in the courtyard below. A rider jumped from his horse, leaving a page holding the reins, steam rising from his horse's heaving flanks. He shouted the password to the guard and ran inside. Perhaps this was the news he had been waiting for.

He remembered what Gülbehar had said to him: "It made no sense to kill my son. But he did it anyway."

How many times had he gone over it in his head? What else could he have done? Mustapha did nothing and Suleiman executed him; he had acted like a true ghazi and Suleiman had thrown his entire army against him. How was it possible to understand such a man?

A log cracked and broke in the grate in a shower of sparks. There were footsteps on the stone flags outside and the door was thrown open.

The Shah entered, smiling like a jackal. I don't want to trust you, he thought, but once again I have no choice. "I have good news for the young shahzade of the Osmanlis," he said.

"Your chaush has returned from Stamboul?" There had been many messengers riding to and fro in the last few months. Had his father finally relented?

"Yes, the chaush has returned. A time and a place has been agreed. He wants to meet with you!"

"Where?"

"Tabriz. He is coming there in secret. Everything is arranged."

"And Selim?"

"Selim knows nothing about it. Perhaps your father has had a change of heart. The Shadow of God Upon the Earth has remembered he is mortal like the rest of us."

"May I see the letter?"

The Shah hesitated. "There was no letter. The message was entrusted to my man's memory."

You're lying, Bayezid thought. "That is unlike my father."

The Shah did not reply.

"Did he commit to your chaush's memory any intent of his purpose?"

"Only that he wishes a reconciliation with his son - he believes him now to be a true ghazi."

Unlike my father not to put his words under his tugra. There is something wrong here. But what can I do?

"When?" Bayezid asked him.

"We leave tonight," the Shah said.

## Konia

Selim is just thirty four years old, Abbas reminded himself. But he already looks like an old man. His face is so bloated from drink that his eyes look like two small currants sunk into a custard. His body is gross no matter how fine the gowns that he wears.

Prince Barley Pudding indeed.

He was slumped on the divan picking at a large tray of halwa on the silver table beside him. He selected three of the pastries and popped them in his mouth.

"You have news, Kislar Aghasi?"

"I do, my Lord." He wondered how he would react when he heard. Even Abbas wondered what to make of it.

"From my father?"

"He has left Amasya and rides east."

The negotiations had dragged on for more than a year. It seemed the shahzade was worth much less to Suleiman than the Shah Tamasp had hoped. It had been whispered that the starting price had been Mesopotamia.

"He looks sick, I hope?" Selim laughed and sprayed half-chewed pastry over Abbas" robe.

"The Lord of Life cannot spend as long in the saddle as he once did."

"Does he have his army with him?"

"No, my Lord. My spies say he has a squadron each of solaks and Spahis and an oda of yeniçeris."

Selim clapped his hands. A page appeared holding a pitcher of wine and a jewelled cup. Selim held the cup out to be filled. He swallowed it in one draft. There was halwa and wine in his beard.

The page refilled the cup and withdrew.

"For what purpose do you think?"

"They say he will meet Bayezid at Tabriz. There are whispers of reconciliation."

Selim jumped to his feet and the wine spilled across the carpets. He uttered a shrill wail and began to shake. Not again, Abbas thought. This is like minding a small child.

No one moved, not the pages, nor the guards, nor the pashas. Finally Selim fell back onto the divan. He had bunched the corner of his robe in his fist. His eyes were out of focus. "I have been betrayed," he said. "Wine! Where is my wine? You!" He pointed to the bostanji standing in readiness by the door. Selim pointed to the page holding the silver ewer. He gave the signal and without hesitation the executioner did as he was bidden, lopping the poor boy's head neatly from his shoulders.

Abbas silently withdrew, drawing no attention to himself. He had no interest in the aftermath of such a spectacle. He had lived too long under the tyranny of princes.

# CHAPTER 115

## Tabriz

Moonlight rippled on the tiled domes of the Blue Mosque and burned like phosphorus on the chill ribbon of the Aji Chai River. The sound of flutes and drums carried on the cold air; yellow light flickered from the shuttered windows of the citadel.

In the great hall slave girls in gaudy silk and gossamer danced while the guests gorged from the silver plates on the carpets in front of them. The Shah sat in the centre of the room with his guest of honour, Bayezid.

The Shah leaned towards him. "Suleiman regrets what he has done to you," he said. "Perhaps you will allow me to mediate. It is not too late. I will help you now and when you are Sultan, Persia and the Osmanlis will be allies."

"What does he want from me?"

"Just that you stay your hand until his death. Selim will take the throne of course but it will not matter. When you return the yeniçeris will never support him over you."

Bayezid had no appetite for the food, or the promise of women later. The delegation was due in the morning. He must learn patience and cunning from now on. He had been too impulsive in the past. Time enough to see Selim's fat head on a pole.

Bayezid was aware of a cold draught on his back, realized that someone had entered the hall behind him. Latecomers. He felt the short hairs at the back of his neck prickle with alarm. The Shah was seated opposite Bayezid, facing the door. He glanced up for a moment, then returned to eating.

"Who are our guests?"

"They are expected," he said.

Then Bayezid heard it; a familiar sound if one had lived in the palace, something between a bark and a cough, like a dog trying to swallow a piece of gristle. It was the noise men made when they had no tongue to speak. The sound of a mute.

The Shah smiled, with genuine regret. "I am sorry," he said. "Your father insisted."

"On what?"

"It is a poor bargain. Four hundred thousand gold pieces. My mullah's thought I should hold out for Baghdad. All very well for them, they would have gone to hide in the mountains of your father had marched here with his army. I decided to take the money instead."

"You pledged me protection!"

The Shah shrugged. ""It is what they call diplomacy. You say what it is best to say at the time. I am truly sorry. It is a very poor example of our hospitality. I wish it could have been another way."

Bayezid span around. There were five of them. One of them was the man they said had murdered Mustapha, the head gardener, a huge, ugly Sudanese. Each of them held in his hands a loop of razor thin silk.

Bayezid's hand went to his killiç but one of the Shah's bodyguards had anticipated this and caught his wrist. Two more guards pinned his arms behind him. Bayezid looked at his sons. God help me in my sorrow; they were too young to understand, too young to die. His eldest started to run and one of the Persians caught him, laughing.

"Could you not have spared my boys?"

"Especially not the boys. Boys grow up to become men. Suleiman was quite specific in his demands."

"Then let Selim be his epitaph," Bayezid said. The silken bowstring was around his neck and he was jerked backwards over the head gardener's knee, choking. His hands clawed instinctively at his throat but once the bostanji had the noose in place there was no reprieve.

"The children were next. The Shah watched with a frown of disgust. He did not hold with the assassination of children. But what was to be done? He selected a sliver of spiced lamb from the plate in front of him and chewed reflectively. Statesmanship was an indelicate business at times, but it had to be borne.

## Bursa

A woman was screaming in the courtyard below the window. The eunuch wished the guards would do something to keep her quiet.

Bayezid's youngest son was still only nine months old. He had been conceived before the battle of Konia and his father had never seen him.

As the eunuch bent over the cot the child smiled at him and put an arm around his neck and kissed him. His hands began to shake and he dropped the bowstring.

He went outside and gave the porter who had led him here two gold pieces and a new bowstring. He waited. A few minutes later the man reappeared and fled down the steps. The coins tinkled and rolled on the stones.

He sighed and went back inside. The child was still smiling.

"Would that you have been a girl," he said. He felt for the leather pouch at his waist. If he did not return with it filled, Suleiman would have his own head.

He tested the string and closed the door behind him. As he approached the child giggled and held out his arms.

# CHAPTER 116

## Konia

A long journey from Venice to Konia, from the Campanile di San Marco to this lonely place surrounded by stone caravansarayas and the black yurts of nomads.

A lonely place to die.

They found Abbas in his cell slumped face down on the rug. A white kitten was licking at the bloodstained handkerchief clutched in his left hand.

"Consumption," the physician muttered. Or perhaps poison. Still, death was infinitely preferable to being the Kislar Aghasi to the shahzade Selim. Or perhaps there were other reasons. Who could know? The less you knew, the better. Knowledge could be dangerous.

It took six pages to lift him and carry him out of the iron-studded door of the Harem into the waiting cart. The physician remained behind to examine the room. Abbas had been writing a letter. Quill and parchment lay on the table beside the body. The letter was unfinished. In fact he had only written the salutation.

"Dear Julia".

The Chief Eunuch writing to a girl? Perhaps it was his pet name for another of the black boys. Well it did not matter now. He screwed it up and threw it in the fire.

## Cyprus

Ludovici joined Julia on the terrazzo, the sun glittering in the distance on the blue of the sea, beyond the vineyards. They sat for a while, holding hands, listening to the murmur of insects.

"I had a letter today," he said, finally. "Abbas is gone."

She nodded. "Oh. Oh, my poor Abbas. Finally, then. Was it a good passing?"

"He did not suffer."

"Not at the end, at least."

"No, he did enough of that in his life. He is free now."

They were silent for a long time. He watched a tear roll down her cheek. She brushed it away and offered him a sad smile. "This may seem a strange time to say this, but I love you, Ludovici."

"I love you, too."

"I wish I had been able to give you children."

"Don't regret it. I don't. I regret nothing, nothing at all. We are given gifts in life, others are withheld. I am grateful that I found you, I am grateful for a friend like Abbas. I am grateful that I found peace here at last. To wish for more would be to forget how rich these gifts have been. I only hope that Abbas has found his peace too, now, wherever he is."

"You're a good man, Ludovici."

"Thank you. In the end, it's all I ever wanted to become."

## Topkapi Saraya

After the wardrobe page had left, after the final offering up of prayers, Suleiman was alone. He lay on his quilt listening to the sound of his own laboured breathing, but sleep would not come. He got up and went to the latticed window and looked at the stars.

"Please tell me you lied," he said aloud.

"I was ill, I was dying. How could you have believed what I said at the last?"

"But how can I be sure?" He stared at her, so lovely, with her burnished copper hair braided with glittering pearls, the green taplock pinned rakishly on her head.

"You said Bayezid belonged to Ibrahim."

"Do you truly believe I deceived you for thirty five years?"

Suleiman could not answer her.

"I would not have betrayed you that way," a man's voice said. There he was, swaggering with his thumbs in the sash at his waist, a livid raw wound at his throat.

"You had the opportunity, Ibrahim. I loved you and gave you my trust. I allowed you into the heart of my seraglio."

"She lied to you."

"Tell him!" he screamed at Hürrem. "Tell him what you told me!"

"I was sick, it was the Devil who spoke, not me."

Suleiman cried aloud and covered his ears but it was Mustapha who spoke next. Even with his eyes tight shut he saw him standing right there in front of him, in flowing white kaftan and silk turban, beard neatly combed, head held high. "I did not betray you, Father."

"The evidence against you was plain."

"No, it was you who betrayed me! You gave our Empire to Selim, a lecher and a drunkard."

"He is of my blood at least!"

"I loved you, my Lord," Hürrem said. "How could you ever believe that I hated you?"

"Of course you loved me! I gave up my harem for you! I made you queen! Of course you loved me!"

"Then why did you murder our son?"

"Because I can never be sure!" he groaned and sank to his knees. The mutes, deaf to his screams, watched him, terrified, but did not move from their posts at the door.

Night closed around the place of silence, a paradise of marble and gardens and glittering stones, leaving the King of Kings, the Lord of Life, to rail at the phantoms that returned to torment him, and to writhe for five more years in his hellish heaven upon the earth.

> "What men call empire is worldwide strife and ceaseless war
> In all the world the only joy lies in a hermit's rest."

(From a poem written by Sultan Suleiman, the one they called the Magnificent, discovered after his death in 1566).

# EPILOGUE

The Suleimaniye mosque dominates the modern city of Istanbul, its minarets and massive domes towering above the Golden Horn, dwarfing the mosque of Rüstem Pasha on the slopes below it. It is a memorial in stone to the man the Turkish people remember as the greatest of all Ottoman Sultans. In the first three hundred years of the Osmanli dynasty, ten sultans, culminating with Suleiman, built an empire of thirty million people, encompassing twenty different languages, all of it won in battle from the saddle of a horse.

After Suleiman there were twenty five more Sultans; an unbroken line of weaklings and degenerates who debauched themselves in their Harems, bled the empire's finances with their extravagances or satiated themselves with acts of unbridled cruelty against those unfortunate enough to fall under their power. The Osmanli tradition of soldiers and statesmen ceased with Suleiman's son, Selim II, the one they called The Sot.

Scholars have speculated that the line was broken. It can never be proved. The loss of greatness may simply have been the natural result of an excess of power, riches and ease.

Anyone interested in the history of the Ottomans can consult the facts. I have not strayed from them, but there is much about the history of Suleiman's reign that historians have never completely understood. This book is fiction only in that it speculates on why things happened the way that they did. Perhaps it is wholly fiction; perhaps it is not. The only ones who know the truth are long dead.

THE END

# NEW HISTORICAL FICTION
# BY COLIN FALCONER

She was taught to obey. Now she has learned to rebel.
This is the story of Isabella, the only woman ever to invade England -
and win.

In the tradition of Philippa Gregory and Elizabeth Chadwick,
ISABELLA is thoroughly researched and fast paced, the little known
story of the one invasion the English never talk about.

# ABOUT THE AUTHOR

"I was 18 years old, I'd just left school and got a job in London, working in an insurance company. I was working inside - in an office! My mother thought that was like being CEO of Shell Oil.

"I was late one morning, I took a short cut through the church yard to the station to catch my train. I'd just finished reading The Sun Also Rises the night before; and here I was looking at all these gravestones, I remember thinking: Gee, we're not here very long. Better make it count.

"So I went home, told my mother I was quitting my job and going to Morocco. She damned near fainted."

After travelling through Spain and Africa, Colin hitch-hiked across Europe to Sweden to visit a girlfriend he'd met the year before on a football tour. When he finally got back home, he was still restless. After failing to make the grade as a professional football player, he travelled around Asia; his experiences in Bangkok and India later inspired his thriller *Venom*, and his adventures in the jungles of the Golden Triangle of Burma and Laos were also filed away for later, the basis of his *Opium* series about the underworld drug trade.

He emigrated to Australia where he helped a mate establish a new advertising agency. "We could only afford this derelict building for an office. Once we were pitching to a client during a thunderstorm and the roof flooded. A piece of the ceiling fell down and just missed his head. Fortunately he had a sense of humour. We got the account!

"After a couple of years we were doing much better. We could even afford to pay ourselves a wage! But I really wanted to be a writer, not a copywriter. When I told my mate I was leaving to try my luck in the Big Smoke, he offered me 40% of the business. It was 40% of nothing at the time. I saw him a couple of years ago, and he'd just sold the agency for twenty million dollars.

I worked out what 40% of that was on a pocket calculator. It's quite a lot of money, apparently."

Colin went to Sydney and worked in TV and radio and freelanced for many of Australia's leading newspapers and magazines. But he got his dream, publishing over a dozen novels in the UK and US and having his work sold into translation in Brazil, Belgium, the Czech republic, France, Germany, Greece, Hungary, Italy, Korea, Mexico, Poland, Portugal, Romania, Serbia, Slovakia, Spain and Turkey.

He lived for many years in the beautiful Margaret River region in WA, and helped raise two beautiful daughters with his late wife, Helen. While writing, he also worked in the volunteer ambulance service. "I'd be at my desk typing, then thirty minutes later I might be crawling into an overturned car or running along a beach with the oxygen for a near drowning. It was an interesting time."

His marriage ended in tragic circumstances, a story he has told in 'The Naked Husband,' and its non-fiction sequel, 'The Year We Seized the Day,' written with a writing partner, Elizabeth Best.

He travels regularly to research his novels and his quest for authenticity has led him to run with the bulls in Pamplona, pursue tornadoes across Oklahoma and black witches across Mexico, go cage shark diving in South Africa and get tear gassed in a riot in La Paz. (He was actually trying to cycle down the Death Road. In the end he had to abandon the attempt and take the bus down.) He also completed a nine hundred kilometre walk of the camino in Spain.

A few years ago he stopped writing. 'I suddenly found I couldn't do it anymore. It was after'The Year We Seized the Day.' I was ridden with guilt and I remember standing on a beach in Thailand late one night, and I said to God: 'Okay I've had enough now.'

A week later I was in a Thai hospital, only time in my whole life I've ever been sick, I'd got some sort of tropical infection and I was close to multiple organ failure. I remember praying again (that's twice in one year!): "Hey I didn't know you were listening, Big Guy! I didn't mean it! I have two girls to look out for!"

"I survived but when I got home I started drinking too much and I couldn't find my writing mojo. It got ugly there for a while. Thought I'd never write again."

Then he published *Silk Road*, and got a three book contract in London, and his love affair for life and for writing returned. "For me, the two things are inseparable. My passion for one infects the other."

His fiction comes from dedicated research and what he calls a quest for Hemingway's ghost; characters with a passion for life, for love and the courage to face down their demons.

Istanbul, Bucharest, Colin Falconer'When I was walking through that graveyard I made two promises to my gawky 18 year old self; one - that I would not die feeling that I had not lived, and two - that I would follow my siren call to write, no matter where it lead. I feel like so far I have kept that promise and I intend to see it all the way through.'

You can now find Colin's books on Kindle where his entire list will be available by the end of the year; *Silk Road* was published in hardback and paperback by Corvus-Atlantic in London in 2011 and his new novel *Stigmata* has just been released. For more information see colinfalconer.wordpress.com.

## OTHER BOOKS BY COLIN FALCONER

## THE FAMOUS WOMAN SERIES

"A wonderful story ... not just a rehash of history but rather a refreshing look at this clever and charismatic leader ... pulsating with the passion of a woman."~ *Womens Weekly Book of the Month*

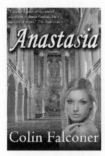   

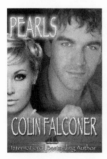  

## THE OPIUM SERIES

"We have every respect for persons entertaining strict religious principles, but we fear that very godly people are not suited to the drug trade."~ *James Matheson co-founder of Jardine Matheson.*

# THE JERUSALEM SERIES

The story of how Palestine became Israel.

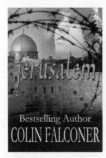 

## EBOOK SHORT STORIES

"Falconer weaves a pacy story of obsession, love, greed and corruption … Really well done." ~*Sydney Morning Herald*

## OTHER HISTORICALS

"If you haven't read one of Colin Falconer's novels, then I promise you are in for a real roller-coaster ride of never ending intrigue ..." ~*Mirella Patzer, Historical Novel Review*

## OTHER BOOKS BY COLIN FALCONER

"I just figured what with guns going off and things blowing up, there'd be plenty of deep truths and penetrating insights."~*P.J. O'Rourke, Holidays in Hell*

"Another man would have made it an affair and nothing else. Another man would have been more ruthless, more cynical. The naked husband falls in love."